THE
UNDERHANDED

THE
UNDERHANDED

A NOVEL

ADAM SIKES

OCEANVIEW PUBLISHING
SARASOTA, FLORIDA

ISBN 978-1-60809-600-8

Published in the United States of America by Oceanview Publishing

Sarasota, Florida

www.oceanviewpub.com

10 9 8 7 6 5 4 3 2 1

PRINTED IN THE UNITED STATES OF AMERICA

"History is a set of lies agreed upon."

NAPOLEON BONAPARTE, 1769–1821

AUTHOR'S NOTE

In December 2022, the German authorities arrested over twenty-five conspirators planning a coup d'état to reinstitute the monarchy and return the German state to a government akin to the former Reich.

On 31 January 2020 and following the 2016 popular referendum, the United Kingdom formally withdrew from the European Union, of which it had been a member for some forty-seven years.

And in the late nineteenth century, a French general and politician named Georges Ernest Jean-Marie Boulanger pursued an aggressive form of nationalism that was fueled by France's defeat in the Franco-Prussian War, which some have described as a precursor to fascism.

In this light, *The Underhanded* is a work of fiction as are all the characters and events contained within, and similar to my previous novels, a board reviewed this manuscript to ensure it did not contain any classified or sensitive information. Yet, the numerous historical elements that underpin the plot—like those above—did indeed occur, and while endeavoring to write about what I know, much of this story is inspired by events and people I encountered while I wore the uniform or worked as an intelligence officer.

Thus, *The Underhanded* seeks to peel apart a world of espionage, international criminal activity, political extremism, and family betrayal that is cruel, twisted, and unforgiving. Those souls who choose to live and work in these spaces trying to do right—the *good guys*—must lie and manipulate and constantly look over their shoulders, while at the same time adhering to a complicated and at times conflicting sense of integrity, honor, and loyalty. It is not easy, nor is it clean, and often the lines between right and wrong are blurred. And sometimes there is no right answer or good option, only something less bad.

Having seen this world up close, my hope, then, was to tell an entertaining story with a taste of realism.

And for my friends and former colleagues still out there on the edge, stay safe.

Adam Sikes
www.adamsikes.com

THE
UNDERHANDED

PROLOGUE

Moser trudged down the sidewalk, the overcast sky making it appear later than it actually was. He was on his way home after a scheisser-day at the auto shop and, of course, it had started to rain. It always rained here. Always.

He popped the collar on his leather jacket and thrust his hands in his pockets. Water droplets trickled down his neck to his back, giving him gooseflesh. He missed the snow. Snow was clean, picturesque, even dry, relatively speaking. Rain was wet—it was only wet—and on days like today it was miserably cold.

Rounding the corner onto Prühßstraße, he sidestepped a puddle and spat, muttering a curse that only he could hear. Then, as he did every day at about this time, he looked up. His eyes honed in on the second building from the corner, three floors up, fourth window in. Except for the occasional light inside, the window was usually empty . . . but tonight, a clay pot with white flowers rested on the sill.

Calla lilies.

Moser stopped in the middle of the sidewalk, a knot forming in his stomach. He pulled a crinkled pack of cigarettes from his pocket and lit one. Raindrops fell on the shaft, causing the smoke to go limp, but he didn't notice. He glanced at the window again just to make sure he wasn't mistaken.

Yes. The flowers were displayed in the fourth window in, third floor, second building from the corner.

Taking one more drag, he tossed the soggy smoke on the wet pavement with a hiss and continued his walk home. He fought the urge to hurry—he wanted to—but he didn't. He followed the same route he always did and maintained his usual pace, but on the inside his mind churned and all his senses tingled.

Once in his apartment, he took a Märzen from the fridge, popped the top, and took a long pull. He grabbed a worn paper map of the city from his bookshelf and spread it out on the table, surveying Berlin's streets and underground stations. It'd been a while since he'd used this route, but that didn't matter. He knew it blind. Polishing the pavement would be the easy part.

Moser woke at five the next morning and got dressed. He didn't put on his mechanic overalls like a typical Tuesday; he wore jeans and a T-shirt, along with his black leather jacket. He called his boss at the shop and said he wasn't coming in. He was sick. The cranky bastard could piss off, too. He didn't expect to be working there much longer.

The sun was cresting the tops of the gray apartment buildings as he set out, and for the next two hours he walked around the city, rode the U-Bahn twice, and took a taxi. He visited a café where he got a coffee and a strudel, a hardware store where he purchased three twenty-centimeter lengths of pipe, an outdoor store for a new pair of gloves, and a handful of other stops at precisely timed intervals.

There was no evidence of any shadows on his tail, so he decided he was clean, reaching Bahnhof Alexanderplatz at exactly 8:48 a.m.

Inside the main level of the terminal, he sorted his way through the morning crowd until he reached Blumen Röwer, a flower shop run by a woman with short white hair and bottle-cap glasses. He'd always thought they made her eyes look like blue marbles ready to pop out of her head.

"Guten Morgen," Moser mumbled, browsing the fresh bouquets. Carnations, lilies, roses, tulips. His mother would have liked the yellow tulips, though he'd only ever given her those kinds of flowers once, and that was twenty years ago. She was dead now, but she deserved to have some flowers placed on her scratch in the earth. Perhaps soon.

But this morning, blossoms and memories of his mother weren't his thing; he was more interested in what was happening outside.

He maintained a clear view of the escalator, able to see everyone coming down from the S-Bahn platform one level up. Checking his watch, he saw it was 8:56 a.m. The train from Jannowitzbrücke would have just pulled in.

He pictured the passengers debarking the train on the level above, some hustling across the platform to get to work, others taking their time. There would be a man with a gray beard and black raincoat among them.

How long had it been since he'd seen him? Five months? Maybe six? The time didn't really matter. All according to protocol. That's how things worked. It's why he'd been sent to Berlin.

He fingered a green plant and shifted his bag to his left hand. Out of the corner of his eye he looked at the escalator. A line of passengers was descending. A businessman, two teenagers heading to school, a grandmother carrying groceries, the man with the gray beard, three more businessmen and -women.

Moser took four steps toward the shop exit and admired an overpriced piece of pottery while anticipation scratched the inside of his chest.

The man with the gray beard stepped off the escalator and headed toward the north exit. He wore an expression like granite, impervious to the noise and distractions swirling around him, yet he didn't stand out. His features and clothes were easily forgettable unless you knew to study the man, and then you would feel it more than see it—something indescribably murderous.

Moser exited the store and charted a path directly at the man. He forced himself to breathe through his nose, but his heart was firing like a jackhammer. Bump, bump, bump with the blood pumping through his veins and around his ears, muffling the station's unruliness.

When he was two steps away, Moser opened his sweaty palm, fighting the urge to wipe it dry on his trousers. He would have left a clammy smear if he did, but it was too late for that. His legs kept driving him forward threading through the commuters.

Just another second . . .

Now.

As they passed each other, Moser felt the man with the gray beard push a small object into his hand. Moser gripped it in the crevice of his palm and kept walking, as did the man with the gray beard, neither making eye contact nor looking back.

Moser walked and walked and squeezed the object as if he'd just snatched the Orlov Diamond, knowing his life depended on not letting it slip from his fingers. But with each step away from where they'd made the transfer, Moser felt a sense of relief spread through him.

Within moments both men were intermixed with the herd of morning commuters. The entire act had been like the glimpse of a passing shadow, no one the wiser. Not even the CCTV cameras would be able to discern what had happened. They were like two strangers passing in a crowd, exactly as they should be.

Moser headed downstairs to the U-Bahn and took the next train to Hauptbahnhof.

The man with the gray beard disappeared on Berlin's streets.

Once back in his apartment, Moser locked his door and closed the shades. He removed the small object from his pocket and sat at the table. He scrutinized it, each side and edge—a breath mint container. He popped one in his mouth, then took a small pocket knife and cut open the bottom. Inside he found a slip of paper with a series of numbers on it.

Twenty-three minutes later he'd decoded the message, and after he'd read it, he sat staring at the wall, smoking, a quiver forming in his gut.

*   *   *

At 21:15 that night, Moser called Ernst. "Guten Abend. Wo bist du?"

"Betrunken werdend."

"Ja. Woher?"

Ernst said he was at a bar downtown, and Moser said he'd be there in a half hour.

At just past midnight, Moser, Ernst, and seven other men—some with shaved heads but all wearing black—exited the bar on Solmsstraße. They were drunk and loud, except Moser, who only acted the part.

He slung his bag over his shoulder and told the group to follow him.

By the time they reached the remains of the Tempelhof Airport, it was nearly one in the morning. A few Middle Eastern men—Syrians—were milling about outside the southern entrance to the former terminal. Another thirteen thousand refugees were

inside—men, women, children, families—the lucky ones who'd
escaped the civil war in Syria but still had no place to go. Perpetual
limbo.

Some of Moser's group—good, strong, pure-blooded Germans—
began hooting and hollering as they advanced toward the terminal.
A couple carried bats, a few had pipes, one had a chain. A handful
of cars started showing up too. More men in black, more shaved
heads, more weapons.

The front of the mob was fifty meters from the gaggle of Syrian
refugees. They saw the danger coming toward them. A few started
to retreat inside.

Moser looked about, excitement boiling within him with every
step. His group had grown to about twenty-five now, picking up
speed, their shouts getting louder, cruder, more threatening. Just a
little closer.

Faster.

Faster.

He reached inside his bag and pulled out one of the pipes he'd
bought earlier in the day, which he'd since filled with black powder
mixed with aluminum shavings. He lit the fuse and heaved it at the
group of refugees, the burning fuse throwing off sparks as the crude
pipe bomb bounced across the pavement.

It exploded and a metallic echo resounded across the parking lot
and into the terminal.

Six of the Syrian men were blown to the ground; another clus-
ter stumbled for the door. They scrambled, panicking, cries going
out.

The mob of German thugs charged forward. When they reached
those writhing on the ground, they bludgeoned them with their
bats and pipes like a medieval battlefield.

Moser lit another bomb and threw it through the double doors into the terminal. Screams—men and women—came from within. The subsequent explosion sent people scurrying in all directions.

Some of Moser's crew barged into the terminal. They chased the helpless refugees, clubbing the children as well as the adults. Others stumbled into the cube walls, too drunk to stay on their feet as they swung wildly at anyone and anything. Moser threw his last pipe bomb into a common area farther down, the explosion going off in the middle of a crowd trying to escape the chaos.

Before he left, Moser took one last look at the melee going on around him, indifferent to the screams. He didn't have any particular hatred for these people, but they didn't belong here.

The Polizei and emergency services showed up an hour and twenty minutes later. The perpetrators had run off by then—back to their homes and jobs and classrooms and churches—and no one was arrested or charged.

Eight Syrian refugees, however, died that night, including a five-year-old boy and an eighty-seven-year-old woman. Another thirty-four were treated for injuries caused by blunt force weapons and metal shards from homemade pipe bombs.

* * *

Two days had passed since the attack on the refugee camp. The mainstream media had offered pity for the victims and then decried the perpetrators. The politicians on the left and in the center had expressed shock and reeled at the horror, and then vowed to increase protections for the helpless victims. Across the board, they made the usual reactions, and they were hollow.

But on the other side, an uncomfortably large segment of the population applauded the violence, and their right-wing leaders championed their beliefs. These voices—nationalist, Eurocentric, racist—were getting stronger and stronger day by day.

His bosses would be pleased, Moser thought. They'd have to be. After all these years, he'd finally done what he'd been trained to do. And now, it was time to go home and put those flowers by his mother's grave.

He stood on the Gericksteg Bridge. It was dark, and it was drizzling again. But in this instance, he welcomed the rain. Fewer people and fewer eyes.

He lit a cigarette and checked his watch: 20:17.

At the far end of the bridge, the mist was settling on the river, and there was a lone figure coming across. Even from this distance, Moser could see the man's gray beard as he passed each of the amber, dimly lit street lamps.

For as long as he'd known the man—fifteen years, maybe—the man had worn that beard. The man didn't age, either. He probably came out of the womb that way, built for the shadows. In this sordid world of lies and violence, the man was a legend—a dark legend— and despite Moser having worked for him for years, the man was still unnerving. Practically terrifying.

But he was going home and thoughts of tulips kept peeking through his mind. His mother had loved the spring. Such beautiful yellow tulips.

Moser didn't see or hear the person come up from behind. A sharp, piercing sensation cut into his back on the right side. He struggled to turn, but a powerful arm wrapped around his neck. The arm constricted like a snake.

Moser tried to yell, but he had no air. He felt his bowels start to loosen.

What was happening?

The man with the gray beard kept coming, his face expressionless.

The sky, the bridge, the trees . . . they started fading, going hazy. Moser felt another stab in his back. For an instant, everything went dark, but then it became clear again. He blinked and stared into the eyes of the man with the gray beard. They were black, soulless eyes.

Why? He'd done everything right. It wasn't supposed to end like this. He was supposed to go home. It'd been fourteen years. It was time to go home. He was done.

Moser felt himself falling.

There was a splash. Everything was cold, ice cold.

Then nothing.

CHAPTER 1

The unexpected vibration of my phone startled me, and I immediately regretted bringing it out here. I should have left it tucked in my jacket draped over the chair or dropped it carelessly on the kitchen counter. As it was, only a few people had this particular number, and I wasn't expecting a call from any of them. It wasn't that I didn't want to hear from Phil or Gwen or Elliot or Alison—all good people whom I would call friends—but not at this moment.

I'd been enjoying my evening of quiet reflection, lost in my thoughts, mulling over what had happened and pondering what I was going to do next. I needed to do something; I couldn't hide away forever, even if the idea was mildly appealing. I needed to get on with my life and my work, and just a few moments ago before this distraction, some acceptable ideas had started to percolate.

The phone vibrated again, rattling on the table next to me. And the caller ID showed *Restricted*, which made it even more bothersome, particularly now and especially here.

The south of France—with its beautiful beaches, superb wine, decadent men and women, and unbridled past—was where I went to escape or relax. It was a little of both this go-around. Amidst the centuries-old villages, I could read, eat, flirt with socializing, and recharge. I was content here, and after a few days or weeks, I would be fortified to thrust myself into the breach and face the big bad world.

I watched the phone vibrate once more—three times now—and debated whether to let it go to voicemail. I preferred that option. It was the better option. I didn't want to talk to anyone. Although I had my friends and colleagues and acquaintances and could attempt a front of affable charm now and again, in my truest form I was quiet, preferring the conversations in my head to those with actual human beings.

I was a historian and I preferred books to . . . well . . . just about everything. Books didn't need anything, just to be read and understood. They embodied a conversation with the author that was codified with ink on paper, there to be surveyed and contemplated and always available. People, on the other hand, tended to be complicated and unpredictable, some exhaustingly so.

But there it went again. My phone. Four rings now.

Voicemail, I thought. If the call was important, the person would leave a message or ring back, right?

But . . .

The phone vibrated once more, the noise jarring as it clattered on the patio table, demanding attention like the obnoxious party guest who spoke too loudly for the room and who no one could avoid. I think everyone has encountered those individuals at one moment or another.

And again—it vibrated.

Dammit.

I threw back the last of my wine and snatched up the phone. "Hello?"

"Hello. Am I speaking with Professor William Dresden of Princeton University?" asked a woman's voice I didn't recognize.

She had a British accent and a confident tone, like one accustomed to chucking authority around.

"May I ask who's calling?" I replied.

"My name is Adeline, and I have something urgent to chat with the professor about."

"Okay," I replied, remaining polite but noting that she hadn't offered a last name.

"Are you Professor Dresden?" she asked again.

"I am."

"Good. Glad I reached you."

"What can I do for you?"

"I'll get right to the point. Neither of us like having our time wasted," the woman began. "My organization needs your assistance. We're aware that for the past few years you've been researching the lives of some lesser-known men from the nineteenth century. You've argued that they were driving forces during Europe's imperial era, and you recently gave a talk in Washington, D.C., about them. You caused quite a bit of controversy."

I didn't respond but she was right. My latest research had indeed caused a pompous cabal to descend from the Ivory Tower who were intent on ripping up my life's work. By focusing on the people that surrounded the famous personalities of the past—rather than the statesmen and generals themselves—I'd shown that the aides and deputies of history were often as influential as the principals. They worked behind the scenes, pushing here and whispering there, orchestrating events according to their own designs and those of their masters. Their obscurity was their power, and these lesser-known individuals had intrigued me for the past twenty years or so.

Sadly, in recent months, more than a few scholars—people I would call my peers—had attacked my conclusions, picking apart my research methods and analysis and even my misplaced commas. Some went so far as to call me second rate, which I will admit hurt.

It wasn't all that surprising, I suppose. For those who'd devoted themselves to being the renowned authority on the likes of Napoleon or Roosevelt, my analysis had called into question *their* life's work. One historian from George Washington University even accused me of fabricating my research, although nothing could be further from the truth. That comment truly shocked me, something I'd not encountered before and never in all my years of academia heard leveled in front of an audience.

To say it had been an uncomfortable time would have put it too gently.

Thus, I wondered what side of the argument this woman was on and what she wanted. The prospect of thrashing out some minor point of no real consequence didn't entice me. And in my current state, if provoked, I'd likely pop off and say something I'd regret. Being kind was one of life's most important qualities, my dear mother had always said, and I agreed with her. But after a drink or two I could become a little edgy, which might be good or bad, depending on your perspective.

"From my own work," the woman continued, "and in light of what you claim to have uncovered about these men, I have some documents I think you should see."

"Is that so? May I ask what they're about?"

"They pertain to a small group of men of the same era and caliber that you lectured on. Their actions connected."

"Could you be more specific, please?" I asked, now thinking the woman may not have called to put me on the rack. She had another angle, though it was still unclear. Maybe she was nuts. "You said your name was Adeline, and you represent who?"

"I'd rather not say anything more on the phone. All I can tell you is that the papers have been secreted away for a long time. The information they contain, coupled with events in recent years, suggests we're facing a revived threat to both Europe and America."

I sat up. "What? What are you talking about?"

"This may sound bizarre, but you must believe me. What I'm referring to is highly sensitive."

"I don't understand. What information?"

"I shouldn't say any more right now. I need you to trust me."

"Trust you?"

"We shouldn't discuss anything else. It's too dangerous. We must meet in person."

"Too dangerous? Who are you and how did you get this number?"

I raised out of my chair and scanned the backyard of the villa. It was sunset and the shadows were dancing underneath the Aleppo pines that dotted the hills. I felt the hair on the back of my neck stand up and, for a reason I could not explain, wondered if I was being watched.

"Professor Dresden, I've no doubt you're aware that Europe is facing numerous concerning challenges. An immigration crisis, climate impact, a resurgence of ethno-nationalist movements, Russia hammering on the eastern door . . . We need to meet tomorrow morning. Everything will become clear once we speak."

I didn't know how to respond. The woman wasn't making sense. It was as if she'd drenched me with a mass of my own personal strife threaded with societal chaos and nonsense, intending to frighten or motivate me—I couldn't tell. All I could muster was, "Thank you for the call, Miss . . . Adeline. But I'm going to hang up now. Have a good—"

"Professor, wait. There's more. I wanted to tell you this in person, but—" She paused. "I have information about the death of your father. It was no accident."

I slowly sat back down, her words reverberating in my ears, my chest suddenly going hollow. My father had died over twenty years ago in a car crash outside Paris. Images of a crumpled car and emergency workers scrambling about flashed through my mind. "What are you talking about? What do you know about my father?"

"Meet me tomorrow morning at eight at Le Trastevere in Villefranche-sur Mer. It's on the water. Do you know it?"

"Yes," I said without thinking. It was a restaurant in a small coastal town east of Nice.

"Good. See you then."

The line went dead, but I kept the phone to my ear and stared across the countryside at the setting sun. I lost track of time, unable to form a coherent thought. The woman—Adeline—everything she'd said was at once a blur but jostled with vivid points of intense clarity . . . painful memories.

I interlaced my fingers on top of my head and pressed my palms against my temples, trying to stop the whirls of my thoughts.

Then, like one emerging from a storm, I grasped what just happened—what she'd done.

Son of a bitch.

I'd just been cold-pitched—approached without circumstance or context, and done in a manner so as to demand subsequent contact. It was how professionals orchestrated meetings when there was no logical reason for an introduction. Except this woman had done it using fear and pain, knowing enough about me to zero in on issues no normal person would have any idea about unless I'd shared it with them.

As everything began to crystallize, I then realized it was the combination of what the woman had said that was most unsettling.

I was a European historian and, by definition, my work—my life—focused on the past, not the present. Yet she'd brought up my lecture and said something about how it was connected to Europe's current struggles . . . good Lord.

What could she possibly have to show me? What connected my work with the problems of today?

I had no idea.

As for my father—what did she mean his death was no accident? What else could it have been?

It had been nearly two decades since I'd put the man in the ground, and it had taken another year to close the man's affairs and move on. My father—Ambassador Karl Dresden—had been an asshole, and I had no desire to reminisce.

A clap of thunder off in the distance brought me back. I glanced at my watch and saw it was getting late.

Leaning forward, I looked at the half-empty bottle of wine on the table that I'd been working on since dinner. It was a good vintage from a local winemaker, a Rhone blend, full-bodied and earthy, but I debated switching to scotch. I needed something stronger and no longer cared if someone was lurking about. If they were going to do something, they would have already done it.

Taking one last look at the call log on my phone, I snatched up the wine bottle and my empty glass and walked back into the villa. The stone walls were cracked and weathered, and the neglected hedges had overgrown what little there was of a patio.

The place hadn't always been like this—dilapidated and forgotten. I'd spent several summers here as a child doing what young boys do, and I and my dear Olivia had come twice a year ever since we first met. She possessed a heart-stopping smile when she gazed through the back door across the fields. But that was a long time ago.

I made my way across the terracotta floor of the sitting room to the sideboard and opened the bottle of Balvenie. I filled a tumbler with a treble, downed half of it, swirled my glass, and finished the rest.

Shouldn't discuss anything else over the phone. What the hell does that mean?

I poured myself a second glass—just a double this time—ran my fingers through my hair, and dropped down on the leather sofa. I leaned back, sinking into the cushion, and squeezed the bridge of my nose. When I opened my eyes, I beheld the painting above the stone fireplace. It was a landscape by Albert Bierstadt, an original, and one of the artist's lesser-known pieces depicting the Swiss Alps, painted in 1856. It'd been in my family for years.

The interplay between light and darkness was masterful. The snowcapped mountains were brilliantly lit, and the gentle slope of a hill was lush with grass and evergreens. But there were crevices and depths that were nearly black. I had always considered those places the unknown, hiding something sinister, like a troll or an evil wizard. A child's imagination.

I took another drink of my scotch and tossed my phone on the coffee table. I closed my eyes and tried to block out the memories that Adeline had resurrected.

CHAPTER 2

I woke just before sunrise, and despite the previous night's events, I'd slept fitfully. My internal clock seemed aligned with atomic time, and even if I wanted to sleep in, I never could. My eyes would pop open like a shade and that was it—awake for the day.

And I'd been this way since the second day of kindergarten, anxious about arriving late to Madame Rouxel's class. She'd been a broad-shouldered woman with bright red lipstick who would stand at the door to class with her arms crossed while we ducklings passed by. A ruler being smacked in her palm would have been too much.

Rubbing my eyes once, I rolled over and appreciated the morning light breaking through my second-story window. I took a sip from the water glass by my bedside, then padded across the uneven hardwood to the water closet. The cold water I splashed on my face fully shedded the remnants of sleep, and I started putting on my running clothes and shoes.

Ten minutes later, I was on the trail barreling through the foothills of the Maritime-Alps. I could see the sun cresting the hilltops with its rays peeking through the trees, and I could smell the sweetness of the evergreens and hardpacked, brown earth. It was the best part of the day, I thought, and the cool air invigorated me as I pushed myself up and down the rocky paths.

Normally on my morning runs, I would think through a bit of writing I was working on, mull over the argument of a book I was reading, or simply enjoy the view. The movement, the mindlessness of putting one foot in front of the other, the picturesque landscape—it was a creative mind-exercise for me. But unfortunately, other things were bouncing around in my head this morning.

I was replaying the previous night's conversation, trying to make sense of it. To say it was bizarre would be an understatement, so my brain worked to extract the details of what Adeline had said and what she hadn't, and the woman's voice echoed in my ears. She'd flustered me, and I found it irritating that she had. As I said, after a few weeks of lying low, I was starting to emerge from the unfortunate state of being publicly criticized for my work. I'd been stowing away the negativity inside the boxes I kept hidden in the back of my mind, closing them up with a firm smack.

But Adeline had sent things reeling and I couldn't shake it.

An hour later, I was back at the villa and cleaned up, but not surprisingly, I was no closer to making sense of the phone call than when I'd started my jaunt through the hills. The woman had told me just enough to hook me but not reveal anything about her intentions. She'd known what to say and how to say it. I felt like I'd been beset by someone practiced at manipulating others, stringing them along on threads of information. Or, more probably, lies and alternative versions of the truth.

Topping off my cup of coffee, I checked my email to make sure nothing else distressing had sprung up, but aside from a handful of messages from the history department at Princeton, a colleague from Georgetown wanting me to review a journal article, and an email from my longtime ex that I'd been procrastinating on responding to for three months, there was nothing I couldn't ignore for another day.

Noticing the time, I snatched my keys from the tray by the door and walked outside. Once again being greeted by the warm rays of the morning sun, I spotted Madame Channon trimming the lavender shrubs at her villa next door. She wore sand-colored shorts that revealed her tanned legs and a white button-down blouse that toyed with being transparent.

It was amazing, I thought. For a woman over sixty, she had a body like a thirty-five-year-old and a charm that could tempt the Pope. The only time she betrayed her age was when she talked about her steamy fling with one of the Carnegies back in '79 and a sordid affair with a Saudi prince whom she had vowed never to reveal the identity of.

"Bonjour, Professor," Madame Channon said, tossing me a smile that I couldn't help but return.

"Bonjour, Madame. Comment allez-vous?"

"Je vais bien," she replied, using her hand to shield her eyes from the sun. "You must come by for dinner tomorrow night. A few of my friends from Barcelona are coming in. They're absolutely insufferable and I'd prefer to gossip about them behind their backs."

"Merci, Madame, but I might have plans," I said, still smiling.

"Nonsense," she snapped with a dismissive wave. "I already told them you're bringing the wine, and I know for a fact you have nothing to do tomorrow except hide in that shack of yours. Come at eight," she said and went back to inspecting the lavender, humming to herself.

"Very well," I said, not really committing, but thinking an evening with Madame Channon might be just what I needed after this morning's adventure. At dinner, there would no doubt be a collection of eccentric guests engaging in provocative conversation ranging from Catalonian politics to the latest art exhibitions to the drama of love triangles among the region's socialites. An attractive distraction.

With one last wave, I got in my car—a copper-colored 1981 BMW 5 Series—and took off down the windy road toward the coast. I'd owned this machine since I was a second-year student at university, the only non-authentic piece of equipment being the sound system. I'd added a CD player and top-of-the-line speakers a decade ago. Music could set or change any mood—my grandmother had taught me that—and I hoped a little Green Day would settle me on the drive to Nice.

But it didn't.

My approaching rendezvous with Adeline continued to weigh on me.

I arrived at the corner of Rue de l'Église and Quai de l'Amiral Courbet thirty minutes before eight in the morning, and I'd brought along a copy of *America and the World War* by Theodore Roosevelt. I liked having a book with me everywhere I went, just in case.

Rather than taking a seat under the awning at Le Trastevere, I found an outdoor table at the restaurant across the way. I ordered a breakfast of brie, toast, and smoked fish and looked around to get a sense of my surroundings—sights, smells, sounds, people. I tried to settle in to relax.

On the seaside strip of Villefranche-sur-Mer, there was an assemblage of early risers enjoying a morning espresso, as well as a few strolling couples soaking up the mild ocean breeze. Fishermen were bringing in the morning catch and shop owners were opening their doors for the day. Everything seemed benign and sleepy, which was comforting.

And I liked to think I fit in here. I wore a simple white cotton shirt, pair of gray slacks, and loafers, and when I looked in the mirror I saw common Western European features—brown hair, brown eyes, apparent cheekbones, and what I would humbly describe as a trim yet sturdy physique of nearly six feet. My fluency in French often let people mistake me for a local, and although I was an American, I felt more comfortable on Europe's cobblestone streets than in the shopping centers of the American Midwest or swank bars of New York. I'd spent the majority of my life on the Continent in a smattering of places, and I liked that fact.

The food arrived and I ate modestly, washing everything down with a Perrier and a steaming café au lait. I then checked my watch and saw it was one minute before eight, just before Adeline said she'd arrive. I thought about ordering another coffee as I glanced down the street.

Among the clusters of people, I saw a woman with a silver shoulder bag advancing. She was of average height with brunette hair and a pleasing figure. Her walk suggested she was athletic but still feminine. There was a gracefulness to her, like a dancer. She wore a simple pair of cream-colored slacks and a sky-blue button-down shirt, which were accented by a brown belt and a pair of oversized sunglasses. Subtly fashionable for the season.

But then this woman, whom I'd been watching and started to think might be Adeline, turned right to head up the street into the town and out of view.

That's when I noticed a second woman walking behind her. In contrast, she had short blond hair pulled back taut with an off-center part, and she was a little shorter with a sturdier frame. Not overweight by any means, but with a physique that could probably hold up well in a boxing match. She, too, wore cream-colored slacks but her shirt was white and her handbag was a deep maroon and a bit oversized. It made me think if she swung it at someone, the bag could knock the unfortunate soul on their ass.

But in addition to her appearance, I soon noticed her most strik-ing feature—her comportment. She exhibited an air about her that was strong, almost sharp. She seemed acutely aware of everything going on around her, but in a casual way, as if she didn't want anyone to know how alert she actually was.

She took a seat under the awning at Le Trastevere and spoke to the attendant, perhaps ordering a coffee or a double whisky. Then she looked across the avenue directly at me, locking eyes. She smiled and motioned to the chair across from her.

I was intrigued by how easily she'd spotted me, guessing she had my picture. Leaving a few euros on the table, I walked toward the woman I assumed was Adeline. I reminded myself to let her do the talking. If there was silence, I thought it best to let it simmer so that she had to make the next move. I needed to listen and assess.

I approached the mysterious woman's table and rested my hand on the back of the empty chair, offering a polite smile.

*   *   *

"Hello, Professor Dresden," the woman said, removing her sun-glasses and eyeing me through a deliberate squint.

"Good morning," I replied.

As I studied this woman before me, I guessed she was probably in her late thirties. Up close, she had a handsome face that I thought could both be warm like an aunt's or cool like a hatchet corporate raider. Yet, the confidence she seemed to posses reflected boldly off her skin.

"Yes, it is a good morning," she said, her voice feminine but a bit low, which made me think she could bark orders, if she wanted. "Won't you join me?"

I pulled back the chair and sat.

"You do indeed look like a rugby player," Adeline quipped.

"I beg your pardon?"

"You look fit, like you've kept yourself in shape. Like you're not a pushover."

"What are you talking about?" I asked.

"It's nothing. An observation. Nothing more. Forgive me," she said dismissively. "My name is Adeline Parker. And so there's no misunderstanding, I'm an intelligence officer with Britain's Secret Intelligence Service."

My head was still reeling from the rugby crack and now this—Britain's Secret Intelligence Service—SIS—more popularly referred to as MI6. James bloody Bond.

I wasn't all that surprised; I'd been right to think something was off with this woman. Liars and manipulators had that aura about them, and her behavior on the phone last night had been telling. And now I wondered how many people were positioned in the area surveilling our meeting with high-tech cameras and microphones. Perhaps Adeline carried a pistol in her handbag—a nice little hand-cannon.

"MI6," I said blandly. "I guess that makes sense. I suppose you don't have a badge or some other form of identification?"

"You know I don't. Would it make a difference if I did?"

I shook my head.

"Sorry to disappoint. Would you rather I had lied and told you I was a fellow academic, then break the news to you later? That's how we usually do it. Get people thinking one thing and then open up the kimono, revealing ourselves."

I remained impassive, my guard now up infinitely higher than before. "No. In truth, I'd prefer we forgo the banter and be straight with one another. Does that work for you?"

"Of course it does," she replied.

"Good," I said, but not thinking for a moment that she would. "So let's have it. You called my private number and brought up my deceased father. Could you please explain what this is all about."

"My pleasure," said Adeline, her frank demeanor sliding even more stern. She shifted in her seat and laced her fingers, resting her elbows on the edge of the table. "Let's start with you, shall we. Professor William Randolph Dresden, born April 12, 1970, to Karl and Evelyn Dresden. When you were twelve, your mother died in childbirth. What would have been your sister died, too. Your father—a diplomat with your Department of State—struggled with the loss and poured himself into his work, eventually holding multiple overseas positions.

"Consequently, you spent the majority of your life abroad—in Europe, to be precise—growing up in the care of nannies and boarding schools. Though a frail lad, you seemed to adjust decently enough, excelled in your academics at the Harrow School in England, and by the time you were fifteen had mastered French, German, and Spanish, and were flirting with Russian. Am I missing anything?"

"You're doing the talking," I said, crossing my legs and signaling the waiter for an espresso, though feeling a quiver under my skin by how easily she'd rattled off the details of my life.

"Right. At seventeen you entered Balliol College at Oxford, graduating with honors with a degree in history and politics. Cross-country and rugby—seeming to have overcome the bookish frame of your childhood—a few energetic evenings, and the occasional lover. You went on to Princeton to earn your PhD and entered into a long-term relationship with Olivia Batteux, a French gal and fellow grad student from an old Alsatian family.

"But unlike your father, you had no desire for government service. You were more of a humanitarian-type, as one might say. You worked for a few international development NGOs, and in 1995 found yourself in Bosnia-Herzegovina working at an orphanage. According to your fellow aid workers, you were quite comfortable in the relative uncertainty of the environment. But later that year on a visit to Srebrenica, you got separated from the Dutch forces escorting you and who were supposed to protect the city. You hid with a Bosniak family in the forest while the Serbs massacred 8,000 people. That experience changed you."

Adeline paused and met my stare, and outwardly I did my best not to flinch. But inside, harsh memories flashed like tiny shocks as the sounds, images, and smells came back to me. I could almost feel my nostrils burning from the memory of the rancid smoke. Had the circumstances been different, I would have gotten up to walk away—yet I couldn't move.

Whether Adeline could discern my current state, I don't know, but she continued.

"A year later, you and Olivia split, and then your father died in a car crash. A head-on collision. You resigned from your development work and went back to academia, withdrawing for a time, which is understandable. But you eventually got on with things, teaching classes and doing research. Now, you're a Fellow at Princeton and Research Associate at King's College in Cambridge—an expert in European colonialism and the imperial era.

"But, as I mentioned last night, your latest research has caused some debates in your field, arguing the Franco-Prussian War was the catalyst that led to all the major wars of the twentieth century, and that historical figures we've never heard of wielded more power than we ever realized. As it was, just a few months ago your funding was pulled—no reason given—and now you're here, on a sabbatical of sorts, in the south of France."

Adeline sipped her water. "Oh, and you're the last surviving member of the Dresden family and sole inheritor of your family's estate, which your forefathers acquired in the latter half of the nineteenth century, from the steel trade. The skeletons of old money and all that."

With her final statement, I remained silent, endeavoring to appear unmoved, although that was anything but the case. I wondered how thick my file at MI6 was and what else was in there. Everything she'd said was true, but to hear my life summed up so casually, so flippantly, was disquieting.

Things I would have rather kept private were exposed for others to look at, to analyze, to make twisted conclusions about. The analysts and psyches never got it right. Still, I was genuinely struck dumb even if she didn't know everything about me. She couldn't. No one could.

Finally gathering myself, I said, "All right, you've apparently done your homework on me, as uncomfortable as that may be. So what? You already had my attention from last night's call. So I'll ask again. What's this all about, and what do you know about my father's death?"

She smiled. "Have you ever heard of the Strasbourg Covenants?"

CHAPTER 3

"The what?" I asked, leaning forward in my café chair.

"The Strasbourg Covenants. Have you ever come across them in your research?" asked Adeline, again using her tight squint to lock onto me.

Breaking her stare and gazing across the harbor's water, I thought for a moment, probing the recesses of my mind. But there was nothing. "I can't say that I have. Should I?"

"No, and I'm not surprised," Adeline remarked as if she'd expected that to be my answer. "Mind if I give you the abbreviated version?"

"Isn't that why we're here?" I replied, opening my arms in an overly welcoming gesture to obscure the disquiet inside me.

Adeline feigned a smile. "Quite right. You see, towards the end of the nineteenth century, a small group of influential men from across Europe—politicians, generals, industrialists, royals—the upper crust, you might say, and from various countries—came together in Strasbourg and devised what they called the Strasbourg Covenants."

"Quite the name," I remarked.

"Isn't it? Well, these men believed in the superiority of what they considered true European nationalities and citizenry. They were adherents to racial theory, among other things, and they thought that Europe was the epicenter of the world for all things: politics, commerce, military power, high culture. But as you know, Professor, there were lots of people from that era who thought similarly. European superiority, the *white man's burden*—it was all quite common. Even someone who might not firmly subscribe to racial theory would still, more often than not, consider white Europeans above just about everyone."

I nodded knowingly and said, "Thank you for the history lesson. But I'll bite. What made this group different?"

Adeline smiled again. "This group of men, they formed something they called the *Executive* to pursue these *covenants*. Basically, the covenants were their shared understandings of how they thought the world should be and what they should do to achieve those ends. Let's call this the forerunner to the fascism we saw emerge in the early twentieth century."

"Okay, please go on," I said, allowing a skeptical frown to appear.

"Well, since the Executive's formation, their activities have waned and resurged over the years, working to manipulate the leaders and populations of their respective countries from behind the scenes to further their agenda. We don't know what it is for certain—their precise agenda, the particulars of the covenants—and we suspect it's evolved over time following the major events in history, but we assess they center on national strength and preserving *pure* European ethnic groups."

"Fascinating," I said.

"Isn't it?" Adeline remarked amusingly. "Well, starting back in the 1870s, the Executive played no small part in championing European imperial efforts, which I suspect you already deduced. They then encouraged the nationalist movements that culminated in the Great War, and you can probably guess they had a connection to the Nazis. I'm not suggesting they were the determining factor for any of these things, but like a political movement, they tried, albeit secretly, working in the shadows. Their effectiveness is unknown, but it was there, we are certain. But all that's history; not why I'm here."

I tried to digest everything Adeline was saying. It was true that in the latter half of the nineteenth century, the idea of European superiority was mainstream. Darwin, Arthur de Gobineau, and other thinkers used science to argue their theories about racial inequality and the superiority of white, European peoples. Coupled with greed and the ability to project power across the oceans, the European Imperial era took shape. And these ideas served as the foundation for numerous hate groups and nationalist movements, which I was now assuming this Strasbourg group was among.

But what this woman was suggesting was . . . different.

Despite what the conspiracy theorists wanted everyone to believe, there had never been a faceless, secret society that had been able to shape world affairs in a tangible way. Some groups have tried and created some fascinating tales, but when one gets down to the facts, it's underwhelming.

But that's where I stopped myself. There was more *and* something relevant to today. Adeline was from British Intelligence, and no intelligence organization would dedicate time and effort to a mere story in history. Not unless there was something else to it. That, I knew. Academia may invest time and money into topics purely for the sake of knowledge, but governments and spies don't.

"Since the early days of the Cold War," Adeline went on, "the Executive has been relatively inactive. We're not exactly sure why— perhaps it was the crushing defeat of Nazi Germany and Imperial Japan—but we see no evidence indicating otherwise. The Executive went relatively quiet.

"But in the last few years, we detected a significant uptick in activity. We don't know specifically what they're after—today's manifestation of the Executive—but we're convinced they're responsible for a significant part of the resurgence of populist movements across Europe. When right-wing groups like the Austrian Freedom Party and National Front in France start commanding sizeable percentages of the populace, and when Italy elects its first far-right government since WWII—something is off."

I furrowed my brow. "Okay. Secret groups, neo-facists, international plots . . . sounds like quite the story. But haven't you seen the news lately? It's the Russians and their troll farms and right-wing politicians latching on to old ideas. When life was *better* and *simpler* with the clarity provided by selective memory."

"Yes, the Russians are active and promoting internal discord to weaken Western society, but they're clumsy and everyone knows it. Putin's latest aggression into Ukraine to *protect ethnic Russians* is a shining example. And you are correct, the sound bites from many right-wing political groups regurgitate old ideas. But the Executive," Adeline said as she shook her head. "They're the ones who worry me."

"Okay, fine. The Executive is a concern. I'll go along with it for our little exercise. But why are you telling me? If you were going to talk to a historian, isn't this more appropriate for the talking heads on the BBC or cable news?"

"Perhaps. I'm sure they'd be interested. But like you said in the beginning, let's skip the bloody nonsense. This is real. I'm not here to waste your time."

"Of course you're not," I said, smiling just as the waiter walked up, delivering my espresso that I immediately took a sip of.

"As unbelievable as it sounds, William, this group is real, and they are indeed a threat to Europe, more so because no one knows they exist. What I've told you is highly sensitive—only a handful of people in the Service are aware of its existence—but those who do know are on edge."

"I get it, and let's say I believe you," I said, setting my cup down gently and lacing my fingers. "How does this concern me, and what does any of this have to do with my father?"

Adeline paused for a moment, eyeing me. She then said, "For the past two years you've been researching the connection between nineteenth-century imperialism and its impact on twenty-first-century international affairs. Before that, you wrote a book about how the Franco-Prussian War was the precursor to all the major conflicts of the twentieth century. And recently you gave a lecture at the Woodrow Wilson Center, describing four families from the turn of the century who had significantly more influence on international events than had been previously thought. Am I right?"

"We've been over this. Yes. Right on all accounts. You know me well. But?"

"We think three of the four families you've been looking into were part of the original Strasbourg Executive. And now, the Executive of today is shutting you down for fear of exposure. They're the ones who had your funding pulled and made sure you were thoroughly smeared and discredited."

I sat back in my chair and thought. A few months back, the National Endowment for the Humanities unexpectedly rescinded my grant for the project Adeline was speaking of and which had caused such a backlash. Ironically, when I'd originally proposed my research project to the committee—a reexamination of the late-nineteenth-century imperial era and its impact on the twentieth century—the members enthusiastically endorsed me. I had a reputation for being a historian who wasn't afraid to challenge conventional thinking. I was doing the type of work people talked about, and that's what the NEH liked. So when they pulled my funding, I was thoroughly puzzled. The only thing the cancellation paperwork said was, *Project assessed as low-priority, funds reprogrammed*. And then, of course, the criticism followed.

"What does the Executive think I'm exposing?" I asked. "And why would they single me out? Who am I but a mere academic among thousands?"

"It is their past they are concerned about, which will lead to the present. They can't operate if people know who they are or where they come from."

"What?" I asked, while simultaneously thinking about the four individuals she'd referred to, wondering which ones she believed had been members of this *Executive*: Randolph, Gibbons, Waters, Himmler.

"All right. Fine. Let's say this is true. The Executive had the NEH pull my funding and orchestrate a good lashing from my colleagues to thoroughly embarrass me and send me running to lick my wounds in my place of solitude. Ridiculous, but what about this conversation isn't ridiculous? What about my father?"

"Your father. Yes. After he retired from the U.S. State Department, he became an economic advisor to the EU, sort of an investment advisor for national economies. We think he stumbled across something about the Executive. They killed him for it."

"It was a car accident," I said firmly, remembering the night the French police called and then going to the accident.

"Staged. He was murdered," countered Adeline. "They killed him and made it look like an accident. Failed airbag? Airbags don't fail."

The suggestion unnerved me, uncomfortably so, and I did my best to control my reaction. But I have no idea if I succeeded or not. I imagine the confusion and pain displayed clearly on my face. The idea that my father had been murdered—a shamelessly distinguished man—was too much. I nearly laughed, a painful irony welling up inside me.

For years I'd blamed my father for the accident—a front-end collision with an elm tree. I'd assumed the bastard had been drunk and I resented him for it. My father had never been there for me, not once. Not as a child, not as a teenager, not as an adult.

But as much as I hated to admit it, the man was my father. I felt an inexplicable draw to him, even if our relationship had been a series of disappointments. I'd wanted the man's approval. What boy doesn't? What son doesn't? I remembered as a child looking up to him, hoping for a *good job* or *nicely done*, but my father always had a frown on his face—always. I can still picture it. Like he was perpetually irritated at the world around him as well as with me.

And the night my father died, we'd fought. Olivia and I had split the day before and my father had come to see me, but not to offer comfort. Rather, he'd lectured me on how I needed to move on, put the breakup behind me. Like so many other aspects of my life, the relationship had been a waste of time. Love and attachments were nothing but distractions, he'd said.

That was the last thing I'd wanted to hear. It wasn't the moment, and my father's self-righteous attitude infuriated me. It had been less than twenty-four hours, for God's sake.

We both raised our voices, and in a haze of too much scotch, I brought up my dead mother, accusing my father of being cruel to her. If only my father had been more loving, more supportive of his expecting wife, perhaps she would have survived the birth. She'd been a petite woman, a heart of gold, a caregiver, a mother in the truest sense. She didn't deserve to be treated like that.

My father's reaction to my outburst was venomous. He cursed me for going too far, but I was too heated to care.

Those were the last words we ever said to each other.

"William," said Adeline, trying to get my attention.

I was staring at a spot on the tablecloth, consumed in thought. I met her gaze. "What?"

"I need you to come with me to London. We need . . ." Adeline's voice trailed off, her attention suddenly fixated on something over my shoulder.

I turned to see what it was.

"Get down!" shouted Adeline.

An explosion ripped through the café.

CHAPTER 4

"Analytique Internationale is a boutique, competitive intelligence firm focused on providing market research and analysis to clientele. Our specialty is learning everything about your competitors—and the government pitfalls you will encounter—to give you the edge you need."

The woman speaking sat on one side of the table, flanked by two associates. She had blond hair down to her shoulders, blue eyes, and wore a black pantsuit and white shirt that rested over every perfect curve of her body.

She spoke assertively, practiced at speaking her mind and telling others what to do and how things would be. She came across either as that high-flyer on her way to the top, or the bitch that everyone hoped would choke on her martini olive.

Across from her were four businessmen, all of them in their forties and fifties. Typical executives with white hair in dark suits and solid ties. They were in the boardroom on the fiftieth floor of Petroleum Industries' headquarters—a firm that partnered with BP and Exxon, but without the headlines.

"If you were to contract my firm's services," continued the woman, "I can assure you we'd collect and present to you information no one else can."

"We have no doubt, Ms. König," said the Petroleum Industries' president. "Your firm's reputation is well established, and we appreciate your policies on discretion. Rather, we'd prefer to get right to it. Here are our requirements." The man slid a file across the table.

Sofia König glanced at the first page, then passed it to the man on her left. "My VP for Operations, Brecht Herst, will be taking lead on this effort."

Brecht nodded. "Thank you, gentlemen. I suggest we begin by—"

Sofia felt her phone vibrate in her pocket. She removed it and looked at the number, and a shot of nervousness coursed down her spine. "Gentlemen, please accept my apologies. If you'll excuse me."

Sofia headed for the hall and swiped her phone. "Oui?"

"Have you seen the news?" asked a man's voice. She could hear sirens wailing in the background.

Sofia glanced at a television on the lobby wall as she strode by. A newscaster was reporting a café bombing outside of Nice. First responders were rushing the wounded to ambulances and firemen were putting out the flames caused by the explosion.

"Is it done?" she asked.

"They got away."

"How?"

"She spotted me."

"I thought you said that wouldn't be a problem?"

"A setback," assured the man. "We'll know soon enough where they're headed."

"Contact me when it's done."

Sofia slipped the phone back into her pocket and began to pace, wringing her hands. The operation should have been quick and simple so no one could protest her actions. But that wasn't possible anymore. She'd have to deal with the fallout.

CHAPTER 5

The only reason I was still alive was because Adeline had pushed me behind the concrete barrier we'd been sitting next to. The explosion ripped through the outside seating area of the café, turning tables and chairs into ragged pieces of shrapnel, killing four people. Another seven were wounded, bleeding, screaming, and staring at nothing in shock.

Adeline grabbed my arm and rushed me away from the scene, leaving the dead and the dying writhing on the ground with their cries and screams carrying on the coastal breeze. A block away we jumped in her car.

"We need to go," she said between coughs. "That was meant for us."

"What are you talking about? What's going on?" My ears were ringing and my chest ached from the overpressure. My body didn't feel like my own, trying to reject the trauma.

"A briefcase," Adeline said, putting the pedal to the floor and racing down the street. "I recognized the bomber."

I gripped the door handle as we sped through the narrow streets and alleys, with doorways and confused bystanders whipping by. "You know him?"

"Yes," Adeline said, sliding the car around a corner and hurtling down another tight street. "He's MI5. Tim Sanders. Arrogant prick."

"MI5?" I couldn't believe what I was hearing. MI5 was Britain's other security service, similar to the FBI.

"I don't have time to explain. But I told you this was serious. Once we're clear, I'll tell you what I know, but we need to get out of here first."

We weaved down the back roads of coastal France for another twenty minutes until we reached a town I didn't recognize. We were somewhere between Nice and Monaco off the A8. It was a vacation area but in a less crowded locale. Adeline parked in an alley, and then we walked two blocks to a small hotel.

Inside, she led me to a room with a small sitting and sleeping area separated by a partition. As soon as Adeline shut the door, she started unbuttoning her blouse, revealing a full bosom and black bra. Kicking off her shoes, she undid her pants, pulled them off, and threw them on top of the shirt.

"Enjoying the view?" Adeline asked, pulling on a pair of jeans and throwing on another button-down blouse.

"I didn't mean . . . I wasn't . . . Goddammit, what the hell is going on?" I blurted.

"Not now. See that bag over there? It's got some clothes for you. Your size. Change."

"What?"

"Just do it. We were at the scene. They're after us. Change clothes. And do me a favor, sit down and take a breath." Adeline disappeared behind the partition.

I remained standing, staring at nothing, making no movement to sit. I flexed my fingers, willing myself to settle, hoping to make sense of what was happening.

I took a second glance around the room. Two windows looked over the houses across the street, and I could see a few blocks beyond. I stepped back out of view and pulled the shades down, suddenly fearful that someone might be watching us. I then went to the door and double-checked the lock. I noticed the bag Adeline had pointed to, which was on a high-back chair. I knocked the bag to the floor and jammed the chair at an angle underneath the door handle, barricading it.

I ran my fingers through my hair and tried to remember what I'd seen on the way up to the hotel room. There was a back-door exit at the base of the stairs, and I thought I'd seen another stairwell at the opposite end of the hall. Or had it been a dead end? How many floors were there?

Goddammit! I had to start paying attention. I knew better.

I looked at the bag I'd tossed on the floor, which was made of green canvas with brown leather handles. It was perfect for a day trip up the coast with a bottle of dry rosé for a picnic.

I opened the bag. Inside were jeans, a blue shirt, and a brown sport coat. For the first time since the bombing, I looked down at the clothes I was wearing. My white shirt was dusty and spotted black, and my pants were ripped at the knee. Blood from scrapes stained the fabric. I couldn't be seen like this. I started changing, noticing that the clothes fit perfectly. As I buttoned my shirt, I saw the clock on the wall said 9:04 a.m.

When Adeline emerged from around the partition, she carried a small backpack from which she pulled out a pistol. I think it was a semiautomatic or something. She checked the chamber, then slipped it into a leather holster and tucked it inside her waistband.

I took her arm, demanding she look at me. "What have you gotten me into?"

Adeline met my glare. She took a single breath. "You watch the news, yes? Stay abreast of current events?"

"Not like I used to, but yeah," I said, letting her go.

"Then you've probably seen all the controversy about the push for nationalism, anti-Muslim laws, violence against immigrants, yes?"

"Sure."

"There are some in my organization who suspect the Strasbourg Executive is trying to drive governments to the far right, usher in a return to when Europe was for *Europeans* and it had the militaries to keep it that way. Brexit was the first step."

"What are you talking about? This is crazy."

"Is it? That bomb that just went off—this is not a joke."

"How . . . I don't understand."

"We think they're influencing the politicians and diplomats, social media, mainstream news—most people don't even realize it. They think all this talk about the return of nationalism has been simmering for years. It has, to an extent, but the Executive has worked to bring it out in the open, exacerbate it, shocks to the system. Drive us towards the edge until the momentum is so strong we have no choice but to crack down on everything and everyone."

"That doesn't make any sense. For what purpose?" I challenged, still trying to understand what she was telling me and how I was involved.

"We don't know for sure. That's what I've been saying. But it's more than just populist shit. Perhaps some geopolitical realignment, organized suppression of immigrants or minorities, perhaps money, power—could be anything. What we do know is that they're willing to kill whoever is in their way and do Lord knows what else."

"And you think they're after me because I gave a lecture?"

Adeline nodded.

"That's insane," I said, throwing up my hands.

"Think what you want, but you can't ignore the fact that they just blew up a café to get to you."

I stopped, the blood pounding all through my body. It was like every word she said ratcheted up my apprehension, to where now I was on the verge of gesticulating like a crazy man. Jesus Christ! What was happening?

I glanced at the window again, then the door. If what she was saying was true, the Executive could be anywhere, and the mere thought was absurd. They could be crashing into the hotel lobby, about to rush the stairs and storm the room. Or they could be miles away, trying to decide how best to come after us—after me!

I returned my attention to Adeline, searching her face. There was more, there had to be. She was hiding something. I was about to fire off another series of questions at her, but for a reason I couldn't explain, I caught myself.

I looked at the clock on the wall again. It was 9:07. I felt like time was standing still while simultaneously vanishing. "All right," I finally said. "What do we do?"

"I need to check in with my people at our station in Monaco. Can I leave you alone for a moment?"

I frowned at her comment. "I'm fine, Agent Parker. Do what you need to, and get some answers."

Adeline picked up her mobile phone and went behind the wall, not that it afforded any privacy. I could easily listen in.

But instead, I clicked the remote control to the television. On France 24, a female reporter stood no more than twenty feet from the bomb site. She was describing the scene—casualties, damage, reactions from eyewitnesses.

I pulled out my smartphone, saw it was off—probably from the blast—and turned it back on. I reviewed a string of international news sites to see what they were saying. Nothing yet.

The TV cut away from the on-scene reporter and went to the news desk, catching my attention. An anchorman in a crisp blue suit sat behind a desk. "This just in. Interpol is reporting that the bomb in Villefranche-sur-Mer this morning was likely the work of this man—Professor William Dresden."

My faculty picture appeared on the screen.

"Professor Dresden is a historian from Princeton University and has written numerous pieces about the historical problems with European unity. Interpol is not providing many details, but they suspect Professor Dresden's motive was political . . ."

I couldn't pull my eyes off the television. I couldn't believe what I was seeing. It'd been less than thirty minutes, and there I was, framed for all of it. Who were these people?

"Adeline?"

She was still behind the partition. When she emerged, she had a blank expression on her face.

"Are you seeing this? Is this them?"

Adeline looked at the news broadcast. "Yes," she replied, her voice sounding like it was miles away.

"What? What is it?" I asked, realizing that something besides the TV had unsettled her.

"My desk officer is dead. Killed this morning."

"Who?"

"My desk officer. I don't work out of Monaco. I'm out of Vauxhall Cross in London. I work special projects. Kyle was providing back-end support for me—communications, travel, and all that."

"What happened?"

"Shot in his hotel room. I talked to the head of station in Monaco. He was furious. Demanded to know where I was, why there wasn't any coordination in the cables. Wanted me to bring you in immediately."

"What's the problem? Can't they protect us, help us figure out what's going on?"

Adeline shook her head. "Something's not right. An MI5 officer leaves a briefcase that blows up a café—with you as the target. A senior desk officer working this case is killed the same morning—shot in his hotel room. And now someone is tearing into me about why he wasn't briefed on the op. I don't work for him. He shouldn't know anything about what I'm doing except that I'm in his area."

"What are you saying?"

"Whoever is after us, they've breached my service. Who knows, maybe even has someone on the inside."

"My God," I murmured, then thought, "What about the U.S. Embassy?"

Sirens sounded in the distance and Adeline peered out the window, then she noticed the phone in my hand. "Did you call someone?"

"No. I just turned it on."

"What did you do?"

"Nothing. I just turned it on."

"Bloody hell. It logged into all your accounts—e-mail, internet, GPS—someone's tracking you and they just tipped off the police."

I stared at my phone, my mind flashing to all the stuff in the news and the movies about people being tracked through phones. Big Brother on overdrive.

"Son of a bitch," I breathed. I just led whoever was after us right to the hotel.

The sirens were getting closer.

Adeline grabbed the bag. "Come on."

CHAPTER 6

Adeline headed for the door, her lips moving in a string of silent curses. I could tell things had gone way wrong—more than the bombing and far beyond my mistake. Our situation was spiraling, and all I could think of was that we had to *get out*.

"Adeline, we gotta go," I said.

Adeline didn't look at me. She removed the chair I'd used as a barricade and perched herself left of the door with her hand reaching for the handle. "Get behind me," she said. "Now."

I did, not daring to question it.

With her fingers touching the door handle, she said, "Everything is crumbling as if the Executive knew all the vectors to hit. You, me, my team . . . They know."

"Know what?"

Adeline shook her head and pursed her lips, then she glanced back at me. I couldn't be positive, but I detected a trace of a smile when she saw me leaning forward like a runner on the block. If only she could hear my heart pounding in near panic.

"Ready?" she asked.

I nodded.

"Stay close," she said, opening the door, and dashing down the corridor, the backpack tucked under her arm. I kept on her heels, passing through a connecting door and descending a set of stairs. When we reached the second floor, we burst into a small communal bathroom for hotel guests. No one was in there. Adeline went to the window and forced it open.

We were two stories up. Too far to jump. But a series of wrought iron balconies jutted out from the hotel's façade. Some of the bolts were rusted, and sections of the stucco were cracked.

"We need to climb down. Can you make it?" she asked.

I took one look, then nudged past her. I straddled the windowsill and got out on the balcony. I lowered myself down to the one below. Then dropped to the ground.

Adeline followed, jumping the last few meters. She hit the pavement and rolled, getting to her feet. "This way."

The sirens were getting louder. They screamed in the wind, bouncing off building walls and windows.

We ran down the alley toward the street, but before we reached the end, Adeline tucked into a small doorway and pulled me in with her. A police car flew past and stopped abruptly farther down the road.

"Fuck," I breathed.

Adeline bolted across the street into another alley. I followed in tow. We turned down a connecting passageway and emerged onto the backstreet where she'd parked the car from earlier. There was no sign of the police, just an elderly woman sitting on the steps of her apartment. We got in the vehicle, Adeline again behind the wheel.

"Wait," I said. "If they're after me, and you think they're also after you, won't they know this car?"

"Let's hope they didn't wire it to explode."

CHAPTER 7

The corporate jet took an hour to fly from Frankfurt to Düsseldorf. Sofia was met by her driver on the tarmac, and they headed north, away from the city in a fully armored Mercedes-Maybach S600 Guard sedan.

She sat in the back, reading a report her firm had drafted. It contained the financials of the New Flemish Alliance in Belgium, the National Front in France, and the Freedom Party of Austria. Her firm had produced this report independently; no one had contracted them to do it.

But the document contained information Sofia was keen to examine—a report on the viability of Europe's three most powerful right-wing political parties. She needed to know how far they could go with their current resources, and what it would take to push them even further.

"We'll arrive within the hour," said the driver, looking in the rearview mirror at Sofia's bowed head.

Fifty minutes later and well into the German countryside, the Mercedes turned onto a wide driveway controlled by a guardhouse. The car slowed but did not stop, the drop arm raising in expectation of their arrival.

They drove down a gravel road flanked by trees that hung over the driveway, creating the illusion of a tunnel. In the distance, a Baroque structure began to take shape. The façade was gray stone that rose four stories into the air and stretched seventy meters in width. The left and right ends of the estate consisted of circular towers, and in the center a grand entrance with double doors greeted visitors. Perimeter lighting projected up from the base of the walls and illuminated the manor home with a yellow glow.

The Mercedes stopped in front of the main steps. A man in a crisp, gray suit with close-cropped dark hair and eyes the color of glacial ice opened the rear door. "He's in the study," he said, his voice matching the hardness of his features.

"Good evening to you, too, Faust," replied Sofia.

"You'll need to make it quick. He has other matters to attend to tonight."

"I'll take as much time as needed."

Sofia made her way into the house, down the grand hall, and walked through the double doors of the study. She stopped just inside and looked at the elderly gentleman sitting behind the desk. He had salt and pepper hair, and his skin was weathered—tanned and wrinkled. He wore a charcoal suit with a blue shirt, accented by a white collar and French cuffs. He was using a gold-plated fountain pen to sign a series of documents.

Without looking up, the gentleman motioned for her to take a seat in one of the two chairs in front of his desk. Faust moved to the back corner of the room and stood, directing his eyes at nothing, yet aware of everything.

"Tell me what happened," said the man.

"Herr Kanzler, thank you for receiving me at such an hour."

The old man waved his hand. "I always have time for you, my dear. Now, what is it?"

Sofia explained that the attempt on Professor William Dresden and MI6 agent Adeline Parker's lives had failed. They'd escaped, their current whereabouts unknown.

The Kanzler leaned back and steepled his fingers. "This is troubling. I don't remember agreeing to such extreme measures."

She didn't respond. The Kanzler hadn't authorized the bombing, but she hadn't sought his permission, either. She believed killing Dresden and Parker would make the problem go away. If the old man didn't like it, that was his problem.

"I wanted the professor out of the way, but this . . ." The Kanzler's voice drifted off.

"I will fix this, Herr Kanzler."

"I trusted you when you told me this would be quick and painless, with no loose ends."

"It will be."

"But it isn't."

"I will handle it."

"I think that time has passed." The Kanzler raised his gaze toward the ceiling as if looking to the heavens for the answer. "I'll assume control from here."

Sofia clenched her jaw but immediately regretted allowing such a response.

"You disagree?" asked the Kanzler, searching her face.

He could read her well, and she knew it. It was infuriating. She was masterful at manipulating those around her—like trained pets sitting at her feet—but not him. She had no such confidence in his presence. She felt like a child being toyed with, plagued by the emotions of a toddler and unable to restrain herself.

After a moment's pause, and consciously working to make her words seem dispassionate, she said, "I'd never oppose your wishes, but you know I feel strongly about this matter. I'm the one to see this through to the end. Besides, who will do the work? Him?" She motioned at Faust, who remained in the corner like a hound.

"I appreciate your passion. I do. But you don't know the professor like I do. For a man as bookish as he is, he's more capable than most give him credit for," murmured the Kanzler, as much to himself as to Sofia. "I think he might be unpredictable. We should proceed with caution."

Sofia curled her toes inside her shoes as the Kanzler spoke, fidgeting in unseen ways. She couldn't believe he was going on like this. He was inconsistent, and he was ignorant to the crux of the matter. The professor was only half the problem.

The Kanzler was a tired, old man, and she knew more than he would ever realize. He needed to get out of the way.

"The matter is settled. Now it's my operation," he said, emerging from his digression.

"Yes, Herr Kanzler," she replied.

"Good. Now, do you have the report?"

The conversation was over and there was nothing else she could say. Not now, anyway. She removed the report from her bag and handed it to him.

"Very good," he said, thumbing through the first few pages. "The board will be pleased."

CHAPTER 8

We didn't explode. The car started up with a gentle purr and off we went.

We'd been on the road for over two hours, heading north cutting through the French countryside. Adeline had taken a circuitous route, periodically getting off the highway to drive down a country road, double back, or switch to another artery. She didn't think anyone was following us, but modern technology muted her optimism.

Someone could have hidden a GPS tracker on the vehicle and monitored us from behind a computer anywhere in the world. And without a tech officer to sweep the car, there was nothing we could do about it, she'd said. We could only hope the people after us hadn't found the car. Her assessment didn't give me much comfort, but what was I to do? Whether I liked it or not, I was reliant upon Adeline and her judgment.

I knew nothing of this world. She could have told me to put a foil helmet on to prevent the Executive from blasting my brain with microwaves, and I would have wondered if that was, in fact, true. There was so much I didn't understand—so much.

When we reached Avignon, we parked in an underground garage, took what few belongings we had, and made our way across town. Adeline rented another vehicle with an alias, claiming no one in

MI6 except her boss knew about this identity. She'd had it built *off the books*, though I didn't much know what that meant, either. Since the café, Adeline had begun using a language—a vernacular—that I was ignorant to. I may have understood the words she spoke but not how she used them.

Once in the new car, Adeline handed me a worn passport, which I folded over in my hands. It was maroon and had *Union européenne République française* on the cover. When I opened it, I saw it was me but not me. It was my picture, my birth date, my first name, but the last name was something else: *La Fontaine*.

"What's this?" I asked.

"A precaution. You're marked. Can't have your name popping up on any databases as we cross borders or, God forbid, get stopped by the authorities."

I had guessed that much. I knew why someone would use a false identity. But that wasn't my question. "I know. I meant how and when did you make this? It's me . . ."

Adeline continued getting settled but said, "We have our methods."

I flipped through the passport pages one by one, noting the various stamps: the U.S., Israel, Bosnia-Herzegovina, Germany, the U.K., Switzerland. I found the list unsettling because, at some point in my life, I'd been to all of these places. I'd visited them at different times throughout the course of my youthful fifty years, but still, the accuracy unnerved me.

"How long have you been planning this?" I asked.

Adeline put the key in the ignition and readjusted the seat, but she didn't acknowledge my question. Finally settled, she said, "Give me your wallet and anything else that has your real name on it."

"No," I said without thinking, abruptly tired of being ordered around and led through the darkness that had become this new reality. Maybe it was because I knew we had a minute to breathe that this defiant pulse appeared. I believed Adeline was trying to help me, to keep me safe, but I had doubts about her ultimate intentions. There was too much she hadn't shared for me to go on blindly trusting her.

"No," I said again. "Not until you tell me how long you've been watching me."

Adeline appeared to weigh what she would and would not say. The uncertainty I'd detected in her back at the hotel was gone. She was now back in control with a plan—a plan I desperately wanted to know about and understand.

"We've been watching you for over a year and a half," she finally said.

A year and a half? Eighteen months. Eighteen bloody months!

I'd been at Princeton back then, finishing up a post-graduate seminar, and I'd just started researching the lives of Gibbons and Waters. I'd only begun my research, and it was long before I'd found any of the material in question or published my conclusions that caused such a stir.

What had I done back then to attract the interest of British Intelligence? Had they been watching me the entire time, reading my email, listening to my phone calls, sitting next to me in Rojo's Roastery while I sipped my coffee?

The hair on my arms stood up. I had so many questions, but every time she answered one, more questions surfaced. It was like an onion, yet with every layer removed, three or four more appeared. And they were rotten, all rotten.

I took one last look at the passport and put it in my jacket pocket. Adeline had tossed my phone before we'd cleared Nice's city limits, but I still had my wallet. I pulled it from my pocket and searched the worn leather for an old photograph folded and creased. I put that back in my pocket and handed everything else to Adeline.

"What was that? I need everything."

"Not that."

"William—"

"Don't," I snapped, not bothering to look at her. It was a picture from long ago, from a time when the only cares in the world were how soon summer break would arrive and what book I would read next. It was a picture of my mother and father in the kitchen cooking, both of them smiling while I awkwardly leaned against the cabinet. It was one of the few remaining keepsakes I had left.

"Let's get moving," I said softly.

"Fine," Adeline huffed. She pulled up next to the curb and threw my identity into a trash can. We got back on the road and continued driving north, neither of us talking. The urgency of the past few hours was gone, and the exhaustion that follows an adrenaline rush began to set in. I stared absently out the window, watching the farmlands roll past.

I knew this road. I'd driven it over twenty years ago with Olivia. We were going to Lyon for a holiday, excited to experience the food and enjoy the wine. I had passed through the city once when I was a teenager, but it was Olivia's first visit.

I thought it amusing that she'd never been despite having been born and raised outside Paris. She'd countered by saying it was pathetic that I called myself an American, but I'd only lived in the States for a total of five years—which was less than her time in the U.S. She had that provocative, attractive way about her, a bit of parry and riposte with just about everything.

In the car, we'd listened to old tracks of Édith Piaf and recordings of Monty Python. At one point I spilled coffee all over the map, turning it into a soggy, unreadable mess. We changed a flat tire in a rainstorm, too, Olivia slipping in the mud and ruining her pants.

But problems like that don't matter when you're in love. We'd laughed and laughed about it, Olivia getting what she liked to call the *church giggles*. We'd been happy. We'd been young.

But that was years before everything went to shit. I hadn't gone to Bosnia yet, hadn't witnessed a genocide, nor had I tumbled into a darkness I didn't care to explain. I hadn't withdrawn into academia, either. I'd let my life get away from me. I'd tried not to, but I was like my father, as much as I hated to admit it. I'd let work consume me as I hid from everything.

Consequently, I lost the best thing in my life. Olivia had needed more and she was right. Being with someone who was emotionally absent for so long—even when they were right across the dinner table—was no way to live. Despair can be contagious and she didn't want that. She didn't deserve that. She may have still loved me, but she couldn't go on living with me.

I let her slip away.

"Are you doing all right?" asked Adeline, interrupting my thoughts.

I watched a gathering of dairy cows chew the grass, indifferent to the cars rushing by. "I'm fine."

"You don't look fine."

I again wondered how much of what I was thinking showed on my face. Olivia used to think everything did, particularly if I was embarrassed. She said I'd turn into a red tomato.

"After what just happened and what you've told me," I said, "I think I'm well within my right to have a few things on my mind."

"Of course. Would you care to talk about it?"

"Hell no," I said with a small laugh. "What's in London?"

Again, Adeline seemed to contemplate what to say. "Hungry?"

I rolled my eyes at this woman's ability to redirect.

CHAPTER 9

Adeline took the next exit and stopped at a restaurant just outside Valence. We occupied a booth in the back, and I ordered a caprese salad while Adeline opted for a greasy, delightful croque monsieur.

I devoured my greens and fresh mozzarella, only pausing between bites to take swigs of water. The food and refreshment, coupled with the bustle of the restaurant, let me bury my ruminations that were hungover from the car. I needed the distraction, something mindless to order and reorder my thoughts. There was too much I didn't know, but at least now I had an opportunity to think, ask, think, respond, and think again.

Setting my utensils down, I casually said, "You still haven't answered my question, Adeline. What's in London?"

Adeline stabbed a final forkfull of toasted bread, ham, and cheese to bite into, and then dabbed the edges of her lips with a napkin. "People who can help us."

"Come on. Could you just come out with it, please? Who?"

Adeline sat back and crossed her arms. "We can't go to the authorities. Television has your face all over it. And the frogs would stuff you in a hole until they got what they wanted out of you."

"And what would the French want out of me?"

"A confession."

"But there's nothing to confess," I said.

"Doesn't matter. The Executive has you pegged. MI6 is compromised, too. I can't trust anyone, and neither can you."

"You don't say," I remarked. But I refrained from adding that I didn't necessarily trust her, either. I wanted to trust her—running for one's life does that, pressing you to put faith in the people you're with because you *want* them to be on your side—but I couldn't. Not yet. She was only giving me bits and pieces, and I felt like she was trying to lead me to certain conclusions. I felt myself starting to second-guess most of what she said, wondering what lay beyond or within.

"Right. Well, we're going to meet the one man who can help us."

I gestured for her to continue, tossing my napkin on the table and leaning back.

"His name's Sir Alfred Graham. He's one of SIS's elders."

"What's an *elder*?"

"He's been around for a while. Fought the Soviets back before the days of Thatcher and Reagan and then a bit with them. When the Wall fell, others didn't know how to adapt, but Alfred did, transnational threats and all. And ever since your 11 September, he's been one of the high priests in British Intelligence—a fixture within Vauxhall Cross. Deputy for Counterintelligence. Knows his stuff, as you Americans say."

"Sounds like a jolly fellow, someone I'd enjoy having a martini with. But what else?"

"I work directly for him."

"You? And what makes you so amazing to be the personal scalpel of, what did you say his name was, Sir Graham?"

"It's a delicate matter, but one you shouldn't worry about."

I shook my head gently. "Forgive me, but this isn't adding up. You call me out of the blue, ask to meet, and the next thing I know bombs are going off and Interpol is swooping in from all corners of Europe. What do a deputy chief from British Intelligence and his attack dog have to do with me?"

"You sound irritated, William," Adeline said with a raised eyebrow.

"Irritated?" I chuckled. "Irritated . . . No, irritated would not be the word to describe my state of mind. Put yourself in my position. The things you're telling me—and not telling me—sound that crazy."

Adeline exhaled deeply. "I work for Alfred on special projects. And this happens to be the most important one I've ever touched. Alfred thinks so, too."

"Why do you trust him? You just said we can't trust anyone, yet you want to contact this man directly."

"I can appreciate this is a lot to take in—"

"Answer the question, please. You said we can't trust anyone. Why him?"

Adeline narrowed her eyes, finally feeling the nerves I had unintentionally so wanted to hit. She started to respond but caught herself. There was something about her demeanor that indicated whatever she was about to say, it wasn't easy. And although I was glad she seemed ready to start being more straight with me, I felt contrite by pushing her as I had.

"My parents were close friends with Alfred and his family, and I knew him growing up. My parents died when I was at university— natural causes, nothing sinister—and Alfred looked after me. Took me in, in a way, as I had no one. Then I joined MI6. The realm of intelligence can be incestuous like that. So, why do I trust him? He's like a father to me."

I softened my expression even more. The fearless gaze she'd worn so well had been replaced by the vulnerability of someone—a daughter—who'd just been pushed to admit the pain she felt over the loss of her parents. I knew it didn't matter how old or young someone was or wasn't, how tough or gentle they were—deep emotions from the past are never easy. And this was a piece of her past that she would have rather kept to herself, I believed, and I knew that kind of feeling all too well given my own history.

"I had no idea. I'm sorry," I replied.

"It's nothing," she said dismissively, regaining her composure. "You're right to question things. If roles were reversed, I would have made similar inquiries."

"Okay, then. But I still don't understand what you want with me."

"Alfred will be able to explain better than I. We need your help. You don't know it, but you likely know more about the history of the Strasbourg Executive than anyone else we've come across."

And there it was again, I thought. I felt like I was missing something that I shouldn't. Since her phone call, she'd continuously hinted that I knew something, more than I realized. But the suggestion only baffled me.

Had I come across the trail of the Strasbourg Executive but never realized it? I was as skeptical as anyone when it came to the backroom deals that go on in Washington and the capitals of Europe. And I knew there were groups of men and women outside of government who were just as powerful as those sitting in the official chairs. And the nineteenth century had been infinitely worse. European politics—world politics for that matter—had been dominated by the privileged class.

But the notion that there was a secret group of businessmen, generals, and aristocrats who had worked behind the scenes for over a century in pursuit of European superiority was incredible. It ranked up there with conspiracy theories about the Knights Templar or Hitler's fascination with the occult. Granules of truth that had been blown to absurd proportions.

Still, the possibility of the Executive gnawed at me. There was something familiar about the group, like I'd always known something like it existed. Perhaps an intrigue I'd read about in some dusty tome when I was a child. Whether it was real or fiction didn't matter; it lingered in the folds of my mind.

"Why do you think I know so much about the Executive?"

"Your research," replied Adeline. "It weaves in and around the Executive's activities like nothing we've come across before, you just never address it precisely. There were moments when reading your work or listening to your lectures that I fully expected the next sentence or statement to make a resounding conclusion about the Covenants or Executive."

"You read my work?"

"Of course, William. All of it."

I shook my head again. "Where? Where did you see these references, allusions—the evidence—of the Executive? Tell me what paper, what lecture."

"I'm a decently smart human being," Adeline replied, "but God did not endow me with a photographic memory. But it's there, William, believe me. It's there."

"You'll need to help me see how it does because, before today, I'd never heard of those things. That's the truth. I would remember."

Adeline tilted her head with a smile. "That's why we're going to see Alfred."

"Okay," I said, no more satisfied than when we started, but now, at least, feeling the game Adeline had been playing had become more equal. I decided to switch tracks to something else. "Why does this group concern you so much?"

The question seemed to take Adeline by surprise. "What do you mean?"

"Well, hate groups and secret societies have been around since the time of Abraham. What makes this group so dangerous for it to compel a senior executive with British Intelligence to dispatch his most trusted officer to make contact with a disgraced academic? And why do you speak of them as if they're everywhere, watching and listening to everything?"

"That's a good question. How familiar are you with the term *big data*?"

I shrugged. "Enough. I know the Chinese have it and we in the West are coming late to the game."

"Right. Okay. Big data is what makes the idea of *Big Brother* possible. Thus, the Chinese interest in it. But I'm talking about it in the context of the West. In the twenty-first century, everything we do touches technology: the cars we drive, the credit cards we use, how many steps you walk in a day. And with the explosion of social media, we share everything on Facebook, Twitter, pick your medium. But unlike the physical world where documents can be destroyed and books can be burned, once a piece of information hits the web, it's there forever, and for those who have the power, it's there for the taking. Everything is networked, and with the right tools, it's discoverable."

"You're not saying anything new. I've seen the news, watched the movies. Everyone knows governments can track our movements within a few feet and clicks."

"Wrong," Adeline said. "People think Britain's GHQ and your NSA are listening to their phone calls and tracking their every move, but intelligence agencies don't have the manpower for that. And by and large, they don't care. They've got more important things to worry about than whether you smoke dope or look at porn."

"Okay. Then what?"

"The problem is that this information—this data—is owned and controlled by corporations, internet conglomerates, telecom firms, international banks. Businesses are out to do business, make money, and they don't automatically assume potential clients or partners have malicious intentions. They also don't necessarily consider the collective good when it comes to profits."

"Yes, I've seen the headlines and the backlash against the tech giants. But what are you saying? Are you suggesting that the Executive is duping Facebook?"

"You're not so far off the mark. We have evidence indicating the Executive is gaining access and sucking down all this data, anything that hits the web. They're using AI and ML and big data analysis and predictive modeling to reveal patterns, trends, and probabilities relating to group behavior so they can influence cyberspace and everyone who touches it."

"AI and ML?"

"Artificial intelligence and machine learning."

"Right. Two things I know nothing about. No matter, that's a pretty big assertion," I said skeptically. "The Executive is getting it all to influence everyone?"

"Is it? Think of the Arab Spring, Russia's invasion of Ukraine, the racial unrest and class divisions in your own country. Governments ousted, wars, shocking popular movements—all sparked, instigated, and controlled through the manipulation of information. And the truth—who really knows? The acceptance of false information has become as common as when the population believed the world was flat. That's why the Executive scares me. What else could they instigate and to what end."

I paused for a moment, digesting what she'd just insinuated. I didn't know all the ins and outs of what she was explaining, yet the recognition of the problem—with its severity—shone as brightly as a dark star on the cusp of supernova.

"What do you think they're trying to do?" I asked. "You have to have some theory. You mentioned European unity, but I don't see the connection."

"I don't know. I really don't. I'm hoping Alfred has something for us once we get to London. Before I left to make contact with you, he indicated he may have found something. Which reminds me, when we get there, I need you to do something for us."

I looked at her warily. "Get where?"

"London."

CHAPTER 10

The man reached up and scratched his beard. It was thick and weathered, and not the kind worn by someone accustomed to fine shaves and grooming, but of someone who had suffered in the world. One who'd endured the cold and the darkness. And it was gray, like the steel of a ship or the weathered hue of a concrete edifice. It acted like a piece of armor, and it had been this way since he first grew it nearly forty years ago.

The road before him appeared empty, the yellow streetlights reflecting off the watery lily pads on the asphalt. And the wind gusted. The North Sea wind, strong and chilling, came off the coast and rushed between the houses and through the alleys. It reminded him of other nights when he'd sat waiting.

How many had there been? Too many to recall and often—most often—in the service of other masters.

But those masters had changed so many times that he'd become numb to their whims and ideologies so that the higher calling he'd once followed no longer existed for him. Putin's orders to invade Ukraine had forced his acceptance of that.

And since Berlin—a disgusting business that had been required yet still turned his stomach—events had indeed picked up speed.

Berlin to London to the Belgium coast and now, most likely, on to Germany momentarily.

Checking his watch once more, he saw it was a quarter past four in the morning. Then he saw the shadow emerge from an alley just ahead. The shadow approached the driver's window and stopped, leaning in close to reveal an older woman's face. Those who only noticed the age lines and that she was indeed a female would be mistaken to think she was weak or frail. A quick glance at her hand that rested on the door indicated a coarse, physical strength.

"Did you receive the message?" the man asked.

The woman nodded and in Hungarian said, "He'd like you to be in Essen tomorrow."

"Where in Essen?"

"The estate. My contact said you would know."

"I do. Thank you," replied the man, reaching for the ignition and turning the car on. "You may return home. This is all for now."

"Are you sure I should not stay nearby? I have plenty of reasons. My daughter and her family are in Brussels. I just saw them, but another few days is no trouble."

"No. I must ask you to watch activities in Budapest. That is our ultimate concern. And I will be occupied for the coming days. If I need you to return, I shall contact you."

"Understood." The woman raised back up and continued her walk down the street, the man using his side-view mirror to watch her disappear around the corner.

Alone again with no other movement on the street at this pre-dawn hour, the man put the car in drive and headed toward the main avenue. He wanted to be well on his way before the sun peeked across the horizon. And the darkness on the road would give him time to think.

He needed to decide how to proceed. A great opportunity had presented itself, yet the future—even just a few hours—remained hazy. He must allow the situation to develop further, watching and listening. This rendezvous in Essen would be one of those opportunities. His ultimate desire—his final intent—was and had always been constant, but the path to reach it still needed clearing.

The man with the gray beard, known by some as *the Curator*, reached the autobahn and settled in for the drive.

CHAPTER 11

We abandoned the car on the French coast and made our way to Calais to take the Eurostar railway through the Chunnel. But before we got in line for passport control, Adeline pulled me aside where we could not be overheard and asked, "Do you remember the information on the passport?"

"Yes," I said with a long exhale. "You drilled me over and over in the car. I got it."

"Tell me."

"I just did not ten minutes ago."

"Do it again," Adeline directed.

I did, reciting my name, birth date, place of birth, and a handful of random bits about where we were coming from and what we were supposedly planning to do in England. But although I recited this story to Adeline what must have been a hundred times by now, with each second that passed, I wondered if when the border guard asked me, I would say what I was supposed to.

Adeline touched my arm. "You must believe the lie, William. Believe it. You are no longer William Dresden—you are William La Fontaine. Believe it in your head. You must think it yourself so that if caught off guard, your reaction will be the lie. And remember, the best lies are the ones closest to the truth. And don't overdo the accent."

"Okay," I said, nodding to convince myself as much as her.

"And remember, no matter what happens, even if we get hauled off for a bit of light questioning, *buckle up with a grin.*"

I cocked my head. "I thought it was, *keep calm and carry on.*"

"That's if the Nazis start bombing London again. No, when I was young, I was petrified of failing. Not because I wasn't prepared or didn't know the test information, but because I feared I would freeze up. My mother called me a nervous nelly ever since primary school in Romford. I had this exhaustive drive to do well in my studies. I read everything, asked every question, did the extra credit and then some. My father even applauded me as his *Isaaca Newton.*

"Yet, I was still terrified of failing. There were times when I would nearly hyperventilate, worried I wouldn't be ready for tomorrow's exam. I couldn't let my teachers down, couldn't let my parents down. How it would hurt if I did—almost physically."

"Is this supposed to make me feel better? Because it's not. I was blissfully ignorant not so long ago."

Adeline gripped my forearm. "I just wanted you to know, it's okay to be nervous. Buckle up with a grin."

I tried a smile. "I find it tough to believe you were a nervous nelly."

Adeline shrugged.

"Sounds like your parents were quite special, too."

She allowed a tight-lipped smile. "They were. Now let's get on with it."

*   *   *

The authorities in Calais didn't give my passport or Adeline's a second look. Neither did passport control at Ashford International outside Kent. Part of me was disappointed the gendarmes with their black fatigues and blue berets with dangling submachine guns hadn't asked me a single question. All that anxiety for nothing—but I suppose that was a good thing.

We detrained at Saint Pancras and made our way to a pub in Soho. It was midafternoon with a few committed drinkers at the bar, but it was too early for the crowd of students and office workers who would show up later.

Sitting across from me in a high-backed booth, Adeline asked, "Do we need to go over the plan again?"

"No, I'll be fine. This isn't like Calais. I've been here before, and no one has ever asked for my birth date, and I don't need to go anywhere besides the lobby. Just put the letter in the box," I said, tapping my breast pocket that held the letter Adeline had written out and given me moments ago.

Adeline handed me an ancient-looking mobile phone. "It's what we call a burner. I have its sister. Paid in cash, no connection to you or me. Just another mobile among the millions. My number is already in there, as is yours in mine. If anything goes wrong—call."

"Right," I said.

"You'll be fine."

"Absolutely. See you in ten." I got up and headed for the door.

I could feel Adeline's eyes on me as she watched me go. She would leave a minute later, all according to plan.

CHAPTER 12

I exited the restaurant and joined the mass of Londoners going about their business in the city. It was overcast and the air was damp and brisk, but better cool than hot, I thought. I was already sweating, so no need to compound the situation with a burning sun.

Ahead, the façade of the Oxford and Cambridge Club came into view. I found it ironic that this was the place where I would deliver a secret message to a senior officer within British Intelligence, where merely saying such a thing sounded outrageous to my ears. If you'd asked me a week ago if I ever thought I'd be involved in what I could only refer to as spy-shit, I would have asked how much you had had to drink. Even as a child, I never aspired to live a life of adventure. But now, here I was, approaching an iconic fixture of London's elite with all manner of nefarious concerns roiling inside me.

As it was, I'd been a member of the club since university, but it had been a long time since my last visit. At least seven—maybe eight—years, if I remembered correctly. I pictured the lobby and where I would deliver the letter, assuming not much had changed. In establishments like these, not much ever does. No need to sign in, either, and I doubted any of the staff would recognize me. I was as insignificant then as I wanted to be now.

I crossed Carlton Gardens, then passed by the Royal Automobile Club. Then, as I was about to traverse Saint James Square, a Metropolitan Police car pulled up and flipped on its lights. A uniformed officer jumped out of the driver's seat, moving urgently.

I froze and my heart stopped, and the one thought that flashed through my mind was, *They've found me.* After all the precautions we'd taken, it'd been no use. They'd tracked us and found us. And Adeline, they must already have Adeline. She was supposed to be watching me. She should have warned me. But they'd known to grab her first and then come for me—the weaker one, the untrained one.

The instinct of fight or flight hammered my consciousness, but my feet might as well have been trapped in concrete. I couldn't move. All I could do was tense, ready for the blow to the back of my head or the punch to the kidney. Or perhaps a blindsided strike to knock me silly, followed by a push into a waiting car along with a rush to a dark hole from which I would never emerge.

Balling my fists, I scanned the sidewalks. Businessmen and -women strode purposefully, ladies dressed for the boutiques sauntered, a twenty-year-old with pants too tight strutted, a bloke with blue hair seemed to eye me but then looked away to smile and wave at someone across the street. Everything seemed normal.

Facing back to the front, I saw the officer had opened the trunk of the police car and removed a red and white traffic sign, which he duly placed in the intersection. A moment later a construction van arrived and three men in yellow reflective vests got out, spreading cones around a pothole in the road.

It was a road crew.

My pulse tried returning to normal and, once I'd confirmed I hadn't pissed my shorts, I chided myself for reacting as I had. I looked around, wondering if anyone had noticed my behavior, but

no one seemed to care. I patted my breast pocket, feeling for the
letter Adeline had given me, and for some reason felt comforted
that it was there.

I wiped my brow, gathered myself, and trotted across the street to
avoid the congestion forming at the intersection. A minute later, I
passed through the main entrance of the club. Marble floors, burgundy carpets, frescoes, and gilded crown molding greeted me. An
attendant and a few club members were chatting in the foyer, but I
passed them without acknowledgment as I headed to the rear of
the lobby.

Memories of an earlier time—another life—crossed my mind. A
single malt on the library terrace, decent conversation in the drawing room, top-notch food inspired by Paris' master chefs along with
a solid representation of bangers and mash and kidney pie. An
enjoyable atmosphere, too, even if most people thought it stuffy.
But that was the point. It was the Oxford and Cambridge Club—it
was supposed to be stuffy. You had to embrace it for what it was, just
like a barbeque on the beach with a Corona.

I smiled when I spotted the mail cubbies, approaching the hon-
eycomb of cubes and looking for the *G*s.

Although not prepared for such a sensation and conveniently
overlooking my near panic on the street, now that I was about done,
part of me felt a degree of satisfaction.

CHAPTER 13

Sean McGurry sipped his tea as he watched the four monitors in front of him. He was only two hours into his shift, but his eyes were already feeling the strain, and he had a headache. He needed to find a better job, one that didn't have a direct path to blindness as an occupational hazard.

But this was all he could do right now—contract work watching feeds of CCTV cameras covering London. It might pay the rent, but it barely touched the medical bills. There were just so many. There was no way he could keep up . . . not like this.

Sean reached for the bottle of pain reliever he kept handy when something on the fourth screen caught his attention, followed by a vibration against his leg that was not his phone. He saw a MET police car on the screen supporting road work—routine—but the device going off in his pocket told him there was more.

He removed the small device, which looked like a typical smartphone but was actually an interface connected to the exfiltration tool he'd surreptitiously attached to his system's network. The device communicated with a facial recognition AI platform located somewhere he didn't know about, which ultimately was intended to alert him to people of interest.

Looking at the device in his hand as if he were merely scrolling through photos of his kids, he saw it.

It was *him*.

It was the American professor, the very same man he received a flash alert about yesterday.

The man was in London.

Sean looked to his left and to his right. His pitiful colleagues were glued to their screens just as they should be—as he should be. He looked over his shoulder at his supervisor, Constable Evans, who was either reading a memo about some bureaucratic hodgepodge or skimming the football scores in the *Match* doing fuck all.

Sean rubbed the back of his neck, feeling the tension build. Should he excuse himself? Go to the loo so he could tell *them* that the professor was here? He had orders to contact them immediately. The professor was of the highest priority, they'd said.

But telling a third party the whereabouts of someone whom he'd observed on video surveillance under police authorities—violating protocol and privacy laws—could get him fired, or worse.

Still, he needed the money. Peter needed the money. He needed another surgery. Those bloody medical bills.

The doctors said the surgery was optional—he wasn't going to die; they were past that—but it would alleviate some of the pain. A six-year-old boy shouldn't feel pain like that. It was too much.

Before that horrible day, Sean never really understood what a bomb could do to a human body, what it could do to a child's legs. Metal shrapnel perforates skin, tears muscle, shatters bone. Those were mere words until you saw the effects on a real human body . . . in your own son.

Peter wouldn't be like this—crippled, terrified, scarred—he wouldn't be like this if it weren't for those fucking terrorists. Those bloody Arabs. They were all the same. They'd set off a bomb in the Tube. A terrorist attack in the name of ISIS. Praise be to Allah!

Peter's little friends had died, cut to pieces, but he'd survived. He was lucky, they said. Horrible, bloody luck.

It was their fault. Nasty, dirty animals. People who didn't belong here but came to squat and burden everyone else. Filth.

Sean had to make the call. What other choice did he have?

They were trying to help people like him and stop monsters like *them*. And they were willing to pay him good money. Money he needed. Money that Peter needed. And the politicians and social systems weren't going to give him shit. They were too busy dishing it out to all the immigrants overcrowding this place and draining all the coffers that they'd never filled.

It was the right thing to do to notify them.

Sean signaled his supervisor. "Gotta piss."

Constable Evans came over and got behind the monitors, his mouth stuffed with the last bite of a sandwich. Maybe he'll choke.

Sean went into the hall and made his way to the facilities. He occupied a stall and sent a single text to the number he'd been given two days ago. *Corner of Pall Mall and Carlton Gardens at 1636.*

The text back was instantaneous, causing him to start. *10. Well done.*

He couldn't believe it . . . £10,000 deposited into his account. And all he did was let them know he'd seen some random bloke in London.

CHAPTER 14

I inserted the letter into the cubby marked *M. Gramston*, which was right above the one labeled *Sir A. Graham*. This whole thing was unsophisticated, I thought, but then again, I gathered that was the point. Given the vulnerabilities with technology—my phone debacle back in Nice a perfect example—using "sticks and bricks," as Adeline had called it, was the way to go.

Adeline had explained that the presence of such a letter in Gramston's box was a signal. It was a message that only Alfred and she understood, that an emergency meeting had been set for later that night at a safe flat that only they were privy to, and which changed from time to time.

Alfred was a member of the Oxford and Cambridge Club. But unlike me, a junior member who'd only visited occasionally with years between stays, Alfred stopped in nearly every night for a drink and to converse with the other members. On his way out, he would also check his cubby and, in the process, see if there was anything for M. Gramston—a poor soul who'd died in a boating accident at the age of fourteen, but whom Alfred had *resurrected* and recruited to serve in the machine of British Intelligence.

This method for arranging a meeting was outside official channels and a carryover from the days when Alfred was facing off against the Soviets. The scars of the Cambridge Five endured, and being a CI man, he wasn't about to believe the Service was as impenetrable as some wanted it to be. The USSR may have broken up, but the underworld connections among spies had endured. And Russia's latest extracurriculars—radioactive poisons, disappearing oligarchs, private armies skilled at medieval torture, invading one's neighbors—had reminded everyone that the world was still a troubling place. Adeline had confided all of this to me in the hushed whispers of someone who firmly believed in the infallibility of the dark gospel.

As I stared into the walnut-shaded blackness of the cubbies with the sounds of clinking tableware and muted conversations coming from the adjacent rooms, a surreal sensation struck me. Not more than twenty-four hours ago I was walking the grounds of my family's villa, fully content with the unexciting nature of academic life. But now I was making a dead drop entangled in an MI6 operation I didn't understand with an alleged secret cabal hunting me like a fox.

I shook my head in disbelief, not sure if I should be amused, terrified, or both . . . and then I felt a tickle in my pocket that brought everything crashing back to the present.

It was the phone—the burner Adeline had given me.

I pulled it out and answered. "Yes?"

"Get out now," Adeline said. "They found you."

A shock ran down my spine. "What? How?"

"Never mind. They're coming and they've got the front blocked."

I took hold of a cubby to steady myself, then peeked my head out and looked toward the entrance and saw three men enter the lobby. Their eyes darted about, peering through doorways and riveted on anyone that came into view. They didn't bother being inconspicuous, and the members of the club who happened to walk by gave the three men a wide berth.

I was obscured by the staircase railing, so I didn't think they could see me, but I pressed myself against the wall instinctively. I scanned this way and that for a way out, wishing there was some magical back door I could race through to safety but knowing there wasn't one. Not here, anyway.

I leaned forward around the corner again to peer through the banister. The three men were still there and, much to my astonishment, I recognized the man in the center. I did not *know* the man, but his face was unmistakable. He was the one who had left the bomb at the café in Nice—the MI5 man, Timothy Sanders.

Fear and rage welled within me. The man was dangerous—I knew that. He was hunting me and had somehow tracked me here. The realization was chilling, to know you're being pursued in such a way, but I also viewed him as a monster that needed to be put down. From the bombing alone he'd killed multiple innocent people, and who knows how many lives he'd taken in other ways. I have no idea where it came from, but I felt a sudden urge to confront the man, perhaps fight him. Not that I had any fighting skills, but I wanted to stop him from not just threatening me, but also hurting anyone else.

I almost took a brazen step forward but caught myself. I studied the other two men. One wore a black leather jacket, the other a pair of cargo pants, each built like tree trunks. I didn't recognize them—I hadn't expected to—but I could tell by how they carried themselves that they were thuggish in nature, mercenary-like.

Who are these people, and what the hell do they want with me?

Still with the phone to my ear, I looked around again, forcing myself to focus and think of a way out of the club that wouldn't get me killed.

Then I remembered.

"Meet me outside The Rag," I whispered into the phone.

"Where?"

"The Army Navy Club. It's across the street. The entrance is on Saint James' Square around the block."

"But—"

I clicked off the phone. Just go, I thought. She'd figure it out.

I peered out once more and saw the three men exchanging words. It was only a matter of time before they came my way.

There was no way I could get to the back door of the club. But through the rear of the coffee room there was a hallway that led to the kitchen, and in that hallway was a stairwell to the wine cellars— vaults that were built in the 1830s in the traditional brick-arch style. If I reached the underground cellars, I could escape because, in addition to the Club's forty thousand bottles of wine, there was a way out.

As this semblance of a plan formed in my head, one of the men— the taller one, Leather Jacket—started walking toward me. The other one—Cargo Pants—went up the stairs. MI5-Sanders went into the morning room.

I caught my breath and retreated farther into the club and found the coat check. It was unmanned during the day. I went inside and locked the door, resting my hand on the knob for a sobering moment. I wondered if Leather Jacket kicked it, would the door hold.

I heard footsteps outside, heavy ones, from a man wearing rubber-soled boots. I stepped back and pursed my lips, looking around. I spotted a cane in an umbrella rack, which I delicately withdrew so as not to make a sound. I then gripped it like a club and took another step back from the door.

Someone shook the doorknob, the sound making my heart skip a beat, but the lock held.

Still, I tensed, tightening my grip on the cane. Only then did I notice how narrow and flimsy it was, and how it would probably snap in two if I hit someone with it. My only hope was to slow the man down so I could rush past him and make a break for it.

I shifted my weight from one leg to the other, loosening my knees as if I were stepping up to home plate on the ball field, and silently laughing to myself for having never once played baseball. I'd been to the batting cages on a date decades ago, but that had been an awkward affair. By that time in my life I was athletic, but making contact with the ball proved hopeless and gave my date—who at the moment I could not remember the name of—a wealth of amusement.

The footsteps finally moved away, the sound growing softer and softer. My focus returned to my current predicament rather than long ago memories. I counted to ten, giving the man enough time to turn the corner.

I then held my breath and undid the lock. I cracked the door and stole a look out.

No one.

I returned the cane to its community sheath and hurried toward the coffee room, my head snapping this way and that along my path. A lovely couple was descending the stairs, but there was no sign of Sanders or Leather Jacket or Cargo Pants. I kept moving, my senses now alert to every sound, every movement, every smell.

When I reached the entrance to the coffee room, I hurried in and around the tables to the far door. It was only twenty feet away, but it might as well have been a mile. I couldn't move fast enough, though I refrained from an outright hustle.

I chanced a look behind me when I reached the middle of the room.

Sanders—Mr. MI5—was standing at the entrance.

We locked eyes and recognition flared for each of us.

I hastened onward, nearly knocking down a waiter carrying a drink tray. I banged my leg against another table, incurring aggravated looks from the three women seated there. I muttered an apology but kept going.

When I looked back, I saw the MI5 man rushing toward me.

To hell with it.

I dashed across the remainder of the room toward the back hall, opened the door, and ran down the passage until I reached the middle of the corridor. The lights were off, but I found what I was looking for: the cellar door.

A small padlock secured it.

Dammit!

I ran back to a serving cart and grabbed a heavy metal coffeepot.

Sanders burst into the hall while I was still at the cart. I shoved the cart at him and it slammed into the man's knees. He stumbled. I fled back to the cellar door and hammered the pot against the padlock. Once. Twice. Then again.

The clasp broke loose.

I ripped open the door, but not before I saw that Sanders had recovered. He was barreling toward me, and he'd drawn a gun.

It was dark. There was barely enough light to see the steps. I leapt into the darkness down the stairs, my stomach rising into my chest. I hit the landing with both feet, and my knees and feet seared from the impact. Blocking it out, I burst through the lower door.

I heard Sanders coming down, his shoes pounding the steps. They sounded like they were on top of me. I couldn't move fast enough.

I slammed the door shut, stepped back, and braced myself. My entire body went taut. I couldn't believe what I was about to do.

The sound of heavy boots hit the landing.

I crouched and when the door opened, I barreled into it like I was coming off the starting block. The door slammed into Sanders and crushed him into the frame. Regaining my balance, I reared back and hammered my shoulder into the door again. I felt metal and wood mash skin and bone and I cringed, but I didn't stop. I threw myself into the door again until the MI5 agent slipped to the ground.

Breathing heavily, my heart feeling like it was going to erupt from my rib cage, I pulled the door open and let the man sprawl. I wasn't thinking anymore. I was just acting. As if my body weren't my own, I raised my foot and stomped on the man's face with my heel. And then I did it again.

I looked down. The MI5 man—Sanders—had stopped moving, and there was blood dripping from his nose and mouth. His eyes were closed, and he lay motionless.

I remained still for a long moment, coming to grips with what just happened and what I'd done. I'd just battered a man with a door and my heel, and now he lay bleeding and unconscious at my feet. I was torn between the horror of doing something so brutal to another human being, yet knowing this man was a monster who was trying to kill me.

Revulsion and anger swirled inside me and then I gritted my teeth, accepting the simple fact that at this moment it had been him or me. My right hand started to shake, and I grabbed it with my left. I squeezed as if the pressure would stop the chaos. I closed my eyes and inhaled deeply, and then again, and then again. I told myself I'd had no choice—and it still wasn't over.

I bent down and pulled the pistol from the man's limp hand, tossing it on the floor. I then rifled through his pockets, finding his wallet and identification along with a roll of cash. I was about to take off but had a thought.

I reached for an apron hanging on the wall, removing the waist tie. I rolled the MI5 agent onto his stomach and secured his wrists and his ankles. It was a sloppy hog-tie, but if Sanders woke up, it would take him a moment to get loose. If he didn't, someone from the club would find him soon enough.

I got back to my feet, picked up the pistol and his wallet and ID, and hobbled down the hall toward the old cellar vaults, suddenly aware of the stress my body had just endured with all the aches, pains, and strains starting to reveal themselves. My body had only ever felt like this once years ago, the only other time when I feared for my life. I found it uncanny how the state of mind and physical sensations were unforgettable and also so similar.

I shook my head, telling myself there would be time for introspection later, but what mattered now was getting out of here. There was little light in the cellar, and it took me a few minutes of sorting through the damp rooms, but I finally found what I was looking for behind a stack of wine crates deep in the shadows.

There was a door, a metal one, with a rusty drop arm, and I was relieved that it still wasn't locked even after all these years. It made me wonder if an angel was looking over my shoulder.

Years ago, I'd learned the hatch opened to an underground tunnel that led to the basement of The Army Navy Club. The tunnel had been dug during the Second World War as a way for military officers and politicians to move between buildings during the Blitz. I had happened upon it when I was at Oxford reading a forgettable book that mentioned the tunnel networks. One evening I decided to see if the story was true and ventured down here to poke around. Much to my astonishment, I'd found the old passageway and explored it, confirming that it did in fact lead to the bowels of The Army Navy Club. From then on, I periodically used this remnant of WWII to move between the two establishments, confounding my colleagues with my odd appearances and disappearances. Who could have known the mischievous adventures of my youth would save my life twenty years later.

I entered the tunnel and a few minutes later was walking up to the ground floor of The Rag, as it was called. I straightened my jacket, disguised my limp, avoided the looks of everyone I passed, and walked out the main doors onto Saint James' Square.

After all that, I smiled, taking in the sun and fresh air like I'd emerged from the heart of darkness. Both a sense of relief and exhilaration came over me.

I'd made it.

I'd made it.

I looked to the street and saw Adeline waiting in a car, waving for me to hurry.

I approached and opened the passenger door to get in. I said calmly, "We should leave."

CHAPTER 15

Faust Broch walked beside the Kanzler amidst the evergreens. He wore a pair of outdoor boots, rough pants tucked inside his socks, and an olive drab fleece. He also had an H&K P12 pistol fixed in a pancake holster on his side.

The Kanzler wore a similar pair of boots, but his regalia was more traditional. His sporting jacket was made of tweed with a leather pad on his right shoulder. He had on a felt alpine hat, complemented by a brown pair of shooting gloves. In the crook of his arm, he carried an M98 Mauser hunting rifle, a classic piece modeled after the Gewehr 98 used during the First World War. Attached to the buttstock was a strap holding five 7.92x57mm cartridges. He liked to boast he could keyhole shots at one hundred meters.

For the first two miles, neither man had said anything, but Faust knew the only reason he had been invited on the hunt was to talk. He merely had to wait until the Kanzler was ready.

He didn't mind. He loved the forest and preferred the grass beneath his feet to the Persian rugs and polished floors back at the estate. Being in the wild was meditative, and he believed himself to be clearer in mind.

"Is there any news on the whereabouts of the professor?" the Kanzler finally asked.

"No," Faust replied. "But I'm confident he hasn't left London."

"Why?"

"He has nowhere to go, and my sources would have known if he did."

"But you don't know where he is?"

Faust didn't answer.

"I'm surprised. I would have thought your sources would have mentioned something by now."

The Kanzler was right; his sources should have learned something by now. But they hadn't. He considered their failure a reflection on him, which was embarrassing. Unfortunately, there was nothing more he could do.

"Please tell me once you have something. I know you appreciate the significance of all this. But that's not why I asked you to come with me this morning."

Ahead, the sounds of dogs barking disrupted what had been a peaceful forest. Men emerged from the brush with Caucasian Mountain Dogs—massive beasts well over one hundred kilos—dragging them forward. They'd picked up the scent of their quarry.

"What is your opinion of Sofia?" the Kanzler asked.

He hesitated. "I'm not sure I'm in a position to comment."

"Scheiße. You may not have the legacy some members of the Executive do, but you *are* equipped to judge such things. Your grandfather was a colonel in the SS, and your father—before he was killed—was a leader in the action arm of the National Democratic Party. And you were a soldier of the Bundeswehr, and you know better than most what it means to sacrifice. Now, tell me what you think of Mademoiselle König."

He wondered if he was about to slit his own throat. Criticizing a protégé wasn't a healthy thing. But if he held back, the Kanzler would know. The man didn't ask questions he didn't already know the answer to, and Faust had never been one to temper his perspective.

He hadn't when his commander ordered a reckless attack in Afghanistan, nor when he briefed the politicians about the weakness of the German military. Withholding the truth gets people killed.

"She's smart," he said. "Committed, ambitious—attributes that should be admired. But she's also rash, which makes her a liability."

The Kanzler walked on for a time, chewing on the words of his security chief, and following the trail of the hounds. "Anything else?"

"The bombing in Nice caused more problems than necessary. It was crude, and it failed."

"I agree. Did you know about it in advance?"

"No."

"Curious."

They crossed a clearing and reentered the wood. The hounds were circling the base of a tree, growling with such ferocity they seemed like demonic creatures. Four men, dressed in similar attire to the Kanzler, were positioned a few steps back.

A brown bear was fifteen feet up in the tree, swatting at the dogs beneath. Until recently, bears had been nonexistent in Germany, expelled or killed off by uncontrolled hunting. The last sighting of a bear was in 1835. But in recent years they'd returned, reintroduced to the mountains of Central Europe.

When the four men saw the Kanzler and Faust approaching, they moved in to restrain the dogs. They were large, powerful men, but it was all they could do to control the animals.

The Kanzler gripped his rifle and brought it to his shoulder. He took aim through the scope and fired. The bullet hit the bear in the chest, tearing through its lungs and heart. It fell to the ground—dead.

"It's not exactly a fair sport, but what is," said the Kanzler, more as a statement than a question. "Make sure the professor and the woman are taken care of."

Faust nodded. "Yes, Herr Kanzler."

The Kanzler worked the bolt action of the rifle—ejecting the spent casing—then tucked it in the crook of his arm. He turned to head back to the house but stopped, his eyes fixed on a dark wall of trees from where they'd come.

Faust followed the Kanzler's gaze and saw a man standing at the edge of the wood. He was too far away to recognize, except that he had a gray beard. It was a distinct gray beard.

"If you'll excuse me, Faust," said the Kanzler, his voice distant, detached. "I think I'll walk back alone. Please take the dogs and guides with you. I shouldn't be more than an hour."

"Mein Herr?"

"It's all right. I don't need a minder for everything."

"I meant no disrespect, Herr Kanzler. But who is that?"

"A man I must speak with alone. An uncomfortable recognition. You see, you're not the only one who has concerns about Sofia. We may need to consider someone else for the future of the Executive."

Faust went to say something, but the Kanzler had already walked off, leaving him alone at the edge of the field.

CHAPTER 16

I sat in a chair by the front window of what Adeline had assured me was a *safe house*, though when I asked what that meant, her definition didn't much assure me. No one was guarding it and it wasn't protected by some top-tier government security system; rather, it merely meant it was a place to hide that—hopefully—no one knew about. Nonetheless, it was a modest home—a townhouse—decorated by someone who believed 1960s design was still en vogue. Shag carpet and linoleum, faded pictures, floral drapery, and slim furniture with burlap fabric adorned the home.

I found it nostalgic in a peculiar sort of way. Like something from a visit to an estranged relative, the entire experience uncomfortable for both the host and the guests alike.

But against the wall was an upright piano, constructed from maple with a light coat of stain that needed attention. My grandmother had had a similar one in their home outside of Boston. She'd died before I was ten, but I'd loved listening to her play, watching her fingers dance over the keys. I would read Robert Louis Stevenson and Mark Twain while she filled the house with the sounds of Chopin's nocturnes. It was both odd and fitting that such memories came to me now.

"He'll be here any minute," Adeline said, referring to Alfred. She sat on the sofa opposite me, her hair pulled back in a ponytail, a pistol resting on the cushion beside her. She smiled, then returned her attention to the emptiness of the front door.

So far there had been no indication the authorities had tracked us after the club, but that didn't mean much. I'd assaulted an MI5 officer in the basement of one of London's most prestigious establishments—*Huzzah!*

The incident couldn't possibly go unnoticed.

I'd given the MI5 man's pistol and his ID to Adeline, but I'd glossed over what I'd done to him—how I'd bludgeoned him with the door and then stomped on his face. Rather, I'd said that I'd hit him with the door and rendered him unconscious. I hadn't wanted to say much more. Truth was, I was uncomfortable with the brutality of the incident. I know I shouldn't be, it'd been in self-defense, but I didn't want to talk about it.

Besides, Adeline hadn't seemed at all interested in the details. She'd only asked if I'd delivered the letter as instructed and if anyone had seen me do it. That's what mattered, she'd said—*that the message had been communicated*—everything else was of no consequence.

Though, I'd begun to wonder, if the Executive had found me at the club, didn't that put the club and my presence there under suspicion? Wouldn't the Executive want to know why, of all places in London, I'd gone there? And what about Leather Jacket and Cargo Pants? What if they'd searched the place and found the letter?

But when I'd shared these fears with Adeline, she dismissed them, too. Even if the Executive found the letter, there was nothing in it that identified the time and place of our meeting or the existence of a safe house. And, if they were to suspect Alfred, he knew how either to avoid surveillance or, if unable to, not come near the safe house.

His failure to show up would tell us to shift to alternative meeting methods, which Adeline assured me we had but would not divulge unless necessary. I couldn't do much with that, now could I?

These thoughts were tumbling around as I sat dutifully in my chair. I returned my attention to my newspaper in an effort to distract myself. The day's headlines were out of Vienna. A group of Libyan refugees had vandalized a hair salon because two of their women had inquired about the services available. They'd wanted to get their hair done, but their husbands and fathers had forbidden them from indulging in the carnalities of the infidel. The Libyan men assaulted two of the hairdressers, as well as stole all of the cash from the register.

The police weren't able to identify the perpetrators, but later that night a group of young Viennese men drove by one of the squatter camps, throwing rocks and glass bottles at the refugee families huddled together who most likely had nothing to do with the other incident.

What had political scientist Samuel Huntington called it, a *clash of civilizations*? Perhaps it was, and the politicians were riding every wave they could. Hate speech was the message *du jour*. Xenophobia had become mainstream in Europe and the United States, rebranded under the cloak of *populism*, the *alt-right*, and *patriotism*.

At one time in my life, I had been a voracious consumer of news, going so far as to peruse news sites in different languages to see what the rest of the world was paying attention to. But in recent years, I could barely listen to the headlines without my stomach turning.

It disgusted me, all of it. So much so that I flipped to the arts section of the paper.

*   *   *

"Is it true you witnessed the Srebrenica massacre?" Adeline asked, breaking what had been a long and, speaking personally, a welcome silence.

I looked up from the paper, caught off guard by the question. "I beg your pardon?"

"I read in your file that when you were working with the orphanages in Bosnia, you were trapped in Srebrenica when the Serb forces attacked. The report said you were with a Bosniak family and that you hid with them in the forest until the killing was over. Is that true?"

I felt my face flush and struggled to control my voice. Whenever someone asked me about what happened or if I tried to speak about it, it was like the air was sucked from my lungs and my words came out as nothing but faint utterances.

"I'm assuming it's all in my file," I finally uttered. "What else is there to say?"

"Yes. I've read your file, but that doesn't mean it's the whole story. Could you tell me what happened?"

I stared at a book review in the paper for a title I didn't recognize, but I wasn't reading it.

The faces of the Bosniak father, mother, and little girl flashed through my mind. I could still smell the burning village, hear the screams of those about to die and those being raped. The taste of ash crept into my mouth.

I met Adeline's eyes. "Why are you asking?"

"I'm curious."

I got up and walked over to the bar cart to pour myself a scotch, anything to appease the dryness in my mouth. I stared at the bottle's label but didn't see it.

"I'm sorry but I really don't want to talk about it. I saw quite intimately the horror of that place, and yes, I hid for days with a family in the woods, all of us terrified we would be found and murdered like the others. What else do you want me to say?"

"I'm not sure. But I want to know."

"Why?"

"Because of what we're dealing with now. People who hate. They were the enemy then as they are now, and it's how we understand."

"I commend your . . . er . . . dedication. But I'd rather not go through that darkness right now. I'd put all that behind me, and it took a while."

"Another time, then?"

"Sure. Of course. Over tea and crumpets," I said with a wave of my hand in a forced gesture to lift the heavy veil that had descended over the room.

I was grateful when Adeline nodded and let me be.

CHAPTER 17

Sofia stood behind a well-built man with a shaved head. He was inspecting a crate filled with drab-colored blocks, roughly four inches by two inches, with black stenciling on the side.

"Well?" she asked.

The man shifted to face her. "It's the right stuff. And the courier confirmed he got it clean."

"You trust him?"

"I trust money, and he likes money."

"And?"

"He knows I'd kill him if I found out he made a mistake."

"Of course you would. How'd he bring it in?"

"A simple path. A shipment from a factory in Poland to Turkey, intercepted just over the border in Syria. If anyone traces it, the trail will lead to the Russian arming program for Assad. It will look like former ISIS militants captured it, funneled it through the rat lines back into Europe—the *Balkan route*—and here we are."

"What about the rest of the items?"

"The guns are on the way. Coming from Bulgaria. No end-user certificates, serial numbers traced back to the Warsaw Pact glut from the nineties."

Sofia smiled. It had taken nearly a year to create the network of government officials and couriers to carry out her wishes, but the wait had been worth it. There could be no connection between her and the material. The entire plan hinged on the trail pointing to the Middle East.

A tired, old man from the Cold War had taught her these things. Clandestinity and misdirection—they were essential for this type of work.

The man had been a former officer in the Stasi—the East German secret police before the Wall fell—and involved in active measures against the West. His name was Oscar Mundt.

Sofia was twenty-eight and he was fifty-one when they met, their introduction prearranged. He was to educate her on certain methods and, consequently, they spent much time together. Time to talk, to learn about the other.

Oscar had a tragic story—one that involved torture at the hands of the KGB, a sick wife who despised him, and a son who committed suicide—yet all of it made him brutally effective in his profession.

Sofia absorbed everything she could about plots and counterplots, and even picked up a few things he never intended. She was a good student, motivated.

Then, on a cold night in Prague, Oscar made a pass at her. He was drunk, his hands sloppy and coarse. When she refused, he pushed harder, the vodka egging him on.

She wasn't physically strong enough to overpower him, and the slob did unspeakable things. Sofia became cold, everything mechanical—no emotion or tenderness left in her. Feeling was not worth the pain.

It happened three more times over the next few months. Oscar would drink, and soon enough the professionalism that carried him through the day would devolve into vulgar advances and physical demands.

Sofia wondered if the person who introduced them, the one who ordered the instruction—the Kanzler—if he knew about this side of Oscar. Perhaps he was aware these things were happening. Maybe it was part of her education.

But no training lasts forever. When Sofia realized she'd learned all she could from Oscar, she invited him to a hotel room in Estonia. When he arrived, Sofia was dressed in a negligee that made his eyes go wide. She offered him a glass of apple wine that she'd brought from Frankfurt. He drank greedily, already panting with expectation.

But then he stumbled, and a second later he fell to the floor, paralyzed from the sodium thiopental she'd put in the glass. It was just enough to inhibit Oscar's motor skills and dull his senses, but not knock him out completely. She tied his arms and legs to the bed posts and undressed him. His eyes watched her work, but he couldn't stop her.

Then Sofia put on a plastic body suit, removed a knife from her bag, and proceeded to stab him. She started with his appendages, making jagged punctures and slashes, eventually moving to his groin and stomach. She avoided his chest and made sure not to hit any arteries. Sofia cut him over thirty times, his life slowly dripping onto the floor.

It took Oscar fifty-three minutes to die and, by the end, Sofia was confident the anesthetic had mostly worn off. A good bit of pain at the end of his revolting life.

And that was that. Her education was complete.

She never mentioned what happened to the Kanzler, and he never asked. But there were times when he seemed to study her, as if he was unsure what she was capable of.

Good, she thought. He should be wary.

The door opened across the room, and both Sofia and the smuggler looked up. Sofia's security detail should have prevented anyone from accessing this part of the building, but when Sofia saw who it was, her surprise vanished.

"I don't recall asking you to join us," she said.

"You didn't," replied Faust. "Is everything in order?"

"Yes."

Faust nodded.

"And what about you? Have you found the professor and his protector?"

Faust's phone vibrated. He looked at the screen. "Possibly."

CHAPTER 18

The knock startled both me and Adeline. I rose from my chair as Adeline went to open the door, revealing a gentleman in his sixties over six feet tall with bleach white hair wearing a perfectly tailored beige suit. If he had donned a Bombay Bowler, he would have displayed a quintessential colonial look and would have fit right in on a plantation in Kenya or at a Commonwealth office in India.

"Addie," the man said, reaching out to clasp her hand in both of his. "So glad to see you, dear. You've got yourself into quite a mess, and with the loss of your man Kyle. Shot in his hotel room? Tragic, this business."

"Yes, most unfortunate," she replied, expressing the perfect English understatement and distance in contrast to Alfred's warmth. "Any news on who was behind it?"

"Not a shred. They're calling it a robbery. Of course, the refugee communities are the ones everyone seems to blame."

"Right. Of course. Well, there's no time to waste. We have much to fill you in on."

"Quite right," Alfred said, turning to me where I stood awkwardly across the room. "And you must be Professor Dresden. I'm delighted to make your acquaintance, despite the circumstances."

"A pleasure, Sir Graham," I said, moving closer and extending my hand.

"Oh, please dispense with the sir and just call me Alfred. It's my understanding you've had a rough time of it, too. The bombing. And your latest handiwork at the club when you disposed of that man from MI5. Sanders, I believe."

I glanced at Adeline, wondering how much Alfred already knew.

"Don't look so shocked, Professor. I know generally what occurred and can infer the rest. I *am* a member of the club and a not-so-junior official in the service of her Majesty. You put the bastard in a coma and stole his gun and identification, for God's sake. May I ask where you learned to fight like that? It's not every day a history professor bests an officer from Britain's Security Service."

"Surprised him, I guess," I replied, suppressing the urge to look at the floor or tap my foot like a child in primary school.

Alfred laughed. "Remind me never to surprise you."

"What are people saying?" Adeline asked.

"A spot of confusion, actually. It's a compartmented investigation. Very hush-hush, making it hard even for me to get a straight answer out of my counterpart at MI5. But I did hear Officer Sanders wasn't supposed to be in London."

"What do you mean? Where was he supposed to be?"

"France. On the Continent, at the very least."

"How convenient for the bombing."

"Quite right. But again, MI5 is being tight-lipped, which means they either don't have a clue about what's going on or they're trying to cover something up. Either way, it doesn't matter. The bastard was working for the Executive, I'm sure of it. When he wakes up, we have a man standing by to question him."

"Will MI5 allow that?" I asked.

"Who said I was going to send someone from MI6? I have people all over, but that's neither here nor there. What matters is that you know how to handle yourself and not lose your head. This business is turning troublesome, and I think a drink is in order."

"What about the other two? Two additional men were working with Sanders, one wearing a leather jacket and the other wearing cargo pants. Any sign of them?"

Alfred took charge of the bar cart. "Not that I'm aware of," he remarked, inspecting the bottles before making a selection. "And I suspect there were more than just those three in the area—they were simply the ones you saw."

Alfred tried to hand Adeline a scotch, but she waved it off. He then refilled mine and poured himself a hefty one before sitting down. "Now, Professor, I suppose you want to know what this is all about."

I returned to my chair, but rather than sitting back, I remained on the edge with my forearms resting on my thighs, my glass cupped in both my hands.

"In all my years in intelligence," Alfred began, "the Strasbourg Executive has struck me as unique. They're nothing like the Soviet services we used to go up against, nor anything like the extremist groups of today—al-Qaida, ISIS, Hezbollah—nor the rising Chinese in the East. Those chaps had or now have geography, populations, supporters. We could deter them, target them, kill them—which we do quite effectively.

"The Executive, however, is based nowhere and lacks membership. Yet, it's able to influence millions. Aside from the core leadership, people don't even know they're doing the Executive's bidding. Its weapons are ideas, bloody extreme nationalistic ones. And how do you destroy an idea, William?"

Good question, I thought, and one I didn't have an answer for. In all my studies and what little experiences I had in the real world, I'd never come across an instance where someone was able to *destroy* an idea. The idea always comes back around, and usually worse than the first time.

"You can't," I replied. "Even if you try to wipe out the core thinkers, someone else always picks it up. There are still those who believe the world is flat. The terminology may be different, but it's the same. But why the sudden concern? Extremist groups—right and left—have been around for well over a century."

"Let's just say we think this manifestation of the Executive's ideas are *different*."

"In what way?"

"The Executive isn't a political party nor a weekend club for bloody skinheads. They may use these groups, but they are going after the everyday man and woman," Alfred said. "They manipulate fears, desires, suffering, greed—our base emotions, saying what people think but are too scared to say themselves—and they influence populations to spawn the political vehicles that will push forth their agenda, all the while hiding their hand so no one knows where it originated from."

"Please forgive my reservations," I replied more calmly, "but can you really attribute that much power to someone who hides in the shadows? In all my research, I've never come across a secret organization that had real power unless they were affiliated or somehow influential over a form of state power."

"Ahh. But tell me, what do you know of covert influence or, as the Soviets used to call it, active measures?"

"I'm not familiar with those terms."

"Formal, concerted efforts that are planned and implemented to influence the international stage in the interest of the government behind it. Covert action, covert influence, active measures—all closely connected and done so as to obscure who is ultimately responsible."

"But I thought you said the Executive was not a part of a government."

"You are correct. But now think of those things in the context of the Arab Spring, Brexit, the divisions in your country, a wave of populism—some might call it neo-fascism—across Europe. All of them unexpected, destructive shocks to the system, leaving the rest of us wondering how we didn't see it coming. They weren't grass-roots movements—I don't care what the *experts* say—someone put these things in motion through cyberspace and social media. Then fear and anger took over and the movements fed themselves as mainstream politics propelled them forward."

"But I thought the Russians were the ones behind a lot of it. Fake news and troll farms sowing hate and discontent throughout our utopian democratic systems," I remarked with a small raise of my eyebrow.

"Yes, you're right. When the Kremlin isn't busy invading its neighbors, it puts a few pieces in play. Their attacks have been targeted, too, supporting or defaming one candidate over another, exacerbating a particular issue to muddy the waters . . . But it's been clumsy, akin to a blunderbuss. And to be honest, I don't think they even care if the world knows what they're doing. But the Executive—it's different."

"How so?"

"They're precise—like a scalpel—against specific events as well as broad issues, and seamlessly integrated like a composed symphony. The only way we know this is because of the layers we've been able to peel back. Like a puss-filled scab."

"You sound fairly certain about all this, particularly for something you just said no one has ever seen before."

"The best analysts we have are working this issue. They may not know the full story or have access to every piece of intelligence, but the picture they've drawn—it's impossible to ignore. There are forces working behind the scenes, and it goes far beyond what the cheeky bastards in the Kremlin are slobbering about. It is as if the Executive can read the mood of the mob and respond, react, and push in real time with a click of a button."

Even after everything that had happened in the past forty-eight hours, I found Alfred's description of the Executive hard to believe. The idea of the Executive was simply too far-fetched, something analogous to conspiracy theories and pop history. Secret societies were *a thing*, but because they were secret, the relative power they had was always limited. It took men and women in the public's eye—for all to see—moving things forward for a movement to gain traction.

But maybe that was the point. The Executive didn't have to necessarily *control* a movement; it had to shape the ideas for others to use. Not unlike I'd argued with secondary figures in history, simply replace the individual with a group. And if the core message was simple—hate, differences, us versus them, fear, nostalgia—then responses would be fairly consistent as if there was a guiding hand.

"All right. Let's assume everything you just said is true. The Executive is masterminding these events. Why? For what purpose?"

Alfred looked at Adeline, who'd been sitting quietly on the sofa. "They want to break apart the EU."

"That makes no sense," I said. Ever since Adeline had suggested the Executive was trying to disrupt European affairs, I'd struggled to see the logic. "Ignoring all the platitudes about cooperation and peace—the very essence of the EU is to be a powerful economic and political block. Wouldn't destroying it be counter to the Executive's desires for European primacy?"

"Right," Alfred replied, "but you need to take it a step further."

"What do you mean?"

"In our line of work, what seems obvious is circumspect. If it makes sense, it's because someone has manipulated the environment so you think it makes sense. If it seems right, it's most likely wrong. We're dealing with multiple layers and somewhere between them is the Executive's true intentions."

"Okay. Then what?"

"We suspect the Executive doesn't believe the EU is all that European anymore. With open borders that allow uncontrolled immigration from Africa and the Middle East, certain Islamist leanings and the blending of cultures . . . it's no longer a European institution. It's infected. They want to burn it down and start anew to return to what they believe were better times.

"And, there are some who detest the relative weakness of Europe's militaries. Armies and navies that once conquered the world, now they are ineffectual and a joke. There's jealousy, too, coupled with fear. Those who can remember the tragedies of the imperial wars of the past are no longer with us—therefore, some want to see a return to former glories."

I looked off at nothing to ponder the idea. The EU and its predecessor—the European Economic Community—had been in existence long before I was born, and it was the first of its kind: a supranational and intergovernmental entity of twenty-eight countries. It had its own economy, parliament, councils, an international police force and legal system, and it essentially governed all of Europe. And years ago European unity had been a stalwart in opposition to the Soviet Union. It helped win the Cold War. It kept the peace.

But things had changed. The push for openness and unity had expanded. More groups were vying to either come to Europe or connect with Europe, but they were not assimilating. They were retaining the views and ways from where they came from and it had become publicly visible to the *host* populations. And rather than seeing the benefits and beauty of diversity, some viewed this evolving situation as an existential threat to who they were as a people. Thus, the nationalistic and populist sentiments.

"What would that mean if the EU broke apart?" I asked.

A shadow passed over Alfred's face. "There are three reasons there hasn't been another world war—the permanent positioning of U.S. Military forces on the Continent, China's inability to project real military power outside its region, and that Europe is a fully integrated economic and social system. Take any of these conditions away, and it will only be a matter of time before national interests prevail, bigger states bully the smaller states, and Russia or China picks a fight with a core yet weaker European state. It will be 1914 all over again."

I rubbed my eyes, trying to focus my thoughts in response to everything that was being thrown at me. It was all so . . . unbelievably wild. I saw threads of logic, but they were just so far-fetched as to be unfathomable. Yet, in the past ten years I'd seen our world change in ways I never could have dreamed, not in my wildest nightmares.

"Can we back up? Supposing the threat to the EU is real, how is this *secret cabal* doing this? And if you know what the Executive is trying to do, why can't you thwart it? You must have an idea who some of the leaders are."

"It's not that simple, and we don't know as much as you might think. What we have is conjecture grounded in scarce reporting," replied Adeline, joining the conversation.

"I don't buy it. You've got to know something, otherwise, you wouldn't be able to tell me what you already have. How can the Executive pose a threat to something as large as the European Union and yet nobody knows who's behind it?"

Adeline was about to say something, but Alfred held up his hand to quiet her. "You're right, Professor. We do know a few things. I believe Adeline already explained to you what the Executive's been doing with big data—gaining access to it, analyzing it, manipulating it."

I nodded.

"Well, it all comes down to obfuscation."

"And what is that?"

"It's the ability to make something obscure, unclear, perhaps unintelligible."

"I know what the word means," I said, laughing. "I meant in this context."

"Yes, of course. Forgive me," Alfred said with a twinkle in his eye as he took a drink of his scotch. "We are in an age where some sectors of technology are moving faster than others can keep up. Therefore, when I say obfuscation, I am referring to the Executive's ability to hide their dirty fingerprints."

"Or make their tracks lead back to someone else," added Adeline.

"Quite right. And as you just insinuated, your news media determined quite quickly that the Russians had used various methods to plant fake news and promote alternative messaging during your recent presidential campaigns. Well, I can also assure you the intelligence services knew what was going on long before CNN or the *Washington Post*. That's because there was a trail to follow, and it led right back to Moscow. However, there are other groups and individuals out there, particularly those unaffiliated with the less-than-agile governments of the world, who don't leave trails."

"I thought there was always a digital signature?"

"A few years ago, yes. But lately, methods have been devised to utterly and completely mask the originator of a particular activity as well as misdirect the trail to whomever they choose. The signature is there, it just no longer points to the actual culprit."

"So what's this mean?"

"It means the Executive is better than MI6, CIA, the FSB, and the SVR in how they use the dark web. They launch their platforms, messages, financial movements from the depths of the internet, feed into legitimate sites, and completely distort reality. It's a new form of tradecraft, you might say.

"Consequently, no one knows what is real, what is not, where it came from, who did it, and unfortunately, in this day of blissful ignorance and apathy, no one cares. Deep fakes are just the beginning. The masses will believe anything if it strikes a chord. Therefore, coupled with the Executive scraping everything on the web, their influence is unprecedented and invisible."

"Reality, life, security, prosperity—it's all about perception," Adeline added. "It's relative. The Executive is creating alternative realities which are not factual but become real when picked up and perpetuated by people. It's exhausting when you think about it."

"Yes, it is," I said, pinching the bridge of my nose and feeling a headache coming on. "Still, what does any of this have to do with me?"

"We need your help. You're an expert."

I laughed. "Expert? Technology is not my strong suit."

"I'm not talking about the bloody internet. I'm referring to the *history*."

"That, too. There are a number of historians—brilliant folks—whom I can introduce you to that know far more than I about extremist political movements. They'd love to get a call from someone like you, peddling an international conspiracy."

"Nonsense. We're not looking for historians to talk about the bloody Nazis or apartheid. I couldn't give two shits if Hitler was a homosexual or if the Boers really did whip the British Army.

"No, Professor, you're the man we're interested in. During your lecture at the Wilson Institute, you talked about three men who we believe were among the founding members of the Executive: Waters, Gibbons, and Himmler."

I recalled the lecture. Reginald Waters had been an advisor to Cecil Rhodes, and he was the architect for many of Rhodes' imperial ambitions. Brigadier Gibbons had been an aide to Lord Kitchener and later was rumored to have had a hand in the Sykes-Picot Agreement and the subsequent division of the Middle East. And Ludolph Himmler, the uncle of Heinrich Himmler—the infamous commander of the Third Reich's SS—had been a savant in service to the royal family of Bavaria.

I'd argued how these men shaped events far above their position because of the way they managed information. They were masterminds, orchestrating events five steps ahead like a game of chess, and they intentionally kept themselves out of the spotlight. And I knew there were others out there like Waters, Gibbons, and Himmler, but I hadn't had time to research their stories. I'd intended to, but I'd put everything on hold after the NEH cut my funding and the criticism from my peers rained in.

"Those men you lectured on were instrumental in some of the very things we're talking about—the promotion of imperial agendas, the White Man's burden, social hierarchy. So to say you're not an expert is nonsense. And," Alfred said leaning forward, "you have a family connection."

An awkward silence settled between us as I wondered if Alfred said what I thought he said. I met his stare, my neck and back going taut. The manner in which Alfred had said *family connection* made me think there was more about my father than what Adeline had revealed. She said the Executive had him killed, but . . .

"What do you mean?" I asked.

"Here's the issue. We need your expertise to figure out where these people came from—their beginnings—so that we can uncover who the present members of the Executive are and make sense of their activities and ideology. Only then can we figure out a way to stop them."

I shook my head, still confused. What they wanted from me—historical background—was something I could do. But I didn't believe that was the only reason they'd sought me out. There was something else, something they had yet to tell me. My family. What about my family?

"Fine. I'll help. But before we go any further, I need you to please be forthcoming with me. What about my family?"

Both Alfred and Adeline remained impassive.

"What aren't you telling me about my father?" I said, my voice rising.

Alfred reclined in his chair and sipped his scotch. "I'm going to be blunt, Professor. Your family has been in league with the Executive since the beginning. Every single one of them."

CHAPTER 19

St. Mary's Hospital, Paddington, London

The nurse looked at the MI5 officer posted outside the hospital room. He was an oaf of a man, standing with his arms crossed and feet apart, his jaw set in annoyance at the caregivers and the sick moving here and there. The bulge of his pistol under his windbreaker was visible, completing the image.

"I need to check the chart," the nurse said.

"You're not the sister from before," he replied brusquely.

"Early shift change. She had a party to attend. Her mum's."

The officer eyed her; she carried a pen in her left hand and an IV bag in her right. Without asking, he reached forward to inspect the badge dangling from her breast pocket, and she duly swatted him away.

"Hands off. You want to check my ID, ask." She tore off the badge and thrust it toward him.

He read the name, Judith Halts, studied her face, then took another look at the badge. "All right." He stepped aside, took out a key, and unlocked the door.

"I'll only be a minute," said Judith. But before she shut the door behind her, she turned and quipped, "I'm going to have to change his fluids, too. That won't cause you to come bursting in like a rabid dog, will it?"

The MI5 officer snorted, then shut the door, leaving the nurse alone inside.

In the bed was a man in his early forties, his face almost unrecognizable from the swelling and bruising. He was in a coma due to blunt trauma to the skull.

She read the name on the clipboard: Timothy Sanders. She then checked the respirator, which seemed to be working normally. The heart monitor beeped with a consistent rhythm. As for the IV bag, it was nearly empty.

She wiped her sweaty palms on her scrubs and told herself she was doing nothing unusual. She was changing his IV bag—that's normal. She's a nurse; that's what nurses do.

Still, her fingers trembled as she switched out the empty bag with the fresh one.

She glanced at the window in the door, seeing the back of the agent's buzzed-cut head. She expelled a slow breath, then opened the door. "Your man's fine. See you in an hour."

The guard stepped to the side, letting the nurse pass.

Judith didn't look back as she hastened down the hall. Once she turned down another corridor, she picked up her pace and unclipped her badge. She swiftly descended the stairs to the ground floor, feeling an overwhelming urge to run.

Someone screamed for a doctor from where she'd just come. Then someone yelled *Code Blue*—Timothy Sanders was in cardiac arrest.

Seconds later, Judith exited St. Mary's Hospital onto Praed Street and hailed a cab.

"Where to, miss?" asked the driver.

"King's Cross," she blurted.

"Taking a trip, are we?"

Judith didn't respond. She pulled out her mobile and dialed a number from memory. After two rings someone picked up.

"Hello, Mother," she said, fighting the excitement in her voice. "I'm on my way, and I took care of the plants as you asked."

The person on the other end hung up.

The cab rolled through the evening traffic, and as the cars passed, Judith felt the ecstasy bubble within her. Everything had gone so well! She already had more money in her account than she knew how to spend, and she'd be on a plane to Malta within the hour. And they'd promised once it was done, she'd never hear from them again.

Too easy. Too blooming easy!

She needed to get out of this place. Being laid off and pushed to the side will do that.

The driver turned right and a set of headlights flashed against the window, blinding her.

A van hit the taxi directly in the side, T-boning the vehicle and sending it skidding across the intersection. The force of the impact knocked Judith unconscious. The driver hit his head against the side window, knocking him out.

A man in a black raincoat got out of the van and walked up to the back seat of the taxi. He took out a pistol, aimed, and put two bullets in Judith's head.

CHAPTER 20

I rolled over to look at the clock on the nightstand—4:17 in the damn morning. I'd barely slept a wink since Alfred left the safe house and I and Adeline retired to our separate rooms. I couldn't stop my mind from roiling; I'd been deceived in so many ways by so many people.

Alfred and Adeline had laid everything bare.

The Executive hadn't murdered my father because of something he'd stumbled across; the old man had been one of them, a card-carrying believer.

But while thoughts of my father's transgressions angered me, the revelation about my entire family's complicity caused me to go numb. Confusion, emptiness, betrayal—the emotions were there, but I was helpless to make sense of them . . . and the truth was, I'm not sure I wanted to. I knew that if I allowed myself to feel the sentiments surging around inside my heart, inside my brain, inside my soul—it would hurt too much.

Everything I thought I knew about my family was a lie.

My great-great-grandfather, Heinrich Dresden, emigrated from Germany to the United States after the Franco-Prussian War—to build his fortune from steel contracts for *the progress of mankind*—but, in reality, it was an infiltration, a plot to infect North America with the Executive's agenda. Heinrich's sons, working as diplomats in the administrations of Theodore Roosevelt and Woodrow Wilson—spreading American values and universal ideals to the rest of the world, *a beacon on the hill*—were actually a grand deception bent on imperial ambitions.

And my very grandfather, a man I had dearly loved and looked up to, Maximillian Dresden, a close advisor to Franklin Roosevelt during World War II, heading up policies in response to the treatment of Jews in Nazi Germany . . . I couldn't even bring myself to think what that truly meant, what he'd done or not done.

How could he? How could my grandfather have believed such things?

I'd imagined Grandpa Max could do no wrong. He was the male role model my father had never been, and he'd been there when others chose not to be.

The summer my mother died, my father sent me to camp in Maine. Distract the lad with canoes and campfires, my father had said. But two weeks into it, I got into a scrap with another boy and was thoroughly whipped, tears and mud coloring my cheeks. Of course, such behavior could not be tolerated at such a refined place as Parker Mountain.

It was Grandpa Max who came to pick me up. I could still picture his mechanical limp as he trudged up the rocky path—when he was in his fifties, a horse had kicked him in the knee, necessitating a full replacement with steel rods and screws. When my grandpa got to the lodge, he didn't say anything; he just hugged me.

Instead of going home, we went to the coast and stood on the beach, looking out across the Atlantic. It was high tide and a storm was brewing, the roar of the surf making it hard to hear anything except the crash of the waves and the wind rushing across the dunes.

My grandfather told me to yell, to scream my lungs out. He wanted me to expel the pain from the loss of my mother. And I did, screaming louder than I ever had before, my voice mixing with the fury of the sea.

Then Grandpa Max put his arm around me and said, "You'll be all right, and I'll always watch over you, even when it's my turn to go."

How could he have been part of this!

I sat up, but the sudden movement made me feel light-headed. I ran my fingers through my hair, trying to shake it off, but it didn't help. A queasiness formed in the back of my throat. I got up and shuffled toward the bathroom. Turning on the light, I rested my head against the doorframe.

As I stood there, other memories of my childhood took on new forms. Mysterious visits by bankers to the townhouse in Paris. A vacation in the Alps where my father and grandfather met a group late in the evening. Encouragement to read the works of Darwin and Spencer on the ideas of natural selection and survival of the fittest, as well the writings of Machiavelli and Hobbes to plant the seeds of imperial and nationalist theories.

The Executive had been there before me the entire time, hidden and yet exposed in everyday things.

I wondered how many of my other relatives had been involved and what they'd done as servants of the Executive's ideas—the Covenants. Had they murdered people, set bombs off, conspired in the pursuit of a twisted agenda?

And why had no one told me? What had prevented my father or my grandfather from sharing this secret? Was I not good enough? Was there something wrong with me?

And what of my mother? Had she known? Had she been involved, too?

Oh God, no. It wasn't possible.

I lurched toward the toilet and retched. Bile and alcohol bubbled up from my stomach. When there was nothing left, I dry heaved, coughing until my face hurt from the rush of blood.

I fell back against the wall, pressing my palms against my temples.

What would I have done if my father had told me such a horrible thing? Or what if Grandpa Max had? Would I have joined and followed in their footsteps? Would I have rationalized things little by little, and in time, accepted my position?

No, I told myself. I couldn't have. I was different. That's why they left me in the dark . . . right?

Maybe my dear mother hadn't known anything either. She was innocent. She had to be.

I struggled to my feet and bent over the sink. My stomach was settling down, and the dizziness had passed. I splashed water on my face and gargled a cupful of mouthwash, trying to cleanse the horrid taste from my mouth and throat.

I looked at the clock on the nightstand and saw it was just after five. I gingerly made my way over to the window. It was drizzling outside, though the sun was starting to rise. I could see an orange hue mixed with the fading shadows of the street lamps.

How many mornings had I seen just like this one? Countless, countless mornings with rain and sun signaling a new day. A new day to get on with it, tackle the challenges that lay ahead.

That's what this was, I told myself—a morning like any other. It had to be. My family's involvement had always been there, yet I had never known and had charted my own course in life. Why should today be any different, then?

I took a deep breath and forced my feelings, the memories—all of it—I forced everything down to the depths of my consciousness.

"Quit feeling sorry for yourself," I murmured to my reflection in the window.

It was time to get on with it and figure out what the hell was going on.

I crossed the room and opened the door to the rest of the house. All was quiet.

Five minutes later I was dressed. I made my way down the hall and stopped in front of Adeline's door. I didn't see any light coming from the crack, and when I pressed my ear to the frame I didn't hear a thing.

I tiptoed to the front door, careful not to make a sound as I slipped out onto the front steps. I needed to check into something, and I didn't want Adeline peering over my shoulder.

CHAPTER 21

"Professor Dresden! Blimey, I thought it'd be a long while before you came back. Horrible business, if you ask me. I hear they pulled your funding. Bloody wazzocks. Never liked bureaucrats much, making all kinds of policies and regulations just to move a'piece a'paper from one side of their desk to the other. Waste a' bleeding time if you ask me."

"Good to see you, too, Henry. How's the family?" I asked the elderly security guard.

Britain's national archives weren't open yet, but I'd been here enough to know some of the staff. They were my sensible friends—the archivists, security guards, admin assistants, and cafeteria workers whom I'd become acquainted with over the years. We'd nod in the halls, exchange a few words outside an office, and on occasion grab a cup of tea together. They led the lives I thought I wanted—quiet, predictable, simple.

"Ah, can't complain," Henry went on. "The missus and I celebrated our fiftieth just last week."

"Good for you."

"Thanks. If I'd known you was in town, I would have extended an invitation."

"I would have liked that."

"Ah, perhaps on our sixtieth. As long as the old witch decides to keep me around till then, that is. Now, it's not every day the esteemed Professor Dresden shows up outside my building. What can I do for ya?"

"I was hoping you'd let me in. Like old times."

Henry grinned. "I thought as much. New book?"

"Something like that."

"Right. Good stuff. Come on."

Fifteen minutes later I was in one of the small reading rooms, prints of anonymous landscapes on white plaster walls. There were four work tables spaced evenly apart, worn smooth with dime-sized dents and nicks, and wooden chairs with straight backs that made your spine scream by the end of the day.

I'd been here before. It was the same room I'd done my research in for my dissertation: *Britain in Palestine: The Complexities of Two-Pronged Insurgencies and Hostilities Between Foreign Ethnic Groups.* Quite the pretentious title, I thought to myself. I must have been drinking or in an overly gaseous mood when I came up with it.

Those days seemed like another life, another world—no longer mine. Things were different now, and I felt an unease in my stomach like I shouldn't be here. I felt like I was no longer free to sift through the past. I was too different, soiled by my newfound ancestral roots.

"Need anything else, Professor?" asked the guard.

"Does Wendy still get in early?"

"Arrived fifteen minutes before you did. I'm sure she'd love to say hello. I'll send her down so you can get the files you need. How 'bout that?"

"Thank you."

A short time later, a woman even older than Henry shuffled in. She had straight white hair and an oval face that was wrinkled and pale as ivory, and she wore clothes with polyester fabrics that fell off her shoulders and bony hips. But her eyes were bright as stars, and her face radiated warmth when she smiled. Years ago when I was researching here, she used to bring me homemade biscuits. Sweet, buttery goodness, and you could never eat just one.

She gave me a grandmotherly hug. "William, so good to see you. How are you?"

"Fine, Wendy. Delighted to see you, too."

"I've missed seeing you around. The folks I deal with here can be a bit odd. Always liked helping you, though. You doing okay?"

"Yes," I replied, giving her a curious look. "Why do you ask?"

"Because that's what I do. And besides, you look worn down a bit. Not letting the critics get to you, I hope. Best to tell them to go to hell than listen to their nonsense, if you ask me."

"I'll remember that," I said with a small smile.

"No you won't, but that's fine. Now, what can I get for you?"

I told her what I needed from the back rooms, and no more than ten minutes later she returned with a cart full of archival boxes.

"If you need anything, you know where to find me. And do make sure you get some rest. You work too hard." She clasped my hand between both of hers and held it for a moment, then she shuffled back to her office down the hall.

I watched her go, and for a moment forgot about the mess I was in. She was one of the kindest human beings I'd ever met.

But my respite only lasted a few seconds. The archives would be alive soon.

I sat down and got to work, quickly sorting through the first batch of files—the papers of Reginald Waters. I'd read them countless times before, studying these documents meticulously to prepare for my lecture at the Wilson Center—the lecture that the Executive supposedly found threatening.

It took me less than twenty minutes to find what I was looking for, inscribed on the pages of a cracked ledger. They were there—multiple entries—just like I remembered, but which I'd dismissed as coincidence the first go-around.

Noting the record locator, I moved on to the second set of papers—those of Brigadier Nigel Gibbons. Gibbons had been an aide to Lord Kitchener, the British field marshal of colonial campaigns and the First World War. I found what I was looking for in Gibbons' papers just as quickly—financial movements.

In both cases, there were numerous records documenting transactions between Barclays, HSBC, a smattering of international shipping firms, African holding companies, and a long list of domestic enterprises. These men had substantial assets, and their businesses spanned the globe.

But of particular note, there was a small number of transactions with HG Krautherbank, an exclusive firm out of Prussia. I suspected that if I looked at Himmler's financial records, he'd have similar dealings with HG Krautherbank. Yet, the link between these three men and the bank wasn't the reason to break out the champagne.

A fourth connection existed, one that only I knew.

"Christ," I breathed to myself.

No one else would have seen the clues. And even if they had picked up on the link with HG Krautherbank, without knowing the other half, it would have meant nothing. But to me, there was no doubt.

HG Krautherbank was our conduit to the Executive.

"Professor Dresden?"

A man's voice called from across the room, disturbing my concentration. I looked up.

It was a heavyset man, bald on top but with curly brown hair that wrapped around his skull. He could have been a double for Friar Tuck had he not been an avowed atheist.

His name was Paul Ingrid, a professor at King's College London. He and I collaborated on a panel a few years back. A nice enough man, but odd. Socially off. The kind of colleague one said hello to, but didn't dare go beyond the surface for fear of never being able to break free, perhaps being the recipient of a long soliloquy about the pain in his hip that has also attached itself to the nerve and requires extensive pain medication but not so much as—

I swore. I'd half thought the possibility of running into someone like this existed, and I'd worked out a few things to say, but now that I was in the middle of it, none of my potential stories seemed even marginally believable.

"Paul, what a pleasant surprise," I said.

"Isn't it. What brings you here? I thought you were taking some time off."

"Couldn't stay away," I said, forcing a grin.

"Can't say I blame you. Not sure how'd I'd react after being shut down like that. Never had something like that happen to me. 'Course, our grant system works a bit differently than yours. You know, I never did hear the reason why they pulled your funding."

"Wasn't something I told many folks."

Paul stood there, seeming to wait for me to continue, but when I didn't, Paul leaned forward to get a look at my table. "So what have you been up to?"

I instinctively shifted my body between Paul and the archival material.

Paul craned his neck and said absently, "I heard you were on sabbatical in the south of France. I wish—" Paul's demeanor suddenly went from genial to one of fear. "My God. There was a news report . . . a bombing . . . your picture . . ."

I looked around. Paul was between me and the exit door, his substantial frame blocking the only way out. There was one other researcher in the room, a woman who just a moment ago had been buried in her boxes and letters, but I suddenly felt her eyes boring into me.

Paul took a step back, bumping into a chair.

I turned around and fumbled for my notes, my mind racing.

"Professor William Dresden?" called someone else's voice.

I turned to see who it was—Adeline, standing in the doorway.

She produced what looked like a law enforcement badge and flashed it at me. "Are you Professor Dresden?"

I nodded hesitantly.

"My name is Detective Inspector Potsam with the Yard. You're needed for questioning regarding the café bombing in Nice, France, that occurred four days ago. We have officers standing by, but we'd prefer to do this quietly. Would you please come with me?"

"Of-of-of course," I stuttered.

I could see Paul staring wide-eyed—the arrest of a distinguished historian in Britain's National Archives—a scandal for the ages. No one would have any hope of freeing themselves from his grasp at the cocktail socials of the future.

Adeline took my arm and led me out of the reading room.

CHAPTER 22

KEW, ENGLAND

"What the hell were you thinking?" Adeline demanded once we were in her car and driving out the gate.

Ignoring her, I watched the National Archives fade away in the side-view mirror, wondering if I'd ever be able to go back there. Certainly not before this mess was over. And I had no doubt jolly ole' Professor Ingrid was regaling anyone who would listen about his run-in with *Professor Dresden*—disgraced academic, wanted on charges of terrorism, detained by Scotland Yard right before his very eyes.

Adeline took a right on South Circular Road to head across the Thames and back into the city. "Well?" she repeated. "Why'd you go off alone like that?"

I knitted my brow and looked out the window. I was trying to remain composed, but her tone was grating. "How'd you find me?"

"You're not as quiet as you think. I followed you."

I didn't respond.

"Christ, William. You could have been wrapped up in seconds. Who knows who else was watching. What was so important you had to go off like that?"

"I needed to look into something."

"Oh yeah? And you thought it was a good idea not to tell me?"

"Actually, I really didn't give a shit."

"What?"

"Look. Thanks for getting me out of there, but let's get something straight. Last night you and Alfred asked for my help. But since the beginning, you haven't been honest with me, and you don't tell me a damn thing about what's going on. You wanted to know if I trust you?" I asked. "Well, I don't trust you. Every day I find out you've told me another half-truth or misled me, making me think one thing only to be contradicted later."

My sudden response seemed to startle Adeline, which I guess I intended though hadn't planned. The stress, the lack of sleep, the lies, the confusion—as I spoke, I had a simultaneous conversation ongoing in my head. I was thinking one thing while the words of another spilled from my mouth.

"William—"

"Don't interrupt me," I snapped. "Yes. I admit it wasn't the wisest decision to go off like that, alone. But as I said, I needed to look into something, and I didn't need you asking stupid questions. If you want my help, then stop screwing with me. If this *partnership* is going to work, you *will* be straight with me in everything. No more lies, no more holding back, no more handling me like a pawn." I shifted in my seat to look directly at her. "Are we clear?"

I couldn't be certain, but it seemed like Adeline wanted to smile. She finally said, "Yes. We're clear."

Neither of us spoke for a while, me tapping my foot on the floorboard and Adeline fixated on the road. It was like the aftermath of a lover's quarrel, with neither party willing to extend an olive branch, either, because they were still too angry or because they were scared of what the other might say.

Then Adeline did indeed smile, or perhaps it was closer to a smirk. "Feel better?"

"What?"

"Do you feel better getting that off your chest?"

I eyed her, wanting to stay pissed, but soon found myself unable to hold in a chuckle.

Adeline joined my cathartic laughter.

"It's not funny," I said between breaths.

"It kinda is."

"I'm serious. This crap has got to stop."

"You've made your point. We're good. No more games."

"Sure," I said, shaking my head.

"Right. Well, did you find what you were looking for?"

I spotted a restaurant up ahead. "Park over there. I'm starved."

CHAPTER 23

Adeline sat across from me in a pub named The Eagle. We both had cups of coffee in front of us and two plates of food were on the way.

"All right," she began. "It's a lovely morning, and we've already had our excitement for the day. Mind telling me why you felt compelled to visit the archives without telling me?"

"I have our next move," I said delightedly.

"Why, of course you do."

I smiled. "I know what bank the Executive used when it first formed, and I suspect they're still using it."

"That's something. Go on."

"How much do you know about the city of Strasbourg?"

"Never been."

"All right. I'll try not to bore you, but think of the city as a gateway between West and Central Europe. Kings, emperors, even Napoleon launched their legions from there. Over the centuries, thousands of Frenchmen and Germans lost their lives with that city in the backdrop. Then, after the Treaty of Frankfurt in 1871, Imperial Germany decided to rebuild Strasbourg as *Neue Stadt*: new city."

"Sounds very benevolent of the Kaiser."

"Ambitious. Germany had just defeated France and threatened to occupy Paris. They had demonstrated their power to the world."

Adeline shrugged and sipped her coffee. "And?"

"Enter HG Krautherbank. Have you ever heard of it?"

"Still no, William."

"Right. HG Krautherbank sets up shop in Strasbourg in the aftermath of the Franco-Prussian War. But while most banks start small, this one opens its doors mature and funded."

"What does that mean?"

"The bank's board had connections across the Continent—inroads into all the great empires of the day, including France—and in a few years, the firm is a preferred institution within elite circles. Reginald Waters, Brigadier Gibbons—the men you think were founding members of the Executive—they had interests at HG, and the transactions were significant. In the hundreds of millions."

"What does that mean in today's currency?"

"It's closing in on a few billion, give or take."

"That's significant."

"Quite," I remarked.

"Any indication what the transactions were for?"

"I wasn't able to get that far in light of seeing my—" I waved my hand dismissively—"professor friend."

The bartender swooped in with our breakfast, and both Adeline and I sat back to give her room. She delivered a plate of egg whites for me and I asked for a coffee refill. Adeline then stole one of my chips and cut into her sausage and potatoes.

"Okay. So, these men banked at the same place. What else?" Adeline asked, taking a forkful.

"The Executive is somewhat hereditary, right?"

"Not everyone, but a few."

"Well, neither of these two men had any descendants. They each had their respective versions of a tragic ending."

She held up her hands. "Wait. Okay. I apologize. Before you go any further, can you please tell me who these guys were?"

I flashed her a curious look. "I thought you knew of them from my infamous lecture and file in MI6's basement?"

"I didn't attend your lecture, and I have doubts about the report I was given that was supposed to summarize things."

"All right," I said, looking down at the table to gather my thoughts but also wondering what she meant. "Why would you doubt your own report?"

"For the same reason we can't trust anyone in my service now. It's possible the report I was given—created by a team of analysts who should not have been privy to the reasons behind the report they were writing—it's possible they were compromised."

"Right, sure," I said, shaking my head. "I should have guessed that by now."

"Besides, you're the actual expert. Please continue."

"Of course. How much do you know about European imperialism?"

"I studied computer science at university. I don't think I saw it on the required course schedule."

"Okay. Well, most people know about colonization, exploitation of resources, maybe even the so-called *scramble for Africa*. And most people are familiar with Darwin's theory about the survival of the fittest and the layman's concept of imperialism, right?"

"I think you give people too much credit, but go on."

"Well, the latter half of the nineteenth century was the heyday of these movements. It was the first time in history a people— Europeans, to be precise—had the industrial power to conquer the world—ships, railroads, combustion engines, weapons of war that could kill beyond anyone's imagination. The main players were who you might expect—Britain, France, Germany, Austria-Hungary, the Dutch."

"And the Russians," she added.

"Not as you might think. They were running about—that's certain—but their strength came from their numbers, not their industrial might. They were hard-pressed to project power beyond their borders, and most European states wanted to keep the Slavs in check—fear of the Russian steamroller and their superstitions. Europe has never accepted Russia as an equal and we still don't, which is probably why the Kremlin sees the world as a zero-sum game and decided to invade Ukraine not so long ago. But that's mere context.

"The point I'm trying to make is that European states had the capability to subjugate the world. Then you couple this with the top biological thinkers of the era—racial theories backed up by *science* about superior and inferior forms of humanity—You have a potent combination. Decades later, the biological scholarship of the late nineteenth century served as the foundation for the Nazis.

"This was a dynamic era with monumental changes—changes that were about power and control. It was networks—money, influence, information, brute force. That's what Europeans brought to the world at the turn of the century. Reginald Waters, Brigadier Gibbons—they were in the middle of it."

"How so?"

"Waters worked for Cecil Rhodes, the very same Rhodes the scholarship is named after. But Cecil Rhodes was a racist, the architect of apartheid in South Africa, and a champion of British imperialism. Waters made Rhodes' ambitions possible. He was a facilitator—moving money, negotiating contracts, marshaling men and resources, manipulating back rooms while Rhodes hammered the front rooms. Put simply, Reginald Waters was an influential power broker, but out of the spotlight. And he had extreme views about European superiority. He fits the profile of the Executive. So does Gibbons."

"Okay. What else?"

"Their deaths... They were the founding members. Take Brigadier Gibbons, an aide to Lord Kitchener and someone involved in the drafting of the Sykes-Picot Agreement that divided up the Middle East, leading to so many of the challenges we are confronted with today. Then, in 1919, Gibbons is outside of Munich on a hunting trip. On the second day, he gets separated from the group. They find him hours later—dismembered and partially eaten."

"Good Lord."

"The police report said animal attack; however, some of the photos from the investigation survived and are kept in the provincial records office in Munich. If you look closely, the body doesn't look like it was ripped or torn apart. It was cut, hacked with an axe of sorts, and the face was sliced to shreds, unrecognizable."

"A murder covered up as an animal attack?" Adeline asked.

I could see her gears were starting to turn. But all we had were educated conclusions, nothing definitive, so I shrugged.

"Who was on the hunting party?"

"Among others, Ludolph Himmler."

"You mean *the* Himmler?"

"Yes, Heinrich Himmler's uncle, who was also a savant to Bavarian royalty. Ludolph's papers are located in Berlin. But what I'm getting at—and to answer your question about who these men were—is that they were all interconnected in some way, but they operated in the shadows of history's greats. They had significant power, yet they lived mostly unknown and died in mysterious ways."

"As if there was someone, or something, working even further behind the scenes," she offered.

"Possibly. The timing of their deaths is strange, too. Approximately twenty years between them. Waters in 1899, Gibbons in 1919, and Himmler in 1939. Like clockwork, as if it was time to go, to make room for someone else, or move on to something different."

"What are you saying?"

"I don't know," I murmured, staring out the window, the people of London hustling by. I had ideas—theories—but they were still formulating. "HG Krautherbank . . . that's the connection that spans time."

"What do you mean?"

"I can't explain the deaths of these men, nor why they occurred twenty years apart. But HG Krautherbank is where we'll find more answers."

"How do you know?"

I met her eyes. "Because it's where my family's trust is held."

"What?" Adeline's voice betrayed her. I could tell she had not expected this kind of connection, which surprised me and made me think we were moving into new territory, pulling back the layers that Adeline and Alfred had been unable to reveal on their own.

"Alfred was right," I said. "I have a family connection, but it goes beyond what he shared with me last night. The Dresdens—my family—they used the same bank as those men and have been doing so since they immigrated to the United States in the 1870s. And I meet with my account manager from HG annually and review my family's trust."

"Why didn't you mention this before?" Adeline asked.

"I didn't know about the connection until this morning," I replied.

"Where do you meet your account manager?" Adeline asked.

"He always travels to me and we meet in a hotel suite in whatever city I happen to be in at the time, the meeting lasting no more than an hour. The past few years, that's been Princeton. But there's been times when we've met in Rome, Paris, Tours, even here in London. And now that I think about it, I've never been to the actual bank. I've never once been to his office," I said absently.

"How is the meeting arranged?"

"As any meeting is. He calls me a week or two in advance, asks where I'll be, and sets it up."

"And?"

"And what?"

"How do you meet? Does he send you a key to the suite, do you rendezvous at a restaurant, do you get a gilded invitation?"

"No, nothing like that. He meets me in the lobby, we go to the room, he presents everything, we chat, and I'm on my way within an hour or so. Sometimes he has food brought in, and depending on the hour, we might have a drink together."

"You two sound chummy."

"Polite. I've met him annually for nearly two decades. There's bound to be some familiarity between people with that kind of history, even the stiffest of folks."

"What does he review with you?" Adeline asked, the questions coming as fast as I could answer.

"I just make sure the money is still there. I've never touched any of it. It sits in the account accruing interest."

"Why?"

"As I've suggested, I have a bad taste in my mouth about a few things concerning my father."

"Right. How much is in the trust?"

"Not that much. My great-grandfather set it up decades ago to protect inheritances, but the wealth from steel that you referred to dwindled over the years and long before my time. The account currently has a few million in it."

"Not that much? A few million is nothing to dismiss."

"For a generational trust, it's a bit meager, I would think, especially in today's world where the family home can sell for one or two million and set up the grandkids."

"Right, sure. I don't have a trust," muttered Adeline.

I wrote a name and telephone number on a napkin and handed it to her. "Here's his contact information and home office in Frankfurt. You think Alfred can look into him for us? I've obviously been missing something about the man."

She took the napkin. "Sure, we'll stick the profilers on him to work up a nice little package on who this man really is. But in the meantime, I've got another idea."

CHAPTER 24

Seven men and three women sat around a long, rectangular table. They were all dressed in business attire, their posture rigid, their demeanors humorless. Were it not for the Brioni suits, Armani shoes, and light refreshments presented on fine porcelain, one might think they were senior military officers preparing for a coup.

Some had worn a uniform at one point in their lives, but most came from the private sector or the civilian side of government. Yet they all possessed the poise and discipline of executives accustomed to wielding power.

They were all white, too.

The Kanzler, who sat at the head of the table, stood up and looked at the board members. This was the team he'd created, which he'd handpicked from the ranks of the elite. It had taken years, disposing of some members who did not see things as they should, or waiting for others—who out of respect he could not easily remove—to pass on or willingly slip into retirement. But the wait had been worth it.

"Ladies and gentlemen," he began. "Thank you for gathering on short notice. I recognize every one of you has important commitments, but our work together comes first, always."

The members around the table nodded in agreement.

"As I indicated in my summons, there are two matters that require immediate attention. The first concerns recent events in Nice."

A few of the members frowned, unable to disguise their displeasure with what had happened, but most of the group remained expressionless.

"The bombing was unfortunate," he continued. "It's not a preferred method for doing business. Not how we operate. The days of indiscriminate violence—as some of our predecessors employed— are no more and are counterproductive. Violence should be used sparingly and only for precise intentions."

A man at the end of the table, a former admiral in the British Navy, spoke up. "We know this, Herr Kanzler. Not a person around this table thinks you gave the order. My interest concerns what you plan to do next."

"I've assumed control of the operation. It will be over soon."

"And Ms. König?" asked a German banker.

"Handled. There's no misunderstanding."

Sitting back down, the Kanzler rested his forearms on the table and interlaced his fingers.

The nods from around the table indicated the board members accepted his statements. The matter was over, an unfortunate incident. These were men and women who did not waste time discussing an issue for the sake of tedious collaboration. If it was said, they expected it to be done, and that was the end of it.

"Now on to the second matter. Marie?"

A petite Frenchwoman sitting to the right of the Kanzler cleared her throat. "My associates, Europe and our brethren in America are witnessing a convergence of events the world has not experienced for nearly a century. One could overlay the attitudes of the late nineteenth century and 1930s on those of today, and the similarities would be striking. We're fortunate to be in the position that we are.

"September eleventh was a blessing. Islam started a war with the West, and the United States exacerbated the issues tenfold. Since then, the Middle East has been in a perpetual state of conflict, killing itself. Yet, the exodus from the region has been overwhelming. Select Asian powers have also begun spreading their influence. Whether it's the business interests of the Chinese, the brain drain of India, or the tantrums of North Korea—these groups have ventured into areas they do not belong.

"The results—Europeans have come to reject immigration, and laws are being enacted to force the groups already here to conform to civilized culture. In America, police kill African Americans every day in the name of justice, and the current political climate suggests a race war is brewing. The threat from Asia has become real, too, and the West finally realizes it should be blocked both militarily and economically.

"The world is once again recognizing that there are differences, and those differences can't be assimilated. It is one or the other—there can be no blending. But as the Kanzler just said, ill-conceived violence isn't the way to achieve our goals. We must change the thinking of the public, shape ideology, and entrench beliefs. That's the only way to return our peoples to their rightful position in the world and reestablish our economic and military power. Violence will be necessary, of course, but not yet."

Two attendants entered the room and began passing out folders.

"Each of you have push points in your governments, some of you possess influence in media and culture, and all of you have access to significant funds, either through the Executive's mechanisms, or your own. What you see before you in the reports are compilations of groups, leaders, icons, and officials that we need you to apply pressure to. Reach them, shape them, and if necessary, compel them to fund and support the populist movements. Just as Britain did

with Brexit and the United States in recent elections—we must cap-
italize on the deepest beliefs and fears of our populations, which
have been suppressed for too long.

"We intend to inject significant amounts of funding into political
and social movements across the Continent, and over the next few
years have Europe close its borders, dissolve the EU, and create a
space for our respective countries to assume the power gaps. There
will be a time for decisive action, but that will be addressed at a
future date."

A Dutchman seated in the middle of the table cleared his throat.
"And what of Russia? You talk of influence and pressure, but we can
no longer ignore the activities of the Kremlin."

Marie, who had paused to take a sip of water, opened her mouth
to respond but stopped. A tremor had hit the room and everyone
inside it, with murmurs traveling among the members like an invisible wave. Attempting to regain control, Marie met the Dutchman's
gaze but had to look to the Kanzler. "I—"

The Kanzler lifted his index finger to silence her.

"That's an excellent observation," he said. "And I agree with you.
It cannot be ignored. It's something that weighs on me."

"And?" asked the Dutchman.

"I've opened a line of communication with some like-minded
contacts inside the Kremlin."

More murmurs and whispers shuddered around the table, threatening to devolve into a riot were it not for the restraint of the biscuits and tea. Never in the history of the Executive had substantive
engagement with Russia been considered, much less acted upon.

"When were you going to tell us?" asked an elder Belgian woman.

"When the time was right. And it still isn't. The *initiative*, as I will
call it, is something I've not fully decided. But it has been a consideration of mine for quite some time."

"Yes, we know," remarked the Dutchman. "We remember the discussion. It was 1998, I believe. You'd just assumed your position as Kanzler."

He nodded slowly. "A decision such as this takes time. The impact could be significant. Unfortunately, I'm not ready to discuss the matter in full."

"When will you?" another member asked.

The Kanzler exhaled, followed by a clench of the jaw. He knew his outreach to the Kremlin would be unsettling to the Board, but now was not the time to dive into the matter. The initiative wasn't fully formed, which was why he'd hoped the topic would not have come up at this meeting.

But in a not-so-comfortable way, the topic had come up. He couldn't ignore it.

"In one month's time, after you have commenced your respective efforts, the initiative will be formally presented to the board for consideration. However, given that the matter has been raised, I will end with this.

"Russia is a resilient country. Their fall and rise in the past twenty years is proof of that. And they feel as we do about protecting what is theirs—their actions in Abkazia, South Ossetia, and Eastern Ukraine to protect ethnic Russians serve as prime examples. The key to an arrangement will be a common understanding, and as I said, I am in consultation with like-minded members of the elite."

The Kanzler turned to Marie and indicated for her to continue. Whether the other board members appreciated the abrupt conclusion to the discussion was unclear. Nevertheless, if they were bothered, it didn't matter. To hell with their concerns.

He was the Kanzler. He had been chosen to lead the Executive and, goddamn it, they would do as was directed.

CHAPTER 25

On the drive back to North Kensington, Adeline made a phone call to a voicemail box where she left a message for Alfred. She also sent a text to someone but didn't share with me who it was. And when I asked, she ignored the question, making me wonder if she'd already ditched our agreement to be straight with one another.

But I decided to let it go, not surprised she was still cagey, and electing to choose my battles rather than act from disadvantage.

Besides, I was preoccupied mulling over the Executive's connection to HG Krautherbank—my family's bank. Like so many other things, the evidence had been right in front of me. But my aversion toward my past—my father and every painful memory that went with it—had blinded me.

I was disappointed in myself. I should have known. I should have been aware of what was happening around me. It made me question so many things about who I was as a person—who I am—even wondering if the image of myself was, in fact, at all accurate. Or, was the way I perceived myself a distorted reflection while everyone else saw something quite different?

But I did not come to any resolution about those thoughts because, as they started to swirl, Adeline parked on a narrow street a block away from the safe house. The walk to the safe house was quick and uneventful, and once back inside, Adeline proceeded to inspect the door locks and hinges, then the windows, then the floors around the points of entry. I remained by the entrance out of the way, watching her do her checks and examining the room from afar.

Everything looked as we'd left it—glasses on the kitchen counter, the newspaper haphazardly folded on the footstool, the curtain sheers closed but off-center, a small stain on the carpet in front of the sofa. The sounds were the same, too. The pop of a floorboard, branches tapping the windows, the occasional sound of a car driving by.

Nothing.

In a way, it was like coming home after being gone for the weekend and finding the front door closed but unlocked. It makes one wonder, did I leave it unlocked, or did someone pay me an unwanted visit? Nothing apparently wrong, but the fear tugs at the back of your mind as it did for me now. How close was the enemy lurking about, and would we know it?

Seeming satisfied with her checks, Adeline went to her room and minutes later emerged with an oversized laptop that she set on the kitchen table. Powering it on, she said, "I call it Balrog."

"Balrog," I remarked curiously. "As in *Lord of the Rings*?"

Adeline nodded.

"You name your computers?" I asked, somewhat amused, remembering a genius friend of mine from long ago who also did such things.

"Yeah," Adeline replied. "We're going to use it to hack into the bank."

"Just with that?"

"Not just with this," she said, typing in her password. "Help is on the way."

The text, I thought. "Who?"

"Someone who can help us."

"You need to do better than that, please. Who is he?"

"His name's Miikka."

"Miikka," I murmured, trying to tease out the name's origin. "What heritage is that?"

"Finnish."

"Finnish?"

"Yeah. He's an old friend. From grad school."

"Lovely. A nice little reunion for you."

"In a way."

"Who is he?" I asked.

"He's a specialist, of sorts."

"A specialist in . . ." I waved my hand invitingly, urging her to go on.

But before she could respond, someone knocked. Adeline approached the front door, her hand resting on the pistol tucked inside her waistband. She looked through the peephole, then opened the door.

In walked a man in his early thirties, tall and lean with spiked brown hair. He had high cheekbones and dark blue eyes, and a bit of scruff on his face that was nicely manicured. His black pants, black shoes, and tight black shirt made him look like a fashion model ready for an ice bar. He nodded at Adeline and said, "Iltaa," his Nordic accent crisp.

"Good evening, so glad you could come," she replied.

There was a hint of hesitancy in her voice, revealing that she was pleased the man was here but was unsure how he felt about it. It reminded me of the first few seconds of a reunion between ex-lovers, both wary about how the other might react.

"It's nothing," Miikka said.

Ignoring me, Miikka—the *specialist* in what, I still did not know—made his way into the kitchen where Adeline had set up her computer. "Work here?" he asked.

"Yes."

Miikka produced a laptop from his bag, along with a router and two additional black boxes with associated cables and plugs. He linked his computer and devices, and then connected them to Adeline's laptop. He then sat down and started up multiple programs. Adeline did the same, the kitchen now a pop-up operations center. All we needed were flat screens hanging on the walls and a flashing red light by the door.

"Target?" Miikka asked.

"A financial firm, HG Krautherbank. We need access to client profiles, personnel files of senior officers, and the firm's transaction records," answered Adeline with clipped precision.

"What else?"

"Anything that looks interesting."

"They know we coming?"

"Not sure."

"Government?"

Adeline looked at me. "*Government* what?" I asked.

"Connection to government?" Miikka rephrased, articulating each syllable.

"I don't know. I don't think so."

Miikka kept typing, and Adeline focused on her screen while I watched, not fully understanding what I was witnessing yet rapt at the same time.

"I take control of racks in Dublin. Should give us power we need," Miikka said.

"How many hops?" Adeline asked.

"Four in, four out and rotating. Pure."

I deduced they were assuming control of servers housed in a data center somewhere in Dublin, and that Miikka was bouncing their connection off multiple routes to disguise—or obfuscate—where they were and where they were going. But beyond that, I was at a loss. This was a world and a language I did not understand, yet I knew those who worked in it wielded tremendous power.

And according to Adeline, the Executive knew this kind of power, too.

*   *   *

After a bit of time, with the click and tap of fingers on the keyboards the only sounds in the house, I walked into the parlor. I looked around the room, debating what to do while I waited while also knowing I was of no help to Adeline and Miikka next door.

Oddly, I felt the urge to go for a run, to refresh my mind and loosen the pent-up stress and uncertainty that had coiled itself into my body and thoughts. I might even make sense of the mess we were in, if that was possible.

But looking down at my shoes—a brown pair of leather Oxfords given to me by Adeline back in Nice—the notion of jogging through the streets of Kensington quickly vanished. The picture would be complete if I trotted down the street only wearing my briefs. At least they were mine. Adeline had not supplied me with undergarments, thank God.

Therefore, with nothing but time, I settled on reading the paper from the night before. Markets in Asia were up, an earthquake in Iran killed three hundred, Chelsea beat Arsenal 3–1 . . . but soon enough I found that flipping the pages of a day-old newspaper was no better than staring at a crack in the wall.

I collected up the rest of the paper's sections, refolded them, and placed them in the center of the coffee table. I then grabbed the three empty glasses from the night before and brought them into the kitchen. I washed out the glasses, wiped down the counter, and walked back into the parlor to return the items to the bar cart.

I looked around in search of something else to putter with, hoping the mindless movement would help me think, and I asked myself why the Executive killed my father. It was a question I'd been sparring with since Alfred told me what happened, but it wasn't until now that the question became apparent. If my father had been involved with these people—if my entire family had been involved since the beginning—what had the man done to get killed?

Perhaps he'd been a son of a bitch to them, too, I mused.

His accident was in 1996, over twenty-five years ago. We'd had a few interactions in the months leading up to it—a couple phone calls, a combative dinner, the night we fought. To the best of my recollection, my father had been his usual self. He hadn't been acting stressed or out of sorts at all during that time. Like most memories of my father, he'd been emotionless, cold, unsympathetic to just about everything and keen on maintaining the rigidity of decorum.

Would I have noticed if something was off? Regrettably, probably not.

Going beyond my general distaste and dismissal of the man—my juvenile way of responding to how I perceived he'd treated me growing up—I'd been consumed by my own issues at the time. Olivia had just left me, and I was still adrift after my experiences in Bosnia. Both tragic events: the departure of a genuine companion and lover, a confidante who I suspect knew me better than anyone and someone I cared for with every piece of my soul, and a horrific experience of terror and death and barbarity that I still struggle to believe I witnessed. If my father had revealed any signs worth concern, it's no wonder I didn't see them.

Expelling a heavy breath, I straightened the pillows on the sofa and returned an umbrella to the rack by the door. The room was all picked up and tidy. I looked at my watch and saw only twelve minutes had passed. I doubted Adeline and Miikka had cracked the code in just a short amount of time, so I headed downstairs to the basement.

I'd gone down here the first night to check it out, noticing that it would have been a nice garden flat. There were two rooms sparsely furnished and spacious, with a bookshelf that had been positioned near the fireplace. I thumbed through the volumes and found a few fiction titles I'd never heard of, a collection of Shakespeare's work, a heavy tome on English castles, and a worn hardcover copy of *Winnie-the-Pooh*. I had to admire that. Pooh was a brilliant philosopher on life and friendship, and A. A. Milne's stories and poems had brought me comfort more than once in my life.

But of course, as I pulled out one book only to spot another to inspect, my mind circled back to my father.

Did his death have something in common with the deaths of Gibbons, Waters, and Himmler? They'd died tragically, too, and my father's body had been badly mangled from the accident, just like theirs. Nearly unrecognizable.

But my grandfather hadn't met an unfortunate demise. He died in his sleep at the irritable age of eighty-three. And there wasn't a twenty-year separation between my grandfather's and my father's deaths. But was that even a factor to consider?

Forget the twenty-year thing for now, I told myself. The element of tragic, sudden death was more salient, right? Why did the leading members of the Executive die like that? What was the connection, or association, or point, or whatever?

Perhaps there was nothing. Perhaps the links I thought I saw were, in fact, nothing.

I needed help to figure this out. I knew that. I couldn't do this alone. I needed someone I trusted to sort through this mess, to bounce ideas off. Someone to tell me I wasn't crazy or a total loon.

I reached the bottom of the shelf and removed a worn, leather-bound volume: *Britain and the Origins of the First World War*. Touching the binding and allowing a gentle smile, I recalled this book from university. Professor Goldstein had lent it to me after pulling it from the precarious stacks of papers and books that crowded his office.

I sat down on the sofa and began to read. My eyes dotted over the words, remembering the author's argument from when I'd first read the book at a small wooden table in a corner of the library. In this way and at least for the few seconds when my brain toyed with the ideas set forth on the pages, I enjoyed some brief moments of peace.

CHAPTER 26

NORTH KENSINGTON, LONDON

I heard Miikka's heavy footfalls traverse the floor upstairs, then the front door open and shut. A few seconds later Adeline descended the steps into the basement. Her eyes were bloodshot and her expression looked cloudy as if something had drawn every bit of vitality from her.

"You all right?" I asked.

"Tired," she offered, plopping onto the sofa.

"I can imagine. How'd it go?"

"It all worked out."

"Which means . . . what?"

"I'm not going to lie to you, William. I think trust between us is a good thing."

"That's good to hear."

"It wasn't exactly easy, but Miikka forced his way in. He's good at these types of things."

"You don't say."

"Yes, I do."

"Is he one of yours? One of your brilliant cyber wonders bringing stability to the internet? Or maybe disrupting it?"

Adeline laughed. "No. Nothing like that. Like I said earlier, he's an old friend."

"Right. From uni."

"Yeah. We met during a study abroad in Helsinki. Well, I was abroad, he wasn't. He was a classmate, we had a similar group of friends . . ." Her voice trailed off and she averted her eyes, looking off into an empty corner of the room, unspoken memories coming back to her, I thought.

"Was he someone special, to you?"

"What? Oh, God no. Not him, anyway. It's not important."

"Right. Sorry I asked. Still, must be some friend to get involved in this mess."

"Let's just say he doesn't always stay within the laws of society. This was fun for him. He's what we call a gray hat. He straddles the legality of such things, and doesn't perceive what is right and wrong as the rest of us might."

"I've heard the term."

"Right. Well, we used to have fun together."

"What kind of fun?"

"The computer nerd kind."

"Right. And now, years later, you still have that kind of fun? Things like this?"

"Sometimes."

"But he isn't one of you." I said it as a statement, but hoped for a response.

"No. He's not on the inside. He likes to do his own thing."

"Right. Do you ever think he'd turn on you?"

"What? Why would you ask such a thing?"

I gave her a dumb look. "I thought we couldn't trust anyone."

"Using my words against me. How quaint. No, I don't think he'd turn on me."

"Why's that?"

"A gut feeling. Some things just can't be explained. I'm sure you've had similar experiences."

"Sort of."

Adeline glanced at the bookshelf. "Did you reorganize the books?"

I smiled. "Helps me think."

"Alphabetizing books?"

"Mindless activity, moving and thinking. But running is the best for me."

"You don't say. What did you think about?"

I returned my book to the shelf, not having gotten very far, but enjoying the time with a book in my hand nonetheless.

"I think we should go see what you found out about HG Krautherbank. That's what I was thinking about."

Adeline returned my smile and we went up to the kitchen. I stood behind Adeline's shoulder. On her screen was the website for HG Krautherbank, the internal version, with links for payroll, directories, references, and other areas no firm would ever share with the public.

Adeline clicked on a tab, which displayed a list of names, short bios, and headshots. "Here's the list of operating officials. Recognize any of them?"

"I'm afraid not."

"I thought you had an account manager? The name you gave me to pass to Alfred?"

"Ulrich, but I don't see him."

Adeline clicked on another link, pulling up a personnel roster and scrolling faster than my eyes could keep up. "Wait a minute. Here he is. *Ulrich van Hess* . . . his personnel file is closed . . . deceased?"

"What the hell?" I blurted. I met with Ulrich no more than two months ago in Amsterdam. He was middle-aged but a health nut. I could think of no reason he should be dead unless he suffered an unfortunate accident, or was . . .

"You've been tracking the Executive for a while, yes?" I asked.

"Year and a half, give or take," Adeline replied.

"Do they purge their own?"

Adeline shrugged. "It's possible, but we've never come across any evidence that would lead us to believe as much."

"Except the murder of my father and the seeming twenty-year cycle of tragic deaths in the early days," I countered.

Adeline shrugged again and continued exploring the site. Then she opened a window and clicked on another program.

"What's that?" I asked.

"I'm downloading and imaging as much as I can from their server. We can poke around for a time, but if we stay too long their network managers will see something. And I need to get this to Alfred so he can have the techs in the cellar pull it apart."

I nodded, in no position but to agree.

While the program worked in the background, Adeline switched to another page. "I think this is the account list, all numbered. But there's only eighty or so—not that many. Unusually small. And look at the balances. Over $40 billion."

"Good Lord," I said, whistling.

"I know. Bank of America, Deutsche Bank, USB—they have assets upwards of $500 billion, but they have thousands of clients all over the world, investment arms, funds."

Adeline hovered the mouse pointer over some of the accounts, hoping some identifiable information would come up. Nothing did.

"Do you know which account is yours?"

"There." I pointed. But under the main account—the account that held the funds for my family's trust—was a subaccount that I had never seen before, and the amount took my breath away. The balance said two billion . . . two billion!

"I thought you said your trust was worth a few million?" asked Adeline gently, but somewhat accusingly.

"I had no idea," I said in a hollow voice. "My father, my account manager . . . I've only ever been privy to this." I pointed to the main account. "I have no idea what this subaccount is. I've never heard of it. It's never been on any of my paperwork."

"It looks to be part of your account suite. You're sure?"

"Of course I'm sure. Do you think I would miss a number like that?"

Adeline pursed her lips and continued working her way through the site, eventually reaching the gallery for the board of directors. "Recognize any of these chaps?"

Again, I shook my head.

Adeline clicked on each image, some of which had been taken in the board members' offices.

"Wait a second," I said. "Can you enlarge that?" I pointed at a group picture displayed on the wall of the senior account manager's office. "That. Can you zoom in on that?"

Adeline brought the picture into focus. It was a group photo of nine men in front of a patio garden area—it was a picture I'd seen before. The hairstyles and suits were from the late 1980s, and the gray weather was quintessential of Northern France, near the coast. One face jumped out at me like a three-dimensional image, and a knot formed in my stomach as I uttered, "I don't believe it."

"What?"

"That picture. Him." I pointed at a man in the back. "I know him."

"You do?"

"Yes. He has the same photo, or had the same photo. It was on a shelf by his desk."

"Who is he, William?"

"Rupert Eisengard. He was the head of the history department at Harrow. I used to meet with him once a week, Thursday afternoons, and I'd stare at that picture from time to time. He knew my father, too. He was—is—a friend of mine."

"What else do you know about him?" asked Adeline. The way she asked the question indicated there was something more.

"What do you mean?"

Adeline paused, meeting my eyes.

"What, Adeline? What do you know about Mr. Eisengard."

She pursed her lips and then said, "He wasn't just a teacher, William. He was a talent spotter and access agent for us."

Her words seemed to echo in the room as I tried to understand what she was saying, finally uttering, "Wait . . . what?"

"Until about ten years ago, he provided MI6 with the names of young men and women he thought might make good intelligence officers. It's how we recruit. And his status at the school gave him social connections around the world. He would broker introductions with people of interest. Alfred worked with him."

I was speechless. How could this be? My old teacher and mentor, in a photo alongside board members from my family's bank, and also some kind of *talent-whatever* for British Intelligence! I stepped back to collect myself.

I'd admired Eisengard, one of the few people I'd felt sincerely comfortable around back then when I was young and impressionable and yearning for someone to look up to and trust. The man had even told my father off. I didn't know what the argument was about and neither of them ever discussed the incident with me, but the simple fact that Mr. Eisengard had opposed my father and his domineering ways had endeared him to me.

"When was the last time you spoke with him?" asked Adeline.

Emerging from the fog, I said, "Maybe fifteen years ago. We had lunch."

"And?"

"And nothing. We fell out of touch."

"I've got to tell Alfred." Adeline grabbed the phone from her bag and headed toward her room. She shut the door, leaving me alone with the hum of the radiator.

I sat for a long moment, picturing the face of my old mentor, my friend. A short beard during winter, clean-shaven come spring. Hazel eyes that seemed to change with his moods. He had a refined way about him, and brilliant, utterly brilliant. Just five minutes with him and it was apparent he was thinking on a level most people couldn't fathom. Yet he never flaunted it. He was the epitome of a quiet scholar.

Connected to the Executive? Connected to British Intelligence? Some kind of closet fascist?

It wasn't possible.

I went into the bathroom and locked the door. I splashed water on my face and then stared at my reflection in the mirror. The creases in my skin were more pronounced, and my mouth seemed to have settled into a frown, like it would never recover.

I didn't like what I saw. It reminded me of how I looked all those years ago.

I stripped off my clothes, turned on the shower, and stepped in, letting the ice-cold water hit me in the face and chest. I stood there breathing deeply, the watery needles against my skin. Then I turned the faucet to hot. Steam filled the room and my heart rate slowed, my muscles relaxing. I felt the tension leave my neck and realized I'd been clenching my jaw.

Rupert Eisengard *was* connected to the Executive. There was no other explanation. The relationship with my father, the bank, him—there was no doubt. But this association with MI6 confounded me.

I stifled a laugh. I wasn't hurt by the revelations, even if I should be. I was beyond that. I was more curious than anything. I wanted to know why.

Why was Eisengard a part of the Executive, and why had he taken such an interest in me?

The irony, the ridiculous irony.

I didn't know how long I'd been standing beneath the water, but when I looked up I could scarcely see the mirror through the fog. The steam hung in the air like a spa. I turned off the faucet and hastily dried myself.

The shower had cleared my head, and I knew what we needed to do next.

My skin was still damp as I threw on my clothes, but I didn't care. There was no time. I grabbed my socks and shoes and burst into the hallway.

Where was Adeline?

CHAPTER 27

It took the Kanzler and Faust a little over an hour to fly from Vienna to Dusseldorf and then make the drive to the estate in Essen. Although late, the Kanzler was still working, whispering to himself as he sorted through papers and twirled his fountain pen.

Faust, not yet dismissed from his duties, stood at the window looking into the darkness of North-Rhine Westphalia, what was formerly Prussia. His hands were behind his back, a carryover from his days in the German military. Some habits lasted forever.

Time in the military was funny that way. It changed everything and left a mark no one could shake, no matter how hard one might try. Faust, however, embraced what he'd become on the parade grounds of Berlin and in the mountains of Afghanistan. He was a warrior.

At a young age, his father had instilled in him the ethos of Prussian militarism—austerity, courage, discipline, loyalty, order, honor. There were others, but if one adhered to these few, everything else would fall into place. And these virtues had saved his life and the lives of his men on the battlefield.

He'd fought in Kunduz Province in northern Afghanistan. Among the Afghan and international troops, he'd earned the reputation of a German wolf. When he spoke, people listened. When he was on patrol, everyone knew he would hunt down the enemy and kill them. War had been natural for him, but he doubted he'd ever experience something like that again.

It was starting to rain, droplets splashing on the windowpane. This was his life now, his choice, whether he liked it or not.

His phone vibrated in his pocket. It was one of his team leaders. "Ja?"

The man on the other end spoke quickly and succinctly, then hung up.

Putting his phone away, he announced, "Professor Dresden and Miss Parker have made the connection to the bank."

The Kanzler, standing over his desk, looked up expectantly.

"They hacked the firm's site earlier this evening. My men believe they had help, but not from British Intelligence."

The Kanzler sighed. "All according to plan. These matters are so much easier to handle when people act as expected. Is there anything else? You look like you have something on your mind."

"Nothing, Herr Kanzler. How would you like to proceed?"

"Have Sofia come see me. This can't wait."

"Yes, Herr Kanzler," said Faust as he went to fetch her.

Half an hour later Sofia entered the library. She wore a robe and had the look of someone roused from sleep.

"Sofia, thank you for coming. I know it's late."

"I'm here to serve."

The Kanzler motioned at the chair in front of him, but he remained standing. "It appears the professor has realized the bank is not as he may have thought."

"I'm surprised it took him so long."

"Now is the moment to take care of this, but I don't want a repeat of last time."

"I understand."

"Good. I believe Faust has the details on his location, as well as some assets that can assist you. I trust you can handle things from here?"

"Yes, Father," said Sofia.

CHAPTER 28

I found Adeline in the kitchen staring out the window with her arms crossed.

"What did Alfred say?" I asked.

She flashed me a trivial look. "I didn't reach him. I left another message."

"For him to call back?"

"Yeah. And to meet tomorrow."

"We can't," I said.

"Why not?"

"We need to go to France. Tonight. We have to find Eisengard."

"France? What are you talking about?"

"Eisengard lives near Tours. He's an expat, a true Francophile."

"Wait. Slow . . ." Adeline's words trailed off. Her gaze had shifted from me to something across the room, and her expression had changed from mild irritation to alarm. She was staring at her laptop, the screen flashing and the hard drive sounding like it was spinning out of control.

"I thought you turned this off?" I asked, the hair on the back of my neck rising.

"I did," she said softly. Then her eyes went wide. "We need to go, now!"

I instinctively switched off the kitchen light and stepped back against the wall. I peered outside as best I could, through the drapery into the darkness outside. After three days of being on the run, I was now conditioned—whatever was happening wasn't good. There was no time to think or ask questions, only to react.

Adeline rushed to her room and seconds later emerged with the black duffel. "Come on."

I snatched my jacket from the back of the chair and reached for the laptop.

"Leave it," she said.

I didn't argue. I didn't know much, but I assumed the Executive was attacking Adeline's computer to see what we'd done. A team was probably closing in on the safe house at this very moment, if they weren't already in position.

A shadow passed by the front window. It was low, moving methodically, like someone sneaking underneath the sill to get to the front door. The hair on my arms stood on end, and I felt my pulse quicken. I remained frozen like a statue in a dark museum, holding my breath.

"The back," whispered Adeline.

I nodded and then we both hurried to the patio door. Adeline peeked through the curtain while I crouched against the wall and kept my eyes on the front door, expecting a figure to come bursting through at any moment.

"I don't see anything," she whispered, looking outside. "We're going to the alley."

"Right," I said, taking a sharp breath and getting ready.

Adeline cracked open the door and listened. Not a sound except the rustling of the leaves in the wind. She poked her head out so she could see down the sides of the house, then bolted into the backyard.

I felt a burst of adrenaline course through my body and I followed.

The crash of the door closing behind me cut the night's silence.

CHAPTER 29

NORTH KENSINGTON, LONDON

I ignored the slam of the door and dashed across the patio. I expected to hear gunfire, but no shots came. I kept going. Adeline was just a few feet ahead.

We reached the alley—also empty—and raced toward the street. There was still no sign of anyone.

Adeline held out her arm and stopped.

"What's going on? Where are they?" I asked between breaths.

"I don't know, but we're not waiting around to find out. The only reason that computer would have been hammering like that is if we're blown."

"But the shadow? They should be on top of us."

Adeline scrunched her face, confused. "I know."

Reaching the sidewalk, we saw that the entire street was empty and there wasn't a light on in any of the houses that lined the road. The street lamps cast shadows. That was it. We headed toward the intersection of Wallingford Avenue and Kelfield Gardens. There was no sign of anyone there either.

"I don't understand," said Adeline.

I put my hand on her back to encourage her to keep moving, an extreme desire to get as much distance between us and the safe house as possible. I wanted to get away, far away. Space between us and them was all I wanted.

But then I saw a glint of light up ahead. It was near a treetop. There'd been a reflection for just a second, then it went black, like a hole in the sky—then it moved. It glided to the other side of the street and tucked itself near another tree in front of a row house.

"Do you see that?" I asked bewildered.

"See what?" Adeline scanned the area.

"Oh my God," I breathed.

"Fuck," spat Adeline. "It's a drone. Come on!"

Adeline took my hand and pulled me across the street. We bolted into another alley, hurtling the debris in our path until we tucked into a dark corner.

"What was that?" I asked, panting.

"It was a drone, a little copter or something, hovering in front of us."

"Jesus. A drone? A fucking drone?"

"We need to get off the street."

The first thought that came to me was something big and public, like a market. A place where there would be so many people, a congested crowd, that we could disappear in the mass. But it was the middle of the night. Nothing would be open.

We needed to get somewhere where aircraft couldn't go.

"The Tube!" Adeline exclaimed as if reading my mind.

"Yes!" If we could get to a station, we could go underground. We could escape across the city. Drones couldn't go underground . . . at least I didn't think they could.

"Come on." Adeline took off down the alley.

I took one last look at the drone. It was floating like a wasp. It drifted from around the corner and positioned itself above the center of the alley. It hovered there, twenty feet off the ground. I swore and rushed after Adeline.

As we were about to emerge onto Bassett Road, another quadcopter swooped out from behind a house and hung right in front of us, its rotors whirring. Adeline was in front of me but was caught flat-footed and stumbled backward. I grabbed her arm and drew her to the side of the alley. We ran between two houses and burst out onto Oxford Gardens.

"Where's the station?" I asked.

"Ladbroke Grove, on the other side of Westway."

I could hear the traffic two streets over.

"Come on," she said.

We crossed Cambridge Gardens and then Malton Road. The freeway was above us. We tucked ourselves near one of the concrete supports. We needed to get our bearings and figure out which way toward the station.

And as we sat there, I again tried to make sense of what was happening. The last two run-ins with the Executive had been violent—they'd tried to kill us.

Why not now? Why were they just sending toy helicopters after us? Where were the men with guns? Where was the blacked-out van they would toss us into? Where was the killer with a pistol waiting around the corner ready to put two bullets in each of our chests and then go smoke a fag?

It was as if they no longer wanted us dead. What changed?

"We can't stay here," Adeline said. "They knew we came this direction."

"I know. Where's the station?" I knew London, but not this part.

"There." She pointed a few blocks away. A brick structure enclosed the track that ran parallel to the highway.

"Right," I said, hearing the rumble of a train approaching. "Come on."

I ran toward the station but stayed under the highway. This time I didn't expect gunfire; our pursuers weren't shooting for a reason.

We reached the red-brick entrance to Ladbroke Station and burst inside. A handful of people were milling about. Without breaking stride, Adeline and I climbed over the turnstiles. An elderly woman with a red hat gasped and a young couple with too many piercings hooted.

We took the stairs two at a time, shouldering our way past bewildered passengers. When we reached the platform, the train had already stopped, with a few stragglers stepping into the carriages.

We dashed aboard and the doors shut behind us.

CHAPTER 30

The Hammersmith & City line train pulled into Paddington Station, a major interchange consisting of two separate underground platforms connected by the mainline station on the surface. Exiting the train, we joined the crowd of people hustling through the underground labyrinth. Although my pulse was pounding and my eyes looked nervously into the crowd and beyond, we held hands—putting on the look of two lovers out for an evening—and turned down a tunnel with an exit sign up ahead.

But no sooner had we brushed past a middle-aged wanderer who'd had too much to drink than Adeline's body tensed. A man was leaning against the wall. He wore a black coat and watch cap. I recognized him as one of the men from the club . . . it was *Leather Jacket*.

Luckily, the man's attention was focused in the other direction. He hadn't seen us—at least I don't think he had.

We retreated toward one of the other exit tunnels. With each step, we picked up our pace, and I fought the urge to run. But before we turned the corner, I chanced a look behind. Leather Jacket was nowhere in sight.

"He's gone," I said.

"What?" asked Adeline, focused on the jam of people up ahead.

"Leather Jacket is gone."

"Who?"

"The guy," I repeated.

"Keep walking. And don't turn around again. Don't show your face."

We hastened up the stairs into the cool night air, finding the street nearly empty. Adeline looked around to get her bearings, but I couldn't help myself and took one last look down the tunnel.

My chest immediately locked up. The man from the club was coming up after us, talking on his cell, and his eyes were deadlocked on me.

"He's coming!"

Adeline spun around, drawing her pistol in a smooth, instantaneous motion as if it were an extension of her hand.

Leather Jacket's eyes went wide and he fumbled for his own gun.

Adeline fired four times, each bullet drilling into the man's torso. He tumbled down the stairs in a heap.

"Holy shit!" I blurted.

Men and women on the stairs screamed. Some floundered down the steps while others cowered against the walls.

"Come on." Adeline stuffed the gun back in her holster, grabbed me, and we took off down the street. No one up top had heard the shots. The busy street had drowned out the crack of gunfire.

I should have been in shock at witnessing a man gunned down, but I wasn't. Escape was all that mattered. Survival.

We ducked down an alley, but as we rounded another corner down a narrow passageway between two buildings, we barreled into a man coming in the opposite direction.

The poor man fell to the ground with us tripping over him.

Regaining my balance, I kept moving, muttering an apology but too distracted to notice if the man was all right.

Then Adeline cried out.

I turned to see her hopping on one foot, trying to kick her other leg free. The man we'd bumped into was on the ground, but he'd grabbed Adeline's ankle and was reaching for something in his belt.

What little light there was glinted off something metal—he had a gun.

My state of disbelief at everything that had just happened—drones, trains, gunshots—vanished. A fury surged within me. I kicked at the man's arms and broke Adeline free from the man's grasp.

The assailant retracted, shielding his head and body from my attack. He rolled over and got to his feet like a wrestler. He was at least six feet tall, two hundred pounds, with close-cropped hair. He wore jeans and a black pullover like a thug. His face was fierce, and he zeroed in on me.

The man lunged, catching me in the gut with his shoulder and smashing me into the wall. I tensed my abdomen but the impact made my insides shudder. The man reared back to strike again, but I clumsily spun out of his grasp.

I was no fighter by any means, but a few seasons on the rugby pitch was something. I moved back in, kicking and swinging wildly, aiming for the guy's knees and neck or any part of him within reach. I kept pressing my attack, putting the man on his heels and causing him to stumble.

But as I closed the distance, the man drove his fist upward into my ribs with a precise blow, knocking the wind out of me.

Adeline rushed in from the side. She'd found a pipe in an over-turned trash can and was swinging it like a club. But the man saw it coming. He turned and Adeline's strike glanced off his arm.

She went at him again but overextended and missed, yet her swings drove the man farther back.

But now with additional space, the man tried to draw his gun again.

I lunged forward and tackled him, deflecting his arm, knocking the pistol to the side.

The gun went off with a crack.

My ears rang and the shot's lingering propellant burned my nostrils. I grabbed for the man's wrist with both hands and used my body to drive him into the wall. I felt the air expel out of his lungs. The gun fell to the ground, but the man spun free again and delivered another blow to my side.

I buckled over, pain shooting through my torso. Through clenched eyes, I saw the man pick up a brick and hurl it at Adeline. It glanced off her shoulder but grazed the side of her head, stunning her.

Now against the wall, the assailant pulled up his pant leg and revealed an ankle holster with a second weapon—a compact revolver.

The killer's eyes were riveted on Adeline, and he raised the gun toward her chest.

I snatched up the other gun—the one our attacker had dropped—and wrapped my fingers around the pistol grip and aimed. I didn't think. I pressed the trigger in rapid succession, again and again.

I watched at least one bullet slam into the man's chest.

He went down.

CHAPTER 31

The Kanzler sat at his desk. It was approaching seven in the morning, and before him was a plate of fried potatoes, eggs, onions, peppers, and ham. Known as Bauernfrühstück, it was a farmer's breakfast—rich, decadent, hearty. In recent years he'd grown accustomed to such indulgences, and he preferred to fortify himself in the morning when a demanding day lay ahead.

This morning, however, he felt the weight of history's judgment on his shoulders and his food tasted like ash.

Next to his meal was an old, leather-bound journal. His family had taken great pains to care for it over the years, to protect the cover and pages within. It was irreplaceable, containing secrets known more to the dead than the living. The journal had been his responsibility since his father passed, and he had embraced the task.

The journal was a history, a record of what his family was and what it must be. It embodied the very essence of the Dresden line, like a book of souls.

The first entry was from April 12, 1871, the night the Covenants were drafted and the Executive was formed. It was an important entry in that it articulated the guiding purpose of the Executive, which his forefathers had adhered to for over a century. They'd been leaders in the organization—as he was now—and it was their duty to further the goals of the movement. It was an inspiring passage, one that the Kanzler periodically read to find inspiration.

Though, at this moment he required something different. He needed encouragement, he needed validation, he needed clarity. In contrast to the statements he made to the board the previous evening, he doubted that his decision to engage the Russians—to engage *that man* specifically—was wise.

In fact, he was afraid, deathly so, and the barest hint that he'd betrayed the cause had seeped into his mind. It roiled in him like an ember searing the depths of his throat and stomach.

No, he told himself. It couldn't be. He never could have betrayed his calling—his divine purpose. Betrayal required intent to harm— that's not what he'd done—he'd made a calculated decision. He'd taken a risk. That was his prerogative, and it was his responsibility as the Kanzler.

Still, the man with the gray beard—*the Curator*, as he was called— had displayed desires that weren't in accordance with the Executive's wishes.

Should he be surprised?

No. He shouldn't.

But what to do now? Was it possible to remove him cleanly, to break contact before it was too late?

Yes, it was. He must. There was no other choice but to remove this man, this creature—this *Curator*—because what if the Curator was able to divert—or even transform—the great cause that he had brought the Executive toward? What would happen then? Who would win and who would lose?

No! It could not be disrupted. He had to act now, and he had to ensure that even if he himself was lost, right would be done.

The Kanlzer removed a sheet of paper from his drawer and began to write, etching the words into the page's fibers as if they were divine commandments.

*   *   *

A knock came at the door to the Kanzler's study. Faust, who was standing by the breakfast cart sipping a cup of coffee, looked at his watch. He was not surprised by the visitor; he'd expected her much earlier.

"Come," said the Kanzler after folding the papers and tucking them inside an envelope, which he then handed to Faust dismissively.

Sofia entered the library wearing a black skirt suit and carrying a Louis Vuitton purse.

"Good morning, my dear. Do you have news?" asked the Kanzler, intending to sound more sincere than he was.

"I do," she replied, sitting across from her father. "They escaped, and they killed Fritz."

The Kanzler let the fork slip from his fingers with a clatter. "What?"

"They escaped. They eluded the toys you directed the team to use. They jumped on the Tube, reaching Paddington. Our teams were too thin, too dispersed. Then they ran into Fritz—shot him twice."

"How do you know this?"

"I just talked to the team leader, Peter. His men are upset at the restrictions you placed on them."

"Are you suggesting this is my fault?"

"You took control and required certain—"

"Stop right there," he said, his voice rising. "You are my blood. I've groomed you, taught you, given you all the opportunities in the world, but you don't know everything. How dare you come in here and lecture me."

Sofia remained silent.

The Kanzler leaned back in his chair, regarding his daughter with a critical eye, control returning. "This is unfortunate news, their escape, and it will be dealt with, but do you know what is most concerning to me? You have yet to develop the patience that the leadership of the Executive needs."

Faust set down his cup of coffee and watched the argument between father and daughter. The Kanzler had prepared Sofia since birth to assume the leadership of the Executive. He'd cultivated in her the art of manipulation, executive management, strategic thinking, and fanatic loyalty to the cause, but well-laid plans never came to fruition as one hoped. Her absence from the meeting the previous day had been intentional.

Since Faust had joined the Executive, he'd observed the inner politics of the senior members. Sofia had been designated as next-in-line to assume control of the Executive's board. But a disturbing transformation had occurred in her, something sinister.

Ever since Professor Dresden came to the Kanzler's attention, a darkness seemed to develop within Sofia. There was a ruthlessness to everything, and the Kanzler had noticed it, too.

Was it any surprise? Faust had heard the story—how she'd mutilated one of her trainers but never said a word about it. If someone could do that, what else were they capable of?

The previous night's meeting, and the Kanzler's habit of reading his journal in times of deep contemplation, made him wonder. And as the letter in his pocket was proof, the Kanzler feared something . . .

"Remember, Father, I did as you instructed," countered Sofia.

"Not well enough!" The Kanzler slammed his hand on the desk. "He should have been removed from the equation months ago, quietly, as I instructed. Not with a crude bomb. And Miss Adeline Parker . . . This should not be so difficult."

"Apparently it is."

The Kanzler gritted his teeth. "Your insinuations are starting to irritate me. Don't think that just because you're my daughter you can command me."

"Or what? Will you send me to my room? Or perhaps send me away for another bit of *instruction*? I remember one such lesson being highly effective."

The Kanzler stood. "We'll deal with this later. I suggest you have something to eat. I don't think you're in a right state of mind."

Sofia remained seated.

"Faust," the Kanzler said. "Please escort my wayward daughter to the kitchen. I have no desire to keep her in my presence."

But Faust didn't budge.

The Kanzler shot a glance at his chief of security. "Faust! Get up and do your job."

Again, Faust stayed where he was.

The Kanzler looked back at Sofia; his eyes went wide. She'd pulled a revolver from her purse and was pointing it at him.

"What are you—"

Sofia fired. The noise shattered the quiet of the spacious library and the bullet struck the Kanzler in the heart, knocking him backward to the floor. An acrid smell filled the air, and drops of blood dotted the desk and the gluttonous plate of food.

Faust remained where he was, but reached for his cup of coffee and took another sip.

The seconds passed, but eventually, Sofia stepped around the desk and looked into the lifeless eyes of her father. They stared at nothing, his mouth agape, frozen in shock. The seventh Kanzler of the Strasbourg Executive—her father—was dead.

*　*　*

Maria sat at her vanity in her bourgeois flat in the Saint Germain-des-Prés neighborhood of Paris. She'd risen with the sun, and was fastening a string of pearls around her neck. The sounds of chanson française came from the speakers embedded in the ceiling, giving the sensation that the music was everywhere no matter where you stood in the flat. And on the edge of the vanity rested a half-drunk glass of water with lemon.

Maria had been a board member of the Executive since her twenty-eighth birthday. Her father had died of a stroke, and she'd assumed the mantle. Although she had grieved her papa's loss, taking his place on the Executive's board had been her aspiration since she'd been made aware of the group's existence.

The speech she gave to the board yesterday had thus far been the high point of her work. The Kanzler had picked her to do it, above everyone else, and she believed the Executive's work was her calling.

Maria heard the door open. "Is that you, François?"

No one replied so she looked over her shoulder to see who it was. Only her husband and her personal assistant had a key to the flat. "Eliz—"

A bullet struck Maria's forehead three-quarters of an inch above her eyes.

*　*　*

At a villa on the Italian Riviera outside Genoa, a retired Dutch general named Sten Jansen sat eating a breakfast of cheese and cured meats. He'd moved here after serving forty years in the Royal Netherlands Army, his shining command with the 11th Airmobile Brigade.

His tour was before the unit fell under the Division Schnelle Kräfte, the German Rapid Forces Division. It was a move that had thoroughly pissed him off. He had nothing against his German brethren; he just didn't like taking orders from the swine. He was Dutch.

He was also a devout member of the Executive, as his forefathers had been since the group's founding. He considered himself more devoted to the Executive than he did to Holland. It was a higher calling—as most members believed—and he imagined a momentous time was upon them.

After returning from the meeting in Vienna the night before, he was preparing for a busy day. The Kanzler had asked him to invigorate his network of military commanders spread throughout the armed forces of Europe.

There were thirty-four commanders in all—men secretly dedicated to the vocation of protecting the purity of Europe at all costs. They ranged from tactical commanders of maneuver forces, to staff officers working in the senior echelons of NATO, to special operations soldiers, to commanding generals and admirals. They were good men: loyal, decisive, sharp. He was pleased to be on the verge of activating them.

The sound of the waves crashing against the shore made him smile. Coupled with the warmth of the Mediterranean climate, it was the most peaceful sensation a man could experience. Soon, Europe would be right again.

Another heavy wave rushed against the rocks. The general did not hear the man walk up behind him, or the sound of the gunshot that blew out half of his skull.

* * *

Sofia stood on her balcony in Essen. Over the past hour, she'd received six text messages, all confirming the death of senior members of the Executive's leadership. She expected one more, which came at seven minutes past eight.

Faust, who sat at a wrought iron table behind her, broke the silence. "It's done. And I've confirmed your videoconference for this afternoon."

Sofia didn't say anything but continued to stare at the forest surrounding the estate. The sun was having a look over the trees, rays of light penetrating the darkness. She was about to bring the Executive back to its original, intended purpose. It had been quiet for too long.

CHAPTER 32

Adeline and I reached the second floor of a tired apartment building not far from Gunwharf Terminal, a ferry and cargo shipping port southwest of London in Portsmouth. The only light came from a flickering fluorescent bulb at the end of the hallway, and on the way up the stairs, we'd passed a man asleep on the landing with an empty bottle beside him. In a flat farther back, the sound of a headboard banging against the wall came from within. It conjured an image that I was actively trying to expel from my mind, and I saw Adeline's mouth curl in disgust, too.

We'd taken a series of trains and taxis to get here from London— looking over our shoulders the entire way—and the sun would be up within the hour. There was an unspoken understanding between us that we needed to get to France—to find Eisengard, a man who had been a friend and mentor once—as soon as possible. With the safe house blown, there was no telling what else had been compromised, or who.

And I'd just killed a man . . . shot him in an alley. He'd only been a few feet from me, so close I'd seen the color of his eyes—blue. Of the four or five bullets I fired—I lost count in the madness—one hit him in the chest and another in the upper thigh. There'd been lots of blood. His body had shuddered on the ground for a second or two, then gone stiff. His back had arched at the end.

I could still see everything, like frames to an old, grainy movie.

As we ventured farther down the hall, I saw Adeline steal a glance at me. I suppose at some point she was going to ask how I was doing. But what could I say? And would it matter? It's not like we could stop and dwell on things, have a nice little hug session. What I'd done bothered me—I could feel something inside me was off—but I was also numb because we had no choice but to keep going.

I wondered how she'd felt the first time she killed someone. Contrary to what the movies portray, not all spies are killers. Yet I'd seen her shoot that man in the Tube's stairwell, smooth and clean as all can be. I assumed it wasn't her first time taking a shot like that. Though she hadn't told me she had, I just had this feeling.

But when Adeline stole another glance my way and stopped in front of an apartment door that looked like all the rest, all she said was, "Let me do the talking."

I didn't respond, but I met her eyes and it must have communicated enough.

Adeline then knocked.

Seconds passed.

She pounded on the door again, looking left and looking right until finally the sound of someone's footsteps came from within.

The door popped open, and a bearded man in a white tank top and a grease-smeared pair of trousers stared out at us. He held a wooden bat in one hand while his other arm remained awkwardly hidden behind the door.

"Bloody hell," he said. "What the fuck are you doin' here?"

The man's accent was coarse and thick, and he smelled of beer and cigarettes.

"Let us in," said Adeline.

The man grimaced and stepped aside and swung his arm for us to enter. He checked up and down the hall and closed the door behind us before locking both bolts and securing the chain. He set the bat down against the plaster-cracked wall but in his other hand, he held a knife, which he kept by his side. His hands and forearms were meaty like someone used to manual labor or inclined to brawling.

The flat was small, a single living space with a water closet. There was a jumble of clothes, boxes, bottles, and trash strewn about, and the smell of oil and body odor lingered in the air. It was the kind of place that some folks tried their best not to wake up in, but when they did, they wondered how long they'd been blacked out.

The only item of value was the television, with a ratty football club scarf draped on the chair in front of it.

"Thought we were never s'posed to meet like this," said the man.

"We're not," replied Adeline. "But there wasn't any time for the normal procedure."

"Right—*procedure*—that's what ya call it. So what gives? Better not a'dragged any trouble my way."

"We need to cross the Channel."

The man tilted his head. "I gathered that. When?"

"Tonight."

"Where?"

"French coast, as close to Caen as possible."

"Right, sure. Let me rouse the steward and check to make sure the fresh oysters and prawns are aboard. Care for a cabin with a view of the sea, do ya?"

"We're not playing around, Tanner."

"Neither am I, love. My job is to get who you say across the Channel, but I need at least a week's notice. That's the arrangement."

"Terribly sorry, but this is part of the deal and what I pay you for."

Tanner grimaced. "Right, I get it. I wouldn't turn you away, a'course," now allowing a small grin, his teeth yellow and crooked. "But ya know, ever since this whole Brexit mess, porting here and there hasn't been all that easy. More scrutiny, more money. Bit of animosity, I guess, leaving the club as we did. That's why I need a week to set it up all clean like."

"Yeah, all of England lost its bloomin' mind, but fuck off. We need to go tonight. How much?" asked Adeline.

"You fuck off. It'll cost triple. New hands to grease, and the risk to me and ship. Cash. Now."

Adeline didn't flinch. She pulled out a stack of British pounds from her black duffel, but Tanner held up his hand.

"Euros, love. Pounds ain't too popular where we're going."

This time Adeline hesitated, then pulled out a wad of euros. She offered them to Tanner, who ran his thumb over the edge. "Let me get dressed."

*   *   *

Ten minutes later, Tanner was driving a cargo van toward the port. Adeline and I were in the back sitting on crates facing each other, trying not to topple over every time he made a turn.

When we'd gotten into the van, Adeline had whispered to me that Tanner was the first mate on a small freighter that routinely floated across the Channel, primarily transporting regional goods. The ship's crew had as many Frenchmen as it did British, along with a handful of Eastern Europeans and North Africans and one Lebanese man. Unlike the captain, Tanner didn't live on the ship. He maintained a flat for the other aspect of his job; he was a broker for things like this—smuggling people and things to ports that didn't ask too many questions and who preferred hard currency to a customs form.

Tanner was a support asset, as she'd described to me. Rather than collect information or perform any number of clandestine acts on behalf of British Intelligence, he provided a service. Adeline had recruited him a few years ago, and yet, she never thought she'd be the one he'd be smuggling out of England.

I felt our van make a turn and Tanner broke the silence. "We're coming up on the gate. Shouldn't be a problem, just don't bloody say anything."

I sank further into the corner of the van. Adeline did the same, keeping her eyes riveted on the front cab. Just as we'd discussed, we'd hide in the back and Tanner would drive through the gate of the dockyard in the same van he did every time he drove to the docks. Port security never checked Tanner's stuff; he'd been a mariner for decades and the quid he paid every month—which Adeline provided—ensured things ran smoothly.

Once through the gate, we'd board Tanner's ship and remain stowed below during the crossing. At the French port, we'd go through a similar routine. Tanner would borrow the vehicle he always did, dropping Adeline and me a short distance away. We'd be on our own after that.

When the van finally slowed, a spotlight reflected through the windshield. Tanner rolled down his window. "Hey, guv. Haven't seen you before. Mind opening up?"

There was a pause, then a gruff voice outside the driver's window said, "Gonna need ya to open the back."

"What the hell are you talking about, mate?" asked Tanner. "Where's Rashid? It's his shift tonight."

A pit formed in my stomach.

"He's busy," said the guard.

"Look, mate, am in a hurry—"

"Open the fucking van!"

I held my breath and saw Adeline shift her weight. Her hand moved toward the pistol tucked in her jeans, yet I couldn't believe she'd shoot what was probably just a poorly paid gate guard with an ex-wife, two kids, and a sparsely furnished flat.

A hollow pounding echoed inside the van as the guard smacked his hand on the side panel. "I'm not going to say it again. Unlock the fucking doors!" he yelled.

"What the hell ya talkin' about?" asked Tanner. "I come through here every day. Never have a problem. I'm late, guv."

The guard hit the van again, and I pictured him with a radio to his mouth, about to call his supervisor and then the real police.

"Hey!" Another voice yelled, this one sounding farther away. "Chip! Chip! What the hell ya' doin? That's Tanner, the bloke I been tellin' ya about. Tanner, everything all right?"

"Hey, Rashid. Who is this guy?"

"He's new," said Rashid. "Doesn't know the faces yet. Chip, go back inside. I got this."

I didn't hear the guard named Chip respond, but when I looked at Adeline, I saw the relief in her eyes that I also felt. She still kept herself tucked in the shadows, but I was relieved to see her hand slide away from her pistol.

"Tanner, go on through. I'll get things straightened out here."

"Thanks, Rashid. Thought there was a problem."

"Nah. Kids. Don't know the traditions we have."

Tanner chuckled, put the van in first gear, and rolled through the gate. He turned left and picked up speed. Over his shoulder, he said, "That'll make your balls sweat. Crikey. Thought I was gonna have to run that prick over."

I managed a small smile at Adeline, but the smile she offered back seemed forced, her eyes unblinking.

Boarding the ship went quickly. Tanner parked the van, opened the back doors, and Adeline and I walked up the rickety gangplank. A handful of the crew scurried around, but none of them gave their unnamed passengers a second look. Tanner led us below decks and brought us to a small room barely ten feet by ten feet.

"You've got a bunk, chair, water." He popped open the cabinet, exposing a half-drunk bottle. "Some whiskey, too. We'll shove off within the hour. I'll let you know when we're close to the French coast. Welcome aboard." Tanner shut the door with a clang. It was that quick.

The two of us stood in the tiny room, taking in our accommodations and isolated once again. The walls were painted white but roughly chipped and scratched, revealing the gray hull underneath. There was a metallic smell, too, coupled with the salt of the sea that coated everything. My only maritime experience had been a few sails off the Cape in New England decades ago, but those were of quite a gentler sort. White shorts, bright sweaters, and clambakes on the beach defined those trips. In contrast, there was a starkness to this kind of foray into the sea.

Adeline took a seat on the cot and leaned forward, resting her forearms on her thighs. She stared at the floor, a pensive look on her face.

"Are you all right?" I asked.

Adeline regarded me for a moment, started to say something, and then seemed to change her mind. I sat down on the cot next to her and took a deep breath.

"I think I should be asking if you're all right," Adeline finally said. "You killed a man."

I closed my eyes and let out a slow breath through my nose. "And so did you."

Adeline wrinkled her brow. "But this is my profession. Lies, betrayal, hurting people. It's not easy for me, but I also signed up for this life and have been taught to handle these things."

"What are you trying to say, Adeline?"

"You took a life. That's no small matter."

"I know, but I'll be okay. I have to, right?"

"That's precisely why I'm asking. You're not a sociopath, William. You feel. You know the difference between right and wrong. You know as humans we are *not* designed to kill each other. We do, it happens, but it's not natural. Taking a life is something you will never forget, but you had to do it. So, if you want to talk, I'm here."

Her comments were not unexpected, and I'd probably set the stage for her to ask, yet I stared at the wall, not wanting to engage her further. Talking is what people offer when someone they know experiences a significant event and there is a subsequent pregnant tension in the air. I suppose since childhood we've been nurtured to believe that talking through our struggles is a helpful endeavor. I'm sure some psychology textbook says it's a step forward in the healing process.

Yet I was hesitant to reveal myself to this woman again—a woman I did not trust, *could not trust*—the distress I felt would only be stronger. I was not afraid of pain or hurt or sadness, but only a fool willingly seeks such things. It'd be like cutting the flesh near your wrists for a slow drain that would hurt and exhaust you, but would not be fatal. A simple cloth could stop the flow, yet the scar will always be there as a reminder.

I did not want that, and although at the moment I might be fooling myself, I told myself, *I am okay.*

"I don't need to talk about it," I finally said. "What's done is done, and I'd just prefer to move on."

"I admire your fortitude, William. Good English stock. Yet—"

"Adeline, please. Let it go."

"I am, but I just want you to know that it's okay."

"Okay? Okay?" I shook my head. "Would you like to know why I don't want to talk about this?"

Adeline hitched her chin and nodded.

"You asked me back at the safe house about what happened in Srebrenica."

"Yes, I did."

"Right. Like you just said, there are some things we will never forget. What I witnessed those few days when the Serbs came in and massacred 8,000 men, women, and children, I will never forget. In the orphanages, I'd seen some pretty rough stuff, horrible and tragic. It still breaks my heart to think about those children, whose parents were either dead or had just abandoned them, and the sadness in their eyes. The looks on their tiny faces *touched* you physically and caused actual pain in your heart.

"But in Srebrenica, that was something different. You say we as human beings are not meant to kill other people," I said, taking a breath, "yet, I saw hundreds of men gleefully and grotesquely murder thousands. Sometimes it was with guns, maybe grenades, whatever the hell kinds of explosives; other times it was knives or clubs, even the heels of their boots. Fire, too—they burned those people trapped inside buildings. It was like an evil, barbaric game, and they enjoyed it.

"I hid with a family in the woods. A mother, a father, their four children . . . We cowered together. I don't know if I was protecting them or if they were protecting me, but we hid and we watched, and we listened. We waited, terrified that they would find us. Yet I also know I, the father, and the mother—we would have fought and killed anyone who came near us. I still remember the look in the mother's eyes as she held a kitchen knife. She held it for hours, staring through the trees as her friends and neighbors were murdered.

"There are some people in this world who are indeed evil, and although as a member of the human race I value all life, there are times and there are individuals I have no empathy or remorse for. Maybe it's because I subconsciously have relegated them to something lesser than a person, viewing them as an animal or perhaps merely an animated object—a thing. But that's how I viewed those . . ." I searched for the word. "Those murderers that day.

"And now, to some extent, that is how I view the people that are chasing us—the Executive. They are evil, and they are willing to kill innocent women and children and friends and family—and I don't care," I said firmly. "I don't care. For the moment I am okay with what I just did—killing that fucker who was trying to kill us and about to shoot you. Maybe I won't be okay as time goes on, but with what I saw in Bosnia and how that experience haunted me for years until I accepted it, and now with everything we are going through and what we're up against, I'll be fine. I'll compartmentalize and push whatever trauma I am wrestling with down, deep down, and we will keep going. And then, maybe, if I ever get back to my books, my archives, my writing, and my own fucking little perfect world, I'll keep ignoring it all."

I took another long and deep breath. "So, at this moment, I'd like to rest. I feel like, at least for the next few hours, this is the most secure we'll be, and I'd like to sleep. Whether your friend Tanner will divert us to Tripoli and sell us into slavery is another matter. But I need to sleep. I am exhausted and I just want to sleep."

"Okay, William," Adeline almost whispered, her eyes resting on me. "Sleep. We both need sleep."

CHAPTER 33

NORMANDY COAST, FRANCE

I woke with a start. I'd been in a deep, coma-like sleep, heavy and dark. I didn't dream—at least I didn't think I did. It'd just been black.

Adeline was beside me, also just waking up, looking as haggard as I felt.

"Good morning," I said, rubbing my eyes and stretching the tight coil that was my spine.

A shudder reverberated through the ship's hull and I stood to look out the porthole, seeing the coast and the early morning light. "I think we're here."

Adeline stood and stretched and came up beside me to look herself. "Yep, that'd be a good conclusion." Licking her lips and the inside of her mouth, probably feeling the same dryness that I felt. She asked, "Did you sleep okay?"

I nodded. "Well enough. You?"

"I need a shower."

I chuckled. "I'll keep my comments to myself, but so do I."

Someone banged on the hatch, causing us both to start. "All right, my little stowaways," yelled Tanner. "Make yourselves decent. Pulling into port."

We docked in the port city of Ouistreham on the Normandy coast. The sun was up, with seagulls circling above and squawking relentlessly. Thirty minutes later, Tanner dropped us on the edge of the city.

We took possession of a late eighties–model Peugeot from a local laborer, no questions asked. I suspected the stack of euros Adeline gave him would support his desire for drink and debauchery for the foreseeable future.

We then found a Carrefour grocery store where we each grabbed toothbrushes, toothpaste, soap, deodorant, mouthwash, some hand towels, aspirin, bottles of water, a few granola bars, and some fruit. It wasn't a shower or a continental breakfast, but after freshening up in the parking lot—our new car blocking any curious onlookers—we were on our way feeling bright and bushy.

We headed south, passed through Caen, and spent another hour on the autoroute before pulling off on a secluded back road, flanked by trees and hedges. I stayed behind the wheel, but Adeline got out and moved to where she had a clear view of the sky. She took out the Iridium phone from her bag and made a call to Alfred.

From my vantage point, I saw the conversation was surprisingly short. This was the first time she'd reached out to Alfred after the events in Paddington, and I'd expected Adeline to give him a blow-by-blow of the past twenty-four hours, shootings and all. But there was no way she could have told him everything.

Adeline got back in the car and returned the sat phone to her bag.

"Well?" I asked.

"He had no idea about the attack on the safe house or what happened in Paddington. No police report, no news—nothing."

"They covered it up that fast?"

Adeline shrugged.

"That's crazy."

"It's the Executive."

"What else did he say?"

"Nothing yet on the bank or the numbers we gave him. He said he would pull the file on Eisengard."

"Does he know we're going to meet him?"

"Yeah. I told him. He asked for an update once we made contact."

"Is that it?"

"Yeah. Why?"

"I guess I expected a little more."

"I did, too, actually. But he wasn't in his office."

"Where was he?"

Adeline shrugged. "Sounded like he was in public, or moving somewhere. I don't know. I think he was hesitant to say too much. You never know who's listening."

"Can someone track you through that?"

"We have protocols in place for misattribution."

"So technical."

"We're prepared."

"You and Alfred?"

"Yes."

I thought about her response. I didn't think she was lying, but something about the call troubled her and she wasn't saying what. For a man who she claimed had been like a father to her, their interactions appeared unfulfilling. It was like she was always hoping for more from Alfred—more information, more guidance, more help— but he never quite gave her what she wanted. Or needed, for that matter.

Something wasn't right. It could very well be my paranoia—Lord knows our situation was perfectly suited for a bit of suspicion and unease—but something was off.

"Let's get moving," said Adeline. "We have over an hour drive ahead of us."

CHAPTER 34

At her headquarters for Analytique Internationale in La Défense—the business district of Paris—Sofia sat at her desk facing the picture windows of her corner office. The sleek furniture matched the sparse, modern feel of the suite. It was clinical in many ways, analogous to a chamber for the cold abuse of the body and mind.

It was also in sharp contrast to what had been her father's style: dark wood, antiques, oriental rugs. His tastes had been in agreement with his approach to the Executive's work—outdated.

Now that he was gone, things would change. She'd been planning her putsch for quite some time. Years.

She'd come to him on a despairingly cold day in February and presented her ideas about using virtual platforms to manage aspects of the Executive's key operations. Cut out the middleman, remove the possibility of human error, prevent human compromise. It was the twenty-first century and things were no longer done with paper and pen and backroom conversations with handshakes.

But he'd refused, blustering on about the importance of the *network*. Tried and true methods should not be thrown away, he'd said.

Ignorance, blind ignorance! Might as well assume the cunning of an ostrich and put his head in the sand. Networks . . . networks were different now. They were in cyberspace and went beyond personal connections—they leveraged the masses in near-instantaneous ways.

If the Executive didn't evolve with the rest of the world, they'd be finished, obsolete. The network—his beloved network—old men, old women, bankers still writing paper checks, so-called savants wedded to the past—that was the problem. Progress had passed them by.

But what put her over the edge was when he suggested she spend some time with a few of the senior financial facilitators. They could enlighten her, he'd said.

It was all she could do to keep her face from rupturing. Never again. Never would she expose herself to his idea of *mentorship*. She'd kill them all. There needed to be a cleansing of the past, of the sickness—the old ways. All of them needed to go.

And now . . . they were gone.

The intercom on her desk sounded. "Monsieur Bodmer is here."

Sofia looked at the display, her office manager's face on the screen. "And the others?"

"Coming off the lift now."

"Send them in."

*   *   *

The door to Sofia's office suite opened and in walked three men. In front was Julien Bodmer, a Swiss banker who possessed the look of a blond-haired, blue-eyed wax statue. He was one of the Executive's most senior facilitators, which was a good position for him. After a conversation with the man, one either felt dazzled or smarmy, his sadistic wit often taken less seriously than it should.

Jeroen Bakker followed him, a tech mogul from Eindhoven in the Netherlands, and a relatively recent add to the Executive's board. When Sofia proposed his nomination to the board, her father had balked at him, but he was precisely the type of genius the Executive needed. And he was young, of a recent generation that was unable to compute the ways of their elders.

Bringing up the tail was General Parson, a retired soldier from the U.S. war machine. He was a carryover from the Executive's former regime, but he was not wedded to the ways of the past. He was committed to staying one step ahead of his adversaries, and he probably had assets in place to take Sofia out if he believed he was at risk. A ruthless man . . . the thought made her wonder what he was like in bed.

They took their seats around the coffee table and Sofia joined them, planting herself in an aluminum framed chair that was as uncomfortable as it looked. Pleasantries were brief. They all knew what had transpired in the last twenty-four hours.

"Are you sure no one loyal to your father was left alive to come back and challenge you?" asked the general.

"There's no doubt. All the members and their aides were disposed of," she replied.

"Hmm," he uttered curtly. "I've always been hesitant to use words like *all*, *every*, and *no doubt*. One never knows."

"Good thing you're here, then. To keep things in check."

"That's not my role this time around. That's for you and your traitorous Faust to handle. Speaking of, where is the man? Lurking about like some cheeky Nazi bastard?"

"He's handling other matters, along with my other men. And what you call treachery is loyalty to us."

"Please," injected Bakker. "Can we get on with it? Just because we share a common purpose, it does not mean I enjoy your company."

"Agreed," Sofia said, still holding the general's gaze. Yes, he'd be a rough one in bed, but he'd be the one walking away bruised and cast off.

"The first order of business," she continued, "is my nominations for the new board members. You've received the packages, and I trust you will find them suitable. Please provide your concurrence in the next forty-eight hours."

Bakker and Parson nodded but said nothing.

"As for more pressing matters, we have the issue of the Executive's funds that were formerly controlled by my father and the expired members of the board. Before we can use the money, all of it must be cleaned."

"What?" asked Bakker, leaning forward as if he'd just been told his wife was shagging the gardener.

General Parson also shifted in his seat. "All of it? Why?"

"It appears some of the European security services have been looking into a few of our affairs, and I want to make sure the old ways—the trails—are shut down."

"Why is this the first time I'm hearing of this?" asked the general with a tone even harsher than before. "What *services*?"

"The Germans, the Spanish, possibly the Americans."

"Are you fucking with us? How long has this been going on?"

"It's unclear."

"You better make it clear."

"It's possible my father's transfers for the U.S. election weren't as dark as he thought."

"Dark? I do not know this term," said Bakker.

"My father used a loophole in the American campaign finance laws to funnel money through nonprofits. Donations to nonprofits don't require disclosure, whereas other aspects of campaign financing do. It's called *dark money*. But somehow the FBI may have gotten wind of European injections."

"This is not a good way to start off," the general said.

"Messes are never easy to clean up. That's why they're called messes. That's why Julien is here."

Julien Bodmer opened a pristine leather portfolio in his lap. "The cleaning of funds and closing of accounts is already underway. Our two principle processes involve numerous security firms and real estate ventures in the UAE."

"Julien, would you give us a short overview to put Mr. Bakker and the general at ease?"

"Of course," replied the banker. "The methods we use involve a handful of international security firms as front companies and a smattering of legitimate companies with less than ethical executives. Put simply, there is minimal oversight of conflict zones in the Middle East, Africa, and Asia, and the demand for personal security and site protection is high. Money goes in and out for contracts that never materialize—rents for facilities, government fees, insurance premiums. There is much cash, our cash, which then comes back to our accounts via networks on the opposite side."

"Where are the new accounts?" asked the General.

"Some will remain in Switzerland, but we're also diversifying into Asian firms, as much as it pains me. Europe is still preferred, but the Americans are an unreliable species. It's never clear when they are going to twist the arms of Europe's financiers."

"Fine. And the real estate?"

"Simple. Buying and selling coastal properties in the Emirates. Our brokerages buy in cash, improve the land to increase the value for luxury ventures, then sell. They push the clean funds back into the accounts. It is all aboveboard."

"But the Emiratis, they own a piece of everything."

"And are as corrupt as the next person," added Sofia. "They'll get their cut, which is fine. The cost of doing business."

"Sounds like you got it all worked out," remarked the general, reaching into his pocket and removing a small cigar. "Just one problem—time."

"This will take time, of course," Bodmer said. "I estimate at least two years to wash it all."

"My point exactly. We're about to cross the line of departure, or am I the only one paying attention to the schedule?"

"You worry too much, General," said Sofia, a provocative smile appearing on her lips. "I have the necessary capital set aside to fund our initiatives for the next six months."

General Parson laughed. "Of course you do. Good thing we're all so trusting."

"We're not. That's why we're still alive. Jeroen, do you have any concerns?"

The Dutchman shook his head.

"Good, then would you please show the general what you've been up to."

"Of course," Bakker said. He pulled a tablet from his bag and connected to the LED monitor suspended on the wall via the office's secure Wi-Fi.

"A key issue faced in recent activities—Brexit, the U.S. elections, the Arab Spring, Ukraine—was real-time data. Typically, the dispositions and perspectives of populations can change within hours, sometimes within minutes. A terrorist attack or a breaking story about a scandal can drive perspectives and opinions one way as well as reverse them. This makes traditional polling and demographic trends obsolete. But social media—Facebook, Twitter, Instagram, TikTok—make it possible to determine trends as soon as people start updating their statuses, uploading photos, and trending."

"That's yesterday's hype. Old news," said the general, striking a match to light his cigar.

"You are right. But how we process this information *is* new."

Bakker tapped his iPad and a map of Europe appeared on the screen. Shades of reds and blues started to develop, along with numerous pinpoints. But nothing remained static. The colors ebbed, flowed, and shaded, like a heat map. Dynamic in some areas, imperceptible in others. Mesmerizing to the familiar and uninitiated alike.

"What am I looking at?"

"This is the mood of Europe. The colors represent political leanings—current attitudes—on any topic we choose to monitor. At the moment, we're tracking perspectives toward refugees. Red means anti-refugee and anti-immigration, blue means accepting, and the shades are in between. The pinpoints are reported incidents of refugees or minorities involved in a crime. From the figures at the bottom on the screen, you can see there are a couple a day, a few thousand a year."

"How current?"

"Real time. We have direct access to social media and the latest news, law enforcement reporting, as well as political affiliation and voting trends, which feed directly into our servers. Massive amounts of data but triaged, categorized, and illustrated using AI. And the more data we ingest, the more refined the outputs."

Sofia cleared her throat. "We can ascertain down to a city block what the majority of the people in that location are thinking at that precise moment, what their *mood* is."

"What do you mean *people there at that precise moment*?"

"This tool uses locational information from personal devices," answered Bakker. "We can track mobile phones, tablets, laptops, smart TVs, cars, even the latest generation refrigerator."

"And you're using that to pulse perspectives geographically," added the general, beginning to understand the capabilities of the tool.

"Precisely. Now, if you will please watch." Bakker clicked on a file and activated a feed. "General, do you remember the bombings in Belgium carried out by ISIS?"

Parson nodded.

"I'm going to create an incident outside Brussels . . . there." A pin-point appeared on the map. "That is a shooting at a café."

"What? Did you just order some schmuck to shoot up a café?"

"No. Nothing actually happened. But reports have been sent to the police and local news station that two Middle Eastern men just shot up a café."

A scrolling window appeared on the right of the screen.

"Now, as you can see, I am pushing media reports onto the web . . . which are being picked up by Facebook, Twitter, Instagram . . . including deep fake images of the scene."

The region, which had been a shade of green, began edging toward burgundy.

"There! Don't you see? We can control the sentiments."

General Parson let loose a heavy laugh. "Fucking brilliant."

Sofia grinned. "When I first approached you about joining me, General, you asked what would be different. Here it is—real-time manipulation of political attitudes down to the local level."

"Impressive," replied the General. But after taking a strong pull on his cigar and releasing a cloud of smoke that hung over the four of them, he said humorlessly, "But what of Parker and Dresden?"

CHAPTER 35

From across the lake, Adeline and I observed a provincial manor house. Ivy climbed the façade up to the mansard roof. Stone planters flanked the circular driveway as if welcoming a grand procession of guests in horse-drawn carriages. And the grounds were superbly kept, the edges of an expansive garden sneaking out from behind the house.

This was the home of Rupert Eisengard: a descendant of the English aristocracy, a former department head at the Harrow School, a talent spotter for British Intelligence, and now a suspected member of the Strasbourg Executive.

I recalled the last time I'd seen the man. It was 2012 and we met for lunch at Martin's Tavern in Georgetown. Martinis and cigars were still acceptable behavior back then, and we enjoyed ourselves.

Rupert had been in town for a conference, and I drove down from Princeton for the night. We'd had a casual conversation, catching up on my latest teachings and reminiscing about life at Harrow. Then, when the food arrived, I got Rupert talking about his research—the Napoleonic era—the man could go on for hours about it, and he was a true Francophile despite his English heritage.

I came away from the lunch feeling inspired as I usually did after spending time with my old friend. The man had a way of making even the driest of subjects come to life, which I supposed was why he'd been such a good educator. I'd even modeled some of my own teaching methods after his style, often considering what he might do if faced with whatever pedagogical situation was confounding me at the time.

But like so many other things, it hadn't been real. Rupert had led a double life just like my father and grandfather, and God knows how many others.

Trepidation welled within me. I wanted this confrontation—I did—and I believed Rupert had answers to my questions. Yet I wondered if I would indeed reach a degree of understanding or if more confusion would arise.

"Are you ready for this?" asked Adeline.

I turned to see her staring at me, and then realized I was gripping her hand like a hammer. I didn't remember holding her hand and wondered if I'd unconsciously reached for her or if she was the one who'd reached for me. Adeline did not strike me as a hand-holder, but maybe there were times when even the toughest of characters needed the simplest of human contact.

"I'm fine," I said, pulling away and returning my attention to the estate.

After a short pause, Adeline asked, "So, do you think he'll meet with us?"

"Yes," I said.

"How can you be sure?"

"Obviously, I don't know as much about him as I thought I did, but part of our relationship was genuine. I'm positive. At the very least, he'll hear us out before he has us killed."

"I'd prefer that doesn't happen, if it's all the same."

"Agreed," I said, with a small laugh.

"Arrêtez!" bellowed a voice from behind.

I spun around to see two men in black uniforms pointing rifles at us. One of the men fired. A loud crack shattered the quiet of the forest. Out of the corner of my eye, I saw Adeline buckle over.

CHAPTER 36

I sat on a sofa in the dimly lit room, a parlor of sorts. There was a polished walnut coffee table in the middle of the sitting area and a green stone fireplace nestled in the wall. An oriental rug covered the floor, with maroon and dark blue the dominant colors. Bookshelves lined the walls while multi-pane windows revealed the pampered grounds just outside.

Adeline sat across from me on a matching sofa, still rubbing her hand, trying to work out the soreness. I could see her taking in our surroundings, too.

Just under an hour ago in the woods, two guards had spotted us spying the estate. When they announced their presence, Adeline whipped about and reached for her gun. One of the guards fired a warning shot into the earth in front of her, causing rock shards to pepper her legs and hand. The men then rushed in.

Moments later, Adeline and I were bound, detained, and brought to the estate. Inside the house, our restraints were removed and we were offered light refreshments as if at a cocktail hour. We were encouraged to sit and make ourselves at home.

This space reminded me of Rupert's office at Harrow. There'd been two leather wingbacked chairs that we'd sit in, and we typically had a cup of tea during those meetings. Yorkshire for me, preferring the stronger black tea to the herbal varieties that Rupert enjoyed. The conversation would last until Rupert finished his cup, at which point he'd stand up indicating it was time to go, anything of importance having been said in the first thirty minutes.

I wondered how this discussion would go today. Would it be polite, or would I see a different side of the man? I thought about the fondness I'd felt toward Rupert, believing it had been a mutual feeling for all those years. But now I wasn't so sure.

Everything was in question.

Fidgeting, I looked down and noticed a small clump of mud on the side of my shoe. From where the urge came, I don't know, but I proceeded to rub the dirt off against the leg of the pedestal table next to me, hoping the piece cost a fortune.

Finally, a tall man entered the room who was well advanced in age. He had thinning, gray hair combed back and wore a pair of thick-rimmed glasses not unlike those fashionable during the sixties. His attire consisted of an argyle sweater and a pair of corduroys with scuffed loafers. His frame was trim, almost delicate, but his eyes were intensely sharp.

"My dear William. Has it been so long? I must say you look well," Rupert said, his hand outstretched and his speech as polite as ever as he strode across the floor.

I stood up but held back. Rupert's presence before me—after everything that happened—seemed surreal. I studied the face of my former mentor, recognizing the man I'd known for over thirty years, yet perceiving a rawness that hadn't been there before. The proper air of the British schoolmaster was gone, replaced by something less affable. The instant familiarity and comfort I'd shared with this man—even if we hadn't seen each other or talked for years—I no longer felt. Rather, wariness and sadness unsettled me.

I finally grasped Rupert's hand, noticing that the old teacher was studying me as well. I wondered what he saw.

"And you must be Miss Parker," said Rupert, turning to face Adeline. "I do apologize for the injury to your hand. My guards can be jumpy at times. Although, you did go for your gun. Not a wise move. But then again, I'm ignorant to such things."

"I doubt that," replied Adeline cooly.

The three of us stared at each other, the seconds ticking by as if we all expected someone else to take the next step in our standoff. Nevertheless, although I did not feel anywhere near at ease, I did not think Rupert was about to kill us or hand us over to the more despicable elements of the Executive. Like me, I think he wanted to talk.

"Grant," called Rupert over his shoulder to the guard by the door. "Can you leave us? I've nothing to fear from these two. They are my guests. And you can return their belongings to them, firearm as well."

The guard took Adeline's bag from the table and brought it over, then handed her back her pistol, which she duly tucked back under her jacket.

Rupert then went to a cabinet against the wall and removed three copita glasses. "You used to have quite the discerning palate, William. I just received a shipment of the most remarkable sherry. You must tell me what you think."

When the Englishman returned, he handed each of us a glass of the fortified wine. He raised his in salute and took a sip, his eyes perched over the rim.

Adeline refrained from toasting our rendezvous, but I tasted mine. Yet, I couldn't discern a damn thing. It could have been water, grape syrup, or turpentine—I had nothing.

"Exquisite," I said blandly. I sat back down on the sofa and set the glass next to me on the end table. But before turning back to meet Rupert's eyes, I said, "Why are you trying to kill me?"

"I'm not trying to kill you," countered Rupert as he took a seat in a wood captain's chair. "I've only an inkling of what this is about, though I suspect it has something to do with that ruckus in Nice."

"You're a member of the Strasbourg Executive," I stated. "Do you deny it?"

Rupert remained impassive.

I went on, "If you are bringing up the matter in Nice, then you must know something, though as a former friend I dearly pray you were not complicit in the matter."

Rupert allowed a thin smile. "Ah, I see." Rupert expelled a pensive breath. "You always were one to get right to the point, William. I've always admired that about you. So, how about I answer what I suspect is your second question, and then we can return to the first."

"I don't understand."

"You will, and you are right. Since its inception, my family has been involved with the Strasbourg Executive. Over the decades, the core leadership has evolved—sometimes small, sometimes formal and organized, other times simply the ravings of a lunatic—but in its current manifestation, the Executive has a board, a body of eleven men and women headed by a single chancellor, referred to as the Kanzler. But despite its mutations, the central belief has always been the same—to expand the power of European peoples. It was a vision I believed in for the majority of my life . . . but things change," he said, adjusting himself in his seat. "I would ask you to digest that for a moment."

I pursed my lips, considering what Rupert had just said. Things do change, people especially. The warmonger becomes the pacifist, the conservative becomes the liberal, the preserver becomes the activist, the avowed bachelor a family man. But this change Rupert was alluding to was fundamental. To have once been a supremacist, what could have caused him to change and how could it possibly be real?

"I left the Executive nearly twenty years ago," Rupert continued, "a few years before you and I last met in Georgetown. It was my choice, and one long overdue. Thus, given that I'm no longer a member of the club and haven't been for quite some time, I can only speculate why the hateful bastards are after you."

"You expect us to believe that?" refuted Adeline.

"I don't care if you do or not, Miss Parker. William is the only one that matters to me. You can piss off, along with the rest of your bloody service."

Rupert and Adeline exchanged stares, the air simmering between them. Neither of them had met the other before this moment—I was sure of it—but a history existed that I did not yet understand. Was it Rupert's reputation as a spotter that she'd garnered through Alfred, was it his knowledge of her and Alfred's investigation of the Executive, or was it something entirely different?

"The Executive doesn't strike me as a group that allows its members to just walk away," I remarked in an effort to redirect the tension, but filing away this moment to ask about later.

"You are correct," Rupert said, turning back to me. "But prior to my departure, I enacted a bit of life insurance, you might say. Documents held in the custody of a trusted solicitor to be delivered to select, powerful individuals and institutions in the event of my untimely demise."

"How convenient. Very mafia-like."

"It's the truth."

"Any chance you'll give us a copy of those files?"

"They won't tell you what you want to know, if that's what you're hoping for, so no. Besides, although I wish you all the best in your future endeavors, they are my insurance—not yours. Some personal survival. I'm sure you understand."

I snorted. "Right."

"Now, if we're done sparring over mundane details of no importance, I suggest we get on with it."

I nodded as Adeline leaned back into her seat. "Please continue."

"Good. And I hope you'll believe me when I say my affiliation with the Executive was the only thing I ever kept from you. I had to, for the good of us both. I am sorry for that."

I said nothing, though Rupert's gaze intimated that he hoped for at least an acknowledgment. Yet I wasn't ready to give him that.

"Well," Rupert finally said, a hint of disappointment evident in his voice, "now that we have that out of the way, why don't you tell me what's going on."

"What do you mean?" I asked.

"As I just said, I am no longer part of the Executive so I am not aware of the details that concern your situation. Yet, I do know things. But the only way we can have a meaningful discussion is if you tell me what has happened."

I thought for a moment, part of me suspecting this could be some sort of ploy. But given the absence of any other options, I took a risk, not caring if Adeline agreed with me or not.

Over the next ten minutes, I recounted the events of the last few days. I left nothing out—the revelations by British Intelligence to hacking the bank, the attempts on our lives, even the purchase of the car outside Caen.

Rupert needed to hear it all, I believed, and by the end, the old teacher had a pained look on his face. I trust it was genuine, too, an expression I'd seen years ago. Then Rupert downed the remainder of his sherry and went to refill his glass. His hand shook as he poured the wine.

"I can't say I'm shocked. Just as Miss Parker told you, your family, like mine, has been with the Executive since the beginning."

"Why was I never told?" I asked.

"Your father made that decision. He sent you to Harrow specifically so that I could watch you. Mentor you. Despite what you might think, the death of your mother was hard on him. I've known your father since before you were born, and the loss changed him."

"Was my mother involved with the Executive?" I asked.

"No. Not to my knowledge. Just like I did with my partners over the years, your father kept many secrets from those he was supposed to love, including her."

"Right," I whispered to myself, at once relieved to hear my mother was not complicit in this nightmare, yet still feeling lost. "You were talking about why my father sent me to Harrow, for you to *mentor* me."

"Yes. Your father didn't know what to do as a single parent. It was not in his DNA. So he sent you away as well as for me to guide you. But within your first year at Harrow, I knew you weren't suitable for the Executive."

"Why?" I asked, feeling my stomach drop.

"During the fall semester, a boy a year ahead of you was being harassed by a group of footballers. You didn't know him but you told the boys to stop. When they didn't, you stepped between them. There was a bit of shoving and you got knocked down, but you got back up."

The boy's name had been Kamari, and I could picture his face. We were friends for a brief time afterward, but the boy was pulled out of school the following year. His father had been a diplomat from Kenya, but the family had to suddenly leave England, sparking a rash of gossip. "I never got in trouble for that scuffle. You broke it up."

"I did, and when I asked you why you did it, with tears in your eyes, you said you were terrified of bullies. Then, when I pressed further, you said you were more terrified of sitting things out as they hurt that boy," Rupert said with a chuckle. "Quite principled for a lad of thirteen. I knew right then that you'd never follow in your father's path. The Executive is precisely about being a bully, capitalizing on fear and intimidation to suppress everyone else."

"So you're the one who kept me out of the Executive?"

"Yes."

"Was that why you and my father got into an argument that summer?"

"I'm surprised you remember."

"What did my father say?" I asked, realizing that I was gripping the fabric of the armrest.

"When I told him what happened and about the conversation I had with you afterwards, he understood. I supposed he already knew you were different than him, he just didn't like it. I think he hated it. I saw the venom in his face. Plus, your father and I never really got along, for more reasons than your situation. "We had our"—Rupert waved his hand dismissively—"differences.""

"In what way?"

"He was always more committed than I, willing to do whatever was necessary for the furtherance of the Executive's goals and the realization of the Covenants, no matter how cruel. You do know about the Covenants, yes?"

"Not what they are, only that they exist," answered Adeline.

"Right. Imperialist hogwash. Anyway, as I said, your father was committed. I less so. I'd broken from my family's legacy, too, you might say."

"How?"

"I'd started to doubt, and not just in my own mind, but outwardly."

"Why? What changed?"

"My views and the Executive's are incompatible. It took me nearly six decades to realize that, but sometimes the best decisions take time. It's like the Chinese say—it's too soon to tell if the French Revolution was a good or a bad thing."

"What do you mean *incompatible*? You believed in their agenda once. What changed?"

Rupert laughed uncomfortably. "As flawed human beings, we lie to ourselves all the time and say we believe things that contradict, sometimes vehemently, even when the evidence of truth is incontrovertible. So yes, having been conditioned from the first days of my conscious life to believe that the Executive's perspective was, in fact, the natural state of humanity, I fell victim to such twisted ways. Yet, with age often comes wisdom, and I knew I could not be a part of something that discriminated against one group or another. I knew from history that if you could oppress one group that was considered *different*, then what would prevent them from oppressing another. Longevity in a group centered on exclusivity only lasts as long as you are considered one of the group."

"Is that it? You had an epiphany?" I asked.

"Life isn't always defined by dramatic or profound experiences. Sometimes we simply wake up and realize the courage we have lacked for too long."

I slowly shook my head in disbelief.

"Yet there indeed was a forcing action," said Rupert with a wry smile. "I left the Executive shortly after your father's car accident."

"That would have been around 1996 or 1997."

"Yes, it was. And I didn't much care for the new leadership," Rupert continued. "A new Kanzler had come into existence, and as I said, we had our differences."

"What do you mean?" I asked, dreading the answer but already knowing it.

"Your father didn't die in a car crash, William. He became the Kanzler of the Strasbourg Executive."

CHAPTER 37

For most people, Marseille is a trading center dating back to the time of the Greeks. It had a reputation for being independent, routinely rebelling against the Counts of Provence to maintain autonomy. Even when Marseille was finally incorporated into the French state, it wasn't until the nineteenth century that the city stopped revolting against central rule. The population has been racked by plagues more often than most care to count, and during Europe's imperial era it served as France's gateway to its colonial holdings in the Near East and Africa.

But Marseille has another quality that most people don't realize. As a port city on the Mediterranean, it is a crossroads between North Africa, the Levant, and Europe. In addition to the French, people with all different backgrounds coalesce there—Arabs, Jews, Italians, Africans, Spaniards, Greeks, Palestinians, Syrians, Lebanese—and not all of them come to enjoy the food and culture.

If one looks hard, under the surface there's an unsavory quality to Marseilles, where criminals, terrorists, arms dealers, human traffickers—and the spies who seek them out—conduct their business.

On the sixth floor of the InterContinental Marseille Hotel Dieu, Sofia stood in the middle of the suite. Faust loomed next to her with his arms crossed, and both were watching the video feed on the laptop. There was an image of two men sitting across from each other in the room directly below. They were eating, drinking, and talking.

"We've dispersed and prepared the first shipment for action, ready to commence immediately. When can I pick up the rest of the material?" came a voice from the laptop's speaker, the microphone in the bugged room sensitive enough to hear the two men breathing.

"It will be at the construction site outside Munich," said the other man as Sofia and Faust watched him slide a card across the table. "Here's the address."

Turning to Faust, Sofia asked, "Have you detected any irregularities with this man?"

"Madani? No. Everything we have on him indicates he's a genuine external operations commander for ISIS."

"And his network? What about them?"

"Radicalized refugees, every one of them. They are the enemy in our midst, just waiting to detonate themselves. When the West *crushed* ISIS in Syria, the cockroaches fled and are now among us."

Sofia smiled. "I like your man Fabian. You said his father spent his entire career in the Middle East, yes?"

Faust nodded.

"There's something about the ability to infiltrate an enemy, assume the outward appearance of a trusted member, but all the while hiding one's true self. That is fascinating to me."

Faust looked at Sofia out of the corner of his eye but did not respond.

"That's why he's perfect for this," Faust said as he uncrossed his arms.

"Yes, of course."

The conversation in the room below continued, Fabian playing the part of a disgruntled French citizen with Egyptian roots who had access to ordnance leftover from the civil war in Syria. The ISIS operative—Madani—was an Iraqi, educated in England, but whose parents were murdered by the Americans during the 2003 invasion. He listened intently for how he would obtain the remainder of the weapons and 200 kg of Semtex explosives.

Madani had recruited and trained fourteen refugees who would comprise seven cells, and they were standing by to retrieve, transport, and construct the explosive devices. There would be seven bombs in all, each one powerful enough to bring down a small office building, and the seven attacks would be coordinated with seven mass shootings.

"Now it's my turn to ask a question," said Faust. "Do you think this will work?"

"Yes. I have no doubt," replied Sofia.

"How can you be so sure?"

"Because, every time there is a terrorist attack in Europe, there is a massive uptick in public opinion against foreigners from the Middle East and Africa, along with a surge of nationalism."

"Which is usually short-lived," countered Faust. "People forget very quickly, their tempers and fears assuaged by the liberals and pacifists of the world."

"True. But things will be different this time."

"You keep saying that."

"The scale of these attacks will be significantly larger, and they'll further convolute the view of who is and who isn't an enemy. When this happens, we'll be there to push the populist movements forward."

"And the death of our people?"

"The sacrifice is worth it. My father forgot that Europe has assumed a level of blind enlightenment where the notion of an existential threat seems unfathomable. Where the threat in decades past was invasion, the threat today is dilution. Europeans must realize that if we don't act now, the lands they call home will no longer look or feel like what they remember and what made them strong. They must feel a threat to their livelihood and be shocked by it. Then they'll act to protect what is theirs."

Sofia turned to meet Faust's eyes, and as calmly as she would have ordered a glass of rosé, said, "We will bomb them and shoot them— our own people—and then, when their anger and fear are at their highest, we'll use every form of influence we can to push them over the edge."

A man walked out of the bedroom on the other side of the suite. "Herr Broch?"

"Yes," replied Faust, keeping his eyes fixed on Sofia.

"A message just came in. We've located the American and the British woman."

Faust left Sofia's side and went into the bedroom. It was an expansive room, with plenty of space for two tables holding computers and communications equipment. Three men from Faust's security unit were monitoring the systems.

"It came through the gateway site," said the team lead.

"When's the call?" asked Faust.

"One hour."

"What do you have?" asked Sofia, standing in the doorway.

"Possible location and confirmation in an hour from now. I'm spinning the team up."

CHAPTER 38

I stared out the parlor window, surveying Rupert's expansive gardens. It was like something Louis the XIV would have commissioned for a summer house. The flowers and exotic plants were crisply trimmed. The hedges had grown over ten feet tall with more than a few hideaways inside the labyrinth. And a pergola covered with ivy veiled one corner of the plot—the most useless outdoor structure ever conceived yet common throughout the world.

I peeled my eyes away from the garden and glanced absently at the lamp to my left. Only Adeline and I were in the parlor now; Rupert had been called away as soon as he revealed the truth about my father. The timing could not have been worse, and given everything that had gone on up to this moment, I wondered if Rupert's extraction had been planned to let me grapple on my own with the news, unable to ask a single question more. Yet as I had feared, there were so many unanswered questions.

My father hadn't died all those years ago. The car accident had been staged. The body I identified a fake. It was an elaborate ruse, meant to end one life so he could assume another. It made sense. It was the Executive's pattern.

And there was no way of rationalizing what my father was—a fanatic. If my father truly had taken over the Executive as Rupert said, the man was pure evil. He'd misled me, manipulated me, despised me, then abandoned me. Yet more significantly, he was the head of an organization determined to bully, suppress, and hurt—which was beyond despicable. I tried to tell myself I should feel fortunate I was excluded from such a grotesque affiliation, yet there was also a pain cutting deep inside me.

The man had been my father and there was no changing that. I could hate him, revile him, never want to see or hear of the man again, while simultaneously feeling abandoned by the one person whom I should have been able to rely upon and trust. I even wondered—desperately hoped—if it was all a mistake. But I knew that was a fantasy I couldn't entertain for more than a fleeting moment.

Whether I had fully come to grips with this revelation when Rupert reappeared, I could not say. But an item in his hand—a small leather-bound book—distracted me enough.

"I'm terribly sorry for that," Rupert announced from across the room, "but the matter had to be attended to. Apparently, the yen just overtook the dollar in cross-border trade with China and it has everyone concerned, including the euro counters. Now, where were we? Your father."

I stayed by the window and watched as Rupert took a seat, resting the book in his lap and picking up where he'd left off. "A Kanzler's tenure is twenty years, give or take. And before one Kanzler steps down, the board selects who will succeed him. It's a deliberative process, but preordained in some ways."

"What do you mean?" I asked.

"Most Kanzlers are mentored from an early age—molded, shaped, prepared for the task that lies ahead of them. Once the new Kanzler is formally announced and endorsed by the board, he must *die*—symbolically—completely severing all ties to his former self."

I recalled the deaths of Waters, Gibbons, and Himmler. Each had died two decades apart from the other. They had been the first Kanzlers of the Executive.

"As for your father, like every Kanzler before him, upon his death and after a cooling period to ensure no complications arose from his past affairs, he took control of the day-to-day activities of the Executive. He assumed his role in its entirety, becoming the mastermind behind the Executive's machinations."

"What does that mean?"

"The power of the Executive is not in the core leadership. The board, or whoever is claiming to be in charge, makes the decisions—but the *network* is what matters. Banks, people, corporations, governments—they're fed information and orders to act in accordance with the board's plans. Without the network, the board is nothing but an over-opinionated bunch of old men with no influence beyond what they have for dinner."

"But the network—why does it do it?"

"There are some elements of the network that share similar perspectives as the Executive. Pick your right-wing party or fascist group—it's not hard to incite them. But there are others who do not necessarily adhere to a particular ideology—yet, they can be influenced and incentivized to act on the Executive's behalf. And for both, the majority have no knowledge of the Executive or the Covenants or that they are part of a larger, coordinated movement. The Executive does not reveal it's existence except in the rarest of circumstances.

"And the key is fear and hatred—anger. The Executive manipulates those fears and biases—the ones we don't want to admit we have—to inflame it all."

"And the internet amplifies it," added Adeline.

"Precisely. More than anything ever has in the past."

"The Covenants—what are they?" asked Adeline.

Rupert tapped the book in his lap. "In a moment."

"Is my father still alive?" I blurted. It was the question that had been burning a hole in my gut and I couldn't hold it back anymore. It had been just over twenty years since his disappearance, and I needed to know if my father was the one trying to kill me. Networks, boards, the internet . . . it mattered, but at this moment, I wanted the answer that pertained to me. I needed to know.

Rupert shrugged. "I don't know. As I said, my connection to the Executive ended the moment I resigned, and your father and I never exchanged holiday cards. He might be, and he may still be the Kanzler. Sometimes they stay on past the twenty-year term, but it's rare.

"But I'll tell you this—the Karl Dresden who you knew no longer exists. Don't torment yourself with the knowledge that he may still be alive. Rising to the Kanzlership puts an end to everything the individual may have known before. It is a fanatical calling, with no room for the past."

Rupert's words simmered in my mind, rendering me speechless. I turned again to stare out the window, seeing nothing but a darkness that had consumed the present and the past.

"How do we get at them?" I faintly heard Adeline ask, her voice now distant.

Rupert sat back and interlaced his fingers. "Expose them. The Executive is only effective if the people who lead it can operate in the shadows."

"Go on."

"They can't move assets, funnel money, cultivate propaganda if their identities and intentions are public."

"And what of your *insurance* you said you had tucked away? How can we use that?"

"You can't. It won't serve the purposes you need, and I won't give it up. I fully support your efforts and will help where I can. But I will not be going with you, and if you fail, I still need my safety measures."

"Then what do we do?" I asked, turning back.

"You need to find a man named—"

"I don't think you should say another word, Rupert."

All three of our heads jerked toward the parlor entrance where Alfred stood in the doorway. He wore a casual pair of khaki trousers and a windbreaker, and he was pointing a revolver at Rupert.

"Alfred," breathed Adeline, her voice less shocked than I thought it should be. "What are you doing here?"

"That's not important, my dear. More information has come to light. So glad you're not hurt in any way," said Alfred.

"No, I'm not hurt," replied Adeline.

"I wouldn't believe anything this man says," said Rupert, his jaw clenched, his eyes fixed on Alfred. "He's not what he seems."

"One more word and I'll put a bullet in your head," hissed Alfred.

I looked at Adeline. She was staring at Alfred. Why was she not surprised to see Alfred? Had she known he was coming? She hadn't shared any of this with me. Quite the opposite. Since fleeing the safe house, it'd been as if Alfred—her mentor, the one man we could trust—had abandoned us. Yet here he stood, holding a gun.

"William, please move away from the window and sit down," commanded Alfred.

"Alfred, I wish you wouldn't do that," said Adeline, still all too calmly.

"You know how to follow orders, my dear. Trust me and do as I say."

"That would be unwise," said Rupert.

"Shut up," Alfred snapped.

The muffled sound of an explosion came from outside, followed by a burst of automatic gunfire.

Adeline said something but I didn't hear it because a realization struck me. Every time we'd contacted Alfred, the Executive appeared shortly thereafter. Even after we'd met that first night—rather than provide any level of tangible support that a rational person would expect—he'd left Adeline and me to fend for ourselves. And just a few hours ago, when Adeline had called Alfred to update him, he'd let us go it alone, asking for a report once we were done.

Yet here he was, pointing a gun at us.

"You work for the Executive," I declared.

Alfred trained his pistol on me. But although my throat caught, I remained firm.

"You have no idea what you're talking about," said Alfred. "Now please pull out your pockets and pull up your jacket so I can see you are not armed. We don't need you doing anything rash."

I did as instructed, slowly raising my jacket.

"You're the traitor, aren't you?" I said. "You're part of the Executive. You've been setting us up the whole time."

Another burst of gunfire came from outside, then a loud concussion rattled the windows.

"You always were a—" My old friend didn't get a chance to finish his sentence.

Alfred shot Rupert in the chest, knocking him backward, and I watched my mentor fall and hit the hardwood floor. I couldn't see him breathing, only a hole in his sweater and wisps of smoke drifting upward.

"No!" I shouted.

But when I turned back to face Alfred, the right side of his head exploded into pink mist. Alfred's body slumped to the floor, blood spilling out from the head wound, the heart still pumping, not yet aware that the body was dead.

Adeline, her face cold and impassive, clutched her pistol with both hands. She slowly lowered her arms, but her stare seemed screwed onto Alfred's lifeless body.

"Adeline, you knew . . ." My words trailed off as I took a step toward her, but there was another burst of gunfire, muffled and echoing. Whoever was shooting was inside the house now.

"We need to get out of here," Adeline said, now looking at me with the same cold and impassive stare.

I nodded. I rushed to Rupert's side, expecting to find a pool of blood, but when I bent down to check the wound, Rupert's chest heaved. The old man stirred and let out a groan.

"Rupert, are you all right?"

"Bloody hell," murmured the old teacher.

I leaned in to help him, and when I touched his sweater, I felt a thick pad underneath. It was a vest of sorts.

"Thank God that thing worked," Rupert said between coughs. "I always wondered if it would."

"Are you okay?"

"I suppose so. I put that on after you arrived, figuring you'd dragged one of those fanatics along, though I admit I didn't expect it to be *master Alfred* himself, bloody cock."

Another loud bang came from elsewhere in the house and the gunfire increased in intensity. The battle was constant now.

"Right. Come on. We need to get out of here."

Adeline appeared by my side. "How do we get out of here?" she asked as I helped Rupert to his feet.

"We need to get down the hall. There's a way out."

"Which way?"

The old man winced as he shuffled toward the door, Adeline and me in tow. "We'll go right down the hall. There's a wine closet just before the dining room."

"A closet?" I asked.

"Trust me."

"Right," I replied. Over the last forty-eight hours, a lot of people had asked to be trusted. If I lived through this mess, I vowed never to use that phrase again. "Adeline, you lead. I'll carry Rupert."

"Wait. My journal." Rupert was pointing at the book on the floor near where he'd been sitting. "Get my journal."

I grabbed it and handed it to Rupert.

"Adeline," I called out.

She was already at the door, waiting for us to stack up behind her. Once there, she cracked the hatch. "Clear."

The three of us rushed into the hall and hastened down the corridor. Adeline covered the front and I watched the rear. We eyed every doorway, every corner. Shouts and gunshots echoed throughout the house.

Chancing a look ahead, I saw a door just before a wider opening. I guessed it was the closet. We'd passed it when we'd first come into the house.

Rupert urged Adeline forward. "Here. Inside."

Adeline ripped the door open and all three of us packed in. The closet was more of a medium-sized room, the walls lined with hundreds of wine bottles. A small tasting table was in the center of the space, but there weren't any other doors or windows.

"What now?" I asked, part of me fearing we'd just trapped ourselves.

"Lend a hand," said Rupert, pushing the tasting table.

I joined my old friend, and together we slid the heavy oak cabinet across the floor, revealing a hatch hidden beneath it.

Another boom came from outside, this one closer than any of the others. Adeline double-checked the door lock, then looked at me. Her face finally had a look I recognized—would we make it out?

"All right, time we go. Ladies first." Rupert held up the hatch, motioning for Adeline to get in.

"Go," I said. "I'll cover the door."

Adeline climbed down the ladder into the hole. Rupert followed, easing himself down one painful rung at a time. When Rupert's head disappeared, I backed away from the door and peered down the shaft. I saw a light twenty feet below. Once Rupert was halfway down, I sat to find my footing on the ladder.

Something heavy slammed into the hallway door. Curses and barked orders followed.

They were speaking German.

I hurried down the ladder, closing the hatch and popping the lever into the locked position. Once on the ground, I took in my surroundings. We were in a concrete room, probably thirty feet wide. Workbenches and cabinets lined the walls, and a gunmetal gray Range Rover sat parked in the center of the room. Beyond the SUV, I spotted a dark tunnel, wide enough for a vehicle to drive down.

"My hobby room," said Rupert. "I had it built in case I ever needed to rush away to the Greek Isles, but never thought I'd actually use it."

Gunshots came from above. They penetrated the hatch and ricocheted off the ladder. I jumped back. More shouts, more gunfire.

"Damn it all." Rupert went to a rack on the wall and grabbed a set of keys. He tossed them to me. "You'll drive down the tunnel and come out on the other side of the lake, not far from where my men picked you up."

"Aren't you coming with us?"

Another burst of gunfire peppered the hatch.

"I think not," replied Rupert. He opened one of the cabinets and removed a pump-action shotgun. "Someone needs to slow them down so you can make it out. Now, on your way."

"But, Rupert . . ." The man had lied to me for most of my life. Conspired with my father in a way that plagued me. Yet, I hadn't expected Rupert to stay behind to sacrifice himself. "We can all make it out—you're coming with us."

Rupert shook his head. "We're not arguing. Go. This is my chance to take a shot at these wankers. And believe me, I've been wanting to do this for a long time."

"That's bloody mental," Adeline said with a half-amused smile. She then grabbed my sleeve, pulling me toward the car.

I yanked my arm free. "Goddammit. Wait a minute." I knew we couldn't delay and no sense in trying to drag Rupert along with us, but we couldn't leave yet.

Rupert fired his shotgun at the hatch, worked the action, and fired again.

"Rupert," I shouted. "You never told us who we need to find."

"Right, of course," said Rupert, as casually as if we were back in the parlor. "Julien Bodmer. He's a vice president with Grüber & Cie, another of the Executive's institutions."

"Is he a board member?"

"Hardly. A sniveling schmuck, but he knows everything. He's one of the Executive's senior facilitators. At least he was years ago."

"A what?"

"And you'll need this." Rupert removed the leather book from his pocket and thrust it toward me. "It chronicles my family's involvement since the beginning, every terrible moment."

A hammer started pounding on the hatch above. Rupert turned back, adjusted his stance, and fired again. "Go!"

"We need to get out of here," shouted Adeline.

I turned back to Rupert, who was jamming shells into the magazine tube, smiling.

The adrenaline in my veins went taut, and an intensity welled within me, something I hadn't felt in years. It was a sensation I couldn't explain, nor did I understand it. I wanted to fight and stand shoulder-to-shoulder alongside my mentor, the man who'd been more of a father to me than anyone else in this world.

"William!"

I turned to see Adeline waving at me to get in the car.

Damnit. There was no time. No time!

I got behind the wheel of the Range Rover and tore off down the tunnel.

CHAPTER 39

Sofia slipped out from beneath the covers and put on her satin robe that she found draped across the hope chest at the foot of her bed. Tying the knot around her waist, she looked down at Faust, asleep, the sheet barely covering his toned and naked body.

He always fell asleep after sex. A typical man, and a biological weakness that was just as annoying.

If she wanted to, she could kill him. It would be so easy. Did he know that? Did he know what she could do to him?

No. Men never realized how vulnerable they were.

Pulling back her hair, she stepped into the hall and eased the door closed with a soft click. The passage had tile floors and off-white walls. Metal light fixtures and black and white prints of buildings and bridges lined the hall. It conveyed an industrial feel, sleek and cool.

This was her part of the estate, her touch, her style. Her father had owned the rest—paneling, hardwood, brass, grandiose portraits of men long dead. She couldn't wait to tear it all out.

Entering the study, the ghosts of old cigars and musty furniture greeted her, like something out of a highbrow club for the spoiled and privileged. This is where he'd thought, planned, schemed, and decayed. He'd sat here in the darkest of hours and read his precious journal like a teenage girl and her diary. In this place he'd conferred with other men like himself—dated, ignorant, myopic.

Sofia gazed down at her father's desk—the medieval dagger he'd used as a letter opener, his gold-plated fountain pen, a polished leather mat. The servants must have put it back together just the way the old man liked it. What did they think, that he was coming back? No.

Everything was about to change. It wasn't going to work out as he'd wanted.

She reached inside the bottom drawer and pulled out his journal, the sacred Dresden family journal. The history of the Executive—the plots, the visions—everything recorded here.

There had been successes, and there had been failures. Too many failures. Failures in mind and body, and in action.

Sofia turned to a page near the end, the entry dated 14 November 1985. Her father had written it, and it was longer than most. Sofia knew it by heart. The first time she'd read it she was seven years old, but she'd lost count of how many times she'd snuck in here to read it since. The words were burned into her mind, seared into her heart.

It recorded her father's disappointment. He'd been let down, forced to accept a reality he didn't want to. Her father's ambition to pass the legacy to *him*, his son, her brother, would not happen. The boy was not of the right mind, he'd written. A crushing recognition, such a disappointment—the first choice—unworthy.

It was a pathetic outpouring of emotions. Each word grinding, piercing, excruciating to read—unable to forget. The final line being the worst. A reluctance to look to another, an alternate candidate that would *hopefully be acceptable*. Only dedicated mentorship could possibly overcome the faults and weaknesses of the . . . of the daughter.

Well, Father, you have succeeded. There's nothing weak about me now.

Sofia slammed the journal on the desk and swept the surface clean, everything flying to the floor with a resounding clatter. She strode over to the fireplace, wadded up pieces of newspaper, and threw them in the hearth.

She went to strike a wooden match, but the shaft broke, as did the second, and the third. The fourth finally caught.

The paper ignited, which alighted the remnants of an earlier fire. Small flames began to lick the blackened walls of the fireplace.

Sofia picked up the journal and held it in her hands. It seemed to weigh a thousand pounds. The past was over. It was all over and it needed to be erased. She was the chosen one, she'd always been the chosen one, the death of her mother proof of that.

And she would do what her father never could. She would kill her brother, an unworthy descendant of the Dresden line, an undesirable. No better than any of the others.

She was about to toss the journal into the flames when the study door opened.

"Sofia." Faust stood just past the threshold, fully dressed.

Sofia stopped short, her eyes reflecting in the light. "Yes?"

"We have a problem."

Sofia frowned, threw the journal in the fire, and turned. "What?"

CHAPTER 40

I pinned the SUV's pedal to the floor, the reflectors on the walls guiding me down the tunnel. There was a *thump thump thump* as the vehicle whipped past the support columns. The tunnel had started off with a slight decline, but fifty yards into it, the grade leveled off. Now we were ascending and the pattern of reflectors up ahead was different.

It had to be the exit, but how? Was there some form of a garage door? Would it open automatically? Maybe there was a control? *Fuck!*

I looked up at the visor. There was a small fob with a single button. I pressed it and saw a crack of light appear up ahead, gradually getting wider akin to a hangar door. A brief sense of relief pulled the knot out of my chest.

"What are the odds they have this covered?" I nearly shouted.

"No idea," replied Adeline, gripping the door handle.

"We're not stopping."

The exit was coming up fast, the moon illuminating the land beyond.

Fifty feet.

Twenty feet.

Ten feet.

"Here we go," I said through gritted teeth.

The SUV hurtled from the tunnel. It skidded over hard-packed dirt, rattling across the uneven terrain. We were in a clearing. I kept driving, nothing but trees and foliage to the front. I looked in the rearview mirror and saw the tunnel door disappearing into the rocky side of a hill.

I spotted a road off to my right and steered toward it. "See anything?"

"No, but don't turn the lights on. We need more distance," Adeline said.

The SUV jumped onto the pavement and I held the wheel into the turn to maintain control. I stomped on the gas, reaching 120 km/h in seconds. Without headlights, I was pushing the edge with my speed.

"Where are we?" asked Adeline.

"Somewhere in France." I glanced at the electronic compass on the dash display. We were heading southwest. "How likely is it the Executive has this vehicle marked?"

"Fifty-fifty."

We screeched around a bend.

"They probably had one of his security detail on the payroll. Not sure how else Alfred could have gotten in the house like that."

The Executive was everywhere, I thought, and had been right with us the entire time.

"You knew about Alfred all along, didn't you?"

"Yes," Adeline replied.

"Why didn't you tell me?"

"Later. We need to get to Zurich."

"Goddammit, Adeline, what the hell."

"You can be pissed at me later. But there was a good reason I didn't tell you."

"Son of a bitch."

"We have to get to Zurich, William. That's our focus right now."

"I know. I know, goddammit," I said, remembering Rupert's final instructions—find Julien Bodmer.

"But not by car," Adeline said.

"I know. We need to go to Tours. It's south of here. There's a train station. We can reach Zurich before dawn."

"We'll need to do something about tickets. My docs are blown."

"I'm sure you'll think of something, but if not, I have an idea."

*　　*　　*

We abandoned the Range Rover on the edge of the city. There was no indication we'd been followed. No other cars had been on the road, and once we'd gotten on the A2B, it'd been a straight shot.

Now in the city, both Adeline and I agreed it would be easier to get around on foot. Like most European cities, the roads were narrow, there was no parking, and it would be easy to take a wrong turn and get stuck. On foot, it was simple to blend in with the other pedestrians. The car was a liability.

Tours was an ancient city, marked by medieval squares, a Gothic cathedral, and world-renowned wine. Every summer there was la Fête de la Musique—a festival where the entire city transformed into a venue for street concerts, dancing, and drinking. I knew the town well, but it had been a while since I'd last walked these avenues.

As we rounded the corner in a residential area, I looked up and down the empty rue. Memories of long ago flashed through my mind. It still looked the same after all these years. France was funny that way—trapped in time.

"Do you think he'll go along with it?" asked Adeline.

I thought again about what I'd proposed we do. "If he's still the man I knew years ago, there's a good chance."

"I hope so. We don't have many options."

"Right," I breathed.

But the truth was, I didn't know. I wasn't even sure if the man still lived here. Our plan, what was my grand idea and contribution to our dire situation, centered on someone I hadn't seen or talked to in over a decade. It was a risk, rather presumptuous, a rash of trouble that shouldn't be levied on anyone, but it's how things were.

I kept telling myself that—we had no choice. We were desperate, and there was no other way. Burdening someone was okay in extreme, grave situations—I had to rationalize this.

But if the man refused, we would not pressure him. I wouldn't let Adeline push him. We'd walk away. He could stay clean and not at risk. It's what I told myself.

We came to the third house on the right and stood before the brown, metal door. It was almost nine, and the only light came from a room upstairs, flickering like a TV.

I scanned the quiet street once more and, seeing no one, I knocked. The sound echoed in the night's silence, but nothing in the house stirred. After a minute, I knocked again, smacking the door with an open palm.

A light came on in the upstairs hallway. A few seconds later there were footsteps, and then the sound of someone jiggling the bolt.

When the door opened, a heavyset man of French-Algerian descent who was well into his fifties stood before us. He wore glasses and had a few days of growth on his fleshy face, and his eyes were sleepy, trying to figure out who was standing on his doorstep at such an hour.

"Mon Dieu. William!"

"Oui. Comment vas tu, Hervé?"

Hervé let out a heavy laugh laced with a smoker's cough. He pushed open the door and pulled me in for a bear hug. "My friend, it's been too long, far too long. And look at you, as old as I was years ago. And who is this?" he asked, giving Adeline a wide grin.

Adeline extended her hand. "I'm Adeline."

"Enchanté," Hervé said.

"May we come in?" I asked, smiling.

"Of course, of course." Hervé led us inside to a small dining area, which was more of an open space between the kitchen and the living room. It was a sizeable house, with two stories and multiple rooms, but it was dead quiet, empty, forlorn.

But it hadn't always been like this.

Twenty-plus years ago while attending Oxford, I'd spent a summer in Tours on an academic program. I'd had the hauteur to study French Renaissance architecture, the abundance of châteaus, castles, and cathedrals making it a superb area for field work, as well as enjoying cocktails with pinkies fully extended.

Nevertheless, Château de Chambord—the largest château in the valley, built in the sixteenth century as a hunting lodge for Francis I—struck me the deepest. Despite being a tourist destination, I enjoyed walking the halls and the grounds for hours, absorbing every detail. And sometimes in the evenings, there would be displays—horses, fireworks, theater—supreme opportunities to flirt with the local and transitory wildlife.

Hervé and his family had been my hosts that summer. We'd gotten along splendidly; Hervé and I drinking scotch and smoking cigars on the back patio, his wife cooking delicious meals, and their two daughters of three and four finding me a tantalizing curiosity. I can still picture them running around the back patio while Hervé and I chatted in the afternoon light.

After I left, we stayed in touch for a time, but a few years later Hervé's wife and daughters drowned in a boating accident.

Hervé's grandfather, Jean, had been a Pied-Noir, a child born into a French family who'd been living in Algeria since the late nineteenth century. Jean had then married an Algerian woman, and when the Algerian Revolution broke out in 1952, he'd joined the ranks of the French Army. But in 1962 everyone had to *go home* to France, the war too grotesque and brutal and no longer safe as a French colony.

The family had initially stayed in Marseille but moved to Tours when Hervé was a teenager. Still inclined to the ocean, Hervé joined the French Navy with service in Lebanon in the nineteen eighties, and after his brief enlistment, had sailed across the Atlantic in a forty-foot cutter. But decades later on a pitch-black night off the coast of Brittany, a freak squall drove his boat onto the rocks. His family—his wife and two daughters—was belowdeck; they never came up.

Hervé fell apart for a time, blaming himself for the death of his wife and girls. But after a few years and too many bottles of whisky, he seemed to come out of it. I saw him ten years ago and he seemed to be doing all right, but I doubted one ever truly comes back after something like that. A part of Hervé stayed in the water with his three angels.

Hervé reached for the decanter that held the leftover wine from dinner, but I stopped him, telling him to grab the Ardbeg instead. Hervé narrowed his eyes, then took the bottle from the cupboard along with three glasses.

"All right, it's been nearly ten years. What brings you to my doorstep in the middle of the night?" Hervé asked.

"We need your help," I said.

"You need to spend the night? Of course. You always have a home here."

"We don't need a place to stay. We need to get out of France."

Hervé laughed. "What? What are you talking about? Buy a plane ticket."

I remained stoic. "There are people after us."

"After you? Come on, William. I'm too old for bullshit. What do you mean *after you*?"

"I don't want to tell you anything that might get you in trouble. I don't want to involve you if I don't have to. These people are serious."

Hervé scoffed, reaching for a cigarette. "What the shit, man. What have you gotten yourself into?" Then he pointed a finger at Adeline. "Who the fuck are you? Is this your doing?"

Adeline started to respond, but I touched her shoulder. "She's trying to help, and they're after her, too. She's British Intelligence."

"Fucking MI6? Merde."

"Hervé—"

The Frenchman raised his hand. "Non. You involved me the moment you came to my door, you know that. We go back too far and we're both too fucked up for you not to be straight with me. Fucking tell me what's going on or we go outside and I kick your ass."

I allowed the suggestion of a smile. My friend's directness was refreshing. It inspired me. Hervé was a good man, dependable, and deserved to know more. And he was right; we'd already put him at risk.

"A bunch of crazy fanatics are trying to bring back the days of Imperial Europe," I began. "They want to regain the national power they once had, shut down borders, expel or enslave all the immigrants—even people like you—and get back on top of the world. The group's been around since before the Nazis. They're trying to kill us."

Hervé gave his two guests a curious look, but he didn't seem as shocked as I would have expected. Instead, he laughed and asked, "Even me?"

"Yes. There's a strong racist component to this group."

"Ha! Fuckers. I'm more French than the damned Parisians, and my Algerian grandmother and her blood is the binding proof."

I nodded but didn't say anything.

"Fuck them. So, were they behind that shit last night?" he asked.

It was Adeline's and my turn to look confused. "What are you talking about?"

"Haven't you seen the news?" Hervé got up and went over to the couch, taking the newspaper from the armrest. "Regardez."

I read the headline: *French Rightists Move to Take Back Their Land*. The article was about a mob of Frenchmen who attacked a refugee camp outside Paris. There were beatings, fires, a few gunshots. The police had just watched it happen, only moving in to disperse the agitators when the fires started getting out of control and the pompiers had to be called in. The group allegedly organized through social media, then disappeared just as quickly.

"Fucking disgusting," spat Hervé. "I don't like the refugee problem either, but then what the fuck am I a descendant of? I saw on the news what happened in Syria and Afghanistan. Fucking Algeria all over again. Those people needed someplace to go." Hervé tapped the paper. "What's next, fucking brownshirts and jackboots?"

I met Hervé's eyes. "Here's what we need you to do."

CHAPTER 41

Faust sat in the copilot seat of the MH-6 Little Bird. They were coming in low and fast, skimming the tops of the trees. The forest below looked like cloudy patches of green and black through his NVGs, and on the horizon he could see the faint lights of villages and solitary homes.

There was also an intense glow up ahead, which concerned him. It was where Rupert Eisengard's estate should have been.

"There. Do you see?" asked the pilot.

"Ja," replied Faust. He pressed a toggle on the side of his helmet, activating his radio. "Alpha Team, Alpha Team, this is Reaper One. Come in."

A few seconds passed, and then the response came. "Reaper One, this is Alpha Team lead. Send it."

"I am two minutes from your position. Confirm you are ready to receive."

"Ja, we are waiting."

"Roger," said Faust. "Interrogative. What's going on down there? Picking up a large light signature."

"Part of the residence caught fire, but under control."

Faust paused for a long moment. "Meet me at the LZ. Full report."

"Roger. Standing by."

The helo flew toward the estate, the scene getting brighter as they neared. The craft banked right and then left, circling the estate grounds. The pilot was lining up with the wind, and the maneuver gave Faust a chance to survey the area.

The south end of the house was on fire, and it didn't look anywhere near under control. Flames were rising above the roof. Elsewhere on the grounds, elongated shadows fell off the men set in a perimeter, the orange light of the fire shimmering on the grass around them. In the circular driveway, the four vans that had carried the assault force sat idling.

Faust took a deep breath.

The operation must have gone terribly wrong. He'd made it clear there shouldn't have been any bloodshed; it shouldn't have been an assault. He wanted everyone alive. But what angered him the most was that his men hadn't notified him of the action—no details on the status of Dresden, Parker, or Eisengard—not until he'd already been in the air and sought to reach out to them. He wondered if he hadn't asked for an update when they would have informed him.

The helo touched down on the front lawn, a swirl of smoke mixing with the darkness. Faust took off his flight helmet, opened the hatch, and jumped to the ground. The rotors powered down, but the wind and noise remained intense.

Scanning his front, he saw two men standing near one of the driveway pillars. He started toward them, unzipped his jacket, and made sure his pistol was secure in its holster.

Both men were fully kitted-out in tactical gear, he noticed. They carried H&K416 assault rifles and wore body armor and helmets with the associated magazines, communications equipment, and optics. Their demeanor further aggravated Faust as they stood there as if they'd just taken down the heart of darkness.

The taller one stepped forward.

"Report," barked Faust, continuing toward the burning house. The two operators exchanged uneasy looks, then ran to catch up.

"Herr Broch," shouted the taller man, two steps behind. "As ordered, we secured the grounds so the Englishman could make entry. Within minutes the local security force was alerted to our presence."

"And what did you do?" demanded Faust, the flames from the house reflecting in his eyes. He spotted another operator standing by the front door like a poster child for an online tactical retailer. He had an obnoxious swagger, the toughest man around. A pompous ass.

"My men were at risk. We were under fire. We neutralized the threat."

Faust turned and smacked the team leader below the throat, grabbing his collar. "*You neutralized the threat?* You fucking imbecile! Your orders were to secure the area, from afar, and then detain everyone quietly and alive! Look around. It's a damned war zone."

"But, Herr Broch, we had to defend ourselves."

"You idiot! Your life and the lives of your men are insignificant. This is unacceptable, and if I wasn't concerned about the mess, I'd shoot you myself."

"Herr—"

"Silence! Where are they?"

The team leader swallowed. "Dresden and Parker escaped."

"How?"

"There's a tunnel. An escape route we didn't know about. We lost them."

"Do you know what direction they went? Did they have a car? Were they on foot?"

"South, we think. An SUV."

Faust thought about the possibilities. There were several villages scattered throughout the valley, but only one major city with continental transportation. "And Eisengard?"

The team leader pointed at one of the vans.

"Has he said anything? Anything about where the other two were going?"

The team leader shook his head.

Faust smacked him across the face. "Speak up."

"No, Mein Herr. He hasn't said a word."

"And the Englishman?"

"Dead."

Faust shook his head and turned to stare at the house. The fire continued to spread. It was only a matter of time before the local authorities showed up.

"Take me to him," Faust said, referring to Eisengard. "I'll question him myself. You, however, will prepare for exfil and clean up this mess."

"Yes, Mein Herr."

Faust released his hold on the man and headed toward the van.

CHAPTER 42

Oblivious to what was transpiring in the shadows around them, groups of young folk made their way to the nightlife, dressed to dance, flirt, and bed one another. Older couples returned home from dinner, taking their time, holding hands, pleased to have shared their lives together. Taxis were scooting in and out of the lane at the square, and a young woman played the cello on the corner, letting the notes of Bach float amidst the sounds of the night. And there was an enticing smell of fresh bread, grilled food, and tobacco in the air.

It was a typical evening in this French city tucked beside the river in the Loire Valley.

But that's how things always seemed with the Executive, I thought. Quiet, benign, normal. The enemy was like a chameleon, blending in, hiding in plain sight. They could be anywhere, waiting to burst forth from the darkness.

From the boulangerie across the square, I watched Hervé walk up Rue Édouard Vaillant toward the train station. The man had a powerful gait, acquired from a lifetime of work in the shipyards, and he looked like he would bowl over anyone who got in his way. There was a defiance to Hervé that exuded with each step.

Given our history, he would help me no matter what—loyal to a fault—and I knew that.

The plan was simple. I would observe Hervé's approach and enter la Gare de Tours. I would then reposition myself at the main entrance and monitor the exterior of the building and the surrounding square. If I saw something, I would send a text alerting both Adeline and Hervé to abort and rendezvous down by the river.

Adeline was already inside the station. She'd thrown on a jacket, tucked her hair under a beret, and worn a pair of glasses. It was remarkable how easily she'd transformed her look. Even if the Executive's gunmen were lurking around, it was doubtful they would recognize her.

Her job was to observe from inside the station and watch Hervé purchase two train tickets. If she thought something wasn't right, like me, she'd give the signal and we would all disperse.

The entire act—buying the tickets and passing them off—should take less than fifteen minutes, perhaps faster if there wasn't a line at the counter. A simple, beautiful plan . . . destined to be a debacle, I mused. Why should this go right when nothing else had?

As I sat at my perch, the time couldn't pass fast enough. I searched the area in front of and behind Hervé. I counted the number of policemen loitering by the hotel across the square, and took note of the few lone individuals—men and women—chatting on their phones or seeming to people watch.

No one's demeanor changed when Hervé arrived on the scene, and no one looked particularly interested in him. The more I thought about it, why would anyone be interested in him. He wasn't on anyone's radar, nor had he done anything—except meet with us. Still, this was the plan Adeline devised, so we were buckling up and going for it.

Fortunately, as far as I could tell, no one had taken a particular interest in me, either. If sentries and pickets had been deployed to snare us in the Executive's web, our visages—Adeline's and mine— would be the ones to set off the alarms, right? Though I suppose at this juncture, if there were individuals with mal intent preparing to make their move, it was not yet time for them to reveal themselves. We weren't boxed in yet.

To hell with it. You could go crazy with the back and forth, this or that. Paranoia never helped anything.

I stood and began trailing Hervé from fifty feet behind. Adeline had instructed me not to get too close. If someone were watching me or Hervé, there needed to be enough distance between us not to make an automatic association.

It made me think that this game of cat and mouse was so isolated. Even when near a trusted friend, there must always be distance. And there had to be silence. Although communication occurred and messages were passed, it was done without the natural expression and emotion that human beings display. But to survive, it had to be this way, as I was coming to understand.

Hervé reached the main doors and pulled them open, but before going in, he looked about. Hervé's and my eyes crossed, but they never met. Still, I knew Hervé had seen me, seeking that silent confirmation that everything was all right. And for me, at least, that was something.

A teenage girl passed through the door that Hervé held open, and then he went in himself. I kept walking until I reached the side of the building farther down from the entrance where there was a butt can. A few smokers gathered around, finishing their cigarettes. No one that I observed paid me any attention.

I continued to watch the activity on the square. I envisioned Hervé walking across the concrete floor of the station, past the news kiosk in the center of the lobby, and proceeding to the ticket windows. Given the hour, there was probably only one attendant. The line could be empty, or there might be twenty people in the queue.

I pulled a pack of freshly purchased cigarettes from my jacket, Gauloises. Hervé's brand. I fumbled with the cellophane and removed a smoke, lit it on the third flick of the lighter, managed a hesitant puff with a strained grimace, and turned back to the square to watch.

For reasons I don't understand, my thoughts turned to Rupert. I recalled the last image I had of him—in his tailored tweed jacket, squared off at the base of the ladder and holding a shotgun like he was out on a quail hunt. I wondered if the men who'd attacked his home had killed him outright or tortured him before they took his life. Perhaps they executed him once to make him talk, and then once more to shut him up forever.

A pang of loss hit me. Our final conversation allowed me to see past the deception, but I regretted that I never really knew the man. I would have enjoyed one last cup of tea and conversation with my teacher, if for nothing else than to ask why—to really ask why.

My phone vibrated in my pocket and I clumsily transferred the smoke to my other hand. I pulled out the phone and read the text: *Done*.

Hervé had bought the tickets and was on his way out.

I put my phone away and stubbed out the unsmoked cigarette.

Hervé then busted out through the entrance doors, his face unrevealing, but his eyes looking at everyone and everything. He approached me and asked if I could spare a fag. I offered the pack, and when Hervé returned it, he included the two tickets in the exchange.

"Merci beaucoup. Bon courage," my old friend offered. Then he walked off as easy as that. We'd already said our goodbyes at the house before we split into our respective positions. This adieu was all business.

I looked at my watch and saw it was 21:37. We had eighteen minutes until our train departed, which was plenty of time to get aboard, settle in, and snap open a magazine for a quick read.

I was about to head inside the station until my phone vibrated again, freezing me mid-step.

I wasn't expecting a text. Hervé was gone and Adeline should be waiting for me on a bench inside.

I hastily looked at the screen and the words that appeared made me lose my breath: *They're here.*

CHAPTER 43

Faust raced down the motorway in the Audi sedan. The speedometer hovered at 193 km/h. Every time he passed a car it was as if they were sitting still.

The phone mounted on the dash lit up, and he reached to answer it. "What do you have?"

"There's only one more train to Paris this evening," said a man's voice.

"The others?"

"Caen at 2225, Nantes 2240, Toulouse 2242, Marseille 2251."

Faust calculated the approximate travel times in his head. "Is that it?"

"Yes, Mein Herr. Until 0633 tomorrow morning."

"Any sign of them?"

"Negative, but we haven't been able to search the trains yet."

"Quickly. Call in the teams."

Faust hung up before the man on the other end could respond. He knew where Dresden and Parker were going, but he needed to find them before it was too late. He was running out of time. Everything the Executive had set in motion, everything he'd planned for, was about to start.

Faust reached for the onboard GPS and typed in "Zurich." The navigation system rerouted him and said it would take seven hours and thirteen minutes to reach his destination.

He'd make it in five and a half.

He turned his attention back to the road and saw the on-ramp for the A10. He took the turn, increasing his speed through the bend. Then he dialed another number.

CHAPTER 44

My body tightened with every one of my senses, every muscle on edge. I stepped back against the building, feeling for Rupert's journal in my pocket while gripping my phone.

With my heart thumping, I scanned the square and the front of the train station. A pack of teenage boys were carousing down a side street. An old man with a gray beard was paying his bill at a curbside café. A woman was cussing out her lover. And to my relief, Hervé was out of sight. I prayed he'd done as he'd been instructed: *get out of the city and take a long vacation to the other side of the country.*

Still, I sent him a single text: *Sail.* It meant something had gone wrong—disappear.

A tight moment passed with me still observing the mass of casual chaos around me, not knowing what I was looking for, only that I'd know it when I saw it. Or at least I hoped I'd see it. Then my phone vibrated again.

Another text from Adeline: *North side entrance.*

Recognition was instant. There was a side entrance to the terminal, not widely known. Only local travelers getting off a train and heading to the east side of the city would use it. It was near the industrial end of the tracks and the entrance wasn't marked. Most people wouldn't think to go that way if they didn't already know the entrance was there. But I did.

I responded: *Moving.*

I took another look around—nothing.

Where were they? There had to be a team. Or did they only send one guy into the terminal, the others perched in a perimeter, maybe observing from a distance? Maybe the spotter scope was already on me, watching me fumble with my phone and smoke like a dipstick teenager, now with a rancid shit-taste in my mouth.

I flexed my fingers and took a deep breath. I was tired of running, always feeling like the Executive was about to crash on top of me. Adeline and I needed to get more than just a step ahead—we needed an advantage. This cat and mouse nonsense was driving me nuts and making me jump at shadows. I had to get it under control otherwise there'd be no happy ending with me going back to my books and willful ignorance. But an *advantage*—I hadn't a clue what that looked like.

Screw it.

I walked around the corner of the station, heading east down Rue Édouard Vaillant, the same road Hervé had come up. The street was empty, and the bustle of the square hushed with the darkness that ruled this part of the city.

I moved deliberately down the sidewalk, peering into every shadow, listening to every sound. The façade of the station was to my right, and closed kiosks and empty parking strips were to my left. There was a man and a woman over a hundred yards away on the other side of the street, and a single compact car turned off onto a side street. There was no other sign of life.

It took me forty-three seconds to reach the side entrance, which was tucked around the gray wall of the station and obscured from the road. I slowed before making the final turn.

Here we go . . .

As I came around the corner, there was a massive train in front of me, the passenger cars colored green, the lights off inside. To the left was the industrial yard of the station—tracks side by side, gravel, electrical boxes, control terminals. To my right, heading toward the public portion of the station, Adeline leaned casually against the wall.

"Anyone follow you?" she asked.

"How the hell should I know," I blurted. "What's going on?"

"It's the guy from the club."

"Sanders? The MI5 agent?"

Adeline shook her head. "One of the other ones. He showed up at the departures board five minutes ago."

"Only him?"

"Not sure. Can't tell from here."

I pulled out the tickets. "We're on Voie H." I knew the track was on the other side of the terminal, as did Adeline from the look on her face. "How crowded is it out there?" I asked.

"Not much. It's late."

I thought about exiting the terminal and walking around to the far side of the station, but that would mean we'd have to cross the square. I wasn't sure if there was an entrance over there, either.

"Our train leaves in nine minutes," I said. "You think we can make it without him spotting us?"

Adeline shrugged and let a hardened frown consume her. "I'll walk on your right. You put your arm around me. We'll have a chance if he's focused on the main entrance."

I nodded and we started walking up the side of the terminal, the exterior wall to our right and a train to our left. It served as a barrier between us and whoever was out in the main hall. I then put my arm around Adeline and pulled her close as I would an affair. We fell easily into step.

As we neared the front of the platform, the noise of the terminal grew louder. Voices echoed throughout the cavernous space that rose over three stories, with pigeons nesting in the rafters and crapping on the people below. An old man stood in front of a train's engine reading a magazine but didn't bother to look up when we sauntered past. A young couple nuzzled on a bench, probably thinking romance was still worth the effort.

I could nearly see the entire lobby. There were two kiosks in the center of the hall that contained a newsstand with refreshments and a rental car and travel office. The ticket windows were on the other side of the terminal, a little café on the opposing wall. A few aged men and women smoking and drinking espresso were sitting in the typical aluminum chairs found on almost all of Europe's café patios. A group of teenagers crowded around a large piece of cardboard. They were jamming to *Rage Against the Machine* while one of them did a modern form of break dancing, jumping and spinning to the heavy beat of the music.

And like the appearance in a movie reel, I spotted the man from the club. It was the bigger one—*Cargo Pants*—the one who looked like the muscle rather than the brains. He was standing in front of the ticket windows and talking on his phone, watching the main entrance.

But now having spotted him, I immediately feared the ones I didn't see, and I kept searching for his confederates. I looked into corners, around pillars, and scanned faces. My heart raced and I could almost hear the beats.

Adeline pulled herself closer and spoke into my ear. "See him?"

"Uh-huh," I uttered.

"Keep going," she urged.

We continued past the train platforms, the walkways stretching down the terminal into the darkness outside. A child, no more than two years old, was running in circles and giggling while his mother tried to grab his arm. A father loaded down with luggage called to them to hurry up. They were in front of Voie C, and the platform sign said *Caen*.

I looked at the family again and wished they would get away, board their train, get clear—safe. They had no idea the danger swirling around them. The Executive was here, and they wouldn't hesitate to kill. No more innocents, I thought.

I looked over Adeline's head, close enough to smell her shampoo, and spotted Cargo Pants. He was still talking on the phone, animated now, but seeming to listen more than speak.

Without thinking, I sped up. I felt an earnestness coursing through me, a desire to get out of sight. But Adeline held me back, and she was right. We had to appear undisturbed despite feeling anything but.

We crossed in front of Voie F. The train was large and clamoring, the engine popping and clicking as the operators went through their last checks. The platform sign said *Paris*. It would depart in two minutes. Eight more feet and we would turn down the length of the platform where we could board.

I glanced again toward the ticket windows and departures board. Cargo Pants was still there, still on the phone. Thank God.

But where were the others? They had to be here?

Adeline and I made the last turn and headed toward the entrance to the first car. We fell out of step for a moment, stumbling into each other. When we regained our rhythm, we reached the passenger car's steps.

I ushered Adeline aboard and then grabbed hold of the handles myself. I chanced one more look toward the front of the station, trying to catch a final glimpse of Cargo Pants, but he was gone. No one was standing by the departures board.

I leaped into the car and met Adeline by the luggage racks. "I don't see him. I think he moved."

"Where?" asked Adeline, her eyes searching the faces of the few passengers already aboard settling into their seats.

"No idea," I breathed.

"Come on. Farther back," she said.

We passed through first class, a dining compartment, and then reached the bulk of the economy cars, but we kept going. Adeline whispered to keep moving until we were near the end. If we needed to get off the train and make a break for it, better to do it in the industrial area. It was darker and there were more places to hide.

We finally reached a car with only three other passengers and found two seats on the opposite side of the platform. The train would depart any minute. We sat, both acutely aware of every sound the train made and the muffled echoes from the terminal's intercom system.

Then came the sound of someone bounding up the metal steps into the train compartment.

I leaned in close to Adeline and, through the seats, I watched the front of the car.

Cargo Pants appeared sweating and sucking in air but stopped before coming all the way into the cabin. He was on the phone again, but he didn't look in our direction. He appeared scattered, glancing out the windows, at his phone, down the aisle, and in every other direction but never long enough to actually see anything.

I felt Adeline hold her breath, and I realized I was holding mine, too. It was like time had stopped and I was pinned to the seat with nothing to do but sit dumbly and wait for Cargo Pants to look me dead in the eye.

Then Cargo Pants turned and disappeared into the luggage space.

"What the hell?" I uttered.

Adeline shook her head just slightly. "Bend down. Stay here," she whispered.

"What're you doing?"

"Shhh."

I watched as Adeline peeked through the seats in front of us. She then looked out into the aisle. Staying low, she leaned across the aisle and into the other seats. Around the cushions she peered out the window, I assumed trying to get a view of the platform.

The train shuddered, and I felt it begin to roll backward.

Adeline looked over at me and smiled, and she fell back into her chair. An invisible weight seemed to come off her. "He's gone. I saw him walk off."

"You're sure?"

She nodded, tucking deeper into her seat.

I wanted to laugh out loud, all the intensity of the last few moments hanging inside me like a bolt of electricity looking for a point of release to the ground, but I refrained, instead taking a deep breath and sitting back next to Adeline, my head inches from hers. I didn't know what to say. We'd made it!

I turned to face Adeline expecting her to be reveling in a similar state, but my mood collapsed when I saw her expression. She was staring straight ahead but not in focus, as if looking through the seat in front of her, her gaze far away. Without a word, she tilted her head back and closed her eyes, succumbing to the rhythm of the train.

"You can't fall asleep, Adeline," I said. "Alfred—what the hell?"

Adeline's eyes opened but she didn't look at me. "I've known about Alfred for the past three years. I just didn't believe it until now."

CHAPTER 45

FRANCE

I gaped at Adeline, bewildered and shocked, while she stared straight ahead, unwilling or not caring to look at me. I didn't know if I should reach for her to show her compassion or dig in against another lie. But what came forth was simply, "Please tell me what happened."

"About three years ago, I came across some information about Alfred. I didn't want to believe it—I told you, after my parents died, Alfred became a father figure to me—but I couldn't ignore it."

"What was it?" I asked.

"A source claimed that Alfred was connected to the Executive and that he was complicit in the murder of my parents."

"I thought you said they died of natural causes?"

"Natural . . . Right," she said just above a whisper. "For most of my life, that's what I believed. I came home from uni on a warm day in April. We were supposed to go to the beach for the weekend, to our cottage in Whitby. I still have it, actually, similar to your villa, I suspect," she said with a mournful smile. "My father and I, Marty, we were going to run through the surf and skip rocks. And for weeks leading up to the trip, my mother, Betts, she'd been raving about the fresh fish she would eat. Every meal if she could.

"Instead, I found them in bed. They weren't moving, their eyes closed, as if they'd been asleep. But they were dead. A gas leak, they said—faulty pipes. The flat had been built before the war. These things happen, they said. Those *they* people." Adeline looked up at the ceiling and I thought I saw the threat of a tear at the corner of her eye. "But it wasn't a faulty pipe. They were murdered."

"My God. Why?" I asked. "Was your family connected to the Executive, like mine?"

"No. It wasn't like that."

"You're sure?"

"Absolutely. But they were a threat in the most unsuspecting way."

I touched Adeline's hand as I would a cousin or a sister, and she squeezed mine back.

"My father had been a policy man for immigration in the Home Office. Every day he wore brown slacks that were always a size too big, along with a white shirt that, without fail, would attract a food stain by nine in the morning. Yet, his appearance was disarming. He was single-handedly pushing through numerous policies that would have overhauled the face of the U.K.'s immigration laws. They would have been so much better than what we have now—greater freedoms and efficiencies but better security, too, deeper and faster screening."

"And Alfred had the Executive kill him for it?"

"I don't know if Alfred gave the order—the source never said—but he knew. I've no doubt, and today's events confirm everything. But what's just as twisted, Alfred was a family friend to my mother and father, and as a little girl, I have vivid memories of him and his wife during the holidays. Dinners and celebrations. And then, with my parents gone, he swoops in."

"Why do you think he did that?"

"Guilt, maybe? To cover it up, to make sure I never learned the truth? I don't know."

"And then he groomed you to join MI6."

"Yes."

"That's even more twisted."

"I guess I could say something like *more than you'll ever know*, but you *do* know."

Our eyes met—the recognition—the understanding—the pain—the confusion—all of it passing between us. Like me, betrayal in the basest sense.

"I'm sorry, Adeline," I said, squeezing her hand again before pulling away to give her space.

She dragged her index finger underneath her eyelid, then turned to look out the window at the world rushing by. Even in the darkness, the night sky illuminated the lush fields and groves with a deep green. The rural landscape had a peacefulness to it, something I let myself dream about for a moment. But we had to continue our conversation.

"Who was the source that told you about Alfred?"

Adeline didn't hesitate. "Three years ago I was on an assignment completely unrelated to the Executive and not under Alfred's purview. A side gig I'd been asked to help out with in Budapest."

"What were you doing there?"

"I was supporting a colleague doing a high-risk meet with a Russian asset. I didn't know the full details—identity, the kind of access, the work—I knew none of it, intentionally so. That's how these things go—keep it compartmented. But all that's irrelevant.

"I was doing countersurveillance on the meet. I had my perch along the route—I was static—and as soon as my guy passed, I thought all was good. Didn't spot anything alerting. All good, right as rain. I lingered for another five minutes or so and was about to leave when a man walking by nudged against my table and, as he excused himself, he dropped something in my bag. And he did all this without ever looking directly at me, then walked off so briskly I couldn't get up after him without making a scene. And I instantly knew, it'd been an intentional encounter."

"What did he put in your bag?"

"A folded-up flyer to a concert for a string quartet that evening. It had a simple handwritten phrase on the inside, *See you there, My Little Isaaca*."

"My little Isaaca?"

"It's what my father used to call me, after Isaac Newton," Adeline said, her voice drifting off.

"Did anyone else call you that or know that name for you?"

"Only those who would have been close to my family."

"Alfred?"

Adeline shrugged. "And others. If someone did their homework, they could have come across it, talked to a neighbor or a cousin or one of my parents' work friends who'd been around when I was little. It wasn't a secret, but not something you could do a web search for."

"Right, but personal enough to grab your attention, as you did with me when you first called."

Adeline allowed a small smile. "Obviously, my interest piqued and the nature of the encounter put me on edge. The connection to my father, that it occurred in the middle of an op. I knew whatever was going on, whoever it was, they knew intimate details about me and they knew how to find me even though I'd taken precautions to go unnoticed—a load of tosh all around."

"What'd you do?"

"What else could I do? I went to the concert."

"Alone?"

"Of course."

"Why?"

"My gut told me that's how this needed to be. Alfred had trained me not to trust anyone or anything, so a part of me was concerned about revealing the encounter with my superiors until I knew more."

"Geez, Adeline. Well, what happened?"

"Another signal to meet after the concert."

"Right," I said with a huff. "Did you at least get a look at the guy?"

"Gal. It was a woman. And no, a second cutout."

I exhaled, trying to keep up with everything I was hearing. "What do you mean, *cutout*? And why the instructions to go here and then go there?"

"Standard tradecraft. Whoever was behind this, they wanted to observe me to make sure I was clean. So, just like the op I'd been sent to Budapest to support, where I was watching things from the background to make sure my guy wasn't being tailed, they were doing that to me. Telling me to go here and go there so they could see if I had watchers on me. And I say *cutout* because of what I learned later. At the moment, however, I assumed it was a crew working together like I had with my team. Send this person in to make contact or give instructions while the others waited in the wind. But as it turned out, each link in the chain didn't know about the other. One man was orchestrating it all."

"Who was he?"

"I'm getting there."

"Okay. What happened next?"

"I was supposed to leave Budapest that night to go home to London. Instead, I checked out of my hotel and into another, then woke up the next morning at five and went to Gellért Hill, an expansive park that overlooks the Danube with numerous trails and cozy hideaways. The instructions said to go for a jog—a nice way to limit what I had with me and make it difficult for anyone to follow me without also putting on their trainers."

"And you went along with all this?"

"I knew what they were doing. If they'd wanted to hurt me or kidnap me, there were much easier ways to go about it. So yeah, I went along. They were clearly professionals and they were taking extensive precautions, more than the typical bump from a rival service. I needed to know what this was all about. So, along the trail, there was an overlook with a man dressed like an artist with a small sketch pad. And since it was a rather cold morning, he had his face covered with a scarf."

"So you couldn't identify him."

"Precisely."

"Another cutout, another set of instructions?"

"No. This was the man I was supposed to meet. When he spoke, I could tell he was older, and he had a definite accent. Eastern European, I suspected."

"What'd he say?"

"He told me he knew I was investigating the Executive and that he had information that could help me. But he didn't give it to me. Rather, he said to beware of those closest to me."

"That's it? Beware of those closest to you?"

"Yes. He said he'd contact me with information about the core members of the Executive and their intentions but not to tell anyone, including my boss, Alfred, who he named. Then he walked away."

"Did you follow him?"

"The thought crossed my mind, but again, I knew I was dealing with a professional. He'd taken measures for what I could only suspect was a secure meet with no unwanted observers. With all that together, I wasn't going to blow it by running after him like a scorned mistress. No, I understood there was more going on and I needed it to play out. He'd been too specific in the right ways to convince me of that—my father, the Executive, Alfred—I wanted to know what information he had."

"And how did it play out?"

"Three months later, I found a tiny package in my gym locker back in London. It contained a thumb drive with documents making loose connections between historical and recent events and individuals I suspected were members of the Executive."

"What events?"

"Things I've already mentioned. Political movements, elections, new bills. Nothing over the top, a lot of what I already knew. But again, what was unnerving was how well it aligned with the gaps I had in the Executive's activities, as if this man was reading my files and plugging the holes for me."

"Establishing his credibility."

"Precisely. He was proving the integrity of his information so I would believe him."

"Because of what he knew about your parents and Alfred," I remarked, following the train.

"Yes, but that came over a year later and after he provided more small yet illuminating pieces of the puzzle. Then, the mysterious man and I met again. Similar protocols—multiple cutouts and his face obscured. He also gave me a means to contact him—a number with instructions. And this time I asked him who he was and whom he worked for."

"Did he tell you?"

Adeline snorted. "No, except to say that although a government employed him, he no longer worked for them."

"I don't understand."

"He was saying that he was working outside the bounds of his service, just like he had instructed me to. Not rogue, per se, but his own agenda, I believe."

"Off the books?"

"You're learning."

"Still, who do you think it was and why?"

"It could be anyone really—Russia, China, the Israelis—they all possess the wherewithal to do what he did."

"Right. But the connection to your parents?"

"The man I came to refer to as *the Artist* told me that Alfred was connected to the Executive, not necessarily at the top, but without question an active member. He then said that my parents were murdered and Alfred was complicit in their death. He gave me a time-stamped CCTV report of Alfred meeting my parents minutes before their death, and then being on the street as the killers went in."

"Jeezus."

"Yeah."

"What did you do?"

"I told him to fuck off, that it was bullshit. A deep fake. Made up to force me against the wall. My CI instincts kicked in and I smelled a setup. And I left—there was just no way."

"But you knew it was true, didn't you?"

Adeline nodded. "I knew. But I couldn't hear it. I didn't want to hear it. Hell, my investigation into the Executive hadn't been at the top of my list back then, as it was."

"What'd you do?"

"I kept it to myself, tried to verify the CCTV report but couldn't with any certainty. There were anomalies in the official records that told me something was off, but nothing conclusive. No smoking gun, as you Americans say. So I watched. The next time I saw Alfred, everything seemed peachy. Nothing had changed. But I paid attention. And in truth, it wasn't until he sent me to meet you and things went off the rails that his behavior changed.

"Anyway, after that meeting with the Artist, I didn't hear from him again, And when I tried to use the number he gave me—nothing, no response or meet. So, I went about my work. But as you might have guessed, my interest in the Executive grew and Alfred encouraged it, especially in recent months. But still, the Artist stayed away . . . until a few days ago. That's when I found this."

Adeline removed a slip of paper from her pocket. It was folded and creased as if it'd been hiding in there for days. She surrendered it to my outstretched hand and I read the note.

Little Isaaca, Dolos is plotting to assume control of the Executive and he is using you to do it.

"Where did you get this, and who is Dolos?" I asked.

"Dolos is how the Artist refers to Alfred."

"Dolos from Greek mythology?"

"The spirit of trickery. Yes."

"This man, your source, is a curious fellow."

"Yes. When you took your field trip to the archives, when I went to follow you, I found this note on the front seat of the car. Someone must have been watching, to break into the car to put it there knowing only I—and not you—would find it."

"What the fuck . . ."

"Yeah, he's been watching the entire time."

"How did he know about the safe house?"

"Alfred, I suspect."

"So he could have tracked us to Eisengard's, too. And Tours."

"Yes."

"And perhaps on this train right now."

Adeline shrugged once again. "I don't know. It's unnerving, though, to think all this time we've been eluding the Executive, yet this man may have been on us since the beginning, watching."

"Who can do that? We've been staying off the grid, right? MI6, Interpol, the Executive, whoever the fuck else—we've been staying clear as best we can. Yet this man can find us and pass notes in class that the teacher doesn't see? Geez," I said.

"What do you want me to do, William? I'm doing my best to get us through this."

"I want you to stop lying to me. I want you to stop keeping things from me," I said, holding up the note between my fingers and then tossing it back in her lap. "We're in this together. I can't keep finding out about some clue or shred of information after the fact. I mean, what the hell, what if this *Artist* has been on me, too? What else is there, Adeline? What else haven't you told me?"

"This is it, William. This is everything."

"Am I just supposed to believe that? The lies never stop with you, Adeline. From the beginning, there's always one more truth, one more angle, one more layer. I mean, come on."

Adeline lowered her head for a moment, looking into the depths of her lap. Whether it was regret, shame, or remorse, I didn't care. But then she looked up at me, her face at once biting the sadness while also pushing back.

"You think this is easy? There are so many twisted pieces to this whole thing. And I don't always know what's right or wrong, true or false. I just told you that the man who took me in after my parents' death was also an accessory to their murder and part of the group trying to hunt us down. The lies, the falsehoods, the contradictory layers—I'm wading through them, too. I'm not hiding anything from you, William. And maybe I should have shown you the note sooner, but then how would you have behaved in the presence of Alfred, knowing what I suspected? Would you have kept a level head so that Alfred wouldn't have suspected?"

I exhaled, exasperated yet recognizing her rationale. I sat back in my seat and broke Adeline's stare, looking at nothing on the TV screen at the front of the cabin. "Just please don't withhold anything more. You're all I've got in this mess, and I want to trust you."

"You can, William. I'm sorry."

"Right. Sure. So what do we do now? Do we try to make contact with Picasso?"

Adeline shook her head. "No, he knows how to find me—how to find us—but this is all he's done. And I still don't know his ultimate intentions."

"We need to ask him."

"Next time we break for tea, I will."

"Right."

"Look, there's nothing more we can do now. It's plausible that he found us at the safe house, and it's possible he could have traced us to Eisengard's, following Alfred's trail. But we've had a clean break. So, we stick with the plan to go to Zurich and find Bodmer. We keep going."

"Sure," I said, settling into my seat and closing my eyes for a second.

"In the meantime, I'm exhausted and need to get some sleep. So should you," Adeline said.

"Yeah, right."

I opened my eyes and looked over to find Adeline crossing her arms and nestling into her seat. And within seconds, I saw her breathing become rhythmic and her muscles loosen.

But I couldn't sleep, not after everything she'd just told me. I imagined the world of spies and espionage was a convoluted gauntlet for the mind and soul. Lies and deception were everywhere, at times even with your own colleagues, and the idea of truth was a mirage that moved, shimmered, and disappeared.

But my philosophical contemplations soon faded. Something else was tugging at me. Ever since Rupert had put it in my hand, it'd been burning a hole in my pocket and my mind—the journal.

I eased it from the folds of my jacket, feeling the leather binding that was worn with age, the pages yellow and brittle. I examined it as I would any historical document, wondering what secrets it held. Would there be answers to my questions inside? It was my past, what had been hidden from me, what I had to know, or so I thought. So I hoped.

I opened it to the first page.

April 12th, 1871, Strasbourg, German Empire

"I am doing a great work, so that I cannot come down . . ."

CHAPTER 46

The staircase was a concrete tunnel that fell away into the black. The only illumination came from the motion sensor lights positioned every three meters. If one looked down or back, the darkness was the same—absolute.

Every time Sofia came this way, about midway down—five minutes into it—she would wonder what would happen if she slipped. How long would it take her to reach the bottom, and would she stay conscious long enough to know her life was over?

Probably not. The descent was near vertical, or at least it felt that way. Death would be a combination of free fall coupled with skull-cracking collisions against the unyielding steps.

But other than that, Sofia was quite taken with this facility. It was her little project.

Behind Sofia were five men, and she could hear their tentative footsteps as they followed her. All of them gripped the metal railing, their breathing labored. For all but one, it was their first time here.

One of the Germans was named Elbert Lecter—a forgettable man—but a member of the European Commission. The Frenchman was Tiago DeForest, a socialite and senior representative in the European Parliament. Sebastien Maes was a lawyer; his sway among

Belgian politicians considerable. Then there was the general—ramrod Parson.

And lastly there was Thomas Kaulitz, the owner and CEO of Verbindung Industries, who built this place.

"How far down are we going?" asked Lecter.

"One hundred sixty-nine meters," Sofia answered. "The equivalent of forty-two stories beneath the surface."

"Mon Dieu," DeForest said. "Are we so barbaric that we cannot install an elevator?"

Sofia smiled to herself but did not respond. There was an elevator, of course, but she'd chosen to take the stairs intentionally—this was theater to her—and she'd withheld a great many other details about this place as well. No need to spoil the surprise.

When they finally reached the bottom, the six of them were greeted by row upon row of metal shelving units. They hummed with the sound of whirring computer servers that had tiny white, green, and red diodes flashing as they processed bits of data at speeds beyond human comprehension. The only overhead lights that were on were in their immediate vicinity. It gave the impression of a vast warehouse.

"What is this place?" asked Maes.

"Gentlemen, this is one of three facilities. The other two are in England and on the East Coast of the United States," said Sofia.

Still with her back to the men, she began walking along the wall, activating more lights as she went. She moved slowly, purposely, allowing each pop of a new light to bring into focus another few feet of the facility.

"And what is the purpose of these *facilities*?"

"If you'll be patient, I'm about to explain. But first I must show you the magnitude of what this project entails." Sofia reached a break between the rows of servers. "Thomas, would you mind."

"Of course," the German tech mogul replied. There was a panel on the wall, and he turned the lever marked MAIN. There was a loud clunk, followed by a high-speed hum.

The other four men muttered in astonishment as the bright white fluorescent lighting lit up the entire space. They could see that the center walkway went on well over the length of a soccer pitch, and the rows of servers extended equally to the right and left. The ceiling was at least ten meters high, giving the space a power that took everyone's breath away, even Sofia's.

"What is this place?" repeated Maes.

"A data storage and processing farm," replied Thomas.

"A what?"

"Gentlemen," began Sofia. "Thanks to DE-CIX, more internet traffic passes through Frankfurt than anywhere else in the world. That traffic is information, and the control of information is power. This facility taps directly into the DE-CIX internet exchange point, and since this and the other two facilities came online, the Executive has been using AI to scrape, collect, catalog, and store nearly every bit of data that is shared on the web. Social media, financial transactions, commerce, correspondence between governments—the scope of what we've obtained is titanic."

"Who knows of this?" asked Lecter, turning slowly around, his mouth agape.

"The Executive's current board, and now you."

"What about the people who built it?"

"Done in stages, compartmented, thanks to Thomas and his companies. And our system managers are few because the power of what we have is within the programming itself. The software catalogs by source, type, and genre."

"Who developed it?"

Sofia smiled. "Three teams. One comprised of developers who would have been wonderful associates for the likes of Julian Assange or Anonymous. There was another team who would fit well in America's NSA or Britain's GCHQ."

"And the third?" asked DeForest.

"One team to integrate them all."

"But once you have the data, what do—"

"Excellent question," said Sofia, cutting him off. "The analysis for macro trends and movements is done elsewhere. Again, AI software looking for specific target points. We can predict the mood of the world before it happens." Sofia grinned. "We are monitoring the pulse of populations."

"You can't be serious," injected DeForest. "No one has the capacity to do what you claim. I don't care how many of these *facilities* you have."

Sofia responded with a bland voice. "Why do you think that?"

"C'est impossible. There's too much and the world is too unpredictable. Just look at the past five years."

"Excellent idea. Let's do that."

"What?"

"As you say. Look at the past five years. What's happened?" asked Sofia, leveling her eyes at DeForest.

"Events that no one could predict, of course. Strongmen who've been in power for decades—gone. Financial powerhouses falling from on high. And don't get me started on American politics. No one could have predicted any of this. Yet, you think watching the internet—"

"I believe that's her point," General Parson said, interrupting the Frenchman.

"What are you saying?" asked Lecter.

"The general is right," Sofia said. "The world is volatile because we've made it so."

Sofia's guests—except Parson, too cocky to be wowed—peeled their eyes from the massive space before them and directed their attention at her.

"Let me start from the beginning. When the Wall fell in eighty-nine, the West suffered an identity crisis. Without a main enemy, no one knew what to do. Politicians, diplomats, generals—they were at a loss over who was *us*, who was *them*, and what the state of the world was.

"The first Gulf War was a joke—more of a team-building exercise for the international community than a real crisis. And the wars in the Balkans were a circus; the once great powers of Europe quibbled and dawdled while thugs marshaled armies under national banners to exterminate their enemies.

"Then al-Qaida and bin Laden's network appeared. It was a blessing. The West finally realized that it's *us* or *them*. The idea that we are all equal was put to the test and truth prevailed. And the best way to ensure the prosperity of *us* is to keep all of *them* out of our respective countries. Follow the natural logic, and our national goals will be met and our economic, diplomatic, and military strength returned.

"So, we began an experiment. In the digital age, humans are quick to believe what they read on the internet or see on TV, and it has been proven that social media has made us less open to diversity rather than more accepting. People gravitate to others who think like them and feed their own beliefs—especially those who say the things they are thinking but are too afraid to say themselves. Plus, people don't like to read perspectives they don't agree with or that discredit what they consider to be right. It's uncomfortable, and very few people choose to be uncomfortable.

"Therefore, we theorized we could deliver messaging across multiple platforms—Twitter, nightly news, podcasts, deep fakes, business sites, blogs—to shape public opinion." Sofia turned to stroll down the main walkway, letting her fingers slip delicately over the server racks.

"The Arab Spring was our first attempt. We flooded social media with calls to action, gave outlets to groups whose voices were being shut down by the government, and made sure the world saw everything in real time. When you think about it, it wasn't that hard—the Arab populations were easily agitated with the right tune and the right setting. They've nothing to lose. Within two years the Middle East was turned upside down—dictators deposed, civil wars raging, governments on their heels."

"You're saying that the Executive caused that?" asked DeForest with incredulity.

Sofia ignored the question. "Our next endeavor was more challenging because we were dealing with an educated population. In 2008 the world witnessed Barack Obama harness the power of social media to become the first Black president of the United States. We needed to prove we could counteract that movement by bringing the antithesis of Obama to power."

"I don't believe this."

"Did you ever get the sense that what was happening on the news, articles in the press, viral messages on Facebook, was surreal? Like the world had gone mad and the clowns were in charge?"

All but the general shrugged.

"No one wants to read the boring truth. The more sensational, the more widely read, the more it's believed. And once people believed they were victims and everyone who was different from them was to blame, those screaming the loudest got the support. Blind, undying, mindless support. It's a tried and true technique."

"That's a fascinating tale," said Maes, "but I'd rather skip the lecture and get to the point. Why are we here?"

Sofia smiled at the Belgian. "Each of you are powerful voices in the EU, and you're also about to be commissioned as the newest members of the Executive's board. Thus, you're in a unique position to bring about the weakening of the European Union so that our national interests can fill the void, and once again, the real powers of the European people will come to the forefront."

"That's a bold undertaking, Frau König," remarked Lecter with a laugh. "The Brits may have gone it alone, but the mainland is—and always has been—something different."

"True, but conditions are unique. Think," she said. "Hatred of immigrants is on the rise, populist movements are assuming power, our old enemies in Asia are resurfacing, terrorist attacks are becoming more and more indiscriminate, and Russia is invading its neighbors every five or six years. The Continent is on the brink."

"So you say."

"I do say, and in the next twenty-four hours a series of events will commence that will usher in a new era."

"What kind of events?"

"They'll be unmistakable, and when they happen, there will be a calling for a crackdown and a return to sovereign nation-states and a reassertion of European preeminence in all things. When this happens, you will then take these actions."

Sofia removed four tablets from her handbag and gave one to each of the men. They began scrolling through the material, their eyes growing wide in astonishment.

CHAPTER 47

FRANCE

Our train cut through the night at 250 km/h. The outside was nothing but a blur of darkness, as if we were skimming across the earth's surface but not a part of the world and its disarray. I felt momentarily detached from everything that had been going on, perhaps even secure while inside this screaming bullet of steel and synthetics. It allowed me to focus in a way I hadn't been able to in days.

I shifted in my seat and looked down at the book in my hands, its worn leather binding demanding I read what was inscribed on the pages inside.

Cracking the cover and turning to the first page, the journal of the Eisengard family opened with:

April 12th, 1871, Strasbourg, German Empire

"I am doing a great work, so that I cannot come down."
Nehemiah 6:3

This morning the eleven of us met at the Strasbourg Cathedral. I'd been to the imperial city once before, hunting with Graf Schumer. But this gathering was of a different nature. The gentleman who called us together for this event was an Englishman by the name of Reginald Waters, a man I had met years ago during negotiations for mineral rights in the southern regions of the Dark Continent.

We were an eclectic group: Germans, British, French, Dutch, Austrian, Belgian—the purest of peoples in intellect and blood. I admit I was hesitant to be in such company given the recent hostilities between France and Prussia—old and new wounds among relations can be problematic. Yet, my fears were soon alleviated.

We are all like-minded and unanimously agreed—we have an opportunity and obligation to ensure that we as Europeans must guarantee the superiority and the power of our nations. And we must do so in spite of the imbeciles who believe they were ordained by God—or worse yet—chosen by the people. Science and philosophy are all that matter, and these disciplines have proven there are those who are fit to rule and those who should be subjugated.

This day, the Strasbourg Executive has come into being and will work to further the realization of Nature's intended order via our Covenants.

As I continued reading the handwritten passages and turning the century-old pages, I found entries of a similar quality—brief and pointed—authored by Bernard Eisengard, one of the Executive's founding members. As Rupert had suggested with his tap of the finger, I expected to see the *Covenants*—a list or something, like a charter or grandiose statement. But there was no list or statement, simply an amorphous reference.

Rather, I found an eyewitness history. According to Bernard, the group had started slowly, first establishing its network of influencers across the Continent. It was the Gilded Age, and the realm of finance was a powerful force in the minds of imperialists. Warfare and methods of state control were evolving as well, and the intersection between the generals and industrialists prospered. The group aimed to create political, economic, and military links throughout Europe and beyond, and by the 1880s these webs were established.

Then the Executive became more assertive in a tangible way.

January 26, 1881, Vichy, France

The Kanzler opened the Summit this morning, the Transvaal Rebellion of most prominent discussion. As an Englishman, the Kanzler had many questions for our Dutch members; he was curious to know the intentions of the Boers in the South African Republic. Hubert Mohren—a gregarious individual I do not particularly care for—spoke the loudest, but it was clear his influence over the Dutch farmers was limited.

Although there were heated exchanges at times, a consensus was eventually reached. As long as Mohren could guarantee the Boers were committed to maintaining Nordic superiority, the wealth and power of the southern coast would remain in European hands.

This was what mattered, we all agreed. And the British were well occupied a good distance north in Rhodesia. The Kanzler was intimately familiar with Mr. Rhodes' ambitions there, and assured the Board of his intentions as well.

Nevertheless, it is apparent the Powers of Europe will continue to rub against each other in the coming years. We must be mindful of this if we are to achieve our ambitions.

* * *

March 27, 1896 Strasbourg, German Empire

A new Kanzler assumed the post today. I say that it is a calling, and only for those who possess unmatched dedication and belief— and we are moving in a new direction.

Whereas in the past our purpose was to manage our respective countries to ensure our great Work continues, he asserts it is imperative that the weaknesses within our domains are not allowed to corrupt the pure peoples.

He believes nationalism is the key—the fanatical belief in the greatness of one's own country. Foreigners, assimilated or not, particularly of the inferior breeds, are an antipathy to this, and must be purged or relegated to a lesser strata.

Although this new ideology for national strength may put our respective homelands at odds some times, it is far better for the good of the Continent and the world. With the need to compete, it will make our peoples stronger. The Kanzler is an admirer of Bismarck and his view on the balance of power, and I daresay I agree with him.

*　　*　　*

May 2, 1898, London, England

The Kanzler is an aggressive one. As a Marshall in the German land forces, he has dispatched agents to Spain and Cuba to engineer a war with the Americans. His goal: spark their imperial destiny.

As a former slave-holding society, America is no stranger to our perspectives, and there are like-minded men in Washington and New York who need to join us. The Kanzler's agents will encourage a fight with the Americans to draw them into battle over Spain's weaker colonies: Cuba and the Philippines. By doing so, the Americans will have no choice but to assert their control over what is in their sphere of influence.

Given his family's status within American diplomacy, Senior Board member Heinrich Dresden will lead this effort. He has a brilliant perspective on affairs of state and firmly believes there are those in America who desire to take a more assertive role in the management of the western hemisphere and those peoples within it. He has already begun shaping national opinion by the use of publishers Joseph Pulitzer and W. Randolph Hearst.

For the next fifty pages, I continued to read the inner thoughts of the Eisengard family, their opinions and fears, their view of the Executive and its dealings. I felt as if I were hearing their voices—old, dry, passionate, disturbing.

And every so often, I would come across references to my family like in the entry above. I found myself seeking out any fragment of information I could find. I yearned to know who my forefathers had been—what they had done.

Yet the thought chilled me—to know the horror of my family's past.

Reading on, I learned that, in hindsight, the Eisengards regretted the fanatical push for nationalism at the turn of the century and it proved costly with the impact of the Great War. The conflict should have been brief, meant to knock the unruly Serbs back in line and frustrate the imperial blunderings of the Tsar. Instead, it proved catastrophic for the powers of Europe when the monarchs allowed their pride to prevail. Four years of slaughter resulted.

The rise of the Nazis was viewed more positively until, once again, war engulfed Europe in 1939. The Nazis perfected racial science and ruthlessly executed control of their society in the 1930s, and they effectively gained the support of like-minded movements in England and France, even as far away as the eastern United States. But Hitler proved grotesquely irrational and overextended Germany's war machine.

There were divisions within the Executive about how to handle the opportunities presented by a world at war. On one side were the hard-liners, affiliates of Himmler committed to the Final Solution and perpetual war. Others believed the Nazi and Vichy regimes should not be so bold—great change comes in time, not overnight.

Neither faction in the Executive came out on top. The destruction of the Nazis in 1945 shook the Executive to its foundation.

In the decades that followed, the Executive withdrew. It took nearly forty years, watching the West and East push, pull, and threaten each other—with the loom of nuclear annihilation hanging over everything—for the successive board members to reformulate a new strategic intent.

Coming to the final passages, I paused to wipe my brow. Rupert had written these final entries, and I felt my chest tighten.

My father, Karl Dresden, was the senior board member who reinvigorated the Executive after the Berlin Wall fell in 1989. A decade later, he cemented his vision when he became Kanzler. Rather than force populations to adhere to the Executive's ideals as the Nazis and other fascist regimes had, he believed they needed to covertly influence perspectives.

He encouraged backroom deals to exploit the resources of the Middle East and Africa, while simultaneously encouraging the influx of arms to the regions. Karl Dresden's view: *with a lack of will on the part of the international community, let them slaughter each other through genocide and unsolvable territorial disputes.*

Karl also sponsored a new board member named Sofia König, a woman Rupert described as someone with a darkness in her character that he could not fully comprehend. He likened her to the psychopaths who had engineered the Final Solution and—

A flash of light broke my concentration. I looked up at the television screen at the end of the car. It was a news broadcast, the ticker at the bottom of the screen saying that a bomb had gone off in Paris.

No longer dozing, Adeline fixated on the television, too.

A large explosion occurred at a political rally near the Arc de Triomphe. The National Front, a right-wing political party, had been hosting a rally when an explosion tore through the edge of the crowd. Initial reports indicated that over one hundred people were dead or wounded.

It had all been caught on video, one of the media outlets having had a camera trained on the blast site. They kept replaying the clip over and over—a flash of light followed by a ghastly image of flying debris and bodies—almost too graphic for TV.

The television switched to another location, this one just beyond the unfolding chaos. Emergency crews were rushing about in the background. Men and women with torn clothes—blackened from burns—were running and stumbling.

But the camera focused on a woman in a dark suit with styled brunette hair. The ticker identified her as Marguerite Alliotté, the leader of the National Front.

"... a cowardly act by Islamic terrorists. They have infiltrated our society through the openness of our immigration policies and our misguided generosity for refugees. But these invaders coming to France—they do not belong here. This is not their home, and they come here to drain our society and harm our children, our way of life. We must crack down and stop the infection of our lands. And if the politicians in Brussels will not act, then we must leave this *Union*. The safety and survival of our society depend on it ..."

I absently closed the journal in my hands, my gaze still on the television.

Fragments of doubt cut through my mind. Islamic terrorists? They were easy to blame, and perfect to incite the nationalists as well as the political moderates. For nearly two decades it had been a rallying cry.

Yet something wasn't right. It was too . . . convenient.

CHAPTER 48

Adeline and I never made it to Paris. We got off in Orléans and found a bar a few blocks away from the train station. Although Orléans was another one of France's historic cities, saved by Jeanne d'Arc in 1432 as well as providing the namesake of New Orleans, this establishment was a place where men went to get drunk. And the few women who ventured inside either drank as hard as the men or plied another trade.

This was not an establishment I cared to be in, yet oddly enough, I did not feel out of place. Rather, the coarse atmosphere seemed apropos of our efforts to stay hidden on what some may consider the edge of civilized society where laws, rules, and norms are only applicable if convenient. Immediate survival is what matters; everything else ventures into the muck.

After a quick survey of the room, Adeline and I sat at a table in the back, the other patrons too interested in their individual silence to take any notice of us. At about one in the morning, a man slid off his stool and shuffled to the door, fumbling with a set of keys. He looked to be over sixty but was probably in his mid-forties, weathered from drink and tobacco and ill-advised choices.

We followed the poor soul to his car, which was down the road tucked in an alley. He fingered the key chain searching for the right one, turning to catch the moonlight as if it would make everything come clear.

I was the one who approached him, asking to buy the car for three times its value. It was a Citroën, a hatchback of sorts, but the man didn't like my offer, eyeing me unsteadily and wagging his finger in my face. He scowled and tilted forward, perhaps to balance as the earth rotated or to intimidate me, but he was of no threat.

Fortunately—or regrettably—I honestly don't know which anymore, Adeline and I had discussed what to do if the man reacted this way.

A queasiness settled in my stomach and then I knocked him out cold with one punch, my fist connecting solidly with the man's jaw. The old man sprawled sloppily, his weary limbs tucking around him like a child. For an uncomfortable second, I stared at the man on the ground, shame flooding through me, aghast at what I'd just done. Yes, I'd been in fights before, and only a few days ago I'd shot and killed a man—someone who was also trying to kill me and Adeline— but this was different. With premeditation, I'd assaulted an innocent person—I wondered who I had become and I hated it.

Adeline nudged past me, bent down, and stuffed the cash in the man's pocket. Maybe that would make his face a little less sore when he finally woke up and found he was a few thousand euros richer. She then propped him up on the back steps of a shop. Someone would stumble across the poor soul in a couple of hours if he didn't come to on his own accord first.

Adeline and I wasted no time. I suppressed whatever guilt I was feeling and jumped in the car beside her. We drove off, the interior of the vehicle smelling like wet fabric and stale cigarettes. On the outskirts of town, we swapped license plates with another lucky vehicle, just in case the unconscious man in the alley decided to report his car stolen, and we kept going.

This time I was behind the wheel, and Adeline and I didn't talk much this go-around except for me sharing snippets of what I'd read in Rupert's journal. She said she'd read it herself later, then tucked in against the door to nod off for the first bit of the trip.

A good time later, we switched out and it was my turn to doze, which I did. Days of little sleep and constant stress will do that— you hit a wall and once you feel halfway secure, a wave descends and you can't keep your eyes open. What I remember most was the rumble of our tires over the increasingly frozen road.

Six hours later we reached Zurich, Switzerland.

*   *   *

We drove partway through Zurich proper before proceeding to the other side of the city to a resort area that overlooked the lake. From another memory of my past life, I knew there would be secluded cabins we could rent. From my description, Adeline seemed to think they would suffice for what we needed to do.

We paid in euros for a few nights' stay, and a mile down a twisty road we found our rustic hideaway down a slope at the end of a sharp curve. The cabin sat nestled between evergreens that softened everything around them, and it had snowed the night before, leaving a white coating over every surface.

Adeline and I trudged through the powder to the front door and went inside. The main room had a sitting area with a fireplace, a kitchen nook, a sofa, and a few chairs. There was one bedroom with a lone bed and a water closet with a tiny shower and sink. All standard mid-grade accommodations.

As expected, Adeline examined the room—the doors, windows, cabinets, dust under the bed—assessing what would be our new base. Her movements were mechanical and thorough, her cold professionalism returned and all traces of the emotional revelation about her parents now tamped down to wherever she suppressed her feelings.

"The room's fine," Adeline said. "Make yourself comfortable. We have a few hours before we need to leave."

"Right," I said, heading toward the kitchen nook to see what supplies we might have.

"If you're making coffee, please make me a cup, too."

"Sure," I said, finding a kettle along with a small container of Nescafé. After filling the kettle and placing it on the stove, I again looked to Adeline who was staring absently out the window. If someone were to snap a picture, the caption could easily describe a romantic holiday inside a cozy cabin with a crackling fire.

For a moment, I wondered if Adeline had ever dated anyone seriously. I'd no doubt she had been on dates, but I had a sense she'd never allowed herself to become serious with anyone, man or woman. The loss of her parents, Alfred's corrupt nurturing, and her work with MI6 made me conclude that she didn't trust anyone with the intimate details of her life. I wondered if she was capable of trusting anyone, even me.

And then, as this random thought about Adeline's love life crossed my mind, traces from our conversation from the night before percolated to the surface and I had to ask, "Was my father involved in your parents' murder?"

"No," Adeline said without hesitation as if expecting the question yet maintaining her gaze out the window. "When I first realized who your father was, believe me, looking for answers to their death was high on my list, but I couldn't find anything. Your father wasn't the Kanzler at the time, and from my understanding of how the Executive operates, many of the senior members act on their own accord in their home countries. He may have known about it. I'm sure he heard about it after the matter. But I don't think he was involved. And at this point, I don't care."

"I beg your pardon?"

Adeline turned to look at me. "You're a good man, William. I don't associate you with your family's past. I may have at one time when I first started looking into you, but I separated who *you are* and who *they were* a long time ago."

"But how can you be sure?"

"When are we ever sure about anything? Math—yes. Physics— yes. That the sun will rise and set and after a few days going the way we have, we're both desperately in need of a shower—yes. But with everything else in life, it's all up to interpretation and perspective and often from where you sit and who you identify with. So, maybe your father did know about it. I couldn't prove it, nor can you prove a negative, and what good would it do for me to fester and stew about your father. He'd done enough elsewhere. And as I told you, Alfred was the main one. If I am to channel anger or sadness or loss or obsessive revenge—he was the one."

I'd stood quietly listening to Adeline speak, and then realized the pot was spitting boiling water out the spout. I grumbled, quickly reaching for the handle and spinning the knob to turn off the burner. I remained silent for another moment before saying, "Right. Sure. I guess I should admire your ability to compartmentalize like that," I acknowledged. "I'm not sure I could."

"It comes with the job. You can't do this work if you can't separate your emotions from objectivity—even if it's cold and sociopathic at times, and even if by all rights you should."

"I think it would cause you to drink."

Adeline pursed her lips. "I think you're right. I'll face my demons later. As you did in your life and as you must do again."

"Yeah," I aired, "I suppose you're right."

"Not right. Nothing's right about any of this."

"So true. So, let me ask you this. If Alfred murdered your parents because of your father's work on immigration, why in the world did he take you in as he did?"

"I've been asking myself that same question for years—hundreds if not thousands of times. *Why.*" Adeline turned from the window and walked over to take the mug of steaming coffee from me. "I suspect that, in some twisted way, he may have been considering whether he could recruit me into the Executive."

"He was grooming you?"

Adeline shrugged. "I have no proof but my own experiences. He undeniably groomed me for a life in the service. *Duty* to a higher calling was always at the forefront of our interactions and was always the often-unspoken foundation of everything. And if you recall that my father was a policy man in the Home Office, it's no real surprise. Duty and service to the Queen, to the country—there was no question for me."

"Right. And if he was indeed grooming you, he could keep his eye on you. And as Rupert said, although not always, there's a hereditary element to the Executive."

"Precisely. He wanted someone loyal to him, and how else to cement loyalty than to shape and manipulate me over a couple of decades. I possessed textbook vulnerabilities for him to work with—tragic loss, a need to please those closest to me, obsessed to do well. I was ripe."

"But you didn't fall for it. I mean, you don't seem to harbor any extremist views, silently wishing Britain would return to its rightful place dominating the rest of the world."

Adeline laughed. "No, but I did get a healthy dose of that from Alfred, but it was subtle. A modern perspective on international relations, you could say. He never came out on the nose with imperialistic views, but he did possess and was not ashamed to suggest that countries like the U.K. and the United States were superior. I viewed it as a modern *white man's burden*."

"Why didn't you fall for it?"

"Alfred wasn't as smart as he thought he was, and I think he misjudged just how close I was to my parents and how deeply their loss was embedded into who I believed myself to be and how I aspired to live my life. And as I go round and round about the Artist's last message, I wonder what Alfred was ultimately up to."

"You mean, was he planning a coup?"

"I don't know. You read the same note as I— *plotting to assume control of the Executive.* There's just so much we don't know about how the Executive operates, and every time we get to talk with someone who might know, who might have answers, the opportunity disappears."

I instantly thought of Rupert. He'd recognized Alfred. He knew about him. They had a history. Rupert had been a part of all this, too. I couldn't forget that, even if the pangs of guilt racked me. He'd sacrificed himself so we could escape. He'd changed, I told myself— that was something. Yet I would never be able to ask him the questions I wanted to. As Adeline said, the answers were out there, but every time we had an opportunity to learn them, we were thwarted.

"William," Adeline said, offering me a forlorn smile. "If we're done cataloging our losses, there's something else I need to show you."

"What?"

She went to her bag and removed a tablet. "While you were dozing in the car, I did a little research."

"While you were driving?"

"Just a little scrolling at speed."

"Geez. All right. What?"

She displayed her tablet for me. "This has all happened in the last twenty-four hours."

"What? What am I looking at?"

"Beyond the bombing at the rally, these are the stories that are trending across all media platforms—social and mainstream."

She scrolled through a series of news sites and blog posts—the headlines were all that mattered. They were all volatile and inflammatory, lashing out against immigrants and refugees.

"This is just the beginning," said Adeline, her voice deadpan.

CHAPTER 49

As a historian, I like to think I know a few things about the past. Some would call it useless knowledge, while others would say it's sage counsel in an out-of-control world. I fall somewhere in between, but like those who study martial arts or those who can speak the made-up languages of a sci-fi TV series, history is my passion because it makes me happy.

Thus, as I took up my position on the street a couple of blocks away from Paradeplatz—the notorious square that served as the center of Swiss banking—of course, the history of Zurich was where my thoughts defaulted. And I do believe these ruminations were relevant.

This city Adeline and I found ourselves in—Zurich—was an old city dating back to the Romans, and it had a fortress-like feel to it, but not in the usual sense. Walls and battlements hadn't protected this city; rather, it was the natural geography that made it formidable. Invaders had to face the altitude, the cliffs, and the cold, and only the hardiest of armies stood a chance.

But today in the twenty-first century, it was Zurich's banks that were world-renowned. Numbered accounts, fortunes founded centuries ago, havens for the nouveau riche, and a devout adherence to privacy. And there were secrets here, personal and collective histories that some hoped would never come to light.

It wasn't widely known—nor readily acknowledged—but when the world chose to go to war in 1914 and again in 1939, the Alpine bankers seized an opportunity. While the Swiss military stood watch on the borders and spies from all sides played their games in the country's hotels and back alleys, the financiers showed no prejudice toward anyone who entered their offices. The only prerequisite was money. The Swiss accepted cash, assets, treasures, and secrets, and sometimes they financed the war machines doing battle in the lands below.

They would never admit it, but hundreds—perhaps thousands—of Nazis and other war criminals stashed their fortunes in Zurich's vaults. Ironclad regulations, impenetrable steel walls, and underground crypts ensured the security of their possessions.

It made sense for the Executive to be here capitalizing on Zurich's expertise.

Thus, here I was leaning against the side of Luzerner Kantonalbank on Claridenstrasse. I looked northwest down the street that was flanked by sterile corporate office buildings. With the cold air and prying eyes of the world outside, the gray facades and mirrored windows hid the financial transactions firing away inside the offices and boardrooms.

Having known I'd need something more than my Riviera blazer, before getting into position I'd picked up a navy-blue jacket to ward off the cold. I popped the collar and exhaled a long, cloudy breath. We were going to kidnap the Executive's facilitator, Julien Bodmer—the man Rupert had told us to find—and it was going to be a pisser.

Had it been twenty-four hours ago, the mere thought of doing such a thing—forcibly detaining another human being—would have turned my stomach. Yet now, I'm not sure what lines I wasn't prepared to cross.

We knew Bodmer worked at Grüber & Cie and that he lived in a well-appointed high-rise on the other side of the city. Adeline would uncover more about Bodmer later once she had time, and I suspected she'd contact her Finnish friend Miikka for a little help. We were going to need every shred of information about the man we could dig up, but for this little bit, we'd just have to go with a location and an ill-informed plan.

It was approaching eight in the evening. The bank had closed a while ago, and it seemed most employees had left for the night. I glanced about once again, noticing multiple surveillance cameras on the corners of buildings and tops of doors, and I wondered who might be watching me and how much longer I could stay before some underpaid night watchman called the police. I believed I was out of view for most of Grüber & Cie's security cameras, but it wasn't like I was practiced in the art of surveillance or ducking it. With my luck, I was square in the crosshairs with a well-trained bloke sipping coffee as he pondered why I was shivering in the cold all by myself.

Which then made me wonder why I was here instead of Adeline. Between the two of us, she undeniably possessed the skills I lacked. Yet, here I was acting as *the eye*, as she put it. And the hat on my head and scarf around my neck weren't doing much for a disguise. Still, I hadn't argued when she'd laid out how we were going to do this. In the rush of things, it'd made sense, sort of.

So I continued to wait.

Then, as the automatic light above the entrance to Grüber & Cie lit up, the oversized double doors opened. Out walked a man in his late forties with a full head of blond close-cropped hair, and a set of nearly black eyes. He wore a dark suit and white shirt, and swung a charcoal gray coat over his shoulders as he descended the bank's steps.

The man didn't seem at all interested in anything going on around him. He didn't look about or take notice of the people he passed on the sidewalk. He was apparently too absorbed with himself or preoccupied so much that, for the moment, he wasn't concerned about the physical world.

I checked my phone, making it appear like I'd finally received the text message I'd been waiting for. I smiled as if *my date* were at the restaurant, martinis on the way. It was my attempt at a little ruse, and I made sure to hold my phone in both hands and drop my head into it like there was nothing more important than my tiny screen.

I then started off at a casual pace down the street—the same path as Bodmer but moving slightly faster so I could close the distance. With another smile for any onlookers, I sent Adeline a text that I was on the move, heading north on Claridenstrasse. There was a tram stop two blocks ahead.

Adeline was on a parallel street out of view. She would manage our larger bubble and, when appropriate, slide in to replace me as the eye. It all sounded so simple, and I imagined a choreographed movement between us as we slipped here and there on the tail of our prey. All we needed now were micro earpieces and glasses that displayed scrolling data along with aiming reticles on who knows what. Very super-spy, I thought.

But to my surprise, Bodmer turned right on Dreikönigstrasse and was no longer heading toward the tram stop, which both Adeline and I had assumed he would do. The Swiss were enamored with their public transportation, so it only made sense Bodmer would use it given the lack of vehicles and parking around his bank.

A pulse of uncertainty shot through my veins. Was he heading across the river to go downtown? Was he meeting someone for dinner? Maybe we'd been stupid to assume he'd simply go home after work like a hermit.

I hurried to the intersection and speed-dialed Adeline's number. "Hello?"

"He's not taking the tram," I said between breaths. "He's heading toward the river. Bahnhofstrasse, maybe. "

"All right. Need to trade out?"

"No, not yet. Where are you?"

"Moving ahead of you."

"Yeah. Right. Okay."

I clicked off the phone. Bodmer's pace hadn't changed, and he still seemed more concerned with himself than with anything going on around him.

For a moment, I wondered if I'd followed the right man. Perhaps Bodmer was still inside the bank and this was someone else entirely. But I quickly disabused myself of that thought. It was him. In the few pictures Adeline had found, he had an unmistakable look.

I was nearly fifteen feet away from him now, perhaps a little too close.

Bodmer turned left down a side street and I followed. It was a strip between two large buildings with cars lined on each side. It was one of the rare spots in the city where someone could park, and it all started to make sense.

I watched Bodmer pull a set of keys from his pocket. The parking lights on a black sedan flashed.

My chest clamped tight as the seconds passed, my notion of time accelerating.

Bodmer was almost to the driver's side. If he got in the car, we were screwed.

Damnit!

I sprinted forward.

Bodmer reached for the door handle but must have heard something. He turned, but it was too late.

Someone barreled into Bodmer from the other direction, the collision stopping me in my tracks. Shock and confusion took over.

I then saw a wave of blonde hair whip around—Adeline.

Within seconds she had Bodmer on the ground. She hammered the edge of her palm into the side of his neck, rendering him nearly unconscious.

"Don't just stand there. Help me," she called.

Coming to, I snatched up the man's keys, clicked the button for the trunk, and grabbed the dazed banker under his arms.

"Where'd you come from?" I asked as we dragged Bodmer behind the vehicle.

Adeline didn't answer. She opened the trunk and looked inside. No weapons, but there was a tire iron. She removed the tool along with a bag of dry cleaning, tossing the items under a nearby car.

Then both of us heaved Bodmer into the trunk.

I slammed the hatch and hurried to the passenger door.

Adeline was already behind the wheel. "Think anyone saw that?"

"We'll find out soon enough," I said, clicking my seat belt as Adeline popped the car in reverse, lurched back, and sped away.

CHAPTER 50

Faust advanced down the sidewalk toward the entrance to Grüber & Cie. He bounded up the steps, yanked open the door, and strode inside.

The security guard at the front desk jumped up. "Halt! Die Bank ist geschlossen."

Faust locked eyes with him.

Recognition and then distress washed over the young man's face. "My apologies. I didn't realize it was you."

Faust kept moving, and when he reached the interior set of doors, the guard buzzed him through. The door swung open heavily, the ballistic polycarbonate weighing ten times that of a normal door.

He passed through the main reception lobby, went to the elevator, and rose to the third floor. Stepping out of the lift, Faust entered the hallway. He strode by an office with glass windows that offered a full view of the space inside. A late working executive looked up, but Faust had already slipped past and was halfway down the hall. The other offices were dark, their daily inhabitants home with their families or out with their mistresses.

Faust reached the end of the hall, turned right, and came upon two doors. He removed a key from his pocket and entered the room on the right. Darkness greeted him, the space empty. He swore, securing the door behind him.

There were two leather chairs in front of the mahogany desk, a laptop and leather portfolio on top. Against the wall was a bookshelf crammed with international banking regulations, and a table in the corner held a half-empty carafe of water.

Faust picked his way around the desk and noticed the only photograph in the room. He'd seen it countless times before, every time he'd visited. It was of a French bulldog held by Julien Bodmer, one of the few men who knew all the names, all the accounts, and all the networks of the Executive—the one laundering all of the Executive's money.

Faust felt a pit form in his stomach.

He picked up the desk phone and dialed Bodmer's mobile number. It went straight to voicemail. He slammed the phone down and stormed out of the office, heading back to the front desk. Along the way he sent a text: *He's missing*.

When Faust reached the lobby he asked, "What time did Herr Bodmer badge out?"

The security guard searched his logs. "Nineteen fifty-six."

"Pull all the security footage starting at nineteen thirty," ordered Faust.

The guard worked quickly, then moved out of the way so Faust could work the monitors. A minute later he breathed, "They have him."

CHAPTER 51

It was dark when Adeline turned down the drive leading to the cabin, the car's wheels crunching over the previous day's iced snow as the night's shadows fled the oncoming headlights. She followed the slow turn down the hill, enveloped by the trees until she reached the gravel lot.

Adeline opened her door and said, "Back in a moment."

From my seat, I watched her bound up the porch steps and into the cabin. I then gathered myself and eased out of the car, the forest's chill fingering my skin. Adeline appeared seconds later. In one hand she held what looked like a black cloth, and in the other was a length of rope. It was the coarse, nylon kind of rope that cuts into the skin. She descended the steps and went to the back of the vehicle. I met her there, now both of us fixated on the trunk.

"Ready?" she asked.

I nodded, the inclination to go along with these grisly tasks all too easy for me now.

Adeline handed me the rope and what turned out to be a brown pillowcase. She then took a step back and drew her pistol, training it on the trunk. Her weight shifted from foot to foot and she let out a slow breath.

I gave her one last glance, then pressed the release on the key fob. The trunk popped open the way slow hydraulics do, and we were met by an unexpected sight.

Julien Bodmer was lying on his side with his knees tucked to his chest, with one hand under his head like a pillow. He seemed comfortable as if being stuffed in the boot of a car was routine for him. Yet, there was something menacing about the man. His face was calm, but his black eyes were intense, unable to hide a festering anger.

As if he'd read my mind, he extended his hands so that I could bind his wrists. He didn't blink or turn away as I wrapped the rope and drew the knot tight. He remained focused on me the entire time.

But when I went to hood him—an act that felt surreal even if I knew it to be necessary—he turned to lock his gaze on Adeline. His head rotated slowly, almost mechanically, like a possessed doll. The image, I must admit, disturbed me.

Then, by my hand, his face disappeared under the shroud.

Shaking off whatever it was that was crawling at my sense of right and wrong, I grabbed Bodmer under the arms and hefted him out of the trunk. I dragged the banker up the porch steps, his feet stumbling across the wood slats. I ushered him across the threshold and inside.

Adeline had prepared a corner of the main room, removing all the furniture except a single chair. It faced the wall, and she'd spread towels underneath the four legs. Minutes later, Bodmer was secured to it, still with a hood over his head and a strip of tape over his mouth, and now wearing a pair of noise-canceling earmuffs.

"How long will this take?" I asked, wringing my hands to remove the offensive impression of the rope that lingered on my skin.

Adeline shrugged. "As long as necessary."

"What the hell does that mean?"

"We'll do what we need to as long as we need to."

I didn't say anything, staring at the back of Bodmer's head, anticipating what I expected to come. People like Bodmer didn't divulge what they knew simply because someone asked a polite question. That's why they were who they were, men and women without remorse, without conscience, willing to beat down or kill anyone in their way—predatory and remorseless.

These types of people needed to be compelled to talk and, depending on the individual, only certain approaches would work, Adeline had explained. The more selfish ones—the weaker ones—typically could be convinced they had no other option. Confession was their only path to personal survival. They would turn on their masters to save their hides.

Others, the more fanatical—perhaps psychotic—required a different approach. They were willing to die or sacrifice themselves, and fear for their mortal existence wouldn't work. Instead, the threat had to expose an issue they cared about more than their own life and the matter they believed they protected. For each person it was different; finding it was the challenge.

All of this was beyond me, yet I believed Bodmer was our best-worst alternative, and it was time to get on with it.

I stepped in front of our captive and Adeline joined me. After a moment's pause, I removed the earmuffs and hood, revealing Bodmer's face.

The man blinked, his eyes adjusting to the light, then he glanced at his surroundings, seeming neither surprised nor scared. He returned his attention to me and Adeline, and I detected the absence of fear in him. He stared at us, revealing nothing.

"Your name is Julien Bodmer," Adeline began. "You were born in 1971 in Zurich, Switzerland. You've been a banker your entire life, and currently, you're a senior account manager at Grüber & Cie. You're also a facilitator for the Strasbourg Executive, an international criminal network pushing subversive and nationalist agendas. You move money, broker connections, and support operations. We know the Executive is planning something big, and we need to know what and why."

Bodmer sat unphased, his close-cropped hair accentuating his pale, chiseled features. His face was like granite, his clenched jaw the only feature that indicated he was less than thrilled about his predicament.

"This is going to go one of two ways," Adeline continued. "You can tell us what we want to know now and this will all be over in a matter of hours. Or, over the next few days, we'll make your existence very uncomfortable, and then you'll tell us what we want to know. Which option do you prefer?"

Bodmer's expression finally broke, a defiant smile appearing. He leaned forward as far as his restraints allowed and said, "Don't hurt yourself."

And that was that.

*   *   *

I woke two minutes before my alarm was set to go off, my internal clock a blessing and a curse. It was four in the morning and time for me to take over. Adeline had taken the first shift watching over Bodmer.

Emerging from the bedroom, I found the TV on but muted, and Adeline still hunched over a hefty laptop she'd purchased the day before, the screen lighting up her exhausted face. Rupert's journal rested beside her on the table. Bodmer was where he should be—tied to the chair and hooded, with his head tilted to the side, likely in some state of sleep.

"Have you been at it the entire time?" I asked, rubbing my eyes and fighting back a yawn.

Adeline looked up and squinted at me. "Morning. Yes."

"Any progress?"

"Some."

I nodded and took a quiet step closer to Bodmer. "How's our friend?"

"He rustled around for the first few hours. But he stopped a while ago."

"Right," I said, expelling a long and slow breath.

"Does this bother you, what we're doing?" Adeline asked, watching me watch Bodmer.

"Would it matter if it did?"

Adeline began to say something but hesitated, which was probably for the best. I didn't want to say anything more, either. It was the idea that if we didn't acknowledge what we were doing, if we didn't speak it, then maybe it wasn't real.

With a regretful smile, Adeline closed her laptop and retired to the bedroom. It was her turn to sleep.

I, as expected, assumed my post behind the chair and waited.

CHAPTER 52

At 9:23 that morning, two Middle Eastern men strode up a quiet Straße on the outskirts of Berlin. They wore loose-fitting overcoats, appropriate for the time of year, but buttoned up like they were trying to ward off the biting wind of February—not a mild autumn breeze.

When they reached the main doors of St. Peter's Church, they unbuttoned their jackets and mounted the granite steps two at a time. They stormed inside the church's sanctuary, each carrying H&K G3 assault rifles. They opened fire.

In three minutes, they killed thirty-four people—mothers, fathers, divorcés, widows, children, infants—and wounded another eighteen. The morning worshipers were slaughtered in their pews, unable to escape the onslaught of bullets. The massacre ended when the Bundespolizei arrived with sirens wailing. The two terrorists then looked at each other, called out to Allah, and detonated their suicide vests. Hundreds of ball bearings ripped through flesh, wood, and stone. Then there was silence—until the screams started again.

Images of the victims flashed soundlessly on the television screen. There was a young girl with braided hair—no more than five or six years old—sitting on the front steps of the church. Crimson dots were splattered on her white dress, her face covered in dust. The bodies of a woman and man were on the ground in front of her—her parents—dead. Their skin was gray, lifeless, bloody.

The little girl simply sat there, looking around but seeing nothing with her tiny brown eyes. All the innocence of the child had been lost, everything safe and secure ripped apart. Her world had been destroyed in minutes.

I couldn't pull my eyes away from the screen. I'd seen the look before in the forests of Bosnia and I'd never wanted to see it again. Yet here it was, in a place that should have been safe . . . a sanctuary. And the news kept replaying it all—the video footage of the assailants entering the church, the images captured by victims' cell phones as the massacre unfolded, the aftermath with the emergency services responding, and the little girl.

I felt the sadness deep in my soul. I wasn't a father, but the helplessness of the child screwed into me. No child should suffer that way. No child.

Yet the little girl sat there—numb.

I wondered who would care for her now that her parents were gone. Who would hold her hand and walk her to school? Who would put a Band-Aid on her knee after a fall? Who would tell her to run away if she sensed danger? Who would protect her?

No one. She would be lost, forgotten. Her parents dead, gone, just like that. A life destroyed before it even started.

Movement caught my eye, finally breaking my fixation on the screen.

Bodmer was still in his chair, hooded and rendered deaf and mute. Yet his head wobbled, indicating he was awake.

Even now I'm unsure where it came from, but the thought *this was his doing* kept repeating itself in my head. The Executive was somehow connected to the attack, I believed, a provocation that was part of their twisted agenda—and Bodmer had helped make it possible.

He hadn't pulled the trigger. He hadn't set off the bombs. But he was no different than those who did. He'd made it possible for others to do the dirty work.

He was just as bad if not worse than them.

Bodmer, and other men and women like him, were soulless monsters. They were grotesque thugs obscured behind the façade of woven ties and pantsuits. They were bullies who preyed upon the weak. They enacted evil.

I edged my way over to Bodmer's virtual cell and stood in front of him. I watched the man's chest rise and fall. I watched his fingers touch the edge of the armrest.

Then, after a moment's pause, I removed the earmuffs. Next came off the hood.

It took a second for Bodmer's eyes to adjust to the newfound light of the room until he eventually glared up at me. Despite being strapped to a chair for the past twenty-four hours—sensory deprived and in the dark—he appeared determined. His black eyes were still sharp and he was focused.

He wasn't ready yet—I knew that. He wouldn't answer questions, and anything he did say couldn't be trusted. He needed more time.

CHAPTER 53

"Have you found him?" asked Sofia, holding her mobile phone to her ear.

"No," replied Faust. "And I won't. Bodmer is as good as dead."

"How can you be sure?"

"If he does as he's been directed, the professor will be overcome, and Bodmer will have no choice."

Sofia paused, contemplating the rationale. "He will not fail. The Executive is a divine calling for him."

"Where are you?" asked Faust, changing the subject.

"That's none of your concern," replied Sofia, looking at the electronic equipment that was secured in racks and filling every inch of wall-space in the mobile trailer. "We're about to enter phase two."

"Why did you start early? I'm supposed to direct the operation. What happened?"

Sofia didn't respond.

At the far end of the trailer were two men with their backs to her. They were hammering away on their keyboards, each with multiple thirty-two-inch monitors in front of them. They were manipulating gigabytes of data and nearly fifty streams of incoming and outgoing messaging, and they were doing it as easily as if they were buying toilet paper from Amazon.

"One moment," Sofia said. She stepped outside into the cool night air. They were in an alley between two abandoned warehouses on the outskirts of Frankfurt. Sauntering in front of the blacked-out trailer, Sofia said, "We had to start phase one. The professor and Agent Parker had found Eisengard. There's no telling what he told them. And he pointed them to Bodmer."

"I told you I questioned Eisengard myself. He knew nothing, and the only thing he could tell them was who Bodmer was. We didn't need to move up the timeline, and I should have been the one giving the final instructions."

"You forget yourself," replied Sofia. "You do not decide when we act. I do. Besides, it was more important for you to track down Dresden and Parker. They could bring everything crashing down."

"Who'd you give the order to?" asked Faust, unwilling to let it go. "I need to speak to him. There're details you don't know about. And you're right, everything could very well come crashing down."

"You need to drop this. It's been taken care of. Get to Strasbourg. Once phase two is in motion, there'll be little time. Our people need to be ready. Strasbourg is what's important."

It was Faust's turn to be silent, and Sofia let the man stew. He was a soldier, and soldiers followed orders even if they didn't like them. She should have never fucked him. The man was indispensable operationally, but men's egos could never handle a woman being in charge after sleeping together.

"I'll be in Strasbourg in a few hours," Faust finally said. "I'll have everything prepared."

"I know, which is why I trust you with these things."

Sofia clicked off the phone and looked up at the sky. The city lights drowned out most of the stars, but a few constellations were visible. Phase one was the easy part—violence always was. Bombings, shootings, suicide attacks—there was no shortage of fanatics willing to carry out such things, and she was quite confident their activities were distanced enough that there would be no attribution to the Executive.

Faust—being a man of violence—considered these attacks the centerpiece of the operation. What he didn't realize was that such violence is soon forgotten. There needed to be a means to make sure that the emotional reaction remained at the forefront of people's minds— the fear, the tragedy, the hate—and that there was someone—or something—compelling them to act on it. That was phase two.

Sofia reentered the trailer and approached the backs of the two men. Like before, they were both engrossed in their work. They didn't bother to acknowledge anything else going on around them.

"How much longer?"

"About seventeen minutes," said the heavyset one with black hair. His name was Sven. He was in his mid-thirties and looked like he'd spent his entire life sitting on the couch looking at television and computer screens while eating food from a bag. But appearances aside, he was considered one of about twenty hackers in the world who could manipulate social media platforms on a global scale.

The individual next to Sven was also a hacker in the same class of techies, but he was barely eighteen and thin as a rail. He used the online handle *Malazan Plague*, and even in the physical world preferred to be called Mal.

Sven and Mal had worked for Sofia for two years under the auspices of her intelligence firm, Analytique Internationale. The irony was not lost on her—hackers aligning themselves with a company intended to perpetuate greedy conglomerates and the soulless elite. They had no idea who they were really working for, nor were they privy to the full extent of what they were doing.

To get them to do what she needed, Sofia had used their tendency for widespread disruption and their inclination to oppose anything government related. The first test had been in the last American election. They'd flooded social media with populist and liberal ideas—on both ends of the spectrum—creating an alternative to mainstream news.

Although they weren't the only perpetrators of fake news, the results were nonetheless impressive—the most powerful, educated, and open society in the world had been twisted and manipulated by primary feelings of hate and fear.

That proof of concept was the forerunner to tonight. With the recent spate of terrorist attacks sweeping across Europe, and with ISIS and other migrants and refugees ready to blame, Sven and Mal were flooding all forms of media with provocative, amplifying messages. The messages were getting picked up by legitimate sites, hitting the clickbate algorithms and then going viral.

The brilliance was in the timing and the origins. The messages Sven and Mal were releasing were coming from all over Europe, and they were being launched on a schedule that would run for the next forty-eight hours. After that, the movement would take on a life of its own.

That's when Bakker's imagery tool would come into play. She would be able to see—in real time—where they could exploit opportunities, or identify a need to apply more pressure.

"It's done," announced Sven. "All streams are running and confirmed."

"Quit the techno-talk and explain to me what's going on," replied Sofia.

Sven smirked, his fleshy face sweating. "The initial six hundred and twenty-three shots have gone out. Another three thousand will release over the next twelve hours. We can shut this place down and monitor statuses through these from anywhere we want," he said, pointing at two laptop bags.

"So everything will run on an automated schedule from now on, correct?"

"For the most part. Depends if you want us to tweak anything. But once the next salvo goes out, we'll need to assess effects."

"I don't think that will be necessary." Sofia removed a sub-compact pistol from her purse.

Sven's eyes went wide.

Sofia fired twice, putting two holes in his chest.

Mal, who'd been focused on his screen, spun around with mouth agape, his complexion white. Sofia leveled the gun at his head and pulled the trigger. Splotchy blood and skull fragments sprayed the equipment behind him.

Sofia returned the pistol to her purse and took out her phone. She sent a text and then walked outside. A van pulled up and two men jumped out. One went inside the trailer, and the other got in the cab. Sofia slid into the passenger seat of the van. Both vehicles drove away.

CHAPTER 54

Thirty-six hours had passed. Not a terribly long time for Bodmer to go without food or water; most people could endure such an experience, even if unpleasant. The body could last upwards of three days without water. Lack of food was even longer, a few weeks. Everything goes into survival mode, tapping into those fat stores everyone is so keen on trimming.

But the sensory deprivation from the hood and earmuffs would strain even the strongest of minds. Initial effects include loss of time, disorientation, and fear. Soon, elevated levels of anxiety and depression set in. Eventually, terror, paranoia, and hallucinations plague the subject.

There was no telling where Bodmer was on the spectrum, but I presumed he was channeling his torment into anger. He'd started to aggressively tap his foot for five to ten minutes at a time, and every so often he'd jerk his body and make the chair jump. He would grunt and thrash, and then return to a state of absolute stillness, only to repeat the behavior an hour later.

It was disturbing to watch, and it needed to end.

Earlier that evening, both Adeline and I agreed we couldn't wait any longer. Since Tours, the terrorist attacks had increased in frequency and cruelty. There wasn't a doubt in either of our minds that the Executive was on the move with the Kanzler blasting out the orders.

I wondered if my father could truly be behind it all, the high probability making me shudder.

The latest attack had been beyond compare . . . a vehicle-borne improvised explosive device—VBIED—went off outside the British Museum. People heard the concussion at Westminster, nearly three miles away, causing the police to lock the place down.

However, the Museum's façade was barely damaged, making it apparent that there was another target.

A group of children between the ages of seven and ten had been getting on buses at the end of the block. They'd spent the day gawking at ancient artifacts, listening to stories of the Egyptians and Greeks, and being far too precocious.

Initial reports confirmed fifty-seven children were killed by the blast, and another one hundred sixty-one children and bystanders were wounded. Some would never walk again, use their arms, or use their eyes to see the world around them.

Images of emergency crews rushing boys and girls to ambulances played over and over again. Distraught parents rushed the scene, some hysterical, others collapsing.

Everyone assumed it was the work of pick-your-radical-Islamist-group lurking under the guise of refugees or disenfranchised European citizens who'd been radicalized. And the chatter on social media documented a wave of celebrations across the Middle East and in Muslim communities around Europe.

After somewhat of a lull following Russia's incursion in Ukraine, some pundits were calling the latest spate of terrorist attacks an escalation in the clash between Islam and the West. An attempt to destroy the next generation of Western society, as one analyst put it.

But I knew better. Even if the attacks were being perpetrated by true Islamic radicals, they weren't the ones ultimately behind it all. It was the Executive; it had to be.

Looking up from my post in the kitchen, I saw Adeline emerge from the bedroom. She'd been on the computer again—four hours straight this time—her eyes red from the strain.

"And?"

"I've got it. Let me do the talking."

"That's probably best," I said.

We put two chairs in front of Bodmer, and I took a moment to consider the man before me, as well as what was about to happen. I then removed the man's earmuffs and hood.

CHAPTER 55

OUTSIDE ZURICH, SWITZERLAND

As the hood came off Bodmer's face, he looked like he was emerging too soon from a groggy sleep. He appeared haggard, his hair messed and his skin oily. His breathing was heavy and the hint of uncertainty escaped from his eyes.

But once his pupils adjusted, he glared at me and then at Adeline.

"I'm going to remove the tape," I said. "If you yell, it goes right back on and so does the hood, and this ordeal of yours will continue. Understand?"

Bodmer nodded.

I peeled off the tape covering Bodmer's mouth, leaving a rectangle of irritated skin. "Would you like some water?" I asked.

Bodmer ogled the glass in my hand and nodded again. I brought it to his lips and he drank eagerly, sucking it down. He then leaned back in the chair, a look of exhausted satisfaction on his face, as if he'd just sipped a cold beer on a hot summer day.

"I don't want you to say anything, Julien," began Adeline. "I just want you to listen and think. Will you do that?"

Seeming to regain his strength with every passing second, Bodmer pursed his lips in a contemplative manner. "Obviously I have no choice." His voice sounded gravelly, which matched his hardened features. He didn't have the appearance of a banker—analytical, meticulous, meek, timid. Rather, he looked like someone who enjoyed physically intimidating others.

"We already know who you are and your connection to the Strasbourg Executive," began Adeline, her speech slow and deliberate. "We also know the Executive—the people you work for—are behind the attacks erupting across Europe. We need to know who is in control and how to stop them. But we don't expect you to tell us what's going on out of the kindness of your heart. We're going to offer you a deal. A way out, so to speak."

Bodmer snickered. "You have no idea who you're dealing with."

"Quiet," I snapped, surprising myself with the sharpness of my tone.

"Here's the situation," continued Adeline. "With one phone call, I can have MI6 release a report about a newly identified extremist organization named the Strasbourg Executive. Then they'll release an alert to the security services across Europe that they have a senior member of the Executive—you—in custody who's cooperating. You may not fear us, but there's no doubt you fear the people you work for. And they can get to you, even in police custody, can't they?"

Bodmer chuckled. "If I may speak—that is a weak bluff, Agent Parker. You're both wanted for questioning about the bombing in Nice. You can't make any calls to MI6 or anywhere else. You must do better."

"You're quite bold for someone who's tied up," countered Adeline.

"It helps to know what one is up against, no?"

"Does it?"

"I know all about you, Agent Adeline Parker of Britain's Secret Intelligence Service, daughter of Elizabeth and Martin Parker, who were removed by your very Alfred, the man who took you in after the fact. An odd business, I will say," Bodmer mentioned casually. "And you, Professor William Randolph Dresden, mediocre historian with a sullied past—a failed life. You're the son of Karl Dresden, the former Kanzler of the Executive, and an unworthy descendant of the Dresden line."

"What do you mean, *former* Kanzler?" I asked.

Bodmer smiled. "Your father's dead. He's been replaced."

"What?" My voice suddenly hollow.

"A few days ago. Shot and killed."

"What do you mean?" The news, although not surprising, was piercing, like an ice pick chipping away at a frozen block. I'd expected something like this—I knew the Executive's history—yet suspecting and knowing were two different things.

My father, dead again . . .

Bodmer looked around the cabin, considering what to say next. "You know, it's amazing you two have lasted this long. Both of you should've died in Nice in that café. But Sanders never did measure up. He was a cocky fuck."

"What happened to my father?" I asked, willing my voice to remain neutral.

Bodmer offered me an expressionless look. I could see he was using the only power he had—the keeper of information who would or would not share. I was about to lean forward and shake the man, to demand he speak, but I suspect Adeline could sense what was happening and spoke up.

"You're right, Julien. We're in a precarious situation, the professor and I. But there's something else you should know."

Bodmer met Adeline's gaze, a flash of curiosity appearing.

"We know about your daughter."

The color drained from Bodmer's face, but he didn't say anything.

"Yes, you have a daughter whom you've hidden since she was born. She should be about eleven years old now, correct?"

Bodmer didn't react to Adeline's question, but his impassiveness said it all.

"Her name is Emma, Emma Drucker, which was her mother's name. But you couldn't tolerate the surname, could you? So you kept Emma but changed her last name to Goltz. If ever discovered, no questions then, right?"

Bodmer still refused to permit himself any expression beyond a flat stare, his eyes fixed on Adeline. But the intensity of his composure betrayed him.

"And speaking of her mother, whatever happened to her? A few months after Emma's birth, her mother has no record. Did you make her disappear? Kill her?"

Bodmer shook his head from side to side as his mouth curled into a frown, which I interpreted to mean he knew what happened to the mother but was not the one who did it. But that was just my assumption.

Finally, Bodmer asked in a taut voice, "How did you find her?"

"How did I find your sweet daughter?" Adeline asked, considering her response. "You've been very good, exceptional really, at hiding the Executive's fingerprints—a brilliant array of cutouts and holdings around the world to move and shelter money. But with your daughter, the money and support came directly from you. It took some effort to find, but the trail existed. Perhaps if you'd used some of the networks you established for the Executive, I might not have been able to find her."

Bodmer spat. "I couldn't. You know that."

"That's right. If your superiors knew about Emma and her ethnicity, it'd be unacceptable. Your purity in the eyes of the Executive would be in doubt."

"A mistake, all of it."

"Maybe. Yet, you've tried to take care of Emma and have for eleven years. You feel something."

"What do you want? Threatening me about my daughter will not encourage me to help you. You should know this."

"No, I wouldn't think so. Still, do you know where Emma is now? I suspect you think you do, but when was the last time you saw her?"

"Don't try this with me. You may have learned some scraps, but she is hidden well and safe. I've made sure of that, even if you found the trail of money."

Adeline eased forward, no longer evincing a stern look to confront Bodmer. Her face was now one of sad compassion. "I'm sorry to tell you like this. No one should hear about the loss of a child under such conditions. But there is no other way. Emma, your daughter, is dead."

Bodmer swallowed. "You lie."

"She was murdered a year ago. We didn't know who she was back then, but we knew about the murder."

"You're a fucking liar."

"Am I?"

Bodmer nodded. "I have corresponded with her this past year. You lie."

"I am not the liar. Your bosses are."

"What do you mean?"

"The Executive killed your daughter. We had no idea why at the time, no idea who she was. But we knew about the event. Alfred knew and I knew—we just didn't know why. Your colleagues have a history of killing innocent family members."

"I don't believe you. The Executive did not know of Emma. I made sure of that."

"I found her," remarked Adeline.

"They couldn't have known. I would have been dead."

Adeline pursed her lips, then stood up and walked over to her laptop on the table. She unhooked the power cord and brought it over, revealing the screen to Bodmer. Displayed was an intelligence report and a color photo of a young girl with shoulder-length brown hair, large green eyes, dimples, and a generous smile. The report described her death on the Danube outside Vienna—a drowning.

As Bodmer read, his face crumbled. His head shook gently to the left and right as he read, physically opposed to what the article said, not wanting to believe it.

"I'm sorry. As I said before, no parent should learn about the death of a child in such a way."

"That bitch," Bodmer snarled.

Adeline closed the laptop and took a step back. "Who?"

Bodmer looked up. No tears in his eyes, but there was rage in every breath. "That bitch. She did it."

"Who is the bitch, Julien?" I asked.

Bodmer tilted his head to look at me. He appeared to size me up again. "Your father told me there was a resemblance, but I honestly don't see it."

"A resemblance? What are you talking about?"

"Two years ago your father revealed something to me. I was surprised at first, but then it made sense. Then, when she killed him, everything became clear."

"I don't understand. We're talking about your daughter."

Bodmer leaned forward against his restraints, closing the distance between me and him if only a fraction of an inch. "Yes, we are talking about *my daughter*, as well as *your father*. The new Kanzler killed your father three days ago, and I have no doubt she killed my daughter. Her name is Sofia König."

"Who is Sofia König?"

"Sofia is your sister—the one whom you thought died along with your mother all those years ago. She's alive, and she is the Kanzler of the Strasbourg Executive."

CHAPTER 56

"I . . ." My voice failed me, the room around me escaping focus with the walls seeming to close in. Images of my mother—smiling, laughing, love in every feature—flashed before my eyes.

I remembered the night she went into labor. It was past midnight, and my mother and father had woken me as they rustled through the house getting ready to head to the hospital. I stood at the top of the stairs watching, my little feet cold on the hardwood. My father spoke hurriedly, making sure they had everything—toothbrush, change of clothes, a baby's blanket. My nanny, in her gentle way, tried to reassure him—everything would be fine. They'd done this before.

Then, just as they were about to leave, my mother saw me standing at the top of the stairs. She walked up, one step at a time, her smile soft and gentle, her gaze upon me. She kissed me on the forehead and touched my cheek. She held my hand as we padded down the stairs together, her warm fingers wrapped around mine. Then she said goodbye.

My parents walked out the door, and my mother descended the front steps gingerly. She wore a long, purple coat, with a patterned scarf wrapped around her neck. My father held her hand, ready to brace her if she stumbled. She turned and smiled once more, her hand on her pregnant belly.

It was the last time I saw her. She died four hours later from internal bleeding. I was twelve, and everything changed after that. And now . . . I have a sister?

Adeline could see I'd been struck dumb, but she knew the opportunity with Bodmer was fleeting. She touched my forearm, steadying me, but she kept her focus intently on Bodmer. "Sofia König. Tell me about her. What is she planning?"

"You won't be able to stop the attacks," Bodmer said. "They were engineered to occur independently from each other and on a schedule. There's no turning them off."

"What are the next targets?"

"Only the individual cells know. They were provided instructions on what types of targets to hit. Final selection was left to them."

"Don't hold back, Julien. You must know something. She killed your daughter."

Bodmer shook his head. "Scheiße. No. That's the genius of this. Fully compartmented, as if each cell was a lone operator. There is no central command or control to change or stop things. The order to execute has already been given, and there is no way to stop the attacks."

"Okay. Then who are these cells? Where are they?"

"You're asking the wrong questions," Bodmer said. "The attacks will continue and then they will stop. You should be asking, what's the point."

"Fine. Stop playing games. What's the point?" I demanded, rejoining the conversation.

"To make true Europeans see that the only choice is a closing of borders and return to national ideals. Immigrant trash is infecting our homes. And they're not coming here to live side by side with you or me. They'd rather kill you, take what you have, and ruin it. We're making sure people know what's going on—that it's undeniably clear—so they can take action before it's too late."

"By killing children? Attacking your own kind? The very people you consider superior."

"A soft approach was not working. Sofia believed we needed extreme measures. And as I just said, you can't stop it."

"There's still a way to disrupt things," Adeline said. "Maybe not instantly, but it would be effective."

"Is there? And why would I care? As you keep reminding me, my daughter is dead, and I'm as good as dead, too, given the little chat we are having."

"Yeah, that's right. You think you have nothing to lose or gain at this point. But your life isn't over. It will just be different. You can never go back to the Executive, that's obvious. You'll never be trusted. But that isn't so bad. You'll be free. And—you hate her. The bitch."

Bodmer allowed a twisted smirk. "If I cooperate, what do you think happens to me?"

"We let you go."

"Ha!"

"Julien, listen to me. We let you go. Even though you have supported horrible things in your life, it is not up to us to try, judge, and execute you. We are not murderers, but we also don't have the means or, frankly, the inclination to turn you over to law enforcement. So, we let you go. You can do whatever you want, perhaps retire to a tiny island with all the money you've skimmed."

Bodmer's face twitched with mischievous acknowledgment. "I see your research has been broad. No matter. Those things are immaterial to me. No. If I'm going to help you, I want something else."

"What?"

"No, no, no, no. First, how do you think you can stop the Executive?"

"You're the Executive's premier and most trusted facilitator. Or, at least, you were. So, we need you to freeze all of the Executive's assets and lock the accounts. That will get *the bitch's* attention, and we'll take it from there."

"You think I still have access?" Bodmer remarked with a chuckle. "By now I suspect Sofia has had someone go in and lock me out. Probably her dog Faust."

"Who's Faust?"

"Faust is Sofia's chief of security. He was the same for your father. A cruel man who I am sure has stopped counting how many people he's killed. You should be concerned about him. If he gets a hold of you, it will happen so fast you won't even know. You'll just be gone," said Bodmer, lifting his chin to expose his neck and making a curt hissing sound, bringing to mind the image of someone slicing his throat. "By the way, how long have I been here? I've lost track of the time."

"Thirty-six hours, give or take."

"Yes, I suspect in light of everything that is in motion, I've been locked out."

"Bullshit," Adeline snapped. "You're smarter than that. You would have created a back door for this very purpose. You had your daughter to think about, and it's apparent from your little skimming that you are inclined to take care of yourself."

Again, Bodmer allowed a dry smile. "Fine. You're right. I do still have access to some things. They can't lock me out of everything. I can do some of what you ask, but not all. The Executive's assets are significant and spread far and wide. But I can get at enough to make the bitch shit herself. And once I do, I will have certainly condemned myself, which is why I wanted to know what you were planning before I agreed to anything. Given the scope of your request, my demand—my recompense, maybe—has changed."

"Go on."

"I will lock out all the accounts that I can. And in return, in addition to letting me go, you will do something for me."

"Out with it already."

Bodmer narrowed his eyes. "You must kill Sofia König, the bitch. Only then will any of us be free."

CHAPTER 57

Adeline removed the binds that held Bodmer's arms to the chair, but she left the other restraints intact. Bodmer did not hide his annoyance, but it did not prevent him from tapping away on Adeline's laptop.

While he worked, Adeline stayed perched over his shoulder to make sure he didn't have any errant keystrokes that would bring the Executive or some other nefarious group running with guns up. Once he finished, he handed Adeline three thumb drives in exchange for water and some day-old bread.

As Bodmer ate, Adeline and I conferred quietly on the other side of the room. I was not surprised when Adeline asked how I was handling the revelation that I had a sister, but I'd become adept at suppressing what emotions remained inside me and told her I was fine. She'd also become accustomed to not believing my dismissal of such matters but letting it go, nonetheless. We were a pair, for sure.

I motioned at the three thumb drives, which Adeline had explained were configured to act as security tokens. These thumb drives and the encryption they held on them would now be required to access the security protocols that Bodmer had just slammed on all of the Executive's accounts he could still get into. Essentially, these were the only keys that could open the locks on the Executive's money.

"So now that we have them, what's the plan?" I asked.

"You and I can't do much," Adeline said. "We're not an army that can hunt down the cells and we're both wanted by the authorities. Nobody would believe us, and by the time they did, it'd be too late."

"Yep, I get all that. So what do we do?"

"We need someone who will find it in *their* interest to oppose something like the Executive but who is also outside and perhaps doesn't trust the Europeans. A country or group that would want to prevent bloodshed and chaos, particularly if it gave them a bit of an edge against the arrogant EU."

"You mean a country outside Europe but still on the same side, relatively speaking."

"Yes, but not the Americans."

"Right. Makes sense. Then who?"

"The Israelis and the Indians."

"Really," I said, drawing it out. "I'm listening."

"Both are powerful countries with capable security services. Both would see the value in stopping a group like the Executive, and not just because of the moral aspect. An imperial-minded Europe meddling around is not something they care to entertain, even if a disjointed EU benefits their relative influence. And according to international agreements concerning terrorism, they're compelled to take action."

"Okay, I get the logic. But will they listen to us?"

"We have to make sure we talk to the right person, and we have to do it face-to-face."

"Okay, how do we do that?" I asked, wondering if we simply call up the *Israeli switchboard* and make an appointment.

"We can't stay here in Zurich. We've been here too long and done too much. The closest country is Italy."

"Is that why you asked me to look up drive time to Milan?" I interjected.

Adeline nodded. "Yes, the closest Israeli and Indian consulates are in Milan. And they're both bound to have an intelligence officer embedded in the consulate staff."

"Okay, but how do we reach them? Do we just walk in and announce ourselves, take a number, and wait to be called? *Hi, we're here to speak to an intelligence officer.*"

"Not really. We need to keep some distance. We can't go inside the consulates because they're hardened structures meant to keep people out as well as in. And, as you jest, we shouldn't announce ourselves because we are still wanted by the authorities in connection to the Nice bombing. If either country had us, they'd be bound to turn us over to the Italian authorities for questioning."

"Okay, what then?"

"We'll create two little packages with these babies," Adeline said, teasing the thumb drives with a little shake, "which will also include a detailed account of what's going on and everything we know, specifically names and locations, and anything else they can potentially use to mount an investigation and alert the Europeans to more attacks."

"Sounds like a long shot. Delivering a secret package with instructions hoping it makes it to the right person in a consulate who's also supposed to be a secret. What's to stop them from throwing it all out or, if they think it's a threat, blowing it up like airport security with an abandoned suitcase?"

"You forget I'm also intelligence. I know what to write to get their attention."

"Okay, if you say so. Maybe on the drive, you can clue me in."

Adeline nodded and glanced over at Bodmer, munching away on the last crusts of bread and taking sips of water. "Let's get on with it then."

I expelled a deep breath. "Right," I said, walking over to Bodmer. "Had enough?"

"I need a steak and a beer," he replied, still chewing.

"I'll order you takeout. Give me the glass."

Bodmer narrowed his eyes but complied. I then secured his hands and arms back to the chair. Bodmer didn't resist, but he asked, "What are you doing? Our agreement was for you to let me go. I've fulfilled my end of the bargain."

"We will let you go," said Adeline, "but don't be surprised that we don't trust you. Once we're gone, we'll make a call to the front desk, tell them something interesting, and someone will eventually come get you."

"Scheiße. That's not letting me go. The front desk will have questions when they find me strapped to this chair ready to shit and piss myself."

"You're smart. I'm sure you'll think of something. But it would not be wise to kill the unfortunate housekeeper who comes to your rescue. That'd only create more complications for your disappearance."

I secured the final knot and stepped back. "You can claim you had a secret affair that didn't go as you'd expected, and you woke up to find your mistress gone and yourself tied to this chair."

Bodmer gave me a look. "How about a gag, then? I so enjoyed that part of the experience."

"We can accommodate you if you want, but even if you were to scream your head off, no one would hear you. Seclusion is a beautiful thing."

I faced Adeline and asked pleasantly, "Ready?"

"Yes, my dear." Turning to Bodmer, she said, "So long, Julien. I'd say good luck, but I really don't care."

"Just make sure you uphold your end of our agreement and kill the bitch. If you don't, I'll know, and then I'll find you, or she will find all of us."

Neither Adeline nor I responded. We turned and headed for the door.

"You hear me, Agent Parker, Professor Dresden?" called Bodmer. "Kill the bitch."

Bodmer's voice disturbed the evergreens outside, but we kept walking and drove off.

CHAPTER 58

We were cutting through the Swiss Alps at a speed just shy of what would get us noticed. One hour had already passed, and Adeline once again pulled out a throwaway phone.

"Would you like me to make the call?" I asked.

"No, I got it," Adeline replied.

Keeping one eye on the road, Adeline turned up the volume on the radio, which I assumed she meant to mask her voice. She then dialed a number from memory and brought the phone to her left ear.

"Yes, hello? Hello?" Adeline said, her accent slightly off from her normal speech pattern, making her sound almost Scottish. "Yes, yes. Can you hear me? Right, good. Look, we had to leave in a rush to catch our flight. We were in cottage seven. It probably needs a good cleaning. One of the kids had an accident . . . Right, sorry . . . I left it . . . No."

Adeline hung up and gave the phone an irritated glare. Then again with one hand, she ripped off the back of the handset and pulled the battery, and then tossed the device out the window over the cliff we were driving along.

"How did that go?" I asked.

"Fine. The man was a bit testy, but that's not our issue now."

"Good. Okay, since we'll be in Milan shortly, can we review the plan one more time?"

"You sound anxious, William. It's not that hard."

"Since I met you, everything has been hard. Now come on. Walk me through it."

Adeline smiled cutely. "Right. We get to Milan and find a quiet spot where we can sequester ourselves for a few hours. I'm thinking a hotel that takes cash. That's where we make the packages, confirm the consulate location and hours, do some map recon, identify ingress and egress routes—all very academic."

"Sounds like it."

"Oh, come now, William. This is the fun stuff. We finally have an advantage. We're not running—we're moving. This is deliberate and we can put some pieces in play."

"It does feel a little—" I felt a tickle in my jacket pocket that cut me off, and which got stronger as I shifted in my seat. "What the hell?"

"What?" asked Adeline.

I pulled the vibrating object out of my pocket, realizing it was Bodmer's phone. It was ringing, but it shouldn't have been, and I dumbly stared while holding it before me like some offensive hot potato.

"I thought you turned that thing off. Did you switch it back on?" asked Adeline.

"No, and I checked right before we left the cottage."

"What the . . ."

I continued staring at the phone's screen. A number wasn't displayed, only the contact name: *Mobile*.

"How could it have turned ba—"

I tapped the green icon to answer the call. As I brought the phone to my ear, Adeline mouthed, *What are you doing?* She then swerved to catch the next off-ramp.

I met Adeline's look of shock, but all my focus was directed at the tiny device pressed to my ear and the accompanying silence that screamed. I stayed quiet, barely breathing, and then after what must have been thirty seconds, a woman's voice asked, "William, are you there?"

The voice possessed a German accent and conveyed confidence. Her tone was almost pleasant, yet at this moment my gut twisted.

Another ten seconds went by, the time clicking off with each beat of my heart. Then she spoke again. "William? Is this you, my brother?"

"Yes," I replied, evoking another astonished look from Adeline as she veered off the road and stopped. I knew she couldn't hear the voice on the line, but she knew whomever it was, they had said something that had upended my world.

"Well, Brother, we finally speak. It's so nice," remarked the woman. "No need to reminisce about the childhood memories we don't share, but I will admit, I'm suddenly feeling a touch of kinship now that we are, in fact, introduced."

"Sofia?" I uttered.

Adeline's eyes went wide as did the rush in my veins.

"Yes, William. It is I, your sister. How are you, my dear brother? Are you getting along okay?"

Of all the time I'd had to think about what my father would have said if he and I ever met again, and then learning of a sister and trying to come to grips with that reality, I never could have predicted this moment.

"I'm unsure how to answer that," I said. "Up until recently, I had no idea I had a sister, nor that our father had still been alive."

"Yes, there are many secrets, aren't there."

"And you've been trying to kill me."

"It's an uncomfortable world we live in, William. Sometimes extreme measures are necessary for the greater good."

"The greater good of violence and antiquated supreme racist bullshit?"

"I have no hopes that you will understand any of this. Father was right to exclude you from our family's calling. But your bit of research you so dearly cherished and that you were so proud of, he felt it would be a problem. You had to be silenced. It's as simple as that."

"Silenced . . . You've been trying to kill me. And for what? I don't care what you're doing. I honestly don't. The violence is one thing—I think it's disgusting. But I don't care about any of this," I said, feeling a heat rise in me.

And with these words, Adeline gave me an anxious look, visibly taken aback at what I was saying. But my gut told me something different—I had an opportunity.

"You don't care, William?" Sofia asked incredulously.

"No, I don't care. I care that you stop trying to kill me—I care about that. But the rest of this business, I don't care. Not anymore."

"Please explain. I'm intrigued."

"The only reason I'm wrapped up in any of this and have done the things I've done is because *you* tried to blow me up. I was effectively shut down, my research stopped, and my ego crushed. Hell, I'd run to the family villa with my tail between my legs to lick my wounds and think about what I would do next. I had no reason to get involved with this Executive shit until you sent that fuck Sanders to kill me. I wouldn't have cared about any of this if I'd seen it on the news—not my bloody problem. I'm not *a man of action*. All those tendencies were clawed out of me back at that damned orphanage. You know about that, right? After that, I never wanted anything to do with the ugliness of this world ever again or to be put in a position where I had to do something about it."

"Of course I know. But Father feared those embers might still be lingering."

I thrust open the door and got out of the car, striding out of earshot. The look Adeline had been giving me in the car was distracting.

"Yeah, well," I said, "he didn't know me back then and he surely didn't know anything about me these past twenty years. He got it wrong."

"Interesting perspective. But you still do care, my brother. That's why I'm calling. You and your little friend, Agent Parker, somehow convinced that weasel banker of a man to put a nasty lock on some of my accounts. How is he, by the way, Julien? Did you kill him?"

"I didn't kill him, but he is dead," I said, lying.

"Perhaps Ms. Parker is more ruthless than I thought."

"Maybe."

"Is she standing next to you, listening in?"

"No, she can't hear a thing," I said, turning back to see Adeline get out of the car and coming toward me. I waved for here to stay back.

"Bravo, Brother. I'm impressed. I suspected you two would be inseparable by now. Perhaps having a nice little dalliance."

"Yeah, well, it's not like I trust her all that much, either. Things are different now."

"Quite. And knowing that, let's get back to the point of this call. You don't care, and I need access to those accounts. They're important."

"No way. Look, you started this bullshit. My ability to keep you locked out is the only insurance I have. Without me, you'll never get into those accounts. If I give that up, after all I now know, you'll surely finish what you failed to do a few days ago."

"I will surely kill you if don't give me access. You can count on that." The ice in my sister's voice came through the speaker and touched my ear. "I will never stop until I find you. And my people *will* find and kill you—very painfully I might add. And, if I never gain access to those accounts again, I will still rebuild those funds. It will take time and perhaps slow some of my initiatives, but we can't be stopped. Yet still, I will kill you."

"So why don't you do that? Why are we talking?"

"Honestly, I didn't expect to be talking to you, but now that we are, since *you don't care*, I have a proposition that will make things easier for all of us. Or, let me rephrase—my proposition is your only chance to survive and not worry about being hunted to the ends of the earth."

"I'm listening."

"My analysts have concluded that the encryption placed on the accounts requires some kind of physical security token to unlock the protocols. Is this true—did Agent Parker mastermind this?"

I looked at Adeline, still standing ten feet away, knowing the three thumb drives—the encrypted security tokens—were in her jacket pocket.

"You are correct."

"Good. Well, then. You and Agent Parker are going to come to Strasbourg to hand those security tokens over."

"And you will surely kill us as soon as you catch sight of our smiling faces. No deal."

"Not quite. Feel free to make a copy of the keys and keep them with a third party. If you don't survive, instruct that party to take action to lock down what they can, and we—the Executive—don't get what we want. Surely you can manage that."

"That sounds too easy. Why in the world would you let Adeline and me walk away?"

"Oh, wait. Let me explain. You, William, my brother, will walk away. But poor Agent Parker cannot. She must die."

"Why her and not me?"

"Because you were right. You wouldn't be in this mess were it not for her. The deciding factor in my coming after you was because of her."

"What do you mean?"

"You were right. I'd already shut you and your research down. I could have killed you long before that incident at the café, but when Agent Parker reached out to you, I was left with no choice. So, she is the entire reason you find yourself in this current situation. And how often has she lied to you? Do you think she's telling you the truth now after all you've been through?"

"I . . ."

"Come now, Brother. You're smarter than this. Almost nothing she has told you is true."

"How do you know—"

"Because I know who she is and what she is after. She's a twisted, selfish, fanatical girl, William, and she's dragged you through all this out of vengeance for her parents and their secrets. Don't kid yourself—there is nothing altruistic in her intentions," Sofia said. "But you can think whatever you want. Fundamentally, she got you into this and she would sacrifice you in a heartbeat."

Had I been walking, Sofia's words would have stopped me in my tracks.

"Go on."

"It's quite simple. If I have the accounts back and Adeline Parker is also eliminated, then there's no reason you can't walk away because you—don't—care."

"You want me to lead Agent Parker into a trap so that I can go free?"

"Something like that. Think about it for a moment."

"I don't have to. No deal."

"No? Are you sure?"

"No fucking deal."

"Fine, I admire your loyalty. Then what about a trade?"

"Trade? I'm not following."

"Your old teacher, of course. The man who became a father figure when ours abandoned you."

"What are you talking about?"

"Rupert Eisengard. We have him."

"I . . ."

"You thought he was dead, didn't you? And why wouldn't you. You left him amid a fight, all alone, so you and Agent Parker could escape. *You abandoned him.* But now you can save him and assuage the guilt I know you carry."

"What do you mean, Sofia?"

"It's as easy as this. You come to Strasbourg and turn over the tokens, and in exchange for Agent Parker, you and Eisengard go free. This is your only chance to leave all this behind and not have to look over your shoulder for the rest of your life."

"And if I still don't agree to your terms?"

"I kill Eisengard now, then I hunt you down and kill both you and Agent Parker, and I still get my tokens. And if you implement some kind of *insurance* where your sudden demise sparks some barrister to destroy said tokens or perform some other type of exposure, it is no matter. We pause for a time and dismiss it as we've done for over a century when exposure is at risk, and then go about reacquiring what we've lost." I heard Sofia inhale. "Now, we have spoken long enough and I have no patience. You can't be too far from Zurich. You have four hours. Bring the tokens and Agent Parker to—"

"All right. I agree, but on my terms."

"So forceful. Were you not my brother, I might be tickled. Please, continue and tell me, what are your terms?"

"The south side of the Strasbourg Cathedral on the Place du Château. Public and in the open for all to see."

"Interesting choice. Be there at eighteen hundred with Agent Parker beside you. You will be approached and the trade will be made."

The line clicked off.

CHAPTER 59

The Curator's boots crunched over the frozen ground, which was the only sound on the forest air. Snow and dusk in the woods always created silence. But that silence only extended to the edge of what one could see, which was why the Curator stopped when he spied the small cabin through the trees.

Again, as he'd done when he first parked on the access road and started his approach in, he breathed in his surroundings. An occasional clump of snow dropped from a branch, the afternoon sun peeked through the overcast sky. There was no movement around the exterior of the cabin and no cars parked in the drive. Light came from the front room's window, but the rest of the cottage was dark.

The Curator assumed they had all gone but he was still unsure what he might find inside. He approached the cottage and ascended the porch steps, stepping on the areas directly over the support braces to avoid any squeaks. But when he reached the door and went to test the lock, he instead leaned over to look through the window.

To his surprise, he saw an individual tied to a chair in the corner of the room. The Curator couldn't see the individual's face but he had a strong suspicion about who it could be.

With his gloved hand, the Curator used a small metal cylinder that had a point on the end to punch through the windowpane.

Large and small bits of glass fell to the ground with a sound that mimicked champagne flutes cheering. He then reached his hand through the hole and unlocked the front door.

As he entered the cabin, the Curator watched the restrained individual jerk left and right to try and get a look at who had just broken in.

"Who's there? Who are you?" said the man in German. "Help me. Untie me. I was kidnapped."

The Curator ignored the man's pleas and instead studied the room's interior, noting the relative order and cleanliness of the holiday retreat that had been transformed into a holding cell. He then glanced into the only bedroom but stayed clear of the man's line of sight. Although he had not expected to find such a situation, as he contemplated the possible scenarios, it made sense.

Satisfied there were no other surprises, the Curator took a wide path to stay clear of the man's reach and positioned himself in front of him. Their eyes focused on each other, one scrutinizing from a position of power while the other tried to hide the fear behind a defiant glare.

"Who are you?" Bodmer asked again. "You're not the maid service. Help me. I was kidnapped, attacked."

"Be quiet, Mr. Bodmer. I am the one who will ask the questions," the Curator said in accented German.

"What? Who are you? How do you know my name?"

"What did you tell them?" asked the Curator.

"What did I tell who? Call the authorities. You can't keep me like this. I will pay you."

The Curator shook his head. "If you don't answer my questions, I will simply kill you and uncover what I want to know on my own. Now, I don't like to repeat myself. What did you tell them?"

At that moment, a shock of recognition registered with Bodmer. "My God, it's you. You are the Russian, the one the Kanzler contacted all those years ago."

"The former Kanzler," the Curator corrected. But the truth was the opposite. Although the former Kanzler did indeed request a meeting with him, it transpired that way because the Curator had orchestrated the preceding events so that the Kanzler would be the one to initiate the first move. The Curator believed it is much easier to get someone to do your bidding when they think it's their idea.

The Curator went on, "My understanding is that there's a new Kanzler, correct?"

Bodmer nodded shakily.

"Now, because I can see that you are a bit unnerved, I am going to give you one more opportunity to answer my question. What did you tell the professor and the English woman?"

Bodmer forced a short breath through his teeth. "If it is you that are here, I am already dead. I have heard the whispers of who you are and what you do, and if you don't do it, the Kanzler's apparatchiks surely will. I have no loyalty to anyone anymore and I see no reason to give you what you want."

"You mistake me, Mr. Bodmer. Despite what you assume or think me to be, I am not here to kill you."

"I have no confidence in anything that comes from your mouth," spat Bodmer, but although his words on their own were meant to convey bravado, the quiver in his voice betrayed him.

The Curator thought for a moment, but the pressure of time increased. He took his focus off Bodmer and looked around the room again, then walked to the kitchen nook. He heard Bodmer ask where he was going, what he was doing, but ignored the man's outbursts.

Standing in front of the counter, he noticed the water droplets on the dishes were almost dry and that the wadded-up hand towel was still damp. Yes, time was indeed running out, but he was not far behind them.

"You want the new Kanzler eliminated, don't you, Mr. Bodmer?" called out the Curator over his shoulder.

"Why would you think that?"

"Her predecessor and I discussed many things. I knew her short-comings and her tendencies. I also suspect that, even as a dead man, which you are, you would like to see her destroyed, too."

Bodmer stayed silent for a long minute before finally asking, "What can you do for me?"

"I will make you disappear, Julien, where no one could ever find you. It will not be up to your posh Western standards, but you will be alive and free to do as you wish in your new home."

"What, like a safe house with a lock and guard?"

"No, there will be no such thing. It will be a town for you to exist," replied the Curator. "Now, enough of this."

The Curator spun on his heel and strode back to Bodmer. He leaned forward to grip Bodmer's wrists and the armrest they were tied to. "Tell me where Dresden and Parker have gone and what they are going to do."

Bodmer recoiled but could not escape the Curator's face just inches from his. "I don't know where they are going. They didn't say. Why would they? But I did reveal to them who the new Kanzler is and the relation to the professor."

"Sister?"

Bodmer nodded.

"What are they going to do?"

"I don't know. They would not say, nor did I ask. But I locked out the Executive's accounts I still had access to. I then demanded they kill the Kanzler. Whether they will attempt such a thing, I can't say. All I know is they took the security tokens and I heard them whispering about other contacts."

"Where is the Kanzler? Where is Sofia König?"

"I would assume Strasbourg. It's where she intended to control the operation from."

The Curator raised back to his full height. "You mean the attacks?"

Bodmer nodded.

"Stupid, stupid strategy," the Curator uttered to the air.

"That's all I know. Now, I have given you what you asked for. You promised to help me."

"I promised nothing. But I do follow through. A woman will come and take you." Although the Curator considered Bodmer a weasel, he could be of value in the future.

"What? What does that mean?"

The Curator ignored Bodmer and headed for the door. He took out his phone and dialed, and the woman on the other end picked up on the first ring. In Hungarian, the Curator spoke a few sentences and then clicked off.

"The woman will be here within the hour. You will go with her and do as she instructs."

"What? No. Untie me!"

The Curator left the cottage and let the slam of the door cut off Bodmer's cries.

CHAPTER 60

"What the hell did you just do, William?" demanded Adeline. "Give me that."

Adeline snatched the phone from my hand, checked the call log to see if there was a number—there wasn't—and then tore the handset apart before stomping it into tiny pieces of plastic, metal, and glass.

"Get in the car now," she snapped.

I did as she instructed, albeit slightly slower than my normal pace of movement. And upon incurring one more dumbfounded glare from Adeline, we sped back onto the autobahn toward Milan.

"You better hope they didn't geo-locate us with how long you were on that damn call. That was your psychotic sister, wasn't it? Sofia—the bitch."

"Yes, it was, and you're going the wrong way," I replied flatly.

"What?"

"Turn the hell around. We have to go to Strasbourg."

"Strasbourg? What are you bloody talking about?"

"She has Rupert. He's alive."

"What? Are you sure?"

"No. Of course I'm not sure; when are we ever sure? But I'm not going to risk it."

"William—"

"Take the goddamned exit and turn the hell around!"

Adeline swerved at speed to take the turnoff and then decelerated fast. But rather than taking the turn hard at the end of the off-ramp, I noticed her grip on the steering wheel relax. Then, in a very casual out-for-an-afternoon-drive kind of way, she proceeded under the overpass and turned to travel back north, the way we'd just come. Back on the autobahn, she reached a precise speed of 120 km/h.

"You better start explaining, William."

"We're going to meet Sofia in Strasbourg. We'll turn over the tokens, Rupert will be set free, and then Sofia will kill you."

Adeline's demeanor suddenly went from simmering anger to mild curiosity. "Well, isn't that interesting," she remarked. Tilting her head, she asked, "Do I have a say in the matter?"

"You damn well better because I have no idea how we're going to pull this off."

"Right. A swap, I'm assuming. Rupert for the tokens and me just because."

"Yes."

"Why only me?"

"I blamed you for everything and said none of this was my business and I didn't care what happened. I just wanted to be left alone."

"Right, okay. Does she think you actually believe she's going to let you and Rupert walk?"

"I've no idea, but rather than contemplating what my psychotic sister thinks, we should probably focus on how we're going to prevent her from killing us all."

"Good idea. Where in Strasbourg did she tell you to meet?"

"I set the meeting place—the Cathedral of our Lady of Strasbourg."

"That's an interesting choice. Why there?"

"No other reason than it's the only public and large open-air space I know."

Adeline gave a quick laugh. "Right. Good thinking. It's better than wherever she wanted. We just need to figure out how to use this to our advantage."

"Yeah, I've been thinking about that. Whatever we're going to do, we can't do it alone, just the two of us. We need help."

"I wouldn't disagree, but who?"

"Your source, the *Artist*."

"Hm, right. Sure. Splendid idea. But what makes you think we can trust him?"

"He's obviously against the Executive. You've known that since your first meeting and everything he's revealed to you since then has, in fact, been true."

"You're right, but I have no idea who this man is or why he's doing what he's doing. He could very well be a member of the Executive trying to manufacture his own takeover, and our connection is part of an elaborate ruse. And besides, he's never responded to requests to meet. He's only ever reached out to me."

"True, but given everything that's going on, I suspect he's watching events unfold and, if you were to try to contact him, now more than ever would be the time for him to respond."

"It's a big risk, William. I need to think through it."

"We don't have time, but I hear you. So, in addition to this *are-tist*, we add another layer of protection—sort of a fail-safe."

"What did you have in mind?"

CHAPTER 61

Faust stood by the corner of the Cathédrale Notre Dame de Strasbourg. From his vantage point, and despite the crowds of tourists and locals moving here and there, he spotted the two men positioned on the Place de Château. Faust then looked down each axis that opened onto the square. One man at Rue de Maroquin holding a paper tourist map. A couple—a man and woman—sat on the ground near Rue de Rohan. A single individual at Rue de la Râpe. And there were the same on the north side of the cathedral, too; teams positioned at every point Dresden and Parker could enter the square.

And he had control. These were his teams, his people—they answered to him. This meet was too important and there were too many things that could go wrong. And they couldn't go wrong, not this time.

Faust pulled out his phone and dialed.

Sofia answered. "Is everything ready?"

"My teams are in position. Where are you?"

"That's not your concern right now."

"It absolutely is my concern. When Dresden and Parker arrive, you have to be ready to show yourself."

"I will be where I need to be."

"What are you planning, Sofia? I run the operations. If you launch another attack without informing me, how can I react as you expect me to?"

"You *will* because that's how it is. I am the Kanzler. Now keep your people alert and notify me as soon as my brother and his trollop enter the square."

The line went dead.

Faust squeezed the phone and cursed.

CHAPTER 62

STRASBOURG, FRANCE

The waiting was killing me. I had to pace around the room to keep myself together.

After our high-speed sprint from Zurich to Strasbourg, Adeline and I sequestered ourselves in a not-so-refined hotel on the edge of the city. The hotel's location and the position of our room—facing the main street—were all that mattered.

Then, as soon as we'd agreed it was our only and perhaps best chance, Adeline called the number the Artist had given her all those years ago but which he'd never answered or followed through on. For the call, she'd also broken protocol and said in her message the time and location to meet—a table at a café across the street and directly in view from our window.

If the Artist was going to show, it would be in five minutes.

I wanted to ask Adeline again whether she thought he would indeed show, but I'd done that a few times already, eliciting the same response—*I don't know*. I'd also asked what she thought we should do if he didn't show, and that answer had been similarly short—*We get on with it and figure it out*. I'd asked a few other questions and probably asked just about everything I should, which is why we were now waiting in silence watching.

And then, much to my surprise because admittedly I was in shock at things playing out as we'd hoped, an older gentleman wearing a worn brown coat that went down to his knees sat down at the table Adeline had specified. He'd arrived at almost the precise second he'd been instructed to.

"That's him," Adeline said.

Holy shit was all I could think. We'd pushed a button here and we'd observed an output down there—the presence of this man. Remarkably, I had no idea he was in the area until he sat down. I hadn't noticed him before that moment despite having been observing the café and street just moments before. The man hadn't approached sneakily. He hadn't approached boldly. The man hadn't approached cautiously, either. Nothing observable. As I thought about it, the man had simply existed, an invisible part of the environment until *he wanted* us to see him. And even as this man—the so-called Artist—sat there, to the casual passerby, he blended perfectly.

Yet, as I watched him, the subtleness of this man's intensity could not be ignored. The mere placement of his hands and feet told me he was primed to shift or move with strength and speed. His gaze seemed casual, yet I realized that in less than a minute he'd looked in every direction and taken stock of every detail in his view.

The other noticeable thing about this man was his steel gray beard. Some people look forced with facial hair as if they don't realize how unnatural it looks. Others, however, wear it perfectly as if they were born to display the ideal mustache or shaped goatee. Tom Selleck comes to mind, who wouldn't be himself without his iconic thick brash of hair above his lip. The man below wore his beard in the same manner.

"I'm going down there," Adeline said.

"Okay. You sure you don't want me as backup on the street? If something is to go off the rails, I have at least one good tackle left in me."

"No. If it does go bad, you need to get away. Besides, I need you as my eye in the sky after I make contact. You'll be in a better position up here to spot anyone tailing us rather than peering awkwardly from around a corner."

"Right. Just be careful."

Adeline smiled gently and left the room to make her way down the two flights of stairs, out the back service entrance, and around the block so she could approach from down the street rather than emerge from the hotel lobby.

I returned my focus to our man at the café, seeing that he'd ordered an espresso. Again, the waiting gnawed at me as I counted off the seconds, anticipating Adeline's appearance at the street corner and what would be her figurative run-up to the mysterious source who'd danced in her shadows for the past three years.

Earlier today, Adeline had tested how long it would take her to make the circuitous route to the street corner, which had come out to approximately two minutes and twenty seconds, give or take. But when I spotted her make the turn at one minute fifty-seven seconds, I suspected the adrenaline was pumping in her veins, too.

I scanned the street up and down as well as scrutinized the other patrons sitting at the café or those pedestrians loitering nearby. I knew not to expect any overt reaction—if indeed the Artist had positioned friends in the area—so as Adeline advanced, I looked for the benign gestures—the opening or closing of a magazine or newspaper, the appearance of a phone, or maybe the sudden convergence of two people. Too bad every one of these and all the other examples Adeline had described were about as common as a teenager texting while walking down the street. One could go crazy either jumping at shadows or missing the one sign that could mean life or death.

At thirty feet away, I saw our man with the gray beard—the Artist—look to his left and make eye contact with Adeline. Even from my perch in the second-floor window across the street, I could tell his composure didn't waver even a fraction. He waited and observed.

Adeline continued, but in contrast, instead of remaining locked on the Artist as she had done to me not so long ago in Nice, I noticed her gaze darting all about. Not abruptly so, but she was definitely attuned to her surroundings and everyone around her.

I spotted nothing of concern but kept watching.

Fifteen feet, ten feet, five feet—contact.

I don't know what I expected to happen when Adeline finally reached the Artist—a handshake, a hug, a curtsy—but the scene played out swiftly.

Adeline had walked directly up to the table where the Artist sat. He, in turn, stood, bringing himself eye-to-eye with her and less than a foot away. I couldn't see either of their faces from my angle but I could tell they were exchanging words.

The Artist then placed a few euro coins on the table alongside his untouched espresso and then he and Adeline weaved through the rows of tables, heading toward our hotel. They moved swiftly but not in a hurry, then waited for a car to pass and crossed the street. They disappeared from my view upon entering the lobby.

I pulled myself from the window and did as Adeline had instructed. Rather than standing in the middle of the room with arms outstretched like a guest at a surprise party, I moved to the wall to the right of the door on the hinge side. Adeline's thinking was if the Artist decided to knife her in the hall and then bust into the room to place a silenced bullet in my forehead, I might have a fighting chance to slam the door on him and get out.

The scenarios and concerns that spies must constantly consider, always with a backup and alternative to the desired—or hoped-for—outcome, were limitless and must chip away at the nerves of these people. I knew it was doing so for me.

I waited against the wall, staring at the door, my body awkwardly between a primed stance to rush the door and standing upright. I counted the seconds and almost reached three minutes when I heard the beep of the automatic card lock.

The door opened and Adeline called into the room, "Can you please put the water on." Which was the code for her to communicate that everything was okay. If she'd said anything else or nothing at all, I would have reacted much differently.

Adeline and the Artist cleared the threshold into the room and secured the door behind them. It was the three of us alone in the room, and I beheld this mysterious figure up close for the first time. I felt butterflies in my stomach, and then he spoke with a thick Slavic accent, "Hello, Professor Dresden. Nice to meet you."

CHAPTER 63

"Hello," I said to the man standing before me. He looked about the same up close as he did from afar, except although he appeared to be in his sixties at least, his frame looked surprisingly fit and his hands at his sides seemed meaty and powerful.

"We've got work to do," the Artist said. "I have been trying to find the both of you for some time."

"And why is that?" I asked.

The man's face brightened slightly. "There is an opportunity unlike any in recent history to disrupt the Executive, of course."

"Before we go any further," Adeline interjected, "why do you want to stop them, and why after all this time did you respond to my signal and meet me?"

The Artist looked at Adeline and then me, and then back to Adeline. He walked over to the kitchenette and began rummaging through the few cupboards. "I thought one of you said something about coffee. I didn't get to drink mine at the café."

"We don't have much time," Adeline said.

"There's usually always time for coffee. Unless someone is shooting at you, of course. Then maybe vodka is better," the Artist said over his shoulder.

"Why do you want to stop the Executive, Mr. . . . what is your name?"

"I go by many names. I've heard that you call me *the Artist*, no doubt from my appearance when we first met three years ago. Others have called me *the Curator*. I have used Sasha, Oleg, and too many names for me to remember. But my real name, and the name I would like you to use, is Károly."

"Hungarian?" I asked.

"Yes, by birth. Although I have lived the majority of my life in Russia serving the Soviets and now Russian security services. But we can discuss our family lineages another time. Both of you are quite interesting, too," Károly said. "But as you say, we have little time."

"No," Adeline said. "Not yet. Why did you reach out to me three years ago? Why are you after the Executive?"

Károly continued prepping the kettle to boil water for his coffee. Once he turned on the burner and shifted to spooning Nescafé into a mug, he looked up expectantly at Adeline and me to see if we wanted some. "No? Okay."

Károly screwed the cap back on the container and said, "The Executive is an evil organization that has no room for anyone but itself, even its own members. I, like you, want it stopped."

"Why? Russia and Hungary aren't exactly known for their embracement of diversity."

Károly chuckled. "Yes, Putin is a xenophobic bastard striving to subjugate the fringes of Russian territory as well as kill Muslims. You know Chechnya, yes? And, of course, the prime minister who has run my homeland for far too long, he is an authoritarian nationalist, too." Károly paused to check the kettle and see how the water was coming along. "I understand why you ask these questions. My interest in the Executive is from my desire to stop its meddling in the place I call home. I do not agree with the Executive's ideology."

"It's about ideology?"

"Yes. Ideology. Years ago it was capitalism and democracy. Then we got distracted by religious fanatics for too long. Now, it is murderous groups who threaten someone like me because of my blood. Is it so hard to understand? The world has seen this performance before."

"But why are you helping us now? You've ignored my messages for years."

Károly snorted. "I was skeptical about how effective you would be or if you would survive. I saw no reason to risk myself to toy with your curiosity."

"And now?"

"You have impressed me. And as I said, we now have a chance and I am here to help. It is a simple risk calculation. Now, enough discussion. Our time is disappearing."

Adeline and I looked at each other. I shrugged and Adeline nodded consent.

I said, "Here's what we know . . ."

CHAPTER 64

I left our hotel room and went downstairs, exiting the lobby onto the street. Within a few minutes, I was heading southwest on Quai des Pêcheurs, boutiques to my left and the Canal du Faux-Rempart to my right.

I moved briskly at a speed just shy of what would grab the attention of a casual passerby. With the afternoon sun descending, I observed what I could but didn't think I would catch everything. I didn't mean to. If the Executive wasn't already on me, they would be soon—which was the point. The plan wouldn't work if they didn't see me coming.

I passed by the Saint-Guillame bridge and kept moving.

Adeline and Károly should have been on the move by now, but they would do things a little differently than me. They had somewhere to be, too, but it'd be best if they *weren't* seen.

Adeline and I had put the third element in motion, as well.

My pace consistent, I turned right onto the Pont Ste Madeleine bridge. Across the way at the end of the street, I could see the T-intersection where I would turn left onto Rue de la Râpe. From there, it would just be a few more steps until I stepped onto Place du Château—ground zero—the square adjacent to the Cathédrale

Notre Dame de Strasbourg. The place I expected to confront my sister or whomever she sent in her stead.

There was no turning back now. I could feel the Executive's eyes on me, the lookers and watchers all around.

Another twenty feet and I would make the turn. If my heart rate had quickened, I couldn't tell. The anticipation—the stress—the fear—the uncertainty—it was constant and it was all the same. I kept moving.

I crested the corner from Rue du Bain-aux-Roses onto Rue de la Râpe, and the square opened up. The midafternoon sun burned down on the square, and the pedestrians—many of them tourists—milling about snapping the ideal vacation shots and selfies or admiring a map or guidebook to take in the history of this place. I said a silent prayer for their safety.

As my right foot hit the square's cobblestones, I scanned my path through the innocents. I quickly spotted two unmistakable figures smack in the middle of the square precisely where I'd anticipated them to be.

I put my hands in my pockets and gripped the encrypted tokens between my fingers.

It would be all or nothing, I thought.

CHAPTER 65

Faust's earpiece crackled.

"He just reached the square and he's heading toward us."

"Roger. Where is the woman?" Faust asked.

"We do not see the woman."

"Scheiß," spat Faust. "Alpha Team, Bravo Team—do you have eyes on Agent Parker?"

"This is Alpha Team. Negative. We are holding at the north entrance."

A few seconds passed before Faust said, "Bravo Team, respond."

Another twenty seconds passed.

"Bravo Team, check in."

Faust's earpiece hissed as someone tried to transmit. "This is Bravo Team—we have her—closing in."

"Negative," snapped Faust. "Hold and observe."

Faust waited for acknowledgment but none came.

"Bravo Team, confirm you are holding. You are NOT to engage."

"Sir, we have different orders."

"Different orders? From who?"

CHAPTER 66

I'd made it halfway to the center of the Place du Château when I felt my phone vibrate. There weren't supposed to be any calls—none. Comms silence unless we had a problem. Thoughts of the club flashed through my mind.

I released my grip on the token and brought my phone straight to my ear. "What?"

"Károly is gone. I think it's a setup. Get out," ordered Adeline.

"What?"

"Bloody hell, William. Abort."

"Are you positive?"

Adeline hesitated for the briefest of seconds and I made my decision.

"It doesn't make sense. If it was a trap they would have grabbed us at the hotel when we were together. It's too late to abort. I'm committed. Make the calls or none of this works."

I clicked off my phone, gritted my teeth, and pressed forward. Seventy-five more feet—twenty more seconds—and I would reach the two thugs waiting for me, the men I knew to be Executive.

Their features became clearer with each step. They were of a similar height and build, around six feet, blocky, and with thick necks. Given that they both wore black, their primary distinguishing feature was their hair—one blond and one black. They both had their hands tucked in their jacket pockets, no doubt wrapped around pistols or radios, or both.

Fifty feet away.

Adeline better have started making those calls or I was a dead man.

Thirty feet.

I took a breath.

Twenty feet.

Ten feet.

I stopped. Close enough to talk but still with enough space between me and them in case I needed to run. I sized up one and then the other, as they did me.

At neither in particular, I asked, "Where's Eisengard?"

Blondie spoke, his central European accent harsh. "Where is Agent Parker?"

"Waiting in the wings," I responded. "I'll call her once we do the exchange, but not before."

"That is not the arrangement, Professor. We are to take the tokens and Agent Parker, then you can have your *friend*."

"There's no insurance in that," I replied, turning my chin up in defiance. "You could simply kill or dispose of me."

"We can do that now."

"I'm sure you could. But are those your orders? Wipe me away before your boss gets all she wants out of me?"

Blondie frowned, then turned his shoulders so I could see past him. Thirty yards beyond near the southwest corner of the cathedral—by the main entrance—I spotted him. Rupert Eisengard stood stiffly, flanked by an edgy individual who stood right beside him. I assumed he was pressing a gun into Rupert's back.

And then, perhaps twenty feet to their left, I saw her. With long blonde hair and a striking figure under her white pantsuit, I knew it was her—my sister, Sofia König, the Kanzler of the Executive.

"There," said Blondie. "Now you see we are true to our side of the arrangement."

"Yes, very upstanding of you," I said, quieter than I wanted.

"Yah. We've had enough conversation. Where is Agent Parker?"

I shook my head.

"When we do the swap, I'll call Agent Parker as she and I planned. I'll tell you where you can grab her."

Blondie raised his right hand to his ear and cupped it. I assumed someone was calling his earpiece. He then said something I didn't catch and returned his focus to me.

He smiled with a twisted upturn of his mouth. "We have Agent Parker. You have no more options. Turn over the tokens or we kill you and your friend now."

I thought to say something more, to stall just a little longer, but then I heard the sweet sound I'd been waiting for. Sirens grew in the distance, riding on the cool autumn breeze coming across the square.

Maybe they had found Adeline. Maybe they hadn't and Blondie was lying to force me to act. But regardless, she'd succeeded in her part of the plan.

Both Blondie's and Dark Hair's faces betrayed them. With the sirens growing, the two men looked uneasily at each other and then back to me.

I smiled. "That's right, assholes. That's the sound of Interpol, the Germans, the French, and every other security service in the area—all of them coming here to arrest me, the Nice bomber, along with my accomplices—you guys."

Full recognition still hadn't landed on Blondie or Dark Hair, but behind them, I saw the man holding Eisengard waver while my sister burned her stare into me.

I chanced waiting one more second, wanting the authorities to get just a little closer to storm the square, then I did it.

With one token in my right hand and the other in my left, I tossed them to each side of Blondie and Dark Hair. The two men initially jerked to draw their weapons, but instead, they reflexively lunged to catch the tiny devices I'd thrown at them, no doubt instructed that the tokens were critical.

Coming off the block like back on the track, I dashed between them heading toward Eisengard.

Emergency lights burst onto the square from all directions, police vehicles skidding through access roads and locking the area down. I saw Eisengard's minder draw his gun while my sister stepped as if preparing to flee.

I reached a full sprint, aimed at Eisengard, then saw our third option join the fray. My dear old friend Hervé came barreling around the corner of the cathedral past a confused couple and slammed into Sofia, knocking her to the ground. That hadn't been the plan, but he'd adjusted perfectly.

I expected the man holding Eisengard to start firing, but to my dismay, he released Eisengard and stepped clear. And Eisengard, rather than running away, stayed put.

The guard then raised his gun, but not at me or Eisengard or Hervé.

As my sister tried to get to her feet, the man took careful aim and fired, putting a bullet into her right shoulder. The round's impact spun her wildly.

I stopped my rush forward, utterly confused, then someone hit me from behind, driving me to the ground.

A strained voice said, "Professor William Dresden, you are under arrest."

CHAPTER 67

Someone had their knee pressed at the intersection of my neck and shoulder, pinning me to the ground while grinding a few decent-sized pebbles into my cheek. But even though it hurt, I still smiled.

I saw Hervé sitting on the ground with two paramedics giving him a once-over. Eisengard was in a similar state, all in one piece and alive and well enduring a few pokes and prods. And although I spotted my sister on a gurney with someone attending to her shoulder wound, two uniformed and heavily armed officers kept a tight watch on her.

"On your feet," ordered a voice in accented English. I couldn't see the speaker's face, but he sounded German.

That was fine with me. German, French, South African, Himalayan—it didn't matter. We'd created enough noise to bring quite a variety of security services raining down upon us. The Executive couldn't control them all and this little ruckus, combined with the evidence housed on the magic tokens—the real ones that were still in my back pocket—would help us expose the conspiracy.

Of course, I was thinking optimistically. I had no idea if Adeline was still alive, nor what the hell happened to Károly. But I needed to give myself a moment to be at ease. Sofia, Blondie and Dark Hair, a few others—I watched as the authorities cuffed them and took them away. As my minder ushered me toward a waiting car, I felt like we'd turned a corner—no longer on the run.

When we reached the unmarked car, my escort pushing me along didn't bother to say, *Watch your head*. He just shoved me in the back. *It is what it is*, I thought.

The driver's door opened and a man got in. I assumed it was the one who'd cuffed me and marched me over here. I thought his silhouette looked familiar.

Then he turned to face me and my heart stopped. The man looking at me over the seat was the same individual who'd been holding Eisengard at gunpoint on the square no more than ten minutes ago. He was Executive.

CHAPTER 68

"Do not say a word, Professor. Do not attempt to run or do anything else heroic. Do you understand?"

I didn't know what to say, part of me thinking I should indeed try to escape, maybe even headbutt the man—but at this moment my instincts told me something else was going on and that I needed to listen.

After a moment, letting his stale breath fester between us, the man continued. "I am on your side. My name is Faust Broch, and for the past twelve years, I have been an undercover penetration of the Strasbourg Executive. I was your father's chief of security, and then your sister's for a time."

Again, my voice failed me and I just sat staring at him.

"What? Do you think you were the only one trying to shut down the Executive? The BfV has been watching the Executive since 1961."

"What the hell are you talking about?" I finally asked.

Faust's lips curled into a tight-lipped smile, but I wouldn't describe the expression as friendly. He then faced back around, started the vehicle, and we drove off the square. This car, although unmarked, had emergency lights wired inside. Faust left them on but kept the siren off, thankfully.

Once through the tangle of armed and unarmed first responders, roadblocks, herringboned marked and unmarked cars, police tape, barriers, and the shocked or panicked pedestrians both on the square and bleeding out into the nearby streets, we reached a normal vehicle speed enmeshed with Strasbourg's afternoon traffic. Soon we turned into a sterilized industrial area and then entered a small warehouse through a garage door that rolled shut behind us.

I couldn't see much of anything in the cavernous space until a light flicked on ahead of our vehicle. We parked near what looked like a prefabricated office—four panels thrown together with a door and window. As my eyes adjusted, I saw a handful of identical structures farther back but no movement or light around them.

Faust turned the car off, got out, and opened my door. "Get out."

I waited a half second and did as instructed. Once I cleared the door, Faust spun me around and removed my handcuffs.

"What's going on?" I asked.

"Follow me," he ordered.

I complied, as much out of curiosity as well as lack of choice.

We walked toward the office that had the light and Faust opened the door, motioning me inside. As I looked around, with the single lamp in the corner illuminating some of the space, I saw what I ascertained were the remains of a police operations center but which had recently been abandoned. The half-drunk coffee cups, scattered pieces of paper with pencil scratches, random unplugged power cords, and other bits of leftover activity suggested this place had once been bustling like an ops center but was now absent of all life.

Then I saw a shadow move at one of the back desks. A woman stood up and came forward. In the low light, I saw she wore a dark suit with her hair pulled back, giving her a severe look.

"Professor Dresden, this is Director Wagner of the BfV who heads the special unit focused on right-wing extremist groups."

"Hello, Professor. I would say it's a pleasure to meet you, but given the circumstances, it's not," Director Wagner said, her voice gravelly as if she'd smoked for thirty years.

"Hello, Director Wagner," I replied almost as a question. "Can someone please tell me what is going on?"

"Yes, but only because we don't have a choice."

"I don't understand."

"You've been caught up in an unfortunate business. We know you were not the perpetrator of the Nice bombing; you were the target. And we know although your family has been behind most of the Executive's actions for the past twenty years and before, it was not you. Again, unfortunate business."

Faust spoke up. "As I said in the car, you're not the only one who's been trying to stop the Executive."

"I'm so confused. You say you are undercover and that you knew about the Executive's attacks, but why didn't you do anything until now?"

"To dismantle a network like the Executive takes time. It's been around in some shape or form since the nineteenth century. Sometimes influential, sometimes not, but the toxicity never went away. A cult of like-minded fanatics with corrupt beliefs that seems to attract new adherents, even decades after the fact. Distorted historical beliefs do that."

"I know the history," I remarked. "But why didn't you do anything?"

"Operational patience," replied Faust.

"What is *operational patience*?"

"Letting a situation develop to ensure we understand what we are up against and waiting for the right moment to act, not prematurely. Panicky people have lost opportunities to stop the real threat more than once because they were scared to wait."

I huffed. "So, while you people were taking your time, bombs were killing children. You were the chief of security for my father and then my sister. How could you not know?"

"Since when does an aide know all the mind of his general? I protected your father's life; I did not run his operations or sit in all his meetings. And your sister, although keenly interested to deploy the lethal aspects of my skills, kept many things from me. She was her own animal."

"Right, of course. And what of my sister? What will happen to her?"

"She'll go into a dark hole," assured Director Wagner.

"Never to be seen again?" I asked.

She shrugged.

"And my friends, Rupert and Adeline?"

"Rupert, like you, will return to his former life. We have no further use of him."

"You're not going to question him? He's my friend but he is also a former member of the Executive. Couldn't he help bring down what's left?"

"We know Mr. Eisengard well and have had many conversations with him over the years," Director Wagner said.

I huffed. "Right, of course you have. And Adeline?"

Neither Faust nor Wagner said anything.

"What happened to Adeline Parker?" I repeated.

"She's gone," answered Faust. "But we did locate a room on the first floor above a shop at the edge of the square where there were bloodstains and multiple 9mm shell casings."

"What do you mean *gone*?"

"The evidence suggests the Executive got her," added Wagner.

My gaze fell to the floor, too many thoughts flooding my mind to meet their stares. Adeline could very well be dead or tied up in some basement awaiting a grisly end in the next few moments. She also could be very much free and alive, the bloodstains having come from whoever made the mistake of trying to take her out. But I would not accept a simple *she's gone* or *the Executive got her*. I would not. But I would keep my thoughts to myself. This discussion— what I wanted to ask and demand—would not happen now. Not with these two—no.

"Everything is over for you, Professor Dresden. We will send you home, and you will not speak of these events again."

I looked up. "Over? Over? And what of my face having been splashed all over TV as a terrorist? And what about the parts of the Executive you can't or won't put away? The lone actors still out there, maybe hoping to put crosshairs on my back, or maybe Rupert's. Or does that fall into operational patience, as you phrased it?"

"Although you were known by your father and sister and some of the senior members of the Executive, myself included, your connection to the Executive was not widely known across the network. And we have arrested many of those who may have known your identity. You are no more at risk of being assassinated than your university roommate," Faust said.

"Am I supposed to trust that?"

"We're not concerned whether you trust it or not, Professor. That is up to you," Wagner said.

"Right, of course. And my record?"

"Your record has been cleared to be followed by public announcements admitting mistakes were made. Mr. Broch will provide you with the details for a story, which you must stick to."

"How convenient."

"Yes, very convenient. About what happened and why you were named as the bomber and how that has all been cleared up. An unfortunate mistake. Nothing else—nothing about the Executive, your family, or anything that's happened in the past week, nor your involvement with Agent Parker—none of that shall be acknowledged or discussed. Do you understand?"

I didn't respond.

"Do you understand, Professor Dresden? This business—the Executive—is a highly sensitive matter that is classified, as you Americans like to say."

"I'm hearing the word *unfortunate* a lot. Is the Executive still a threat? Does it still exist?"

"We are dismantling it now," answered Broch. "Those activities, as the director said, are classified—but yes, the Executive is being shut down as we speak. It is not a threat to you."

"Tell me one thing, then—what are these damn Covenants? Everyone refers to them—throws them around like blessings and curses—but I have yet to understand what they really are. What are the Covenants?"

"They are none of your concern, Professor. You should occupy yourself with the Executive no more," directed Wagner.

I couldn't help but stare blankly at these two. Yet, they'd revealed enough. And I certainly was not about to inquire about the fates of Hervé or Károly. Faust or Wagner hadn't brought them up— perhaps they did not know about them—and I was not about to reveal their involvement.

I would think upon the fates of Hervé and Károly later.

"May I go home now?" I asked, feeling a level of exhaustion in my voice I don't think I've ever experienced before or knew was possible.

CHAPTER 69

After my warehouse rendezvous with the great undercover operative Faust Broch and his cheery boss, Director Wagner, they put me on a plane back to Nice. I found my car where I'd parked it a few blocks away from the restaurant where I'd first met Adeline. Although it'd been just over a week, this vehicle I'd owned for decades now looked like an abandoned ghost to me, cold and foreign.

I checked it for wires, having picked up a few things with all that time with Adeline, and then drove past the seaside establishment where this whole mess had started. The scars were still visible—I'd expected them to be—but seeing them in person evoked a relentless sting. Even from a distance, the sight of the blackened walls and broken windows that had yet to be repaired caused my nostrils to burn as if I'd been transported back there with the smoke and heat and my ears ringing.

By the time I got home, dusk was creeping through the orchards and vineyards and over the rolling hills. My house, too, was as I'd left it, and the stuffy air from being shut up for the past week hung in every room. Everything was familiar—this had been my hideaway for years and I owned every piece of furniture or item inside—yet I was unsettled by how after a few days it all seemed distant as if from another life I no longer lived.

But I did not allow this melancholy to last more than a night's sleep. The following morning, I got up and ran. I ran hard along the rocky paths and up the slopes and hills that decorated my region of Provence. I sweated and gasped for air as my legs burned and my lungs screamed. It hurt but I kept going and going until I'd suffered through at least seven or eight miles. When I finally arrived back at the trail leading to my back patio, I wiped the sweat from under my eyes as if they were tears and then I roared at the trees and breeze around me. When I had nothing left to yell, I breathed a full breath and stood up straight. Enough was enough.

Back in the house, I contacted Hervé using the secure means he and I—and he and I alone—had established before the confrontation in Strasbourg. Adeline had indeed been part of the plan to include Hervé in the mix yet separate from us and from Károly—we knew we needed a backup to the backup—but I had slipped him a separate set of instructions for communication with me in the event everything went off the rails. As my friend, I thought I owed him that. And since flitting away from the square like a guilty child, he'd done well staying off law enforcement's radar.

Hervé came to Provence without so much as a question. He and I then set up another means of clean communications, and with what little cash I'd hidden away, I'd put him up in a nearby hotel under an assumed name.

Like I said, I'd learned a few things from Agent Parker.

Hervé and I maintained a clear distance but we kept tabs on each other. My thinking was, it's better to have us both close by in the event the Executive's remains decide to rise from the ashes and come after either one of us—but most likely me.

For the first month, we didn't see any evidence of the Executive lurking, but we spotted the BfV watchers on me fairly frequently. I knew Faust's assertions that I'd be left alone were bullshit. Hervé and I had a few theories, but the one I kept falling back to was that I, again, was a form of bait and if the Executive was to come back around, Wagner wanted to exercise *operational patience* and perhaps let me take one for the greater good before stepping in, if at all. I sometimes wondered if Faust and Wagner discussed among themselves how this *unfortunate business* would be so much tidier if I were dead.

But now, nearly three months since everything came crashing down, it'd been a few weeks since our last spotting. Hervé and I both agreed I was as clear as I was going to get, the BfV probably bored and focused on other persons of interest.

Hervé had then secured my passage on a pleasure yacht departing from Cannes. The middle-aged couple captaining our voyage was an interesting pair regularly laced with alcohol and undeniably open to a swinging lifestyle, but they respected my privacy and did not mind that I refrained from joining them traversing the ship fully naked at all hours of the day and night.

Nevertheless, I was quite ready to disembark when we reached our destination—a little seaside town on England's northeastern coast.

CHAPTER 70

When I stepped off the yacht onto the dock, as a historian, I couldn't help but immediately search the coastal hills for Whitby Abbey and the one hundred ninety-nine steps that led to the famed ruins. Dracula had walked those steps in 1897, a dark creature who'd come ashore from the East.

I did not associate myself at all with an undead blood-drinking monster, but I could relate to the notion of a foreigner coming into this insular village in search of something secret.

Now, though, standing on the porch of a small family cottage at the edge of town, more tangible matters gripped me. Although no sound came from within, I could tell people were inside. Just like you could sense the absence of human activity in abandoned areas, so, too, could you sense life.

That's why I wasn't surprised when the door opened before I could raise my hand to knock. It also didn't surprise me that Adeline stood just inside, one hand on the door handle and the other by her side. This was her family's cottage, after all.

"I'm glad you remembered I'd mentioned this place, William. We've been waiting for you," she said.

"We?" I asked.

Adeline stepped aside to reveal a homely room with a kitchen and eating space opposite to a sitting area with a fireplace, and Károly sitting in a wooden chair by the hearth. Upon seeing me, he gave a slight nod, then stood and walked to the corner kitchen to make coffee, I surmised. *There's always time for coffee.*

"Please, come inside. The wind can bite at this hour."

I entered the cottage and Adeline shut the door behind me. Károly was indeed prepping coffee, and this time when he looked in my direction, I indicated I would like a cup.

Adeline shuffled about and then placed a tray of biscuits on the kitchen table, which happened to be next to a multi-paned window that offered a splendid view of the hills and the coastal edge. I imagined what it would have been like for Adeline to come here as a child, and conjured images of her and her parents spending the holidays here. Early morning walks to the coast, board games in the afternoon, hot tea and a book by the fireplace at night.

Adeline pulled back a chair from the oval kitchen table and motioned for me to sit. She then occupied the chair next to me and, a moment later, Károly joined us. A steaming cup of Nescafé for me and him and a mug of tea for Adeline.

"What kind of tea?" I asked.

"Yorkshire. A strong black tea."

"I know it," I replied.

"Best with milk and sugar," she said.

"Sure. Well, isn't this lovely. The three of us sitting together in the afternoon on a blustery English day." I took my first sip of coffee and fought back a grimace—it had the strength of atomic fuel. "So, what happened back there?"

"Yes, some explanations are in order," remarked Károly, his first words since my arrival.

"Yes, aren't they? Explanations. What the hell happened to you two?"

"I don't think we need to start at the beginning," Károly offered. "You know those things. How about we explain what happened after you left the hotel room."

"Perfect," I said, interlacing my fingers and resting my hands on the table.

Adeline leaned forward. "After you left, Károly and I waited until the time we agreed—about five minutes—and then headed to our overwatch position on the square. We were just about there when Károly disappeared for what I'll call a brief moment."

"Disappeared for a *brief moment*? What the hell does that mean?"

"I shall explain my actions in a moment," Károly said.

"Right," continued Adeline. "When he *disappeared*, that's when I called you to abort. But you were already committed. I thought, maybe, he'd set us up—betrayed us."

Károly seemed to chuckle at this but stayed quiet.

"But even though I thought that, I couldn't leave you in the breach. I continued and prepared to react as best I could. I ran upstairs to what would be my position overlooking the square from the first floor above a shop. And from the window, I saw you marching straight towards those two men. That's when I started calling the authorities in on you. *Professor William Dresden, suspect in the Nice bombing, was on Place du Château meeting with his terrorist contacts, the Strasbourg Executive. They're going to set off a bomb.* But I only got through two calls before one of the Executive's muppets kicked through the door."

"Jeez."

"Yeah, I got one shot off before—"

"You see," interjected Károly, sucking his teeth after another sip of coffee, "I suspected we were all under surveillance. It had been intentional for you—you were, in fact, the bait, meant to draw your sister out—but experience told me the Executive would be on us, too."

"Why?"

"We shall discuss another time," he said with a hand wave. "So, back to the moment. I broke off from Agent Parker so that I could maneuver on the people maneuvering on us."

"That's when I called you," added Adeline. "I thought it was a trap."

"But it wasn't," I said affirming more for myself than them.

"No, it wasn't a trap. If not for Károly, I would be dead."

"What did you do?" I asked Károly, though I had a good idea from what Faust had told me.

"He shot. I shot. What is there to say? Agent Parker is alive and her assailant is not."

"Right," I said. "And then once you two were reunited and I was in the heat of my mess—you two really did disappear."

"We did," said Károly. "And it worked so well. Like the gears of a clock."

"Did you know about the BfV's undercover agent inside the Executive, a Faust Broch?"

Adeline shook her head but Károly piped up, "Oh, yes. I did."

"Why didn't you tell us?" I questioned.

"Haven't you been paying attention? I wasn't sure you would succeed. Never show all your cards."

"And now?"

"Things are different now. We are here talking, aren't we?" Károly said with a smile.

"We are indeed showing cards. How did you know about him?"

"I've been looking at the Executive for many years, longer than either of you. So, years ago when your father contacted me and we

established our relationship, among many things I used that opportunity to confirm some of my suspicions—clandestinely, of course.
Your father did not know of Faust's true purpose. That would have
been problematic for Faust."

"Wait a moment. My father contacted you? Why?"

"For my help, of course. Well, Moscow's help. He contacted a
minister associate of mine and I made sure that I was the one to lead
the Kremlin's liaison."

"Liaison? What in God's name are you talking about?"

"Yes, allow me to explain. You see, even before your father became
the Kanzler, he considered Russia a potential strategic partner.
Perhaps a limited alliance. He was not as narrow-minded in his
views of strong peoples and he'd been impressed by Moscow's will-
ingness and abilities to crack down on minorities and neighbors.
Which is true—Putin, like his predecessors, seeks to protect ethnic
Russians and oppress all others."

"But you inserted yourself," I said.

"I did. As I said back in Strasbourg, my view of the world and the
intentions of the state I work for has evolved. But you two are the
only ones who know of this. In contrast, my experiences in the world
of spies and secrecy are unique. Thus, Moscow believed I was the
right individual for this little arrangement. But to be honest, my
bosses did not think highly of the Executive. *Inconsequential to
Moscow's interests*, is how one chief described it. They did not care."

"Are you still reporting to them on this?"

"I recently informed my superiors the Executive is no more."

"But there is more, isn't there?" I asked.

"Correct. It's not over," said Adeline. "The Executive is just one of
many discriminatory, nationalist movements on the rise. Whether
they have a daft name with a network of well-placed fanatics doesn't
matter. As you say, William, it's the bloody ideas that matter. History

is indeed experiencing a loop-around of past fears and beliefs, pitting us against one another."

"But what does that mean for us?"

"Károly would like our help."

"Ha. Please do tell."

"Your expertise and research methods helped reveal the Executive," said Károly. "Your research and subsequent activities caused it to act sooner and perhaps rashly, thus exposing it so it could be stopped."

"I think you're giving me too much credit."

"Exposure—even just the fear of exposure—can cause people to make rash decisions, Professor. Coupled with other points of leverage, many interesting things can happen."

"Points of leverage," I said, shaking my head.

"Of course, which brings us back to the Executive. The network we have known as *the Executive* will not be fully dismantled—it can't be—so many elements of the Executive did not know they were even a part of it. They were manipulated and used by the board."

"What are you getting at?" I asked.

Károly smiled. "I want to use the remnants of the Executive's network to oppose, sabotage, and destabilize the politicians in my homeland who are advancing their xenophobic and strongman agendas. Hungary and the Hungarian people—from all backgrounds—do not deserve this. I cannot sit by and see my country fall back into an authoritarian, militaristic society while its leaders sit at the heels of Putin and his thieving oligarchs."

"I can appreciate what you're saying. I indeed do. But I feel like you're assuming I want to be involved in this."

"But you do, Professor. I think you will be very interested in what we have in mind."

"Really? And you're in on this, too, Adeline?"

Adeline adjusted herself. "My world and career have fallen apart—I can't go back to MI6 and I have no family. But I can still go after those individuals and beliefs that should be stopped—wiped from the face of the earth."

I saw a fire in Adeline's eyes that told me there was quite a bit more driving her than what she'd just shared.

"And you, William, I think you see it, too," she said.

I sat for a long moment, feeling a strong pull to withdraw into myself and my books as I had done over twenty years ago when I saw the world go mad. Yet, with these two sitting across from me, both looking at me expectantly, I felt needed as well as curious. I would have to think on things, of course, but a quiet urge caused me to say, "Okay, lay it out for me . . ."

ACKNOWLEDGMENTS

The Underhanded went through many versions over multiple years, and the manuscript sat on the shelf for a time, too. It also went through a few title changes. And although I spent many nights alone adjusting and refining this story to eventually realize the work of fiction you now hold in your hand, it would not have been possible without the team I am so fortunate to turn to, rely on, and work alongside.

Again, I must thank my two agents, Judy Coppage and Sam Dorrance, for seeing something in me. I am also thankful to Oceanview Publishing for believing in me once again. Working with Pat, Bob, Lee, Faith, and Tracy is a sincere joy and I feel fortunate to be part of the family. A special thanks goes to my trusted readers and writing confidants, Mark, Amy, Annie, Spuds, Jeff, Irv, Brian, Eric, Phill, Joel, Rachelle, and Tim. You push me to be better every day. I must also give credit to the late Richard Marek, who worked with me on this manuscript several years ago—and what fun it was. I am indebted to my parents, as well, for all they have done for me throughout my life. And finally, to my wife and children who believed in me and supported me through the ups and downs and everything in between—thank you.

NOTE FROM THE PUBLISHER

We hope that you enjoyed *The Underhanded*.

If you did, we suggest that you read *Landslide* by Adam Sikes, another espionage thriller of the highest order.

Here's a brief summary of *Landslide*:

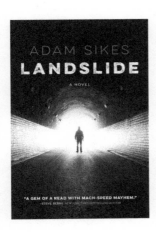

Mason Hackett is struggling with the sins of his past when he sees his best friend—a man long presumed dead—alive on the news. Driven by personal loyalty, tragic love, regret, and guilt, Mason steps into a tangled web of immoral governments and ruthless corporations as he rockets across Europe to uncover the truth.

"A gem of a read with mach-speed mayhem, loaded with rich detail from a writer who knows what he's talking about."

—Steve Berry,
New York Times best-selling author

We hope that you enjoy reading *Landslide* if you have not already and will look forward to future espionage thrillers from Adam Sikes.

For more information, please visit
www.adamsikes.com

If you liked *The Underhanded,* we would be very appreciative if you would consider leaving a review. As you probably already know, book reviews are important to authors and they are very grateful when a reader makes the special effort to write a review, however brief.

Happy Reading,
Oceanview Publishing
Your Home for Mystery, Thriller, and Suspense